MOBILE SUIT GUNDAM SEED

ART BY
Masatsugu Iwase
STORY BY
Hajime Yatate AND Yoshiyuki Tomino

TRANSLATED AND ADAPTED BY
Jason DeAngelis

LETTERED BY
Steve Palmer

BALLANTINE BOOKS · NEW YORK

A Del Rey® Book
Published by The Random House Publishing Group

First published in Japan in 2003 by Kodansha Ltd., Tokyo.
This publication—rights arranged through Kodansha Ltd.

Published in the United States by Del Rey Books, an imprint of The Random House Publishing Group, a division of Random House, Inc., New York, and simultaneously in Canada by Random House of Canada Limited, Toronto. First published in serialization and subsequently published in book form by Kodansha, Ltd., Tokyo in 2003.

www.delreymanga.com

Library of Congress Control Number can be obtained from the publisher upon request.

ISBN 0-345-47179-2

Translator and adaptor—Jason DeAngelis
Lettering—Steve Palmer
Cover design—David Stevenson

Manufactured in the United States of America

First Edition: September 2004

1 2 3 4 5 6 7 8 9

Contents

Honorifics Explained

Throughout the Del Rey Manga books, you will find Japanese honorifics left intact in the translations. For those not familiar with how the Japanese use honorifics, and, more important, how they differ from American honorifics, we present this brief overview.

Politeness has always been a critical facet of Japanese culture. Ever since the feudal era, when Japan was a highly stratified society, use of honorifics—which can be defined as polite speech that indicates relationship or status—has played an essential role in the Japanese language. When addressing someone in Japanese, an honorific usually takes the form of a suffix attached to one's name (e.g. "Asuna-san"), as a title at the end of one's name, or in place of the name itself (e.g. "Negi-sensei" or simply "Sensei!").

Honorifics can be expressions of respect or endearment. In the context of manga and anime, honorifics give insight into the nature of the relationship between characters. Many translations into English leave out these important honorifics, and therefore distort the feel of the original Japanese. Because Japanese honorifics contain nuances that English honorifics lack, it is our policy at Del Rey not to translate them. Here, instead, is a guide to some of the honorifics you may encounter in Del Rey Manga.

-san: This is the most common honorific and is equivalent to Mr., Miss, Ms., Mrs, etc. It is the all-purpose honorific and can be used in any situation where politeness is required.

-sama: This is one level higher than *-san*. It is used to confer great respect.

-dono: This comes from the word *tono,* which means *lord.* It is an even higher level than *-sama* and confers utmost respect.

-kun: This suffix is used at the end of boys' names to express familiarity or endearment. It is also sometimes used by men among friends, or when addressing someone younger or of a lower station.

-chan: This is used to express endearment, mostly toward girls. It is also used for little boys, pets, and between lovers. It gives a sense of childish cuteness.

Bozu: This is an informal way to refer to a boy, similar to the English term "kid" or "squirt."

Sempai: This title suggests that the addressee is one's senior in a group or organization. It is most often used in a school setting, where underclassmen refer to their upperclassmen as *sempai*. It can also be used in the workplace, such as when a newer employee addresses an employee who has seniority in the company.

Kohai: This is the opposite of *-sempai,* and is used toward underclassmen in school or newcomers in the workplace. It connotes that the addressee is of a lower station.

Sensei: Literally meaning "one who has come before," this title is used for teachers, doctors, or masters of any profession or art.

-[blank]:   This is usually forgotten on these lists, but it's perhaps the most significant difference between Japanese and English. The lack of honorific means that the speaker has permission to address the person in a very intimate way. Usually, only family, spouses, or very close friends have this kind of license. Known as *yobisute,* it can be gratifying when someone who has earned the intimacy starts to call one by one's name without an honorific. But when that intimacy hasn't been earned, it can also be insulting.

機動戦士ガンダム SEED シード

MOBILE SUIT GUNDAM

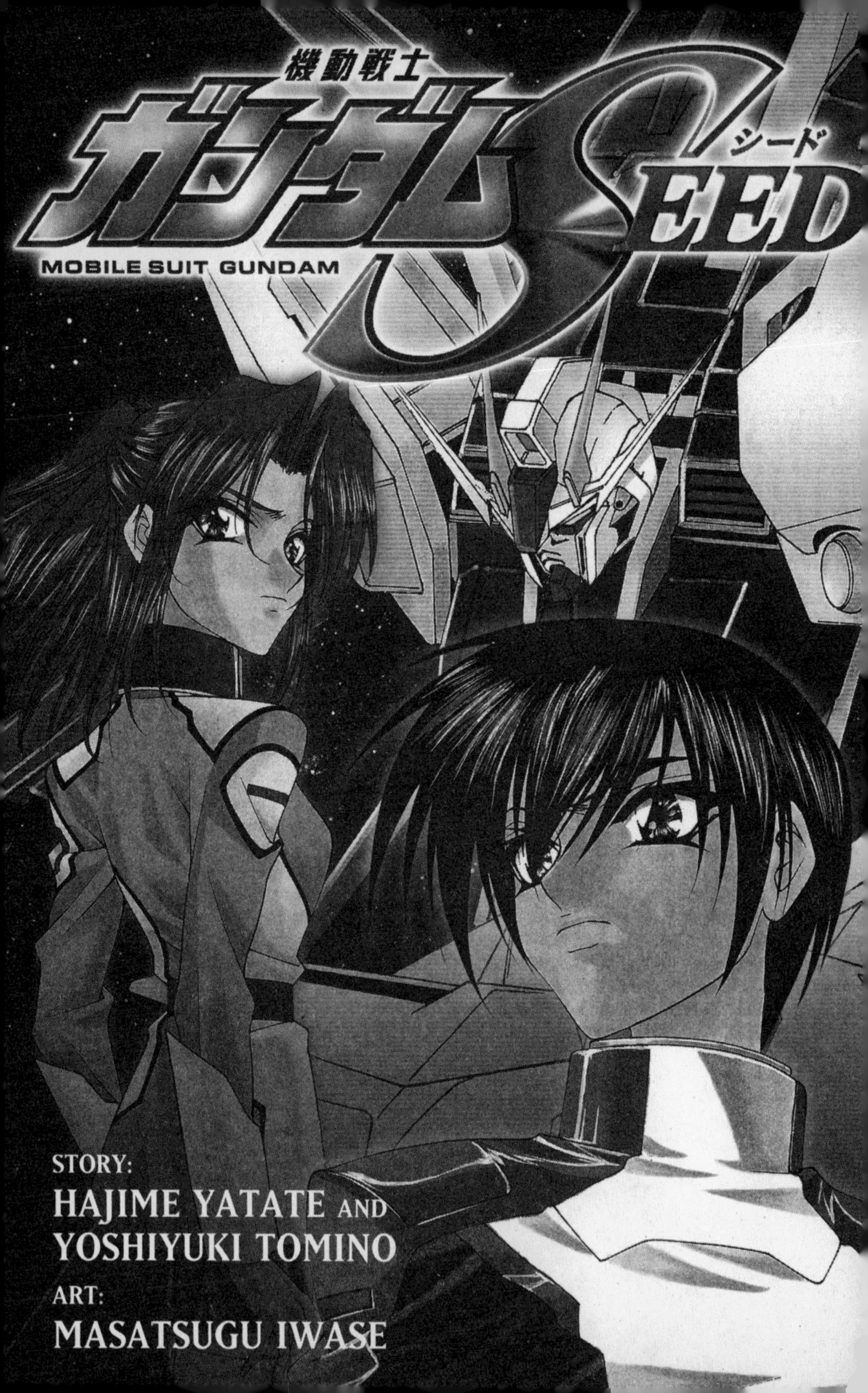

STORY:

HAJIME YATATE AND

YOSHIYUKI TOMINO

ART:

MASATSUGU IWASE

MOBILE SUIT GUNDAM SEED

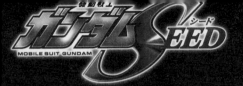

THE STORY SO FAR

71 C.E. (COSMIC ERA). IN THE AFTERMATH OF THE "BLOODY VALENTINE," THE WAR BETWEEN EARTH ALLIANCE FORCES AND THE ZAFT DRAGGED ON AND ELEVEN MONTHS HAD PASSED. KIRA YAMATO, A STUDENT ON SPACE COLONY HELIOPOLIS, BELONGING TO THE NEUTRAL NATION OF AUBE, BECOMES EMBROILED IN THE ZAFT'S PLAN TO CAPTURE THE EARTH'S NEW MOBILE SUITS, AND IS FORCED TO PILOT THE X-105 STRIKE GUNDAM AND REPEL THE ZAFT FORCES. HOWEVER, AFTER BEING EXPOSED TO MILITARY SECRETS, KIRA AND HIS RESCUED FRIENDS END UP STUCK ABOARD THE EARTH FORCES' NEW BATTLESHIP ARCHANGEL. ZAFT'S COMMANDER CREUSET, WHO CAPTURED FOUR OF THE FIVE NEW MOBILE SUITS, LAUNCHES AN ATTACK ON THE ARCHANGEL. AND KIRA, ALTHOUGH RELUCTANT TO FIGHT, BOARDS THE STRIKE YET AGAIN, REALIZING THAT AS A COORDINATOR, HE IS THE ONLY ONE WHO CAN DEFEND HIS FRIENDS. IN THE MIDST OF BATTLE, KIRA COMES ACROSS HIS OLD FRIEND ATHRUN, WHO PILOTS THE STOLEN X-303 AEGIS. BOTH ARE SHOCKED AT THEIR CURRENT PREDICAMENT. MEANWHILE, THE BATTLE ESCALATES, AND HELIOPOLIS IS DESTROYED. COMMANDER CREUSET PURSUES THE ARCHANGEL AS IT HEADS FOR THE EARTH BASE ON THE MOON. KIRA FIGHTS DESPERATELY TO PROTECT HIS FRIENDS, AND IGNORES ATHRUN'S APPEALS, WHICH HE KNOWS WITHIN HIS HEART ARE WRONG. SUDDENLY, THERE'S TROUBLE IN THE ARCHANGEL ENGINES! NOW, DRAGGED BY THE EARTH'S GRAVITATIONAL FIELD TOWARD THE PERILOUS "DEBRIS BELT," FILLED WITH SPACE JUNK AND WRECKAGE, THEY ARE HEADED FOR CERTAIN DEATH. OR ARE THEY?

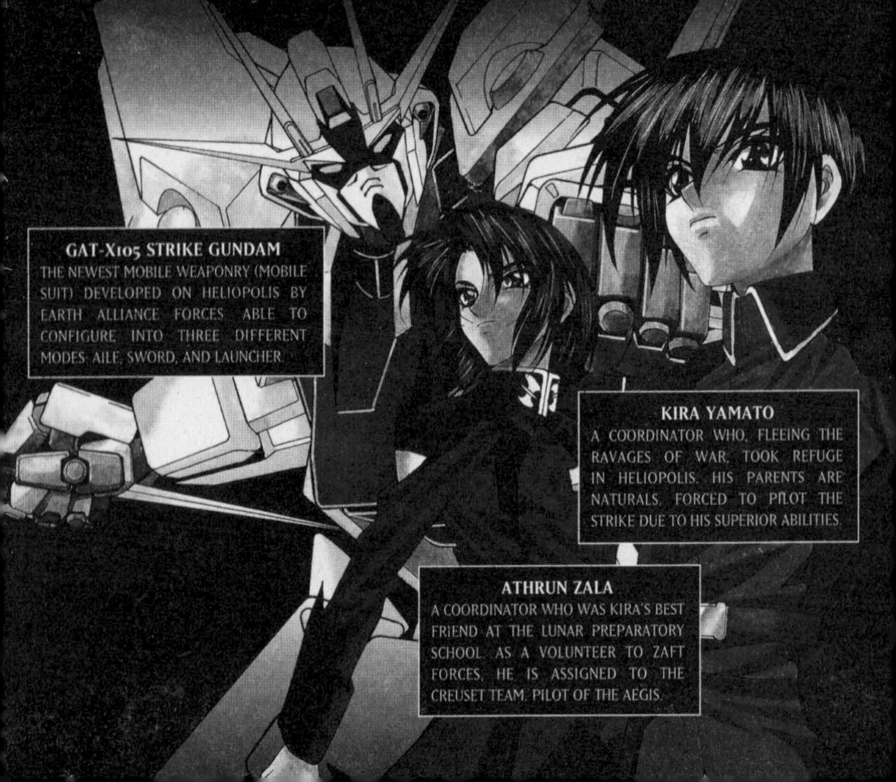
GAT-X105 STRIKE GUNDAM
THE NEWEST MOBILE WEAPONRY (MOBILE SUIT) DEVELOPED ON HELIOPOLIS BY EARTH ALLIANCE FORCES. ABLE TO CONFIGURE INTO THREE DIFFERENT MODES: AILE, SWORD, AND LAUNCHER.
KIRA YAMATO
A COORDINATOR WHO, FLEEING THE RAVAGES OF WAR, TOOK REFUGE IN HELIOPOLIS. HIS PARENTS ARE NATURALS. FORCED TO PILOT THE STRIKE DUE TO HIS SUPERIOR ABILITIES.
ATHRUN ZALA
A COORDINATOR WHO WAS KIRA'S BEST FRIEND AT THE LUNAR PREPARATORY SCHOOL. AS A VOLUNTEER TO ZAFT FORCES, HE IS ASSIGNED TO THE CREUSET TEAM. PILOT OF THE AEGIS.

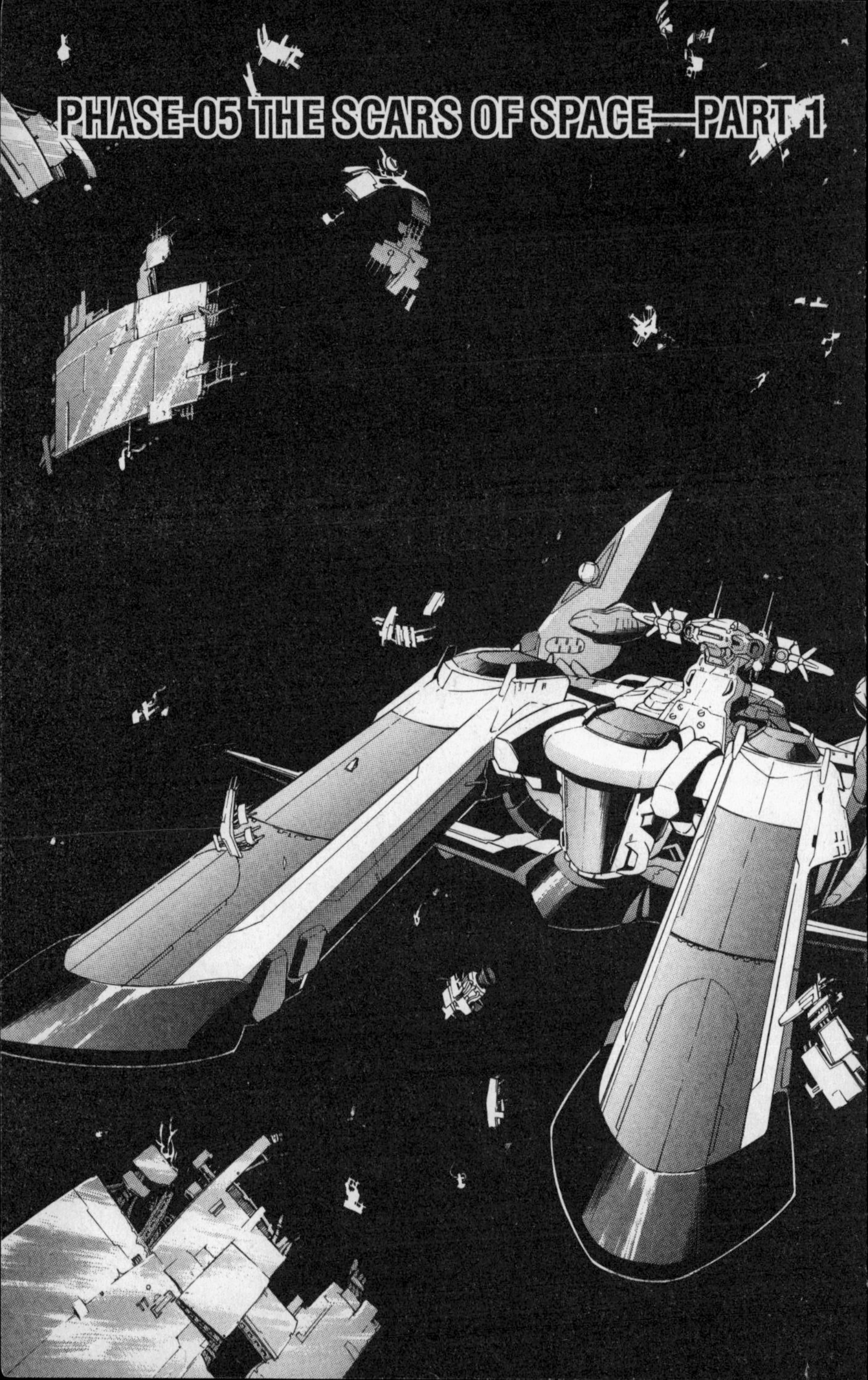
PHASE-05 THE SCARS OF SPACE—PART 1

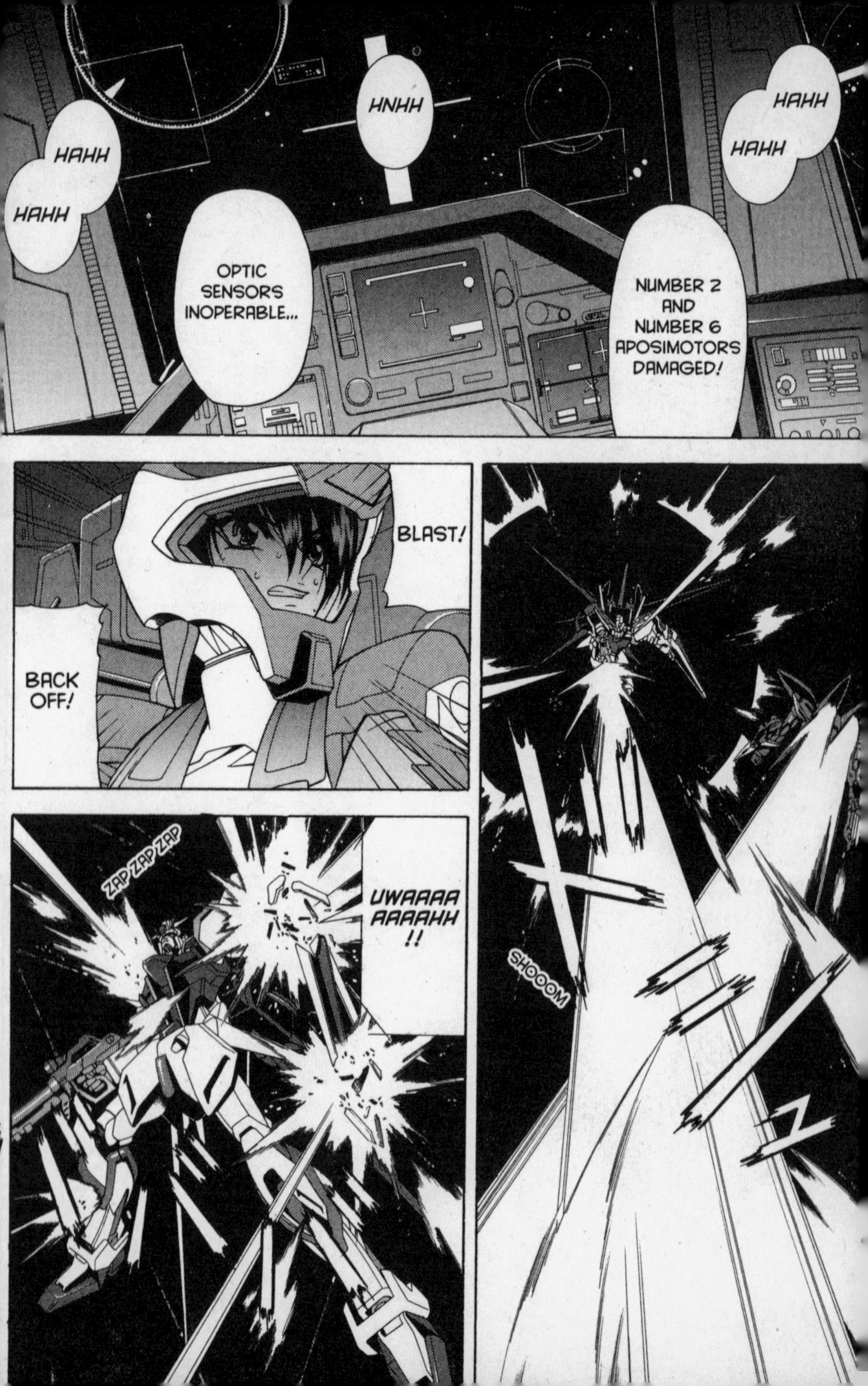
HAHH
HAHH
NUMBER 2 AND NUMBER 6 APOSIMOTORS DAMAGED!
HNHH
OPTIC SENSORS INOPERABLE...
HAHH
HAHH
SHOOOM
BLAST!
BACK OFF!
UWAAAA AAAAHH !!
ZAP ZAP ZAP

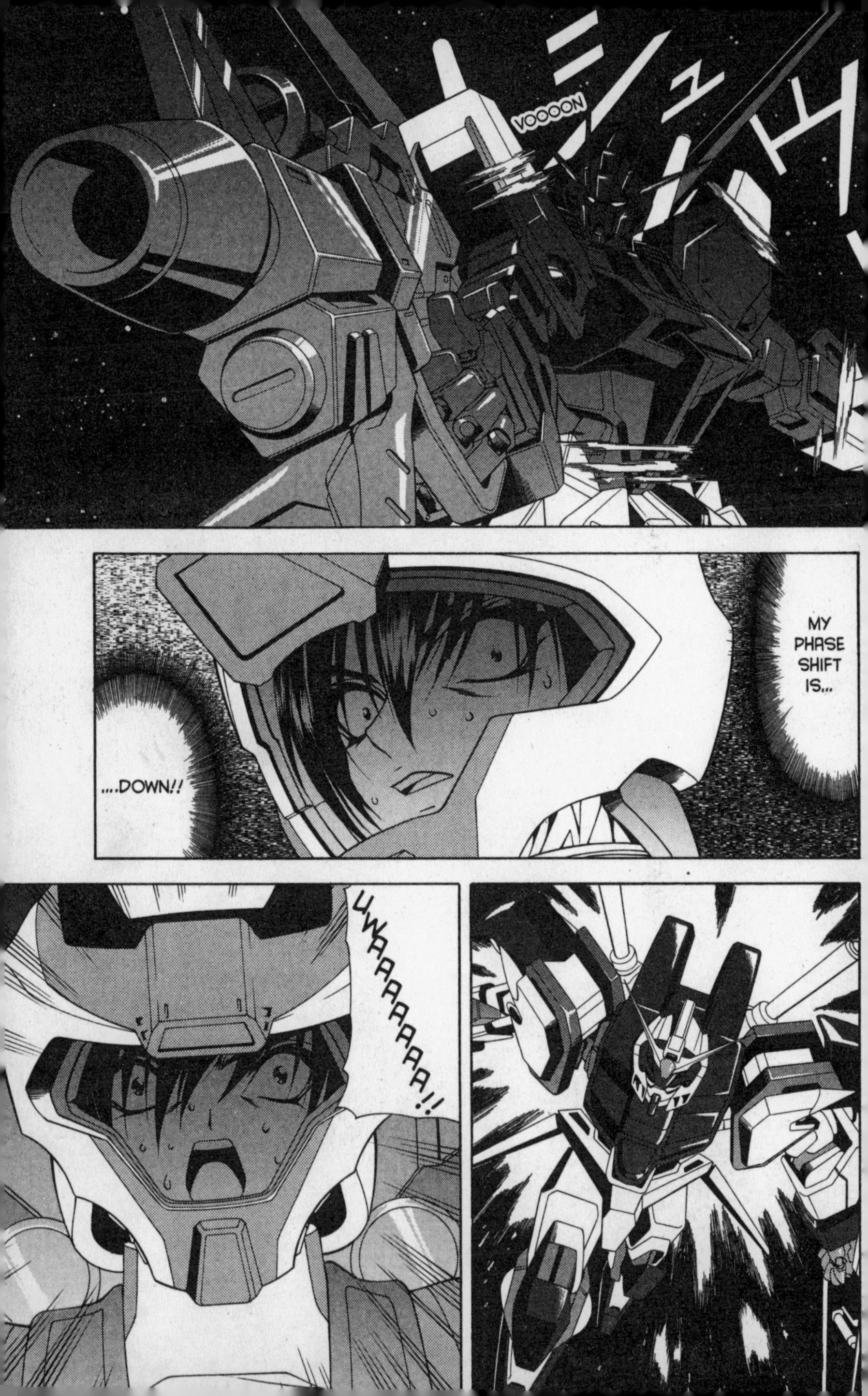
VOOOON
MY PHASE SHIFT IS...
....DOWN!!
UWAAAAAAA!!

WAM!

HAHH... HAHH...

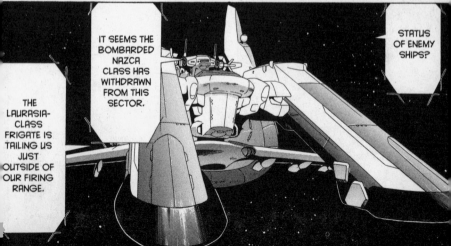

STATUS OF ENEMY SHIPS?

IT SEEMS THE BOMBARDED NAZCA CLASS HAS WITHDRAWN FROM THIS SECTOR.

THE LAURASIA-CLASS FRIGATE IS TAILING US JUST OUTSIDE OF OUR FIRING RANGE.

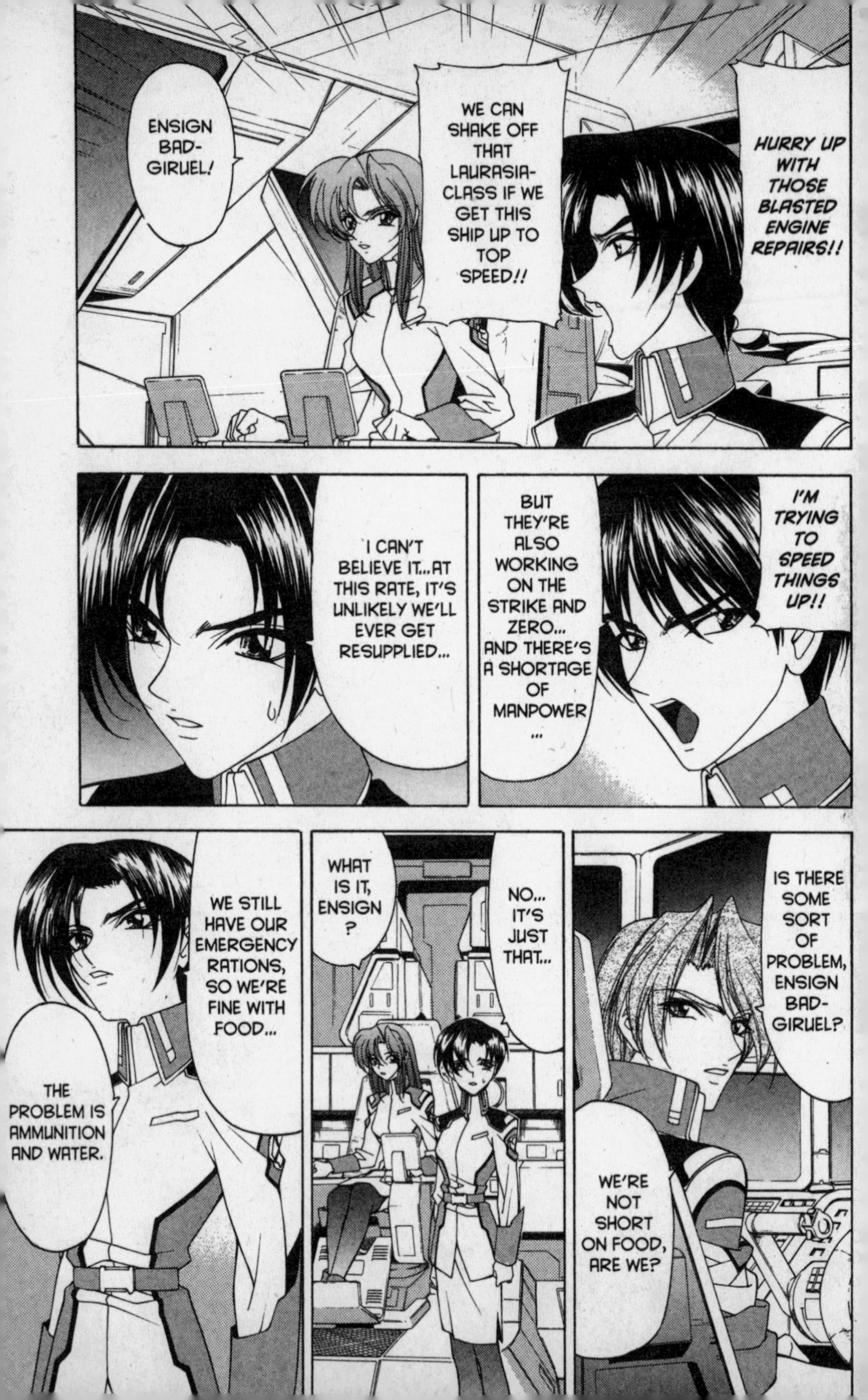
HURRY UP WITH THOSE BLASTED ENGINE REPAIRS!!
WE CAN SHAKE OFF THAT LAURASIA-CLASS IF WE GET THIS SHIP UP TO TOP SPEED!!
ENSIGN BAD-GIRUEL!
I'M TRYING TO SPEED THINGS UP!!
BUT THEY'RE ALSO WORKING ON THE STRIKE AND ZERO... AND THERE'S A SHORTAGE OF MANPOWER ...
I CAN'T BELIEVE IT...AT THIS RATE, IT'S UNLIKELY WE'LL EVER GET RESUPPLIED...
IS THERE SOME SORT OF PROBLEM, ENSIGN BAD-GIRUEL?
WE'RE NOT SHORT ON FOOD, ARE WE?
WHAT IS IT, ENSIGN?
NO... IT'S JUST THAT...
WE STILL HAVE OUR EMERGENCY RATIONS, SO WE'RE FINE WITH FOOD...
THE PROBLEM IS AMMUNITION AND WATER.

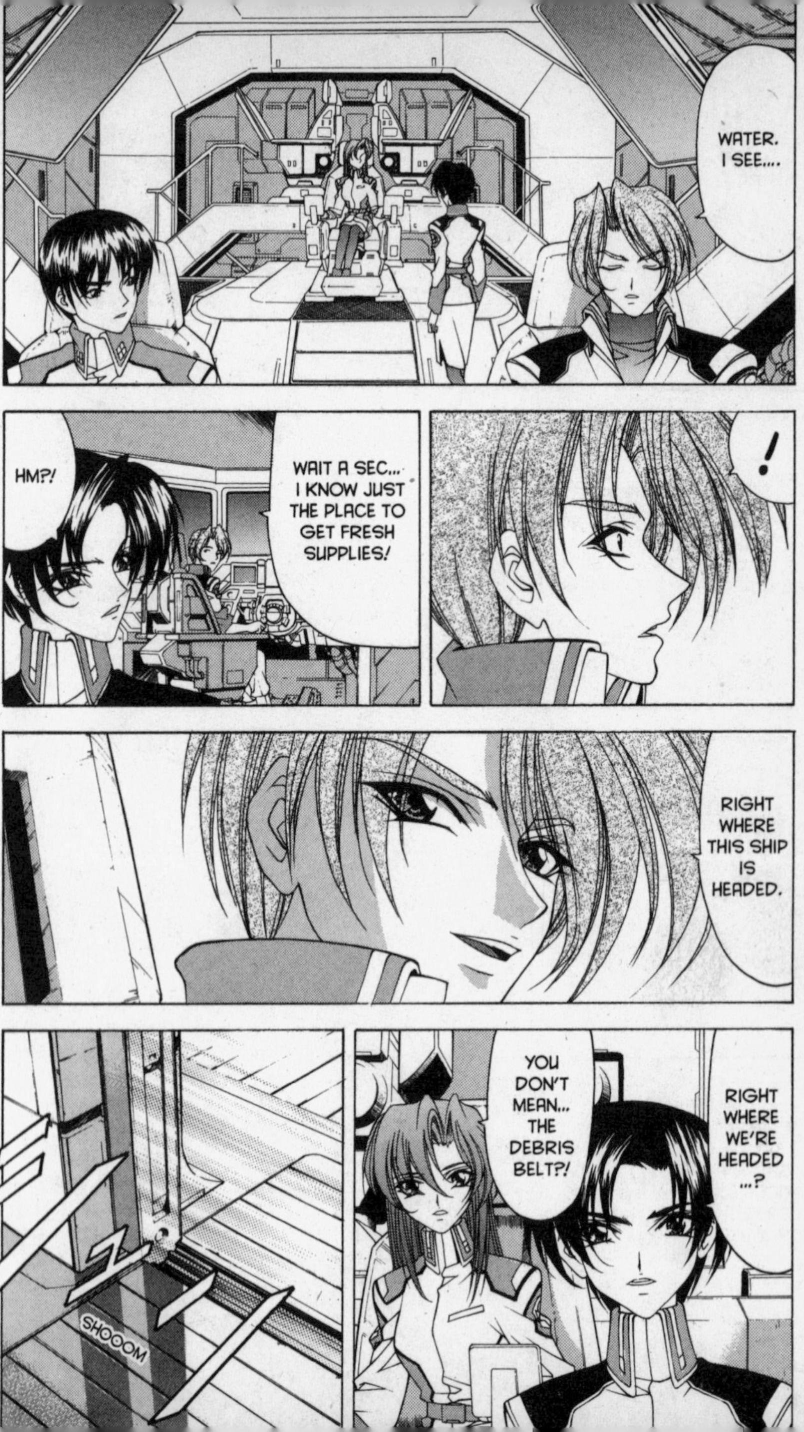
WATER. I SEE....
!
WAIT A SEC... I KNOW JUST THE PLACE TO GET FRESH SUPPLIES!
HM?!
RIGHT WHERE THIS SHIP IS HEADED.
RIGHT WHERE WE'RE HEADED ...?
YOU DON'T MEAN... THE DEBRIS BELT?!
SHOOOM

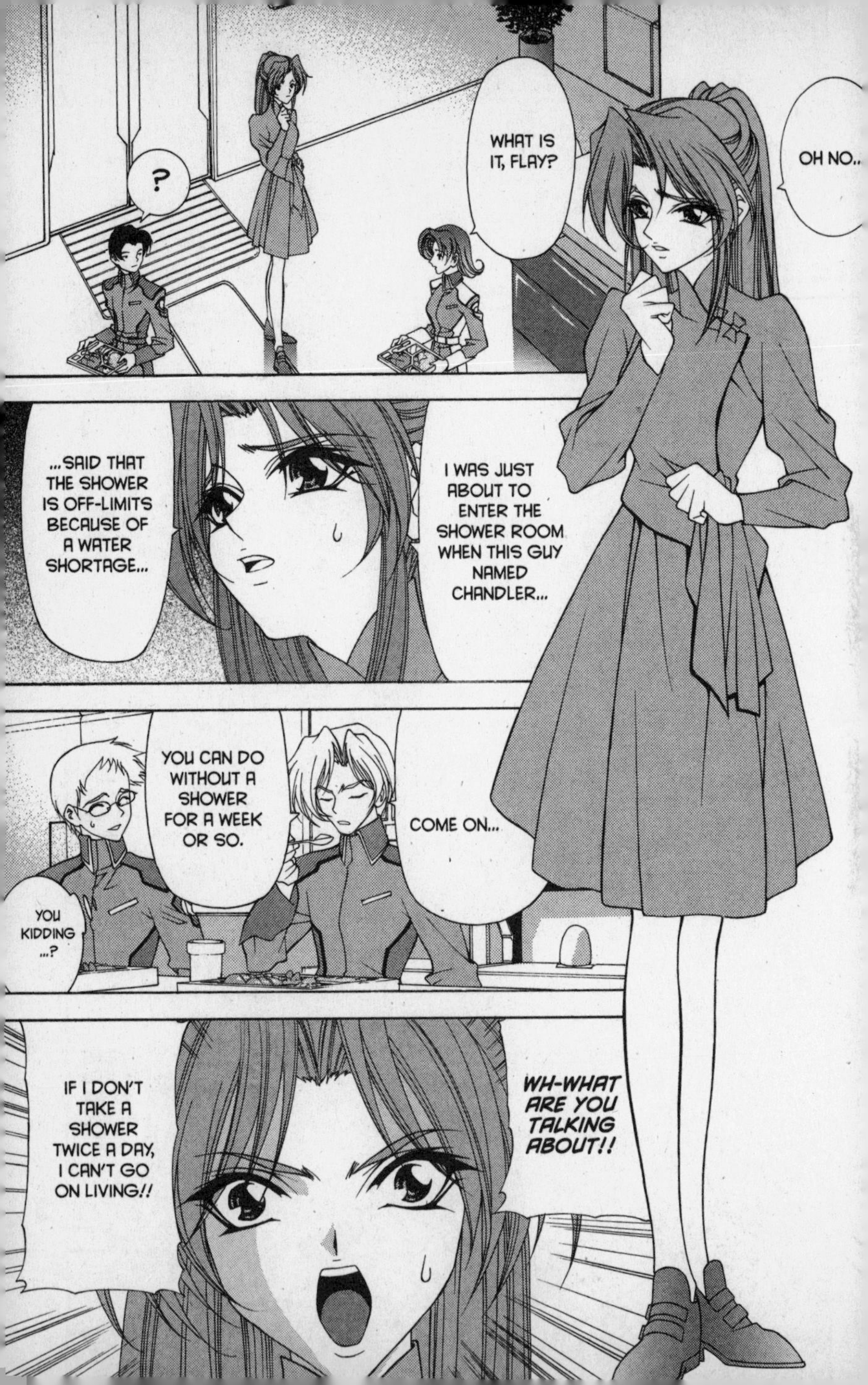
OH NO...
WHAT IS IT, FLAY?
?
I WAS JUST ABOUT TO ENTER THE SHOWER ROOM WHEN THIS GUY NAMED CHANDLER...
...SAID THAT THE SHOWER IS OFF-LIMITS BECAUSE OF A WATER SHORTAGE...
COME ON...
YOU CAN DO WITHOUT A SHOWER FOR A WEEK OR SO.
YOU KIDDING ...?
WH-WHAT ARE YOU TALKING ABOUT!!
IF I DON'T TAKE A SHOWER TWICE A DAY, I CAN'T GO ON LIVING!!

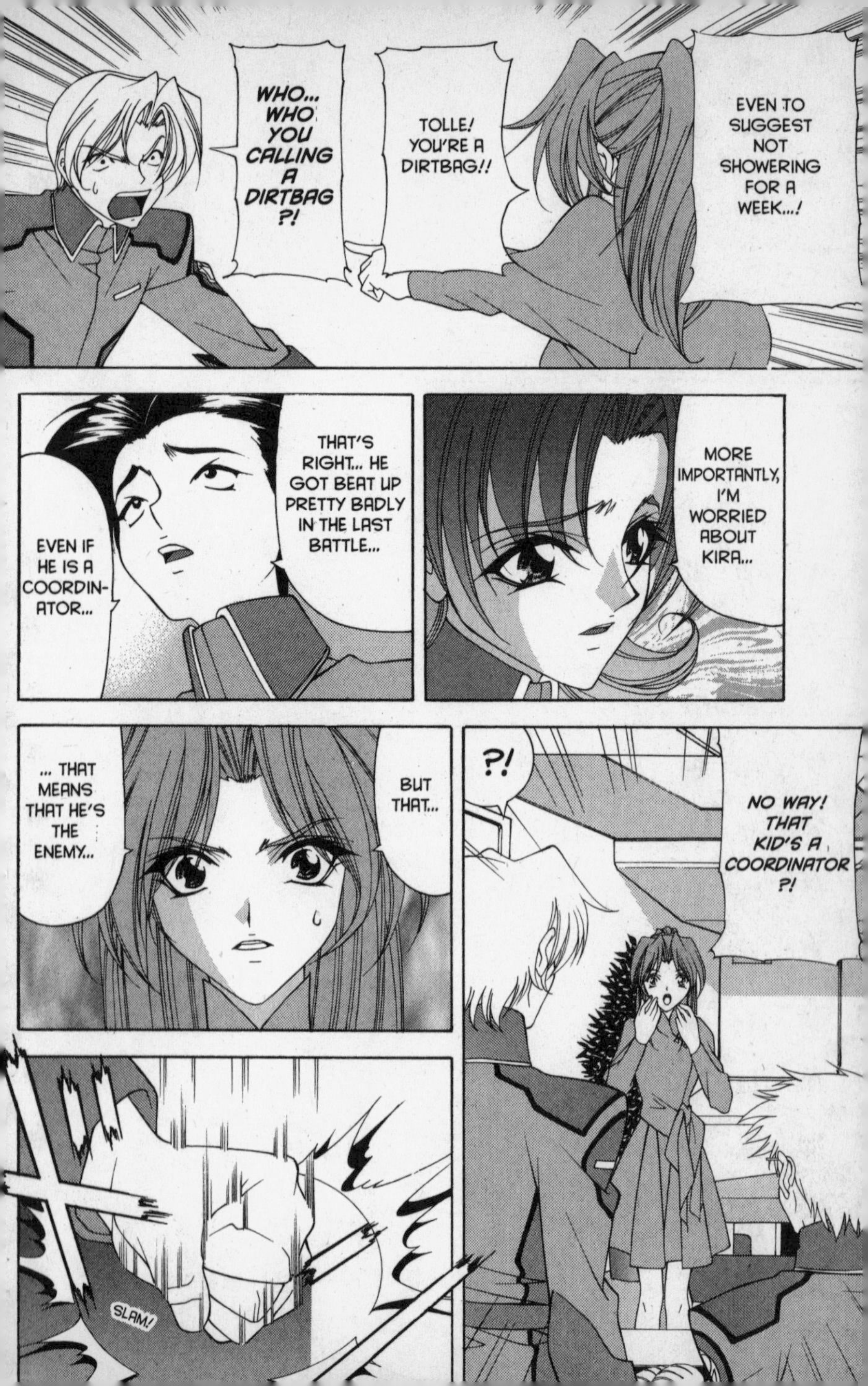
EVEN TO SUGGEST NOT SHOWERING FOR A WEEK...!
TOLLE! YOU'RE A DIRTBAG!!
WHO... WHO YOU CALLING A DIRTBAG ?!
MORE IMPORTANTLY, I'M WORRIED ABOUT KIRA...
THAT'S RIGHT... HE GOT BEAT UP PRETTY BADLY IN THE LAST BATTLE...
EVEN IF HE IS A COORDINATOR...
?!
NO WAY! THAT KID'S A COORDINATOR ?!
BUT THAT...
... THAT MEANS THAT HE'S THE ENEMY...
SLAM!

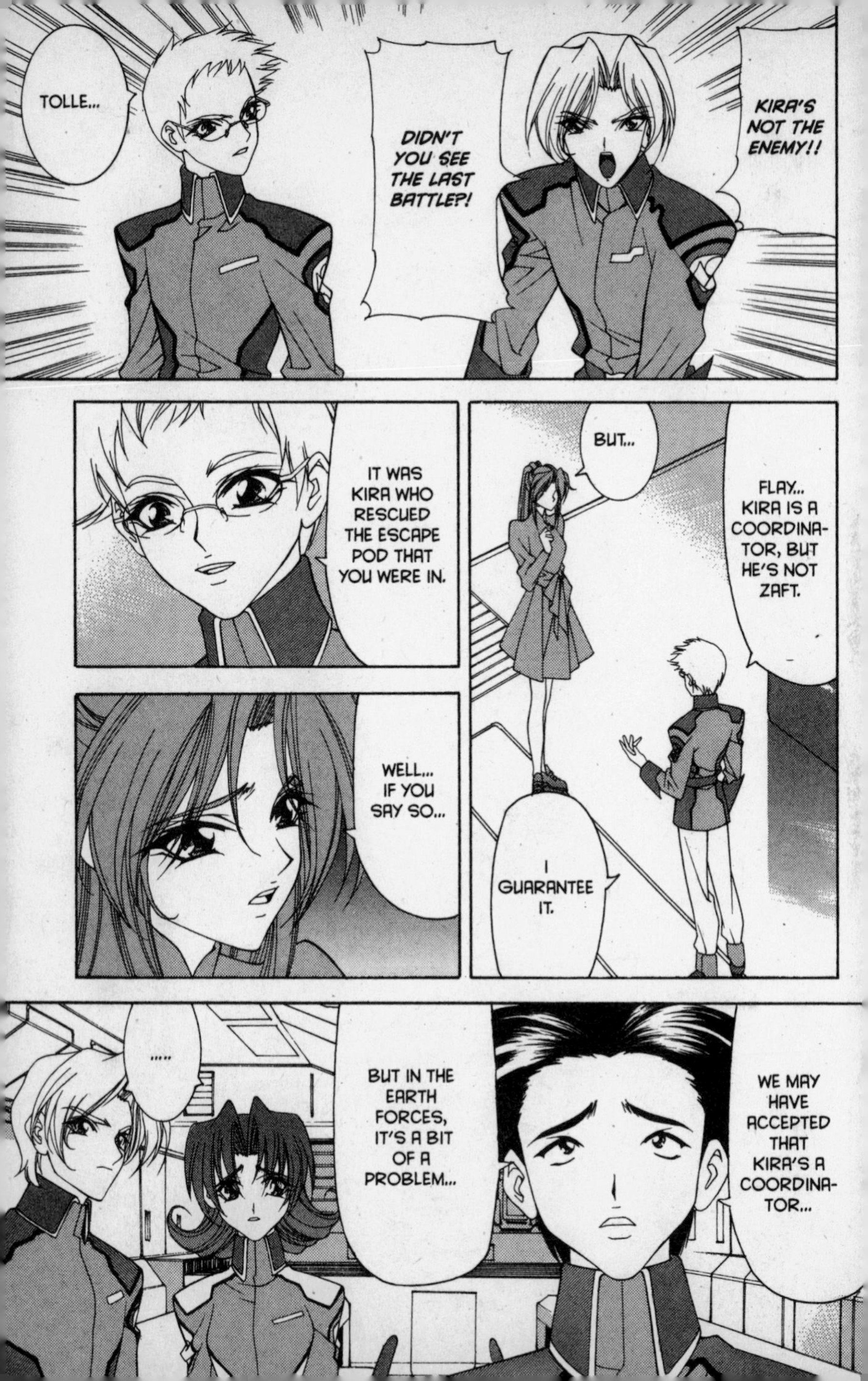
KIRA'S NOT THE ENEMY!!
DIDN'T YOU SEE THE LAST BATTLE?!
TOLLE...
FLAY... KIRA IS A COORDINATOR, BUT HE'S NOT ZAFT.
BUT...
I GUARANTEE IT.
IT WAS KIRA WHO RESCUED THE ESCAPE POD THAT YOU WERE IN.
WELL... IF YOU SAY SO...
WE MAY HAVE ACCEPTED THAT KIRA'S A COORDINATOR...
BUT IN THE EARTH FORCES, IT'S A BIT OF A PROBLEM...
.....

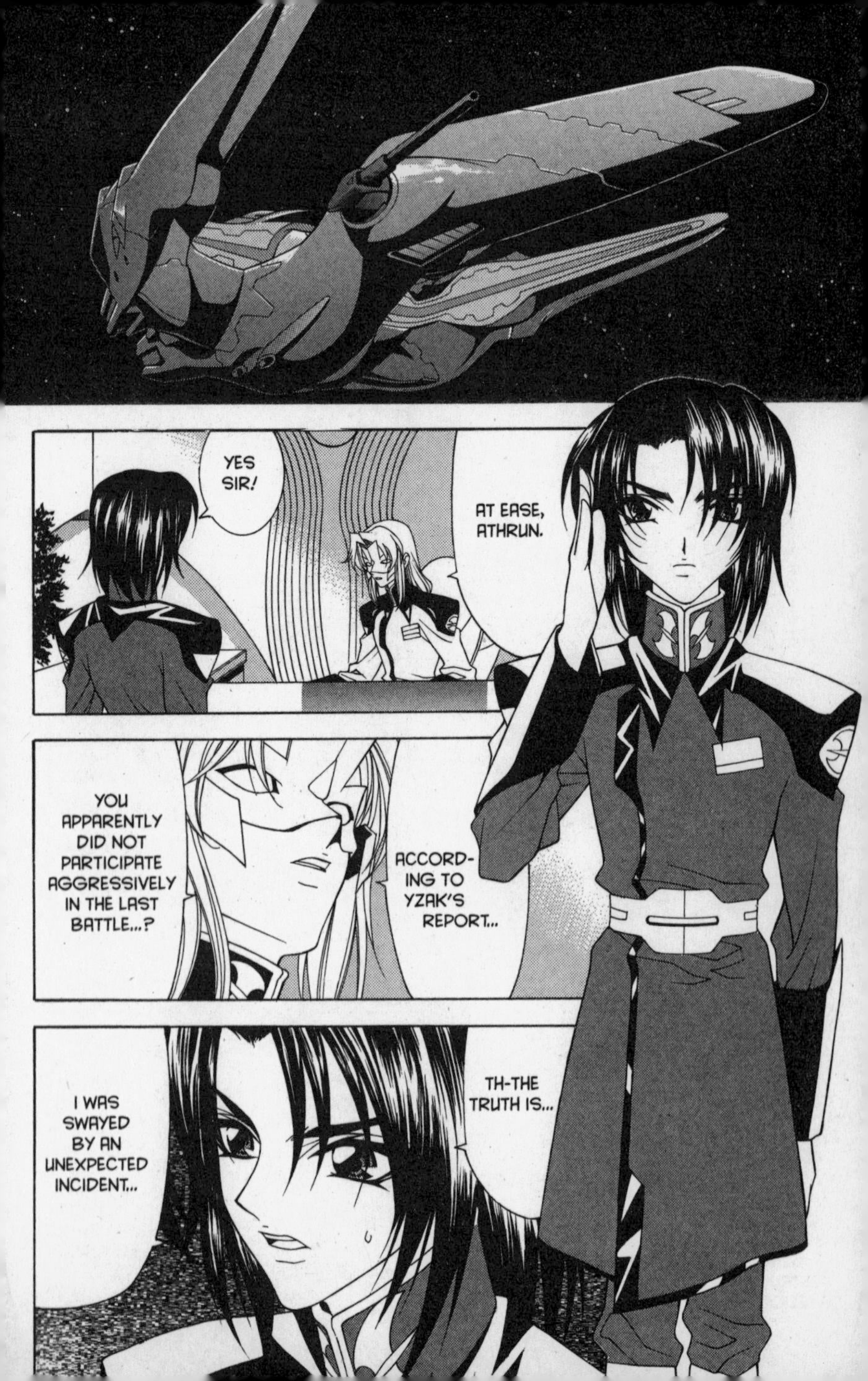
AT EASE, ATHRUN.
YES SIR!
ACCORDING TO YZAK'S REPORT...
YOU APPARENTLY DID NOT PARTICIPATE AGGRESSIVELY IN THE LAST BATTLE...?
TH-THE TRUTH IS...
I WAS SWAYED BY AN UNEXPECTED INCIDENT...

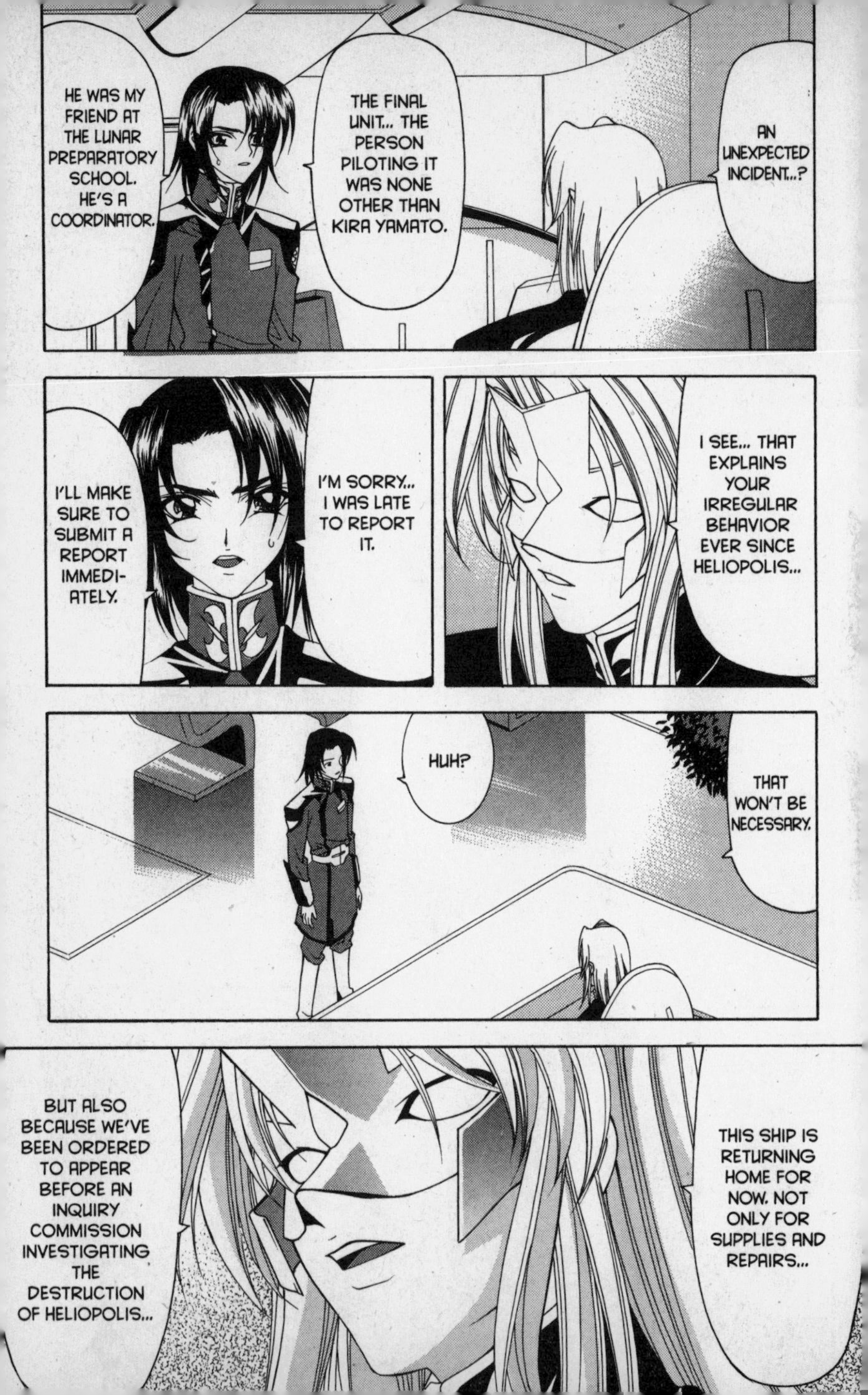
AN UNEXPECTED INCIDENT...?
THE FINAL UNIT... THE PERSON PILOTING IT WAS NONE OTHER THAN KIRA YAMATO.
HE WAS MY FRIEND AT THE LUNAR PREPARATORY SCHOOL. HE'S A COORDINATOR.
I SEE... THAT EXPLAINS YOUR IRREGULAR BEHAVIOR EVER SINCE HELIOPOLIS...
I'M SORRY... I WAS LATE TO REPORT IT.
I'LL MAKE SURE TO SUBMIT A REPORT IMMEDI-ATELY.
THAT WON'T BE NECESSARY.
HUH?
THIS SHIP IS RETURNING HOME FOR NOW. NOT ONLY FOR SUPPLIES AND REPAIRS...
BUT ALSO BECAUSE WE'VE BEEN ORDERED TO APPEAR BEFORE AN INQUIRY COMMISSION INVESTIGATING THE DESTRUCTION OF HELIOPOLIS...

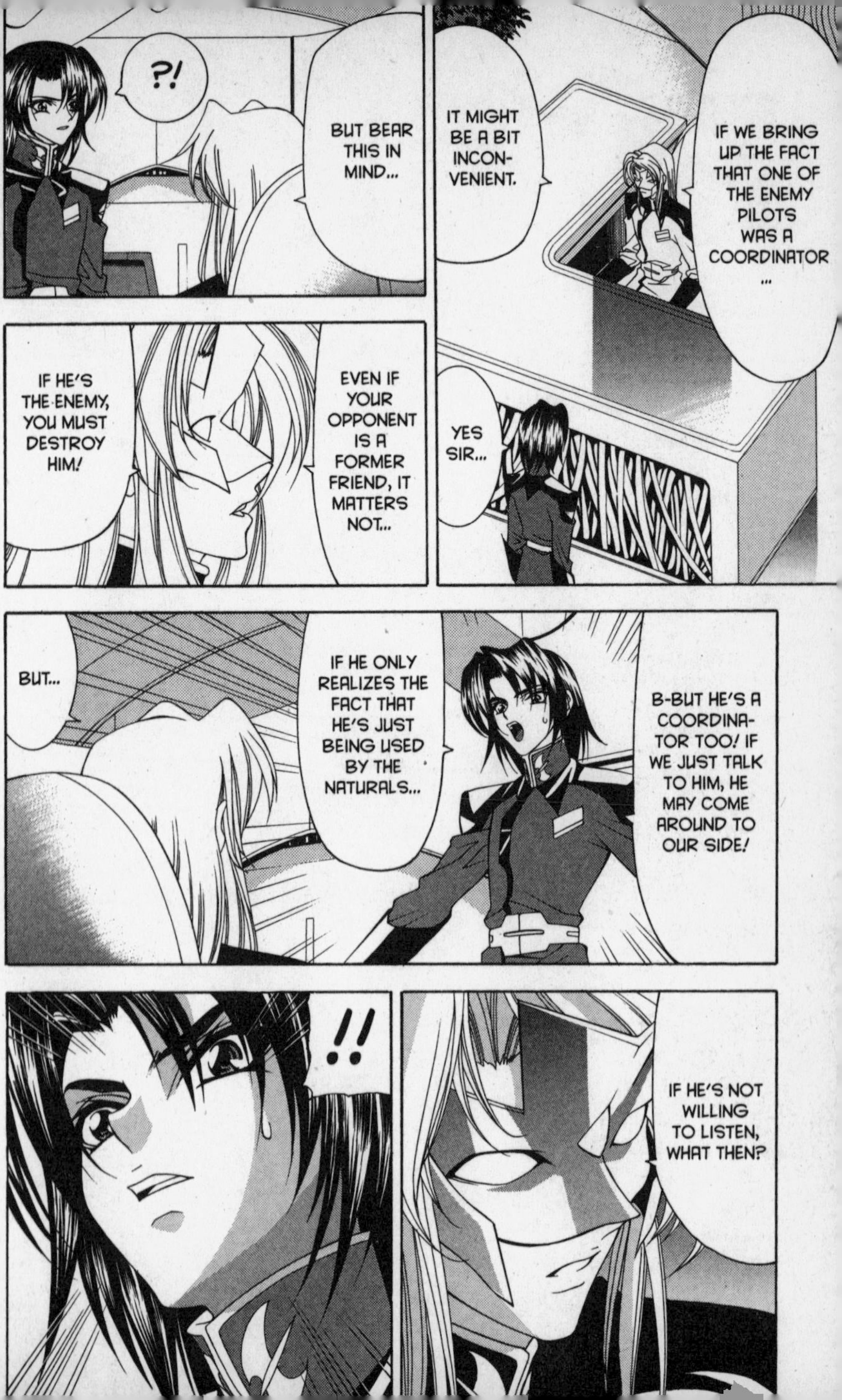
IF WE BRING UP THE FACT THAT ONE OF THE ENEMY PILOTS WAS A COORDINATOR ...
IT MIGHT BE A BIT INCON-VENIENT.
YES SIR...
BUT BEAR THIS IN MIND...
?!
EVEN IF YOUR OPPONENT IS A FORMER FRIEND, IT MATTERS NOT...
IF HE'S THE ENEMY, YOU MUST DESTROY HIM!
B-BUT HE'S A COORDINA-TOR TOO! IF WE JUST TALK TO HIM, HE MAY COME AROUND TO OUR SIDE!
IF HE ONLY REALIZES THE FACT THAT HE'S JUST BEING USED BY THE NATURALS...
BUT...
IF HE'S NOT WILLING TO LISTEN, WHAT THEN?
!!

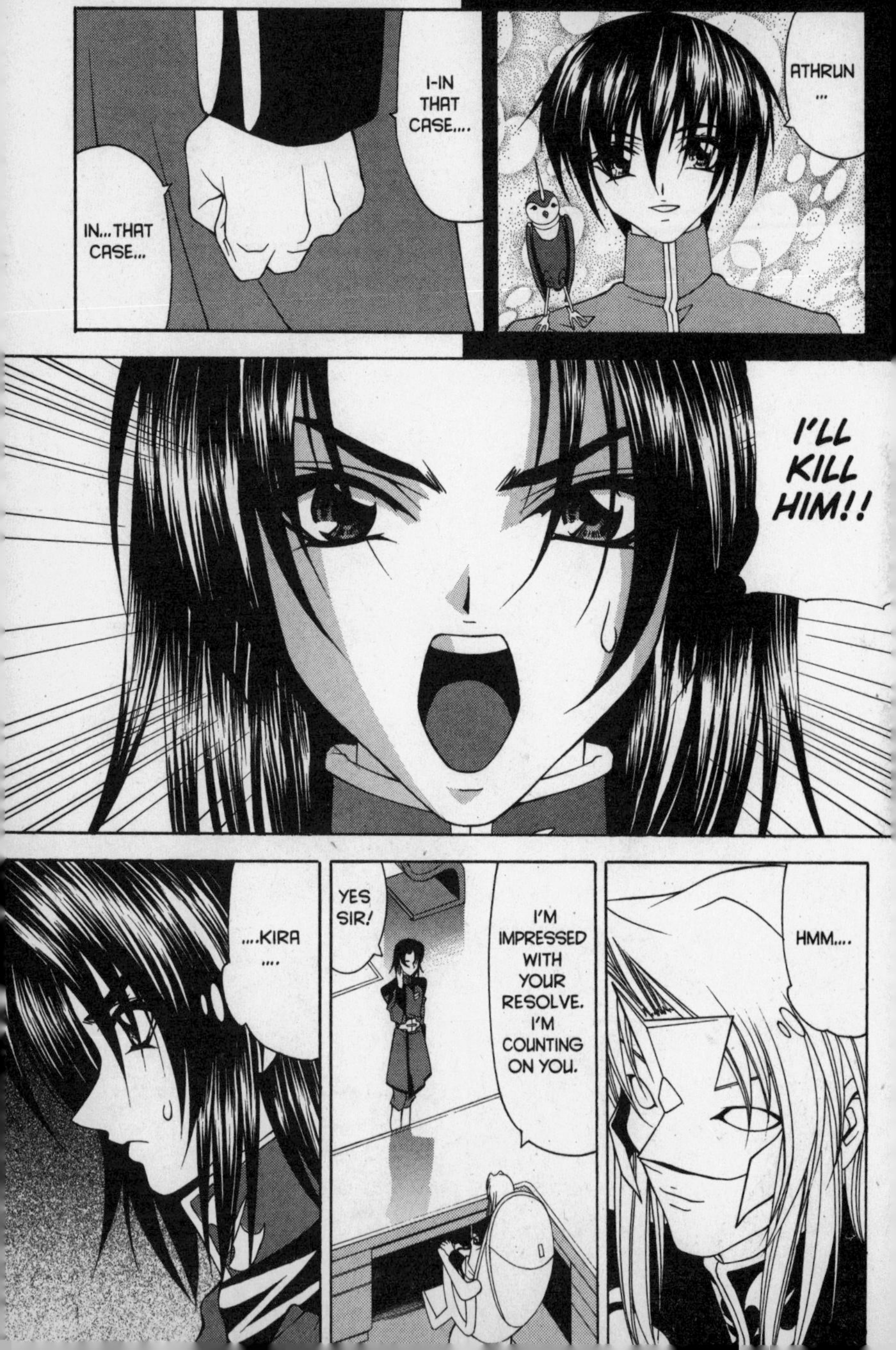
ATHRUN ...
I-IN THAT CASE....
IN...THAT CASE...
I'LL KILL HIM!!
HMM....
I'M IMPRESSED WITH YOUR RESOLVE. I'M COUNTING ON YOU.
YES SIR!
....KIRA ....

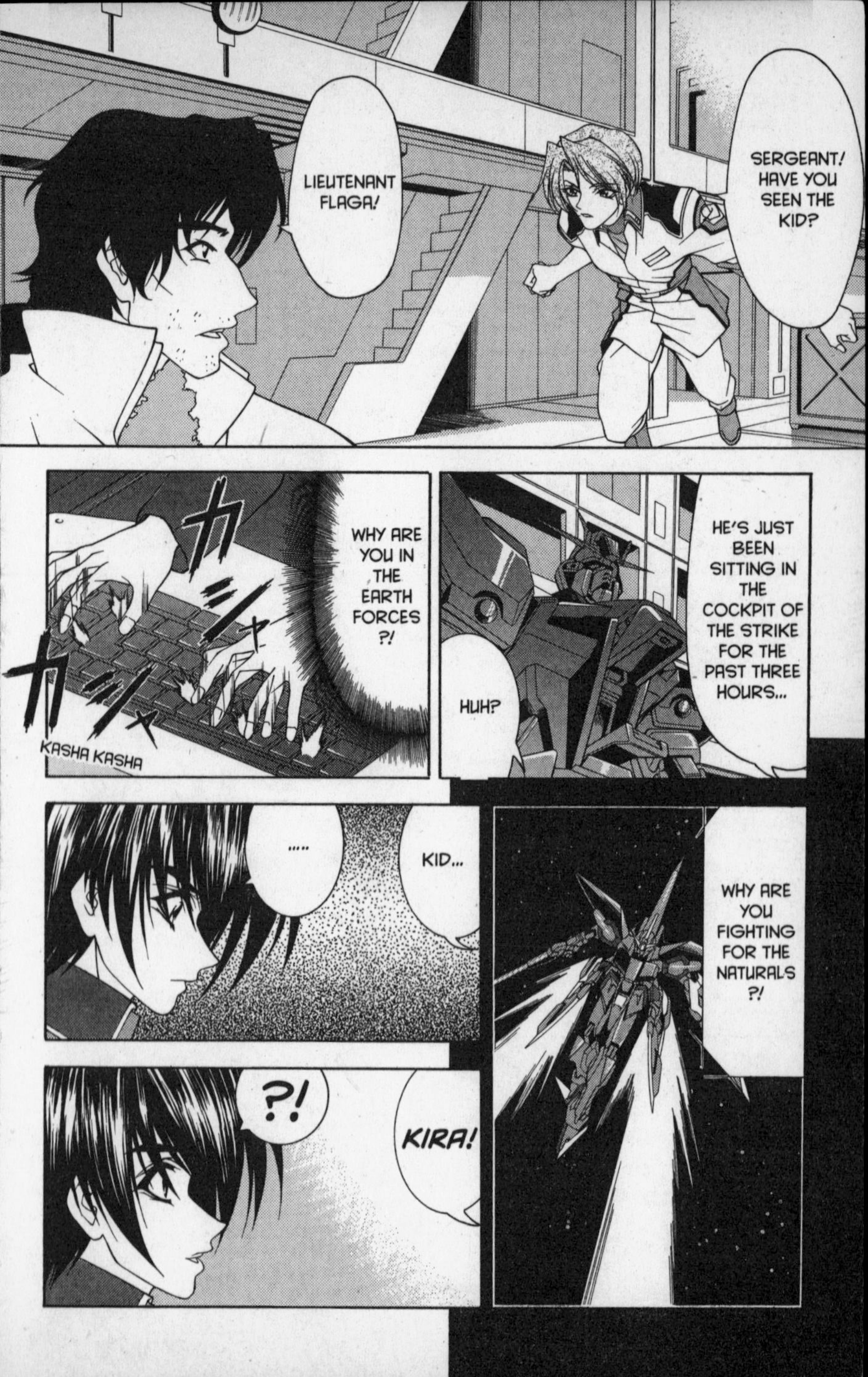
SERGEANT! HAVE YOU SEEN THE KID?
LIEUTENANT FLAGA!
HE'S JUST BEEN SITTING IN THE COCKPIT OF THE STRIKE FOR THE PAST THREE HOURS...
HUH?
WHY ARE YOU IN THE EARTH FORCES?!
KASHA KASHA
WHY ARE YOU FIGHTING FOR THE NATURALS?!
KID...
.....
KIRA!
?!

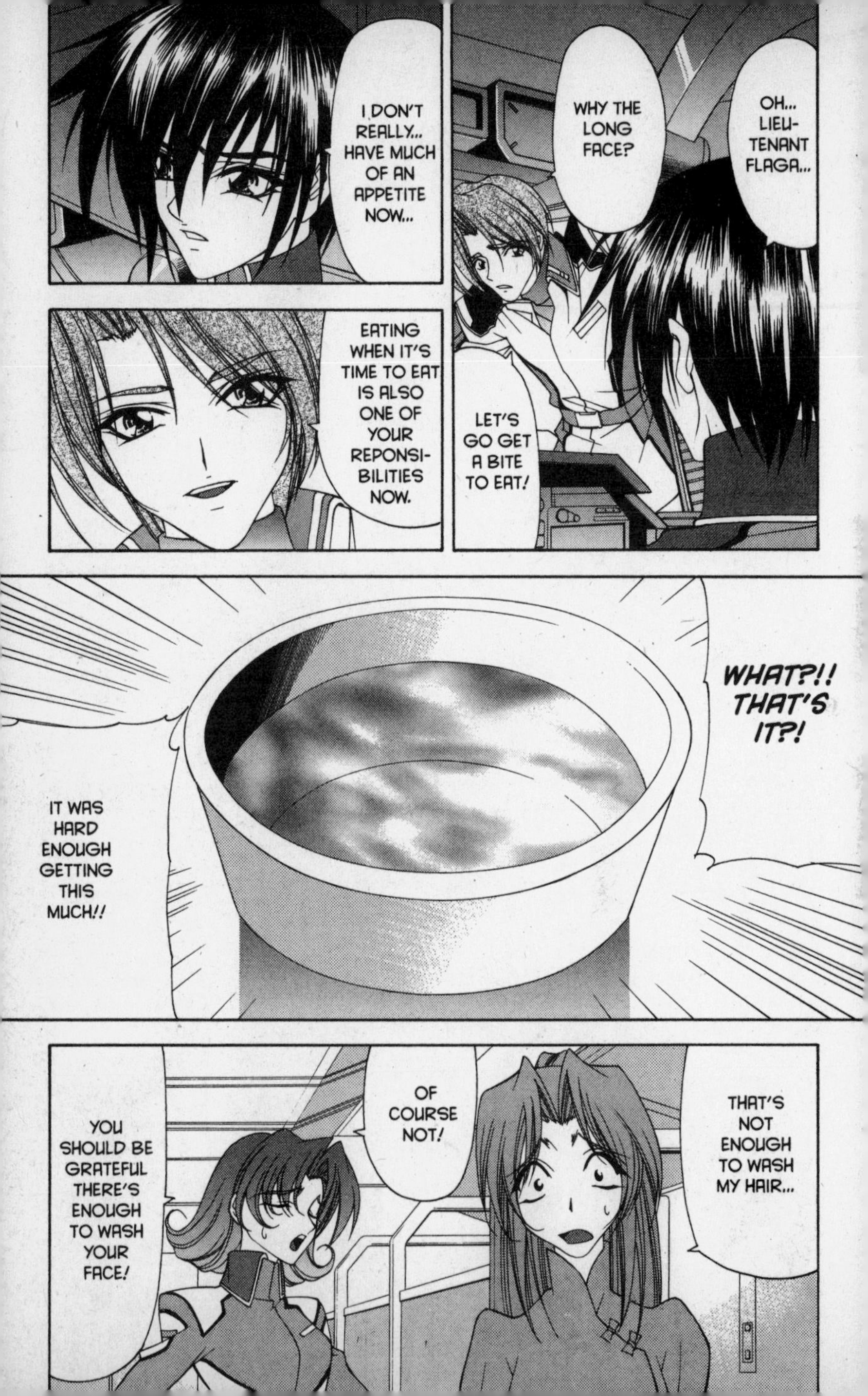

OH... LIEU-TENANT FLAGA...
WHY THE LONG FACE?
LET'S GO GET A BITE TO EAT!
I DON'T REALLY... HAVE MUCH OF AN APPETITE NOW...
EATING WHEN IT'S TIME TO EAT IS ALSO ONE OF YOUR REPONSI-BILITIES NOW.
WHAT?!! THAT'S IT?!
IT WAS HARD ENOUGH GETTING THIS MUCH!!
THAT'S NOT ENOUGH TO WASH MY HAIR...
OF COURSE NOT!
YOU SHOULD BE GRATEFUL THERE'S ENOUGH TO WASH YOUR FACE!

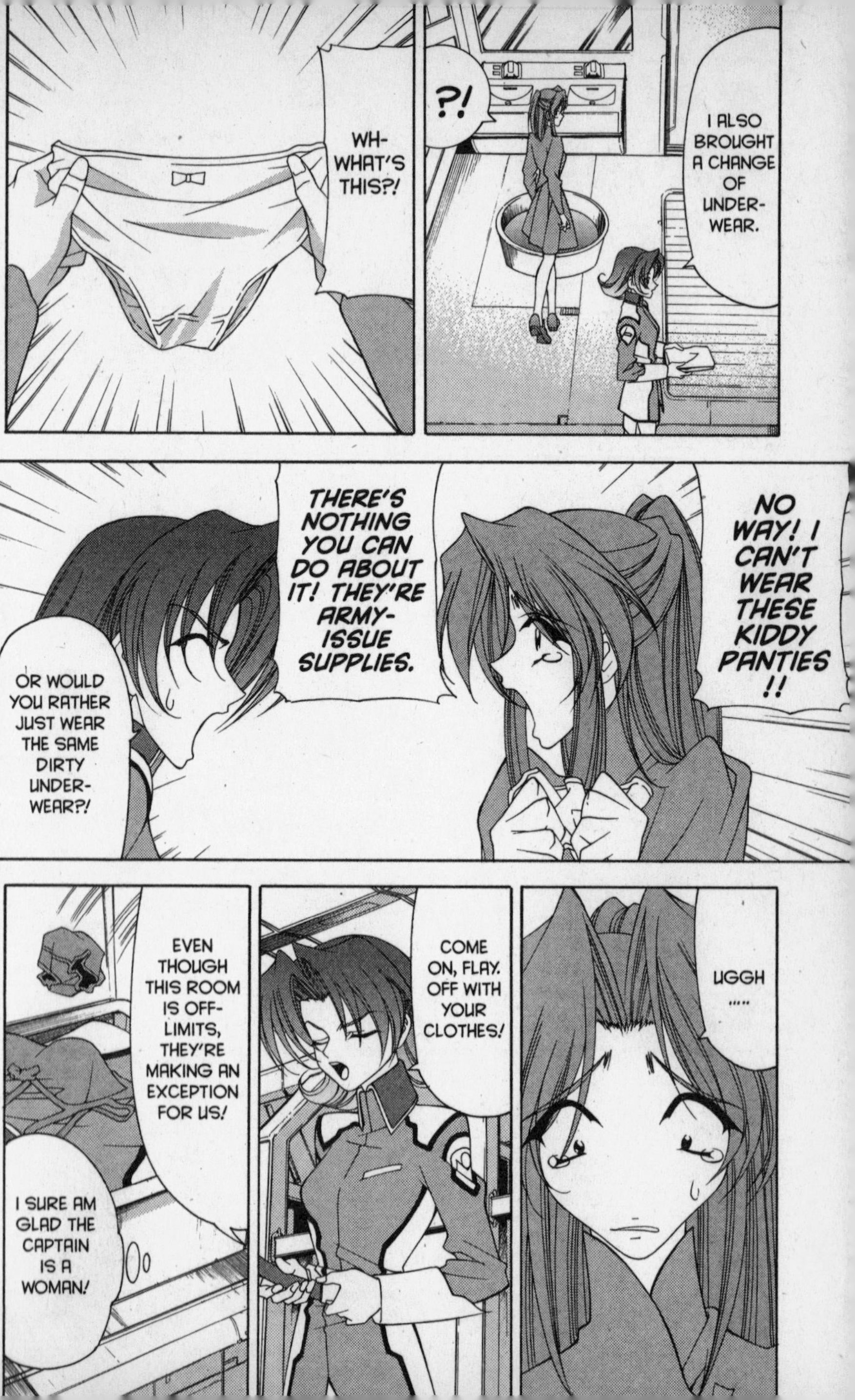
I ALSO BROUGHT A CHANGE OF UNDER-WEAR.
?!
WH-WHAT'S THIS?!
NO WAY! I CAN'T WEAR THESE KIDDY PANTIES!!
THERE'S NOTHING YOU CAN DO ABOUT IT! THEY'RE ARMY-ISSUE SUPPLIES.
OR WOULD YOU RATHER JUST WEAR THE SAME DIRTY UNDER-WEAR?!
UGGH .....
COME ON, FLAY. OFF WITH YOUR CLOTHES!
EVEN THOUGH THIS ROOM IS OFF-LIMITS, THEY'RE MAKING AN EXCEPTION FOR US!
I SURE AM GLAD THE CAPTAIN IS A WOMAN!

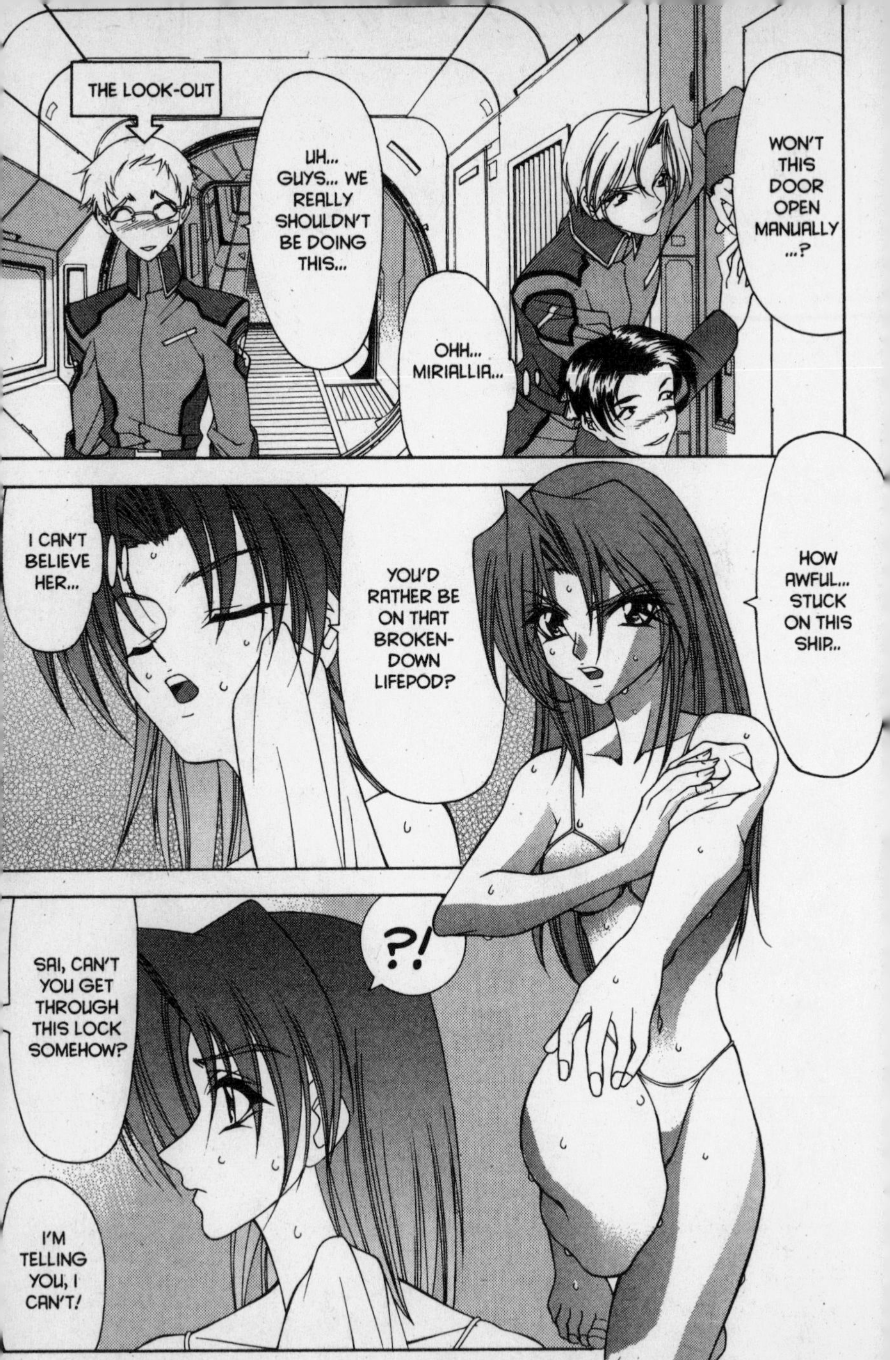

WON'T THIS DOOR OPEN MANUALLY ...?
UH... GUYS... WE REALLY SHOULDN'T BE DOING THIS...
OHH... MIRIALLIA...
THE LOOK-OUT
HOW AWFUL... STUCK ON THIS SHIP...
YOU'D RATHER BE ON THAT BROKEN-DOWN LIFEPOD?
I CAN'T BELIEVE HER...
?!
SAI, CAN'T YOU GET THROUGH THIS LOCK SOMEHOW?
I'M TELLING YOU, I CAN'T!

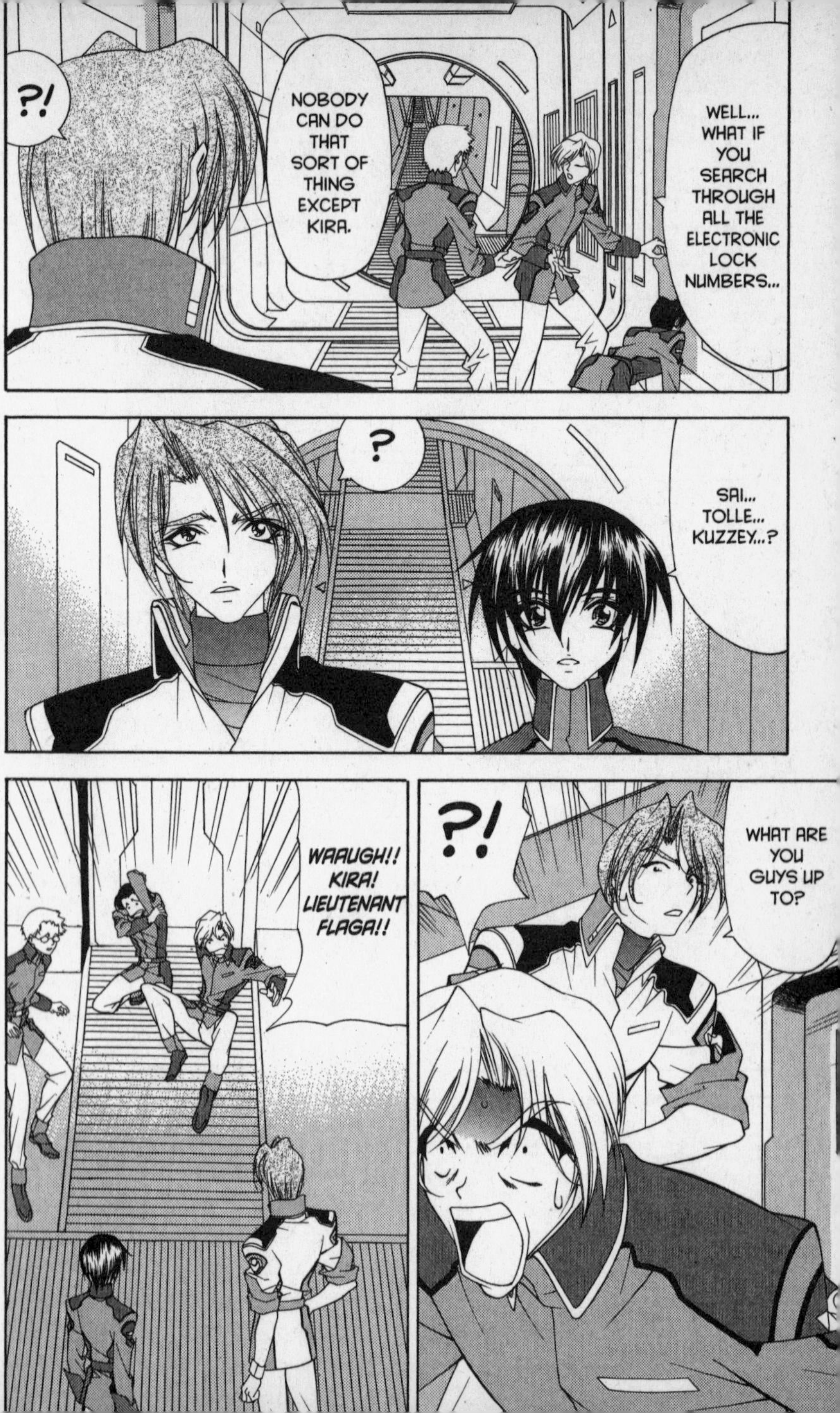
WELL... WHAT IF YOU SEARCH THROUGH ALL THE ELECTRONIC LOCK NUMBERS...
NOBODY CAN DO THAT SORT OF THING EXCEPT KIRA.
?!
SAI... TOLLE... KUZZEY...?
?
WHAT ARE YOU GUYS UP TO?
?!
WAAUGH!! KIRA! LIEUTENANT FLAGA!!

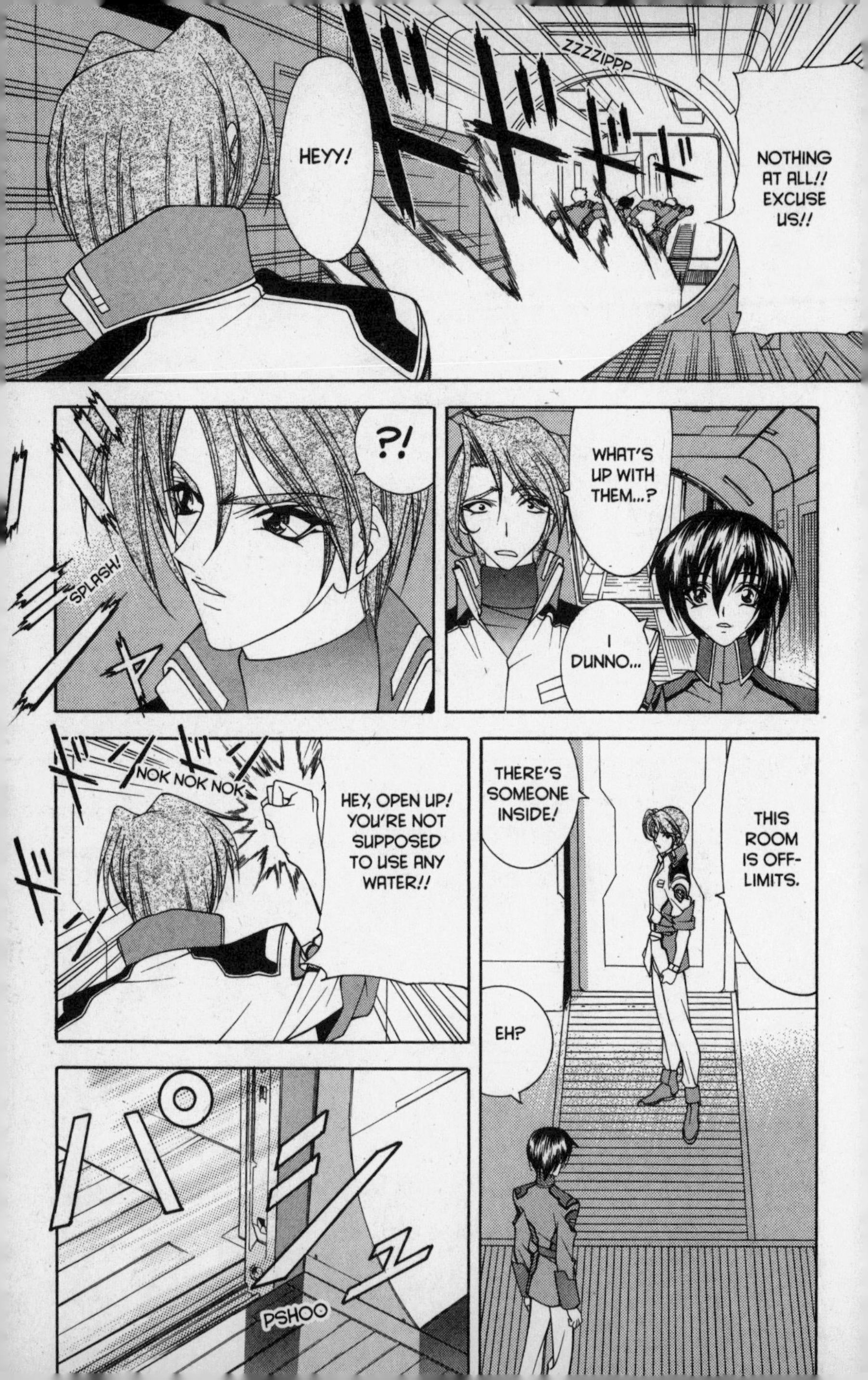
NOTHING AT ALL!! EXCUSE US!!
ZZZZIPPP
HEYY!
WHAT'S UP WITH THEM...?
I DUNNO...
?!
SPLASH!
THIS ROOM IS OFF-LIMITS.
THERE'S SOMEONE INSIDE!
EH?
HEY, OPEN UP! YOU'RE NOT SUPPOSED TO USE ANY WATER!!
NOK NOK NOK
PSHOO

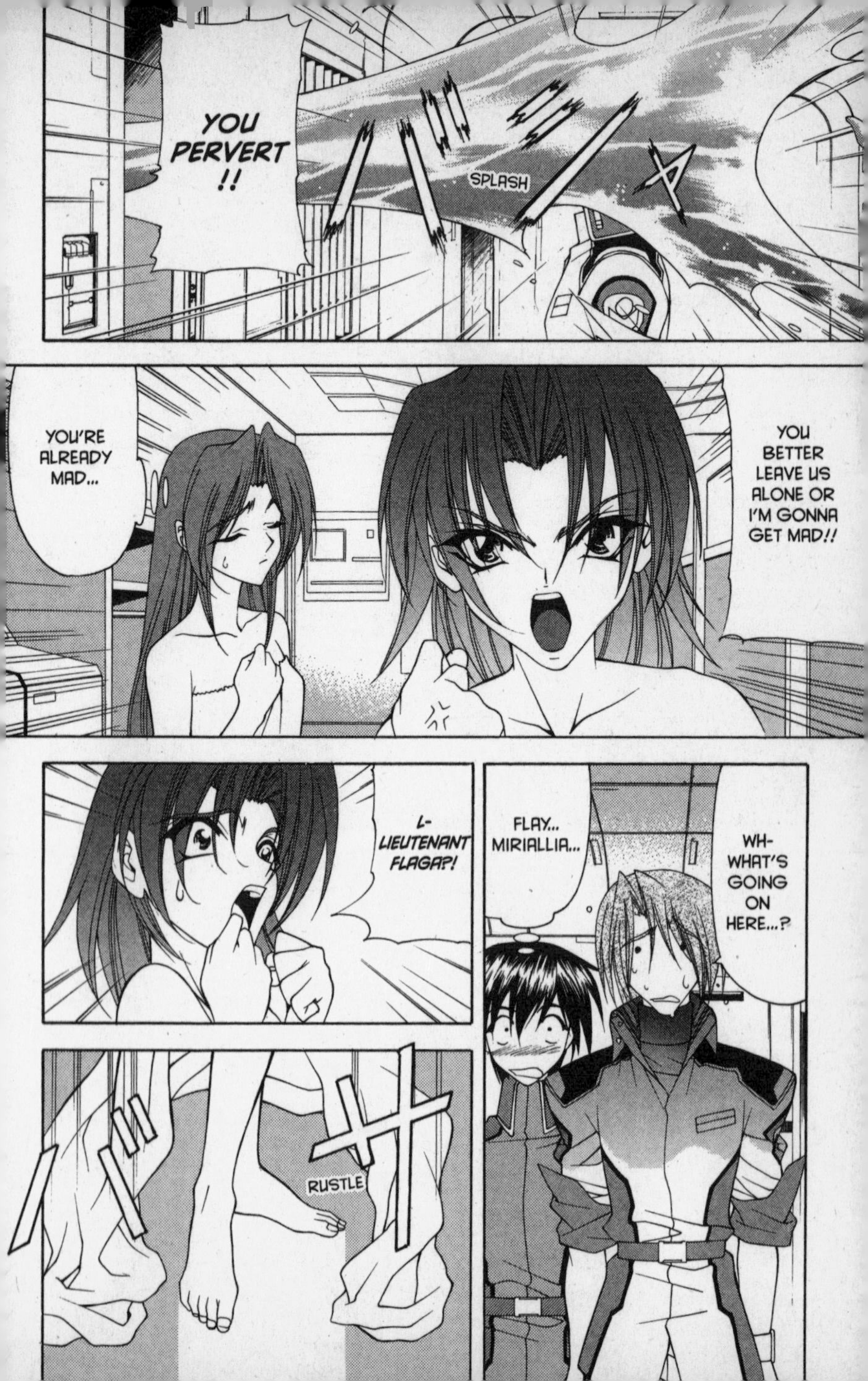
YOU PERVERT!!
SPLASH
YOU BETTER LEAVE US ALONE OR I'M GONNA GET MAD!!
YOU'RE ALREADY MAD...
WH- WHAT'S GOING ON HERE...?
FLAY... MIRIALLIA...
L- LIEUTENANT FLAGA?!
RUSTLE

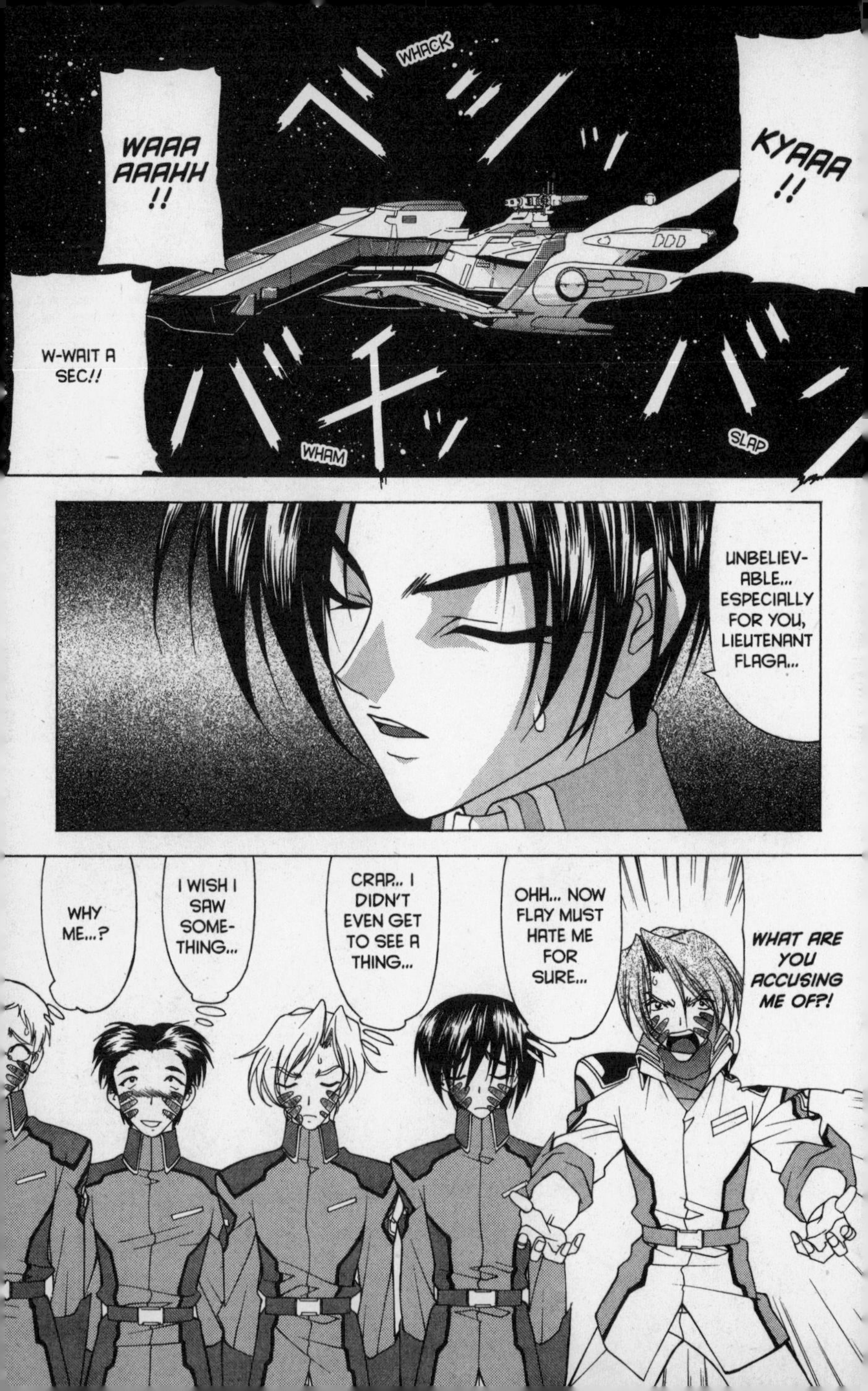
KYAAA!!
WHACK
WAAAAAAHH!!
SLAP
WHAM
W-WAIT A SEC!!
UNBELIEVABLE... ESPECIALLY FOR YOU, LIEUTENANT FLAGA...
WHAT ARE YOU ACCUSING ME OF?!
OHH... NOW FLAY MUST HATE ME FOR SURE...
CRAP... I DIDN'T EVEN GET TO SEE A THING...
I WISH I SAW SOMETHING...
WHY ME...?

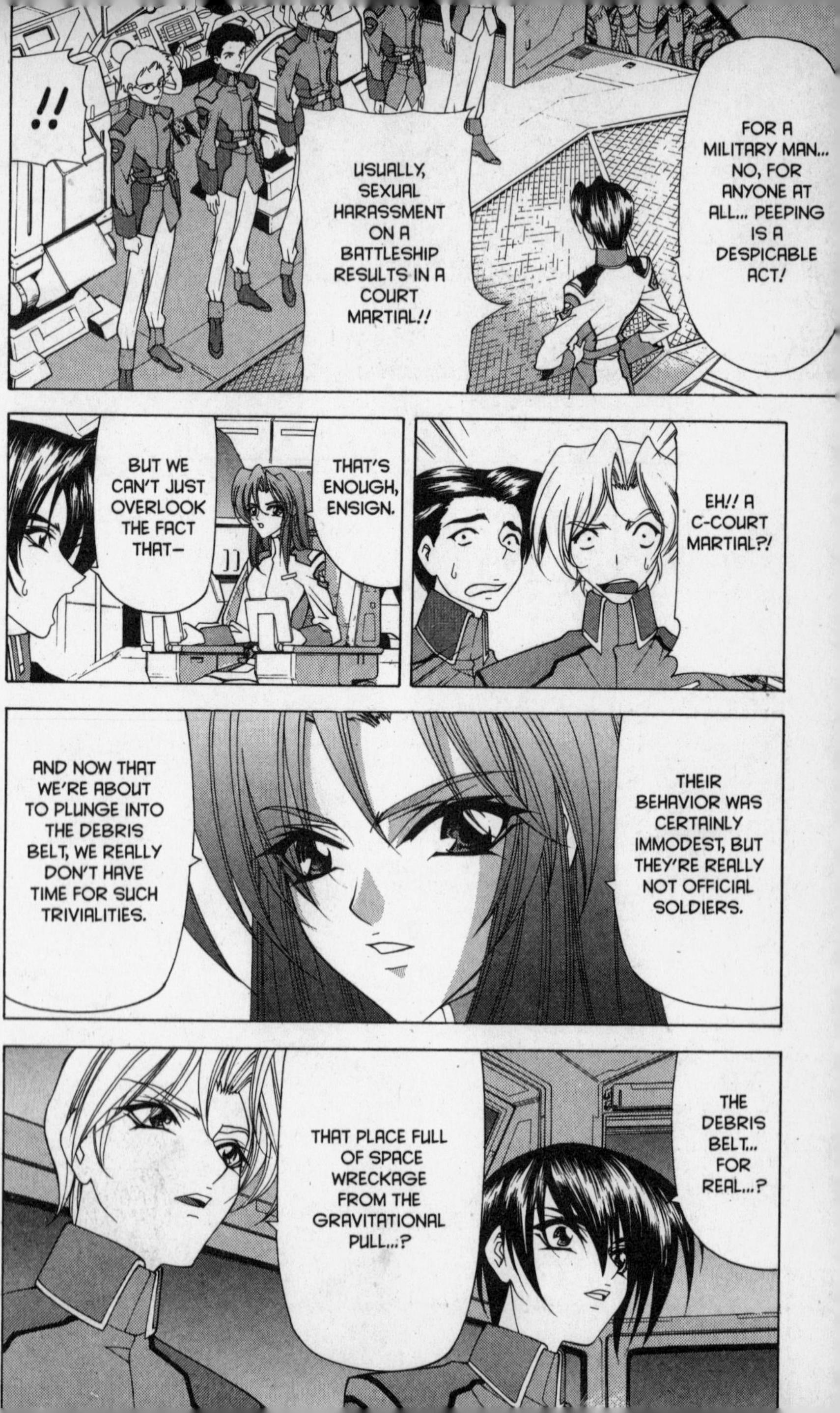
FOR A MILITARY MAN... NO, FOR ANYONE AT ALL... PEEPING IS A DESPICABLE ACT!
USUALLY, SEXUAL HARASSMENT ON A BATTLESHIP RESULTS IN A COURT MARTIAL!!
!!
EH!! A C-COURT MARTIAL?!
THAT'S ENOUGH, ENSIGN.
BUT WE CAN'T JUST OVERLOOK THE FACT THAT—
THEIR BEHAVIOR WAS CERTAINLY IMMODEST, BUT THEY'RE REALLY NOT OFFICIAL SOLDIERS.
AND NOW THAT WE'RE ABOUT TO PLUNGE INTO THE DEBRIS BELT, WE REALLY DON'T HAVE TIME FOR SUCH TRIVIALITIES.
THE DEBRIS BELT... FOR REAL...?
THAT PLACE FULL OF SPACE WRECKAGE FROM THE GRAVITATIONAL PULL...?

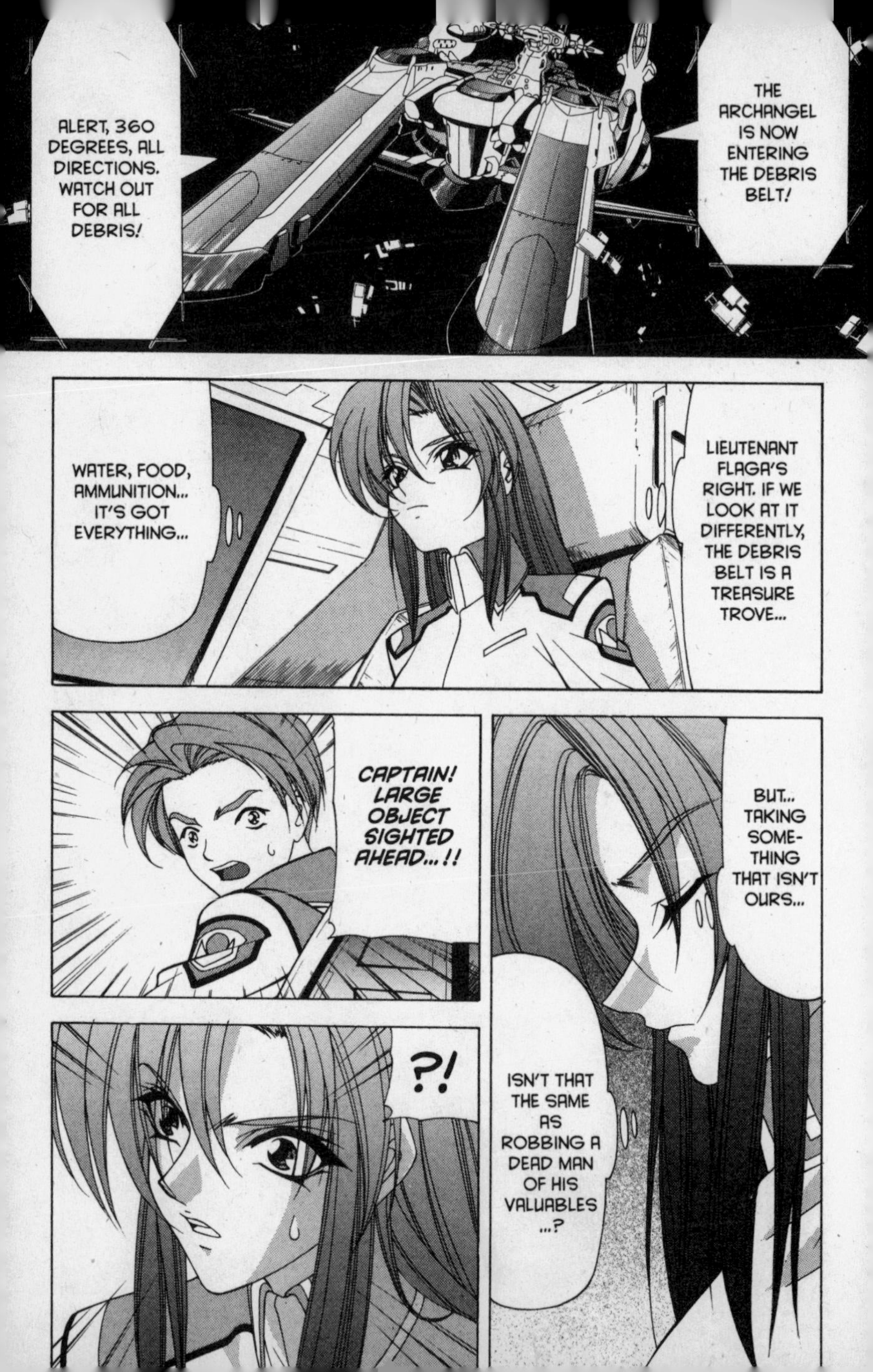
THE ARCHANGEL IS NOW ENTERING THE DEBRIS BELT!
ALERT, 360 DEGREES, ALL DIRECTIONS. WATCH OUT FOR ALL DEBRIS!
LIEUTENANT FLAGA'S RIGHT. IF WE LOOK AT IT DIFFERENTLY, THE DEBRIS BELT IS A TREASURE TROVE...
WATER, FOOD, AMMUNITION... IT'S GOT EVERYTHING...
BUT... TAKING SOMETHING THAT ISN'T OURS...
ISN'T THAT THE SAME AS ROBBING A DEAD MAN OF HIS VALUABLES ...?
CAPTAIN! LARGE OBJECT SIGHTED AHEAD...!!
?!

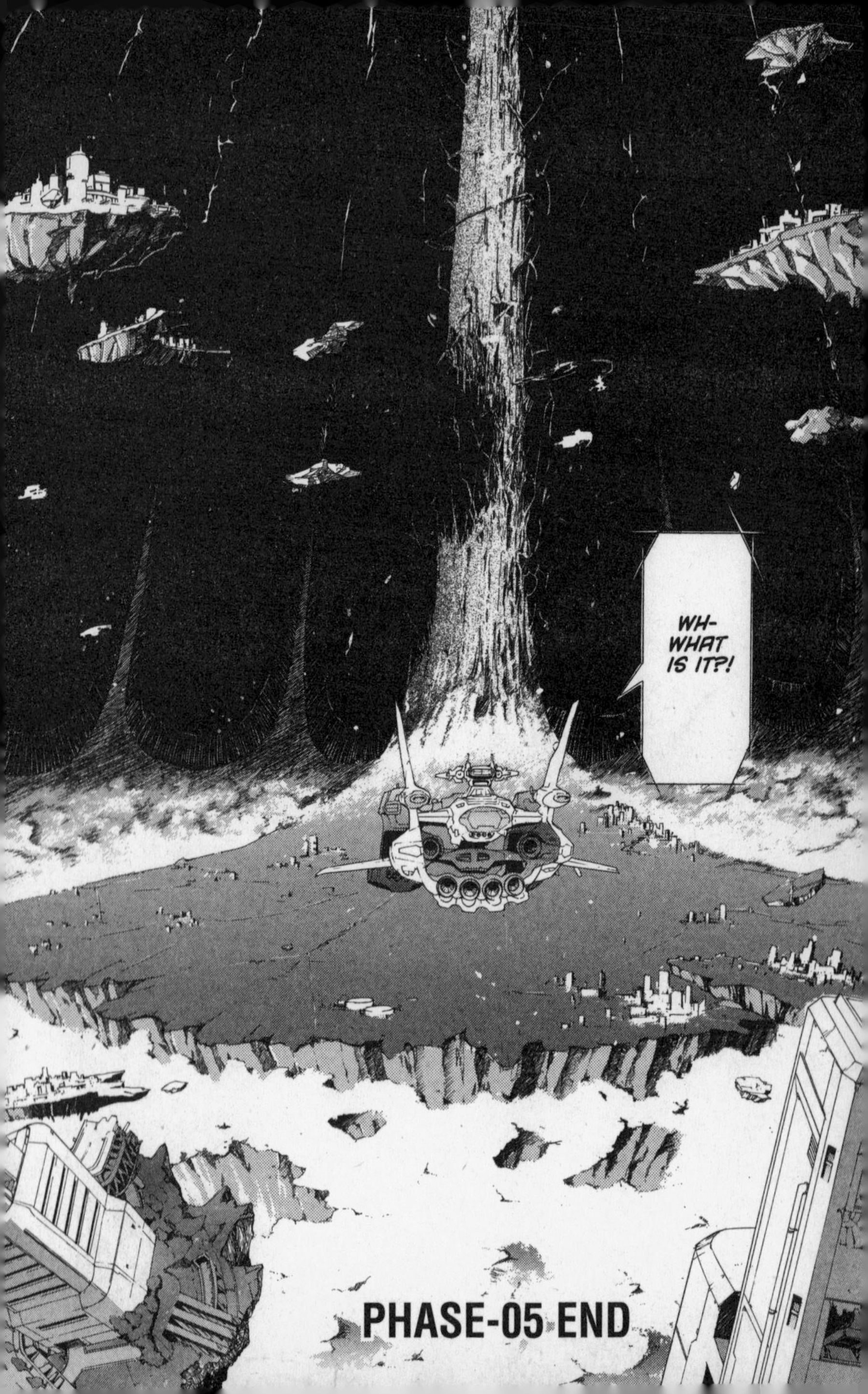
WH-
WHAT
IS IT?!
PHASE-05 END

PHASE-06 THE SCARS OF SPACE—PART 2

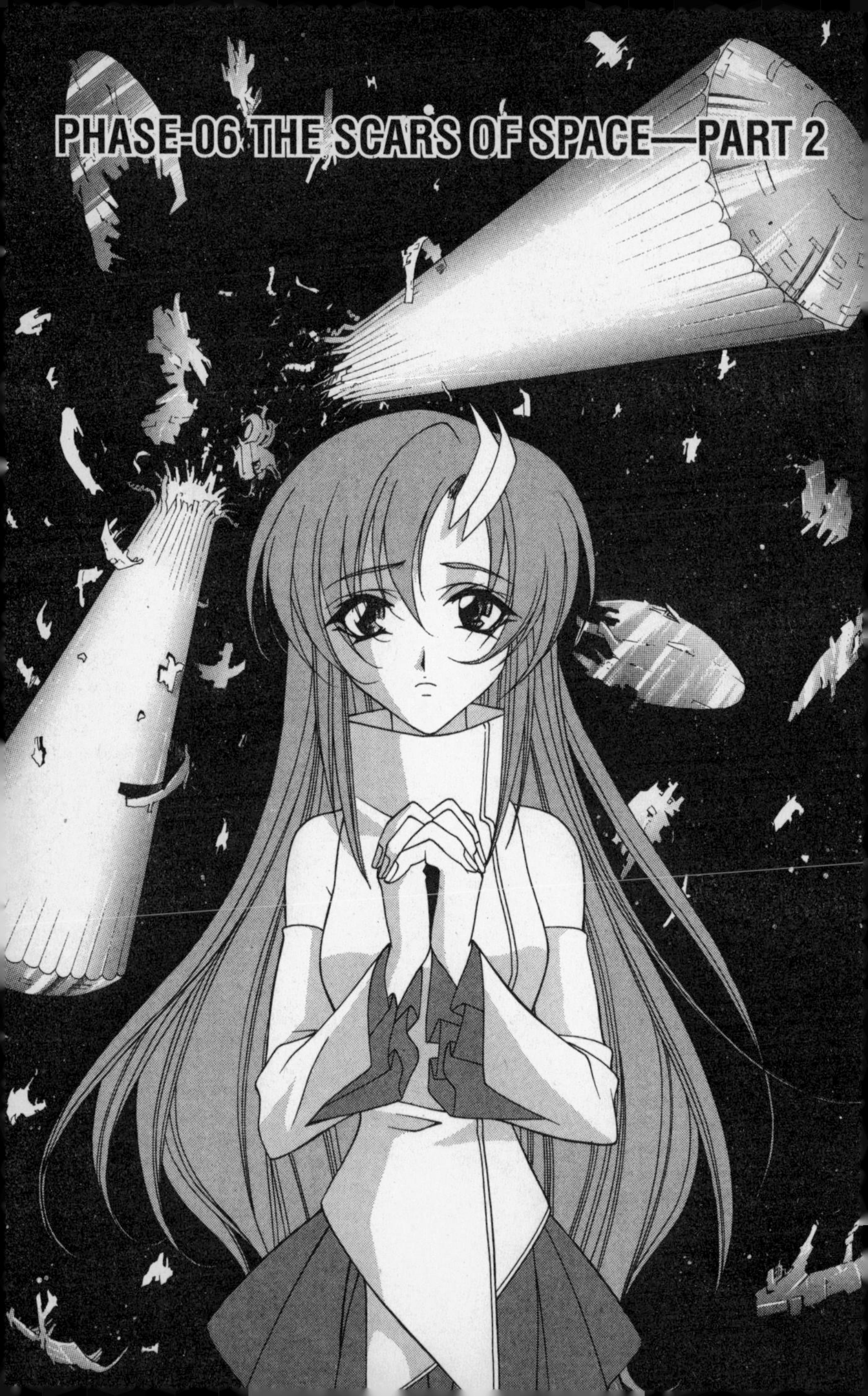

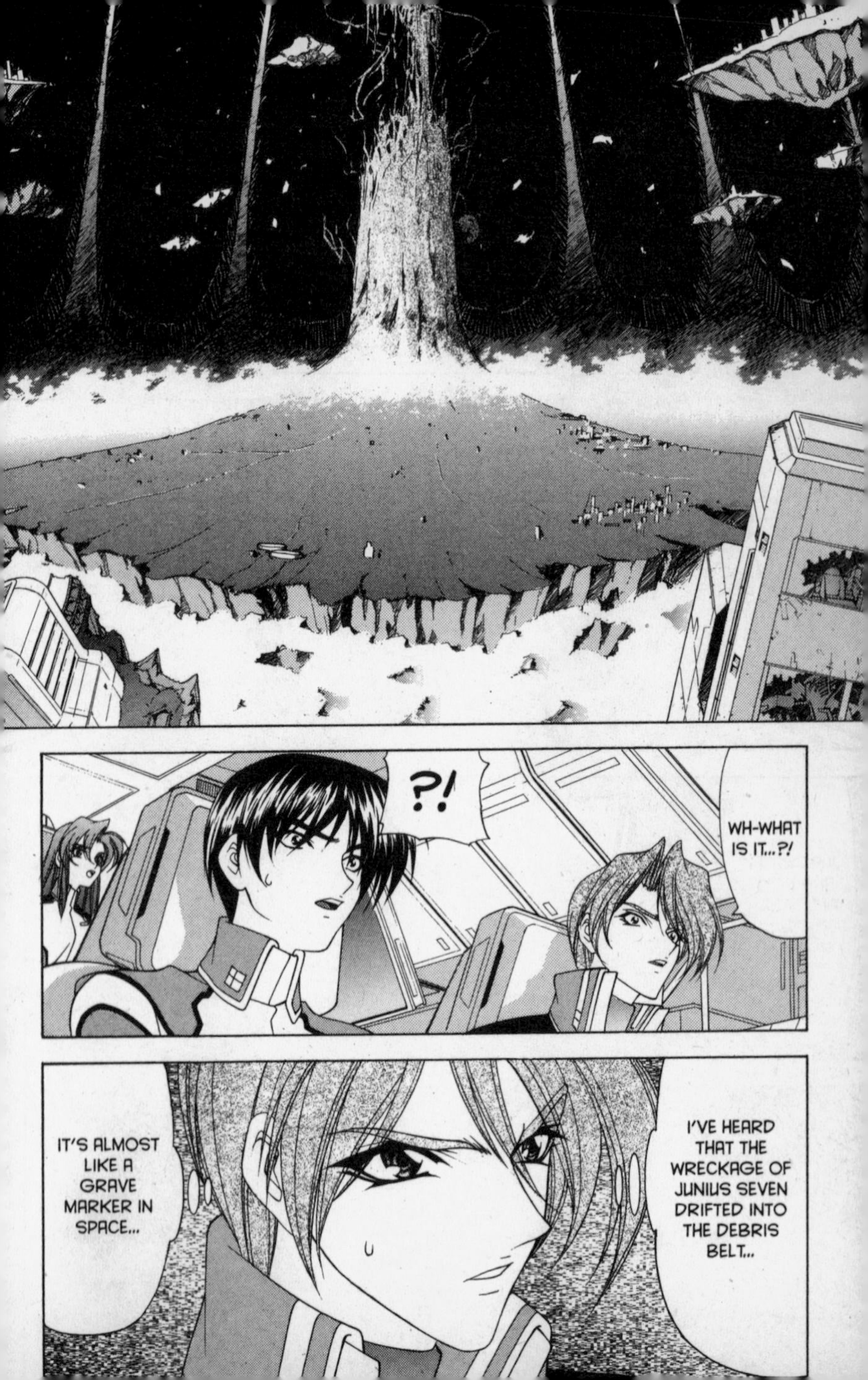
WH-WHAT IS IT...?!
?!
I'VE HEARD THAT THE WRECKAGE OF JUNIUS SEVEN DRIFTED INTO THE DEBRIS BELT...
IT'S ALMOST LIKE A GRAVE MARKER IN SPACE...

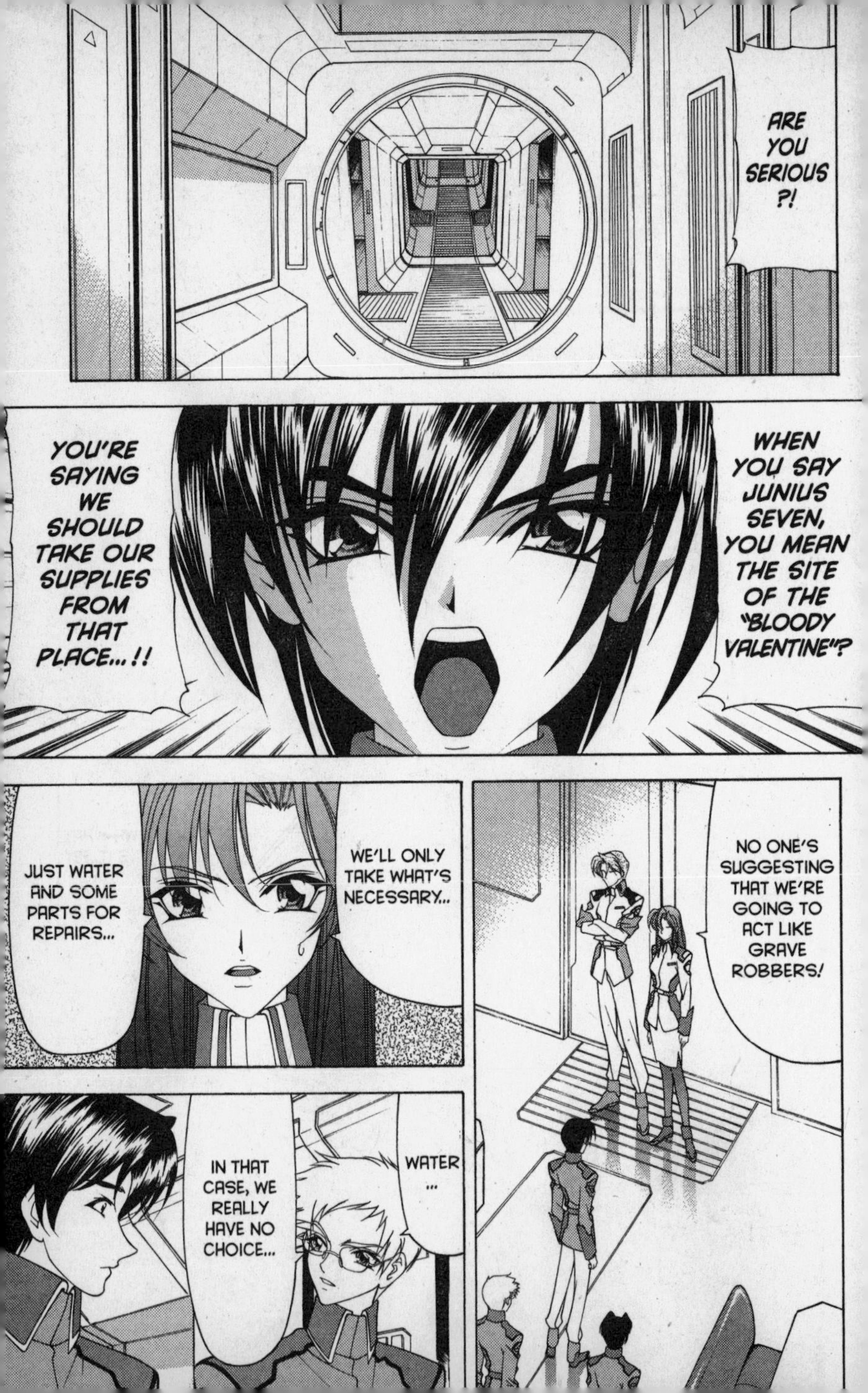
ARE YOU SERIOUS ?!
WHEN YOU SAY JUNIUS SEVEN, YOU MEAN THE SITE OF THE "BLOODY VALENTINE"?
YOU'RE SAYING WE SHOULD TAKE OUR SUPPLIES FROM THAT PLACE...!!
NO ONE'S SUGGESTING THAT WE'RE GOING TO ACT LIKE GRAVE ROBBERS!
WE'LL ONLY TAKE WHAT'S NECESSARY...
JUST WATER AND SOME PARTS FOR REPAIRS...
WATER ...
IN THAT CASE, WE REALLY HAVE NO CHOICE...

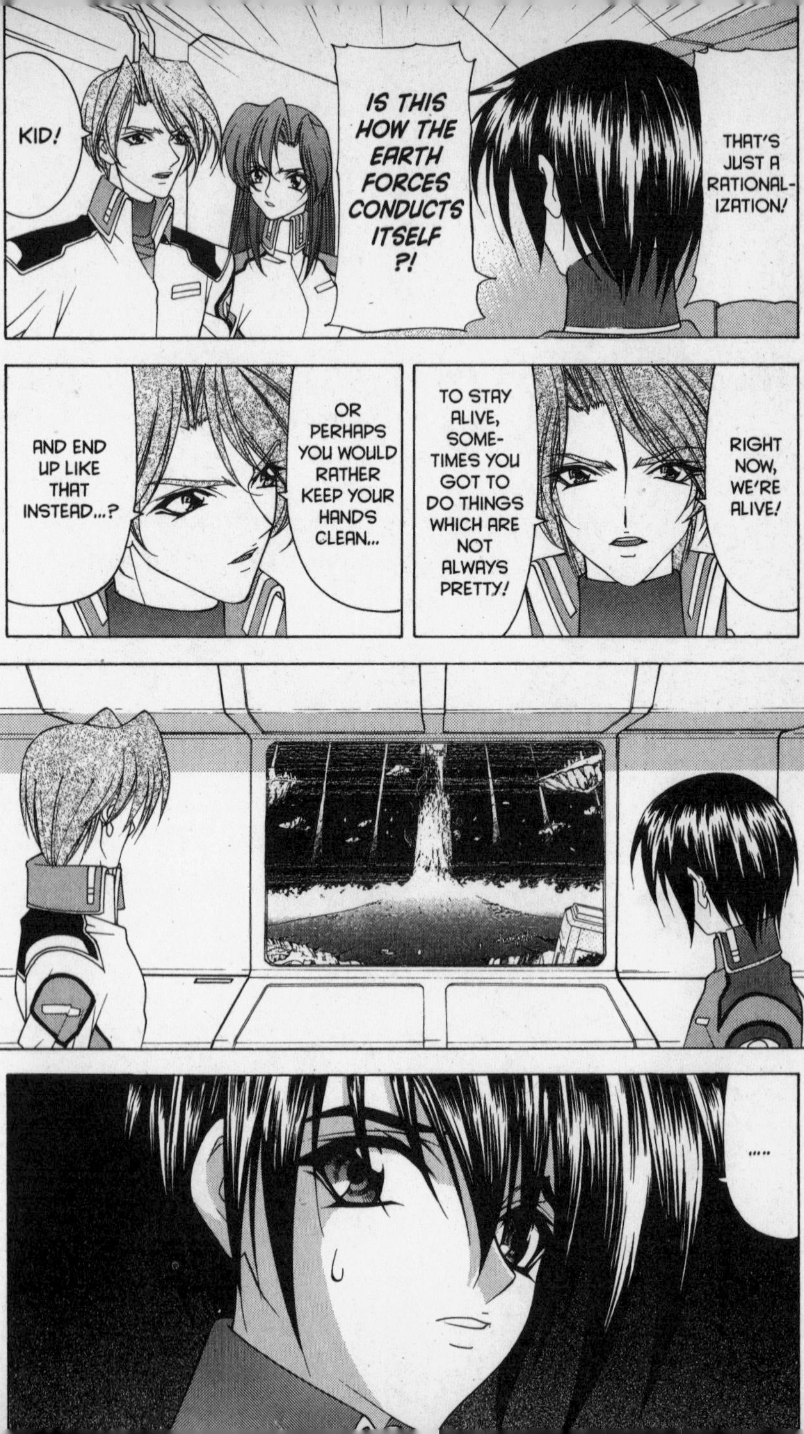
THAT'S JUST A RATIONAL-IZATION!
IS THIS HOW THE EARTH FORCES CONDUCTS ITSELF ?!
KID!
RIGHT NOW, WE'RE ALIVE!
TO STAY ALIVE, SOME-TIMES YOU GOT TO DO THINGS WHICH ARE NOT ALWAYS PRETTY!
OR PERHAPS YOU WOULD RATHER KEEP YOUR HANDS CLEAN...
AND END UP LIKE THAT INSTEAD...?
.....

?!

FATHER!

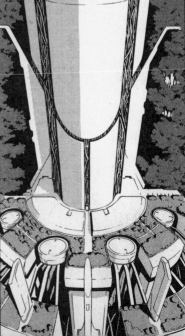

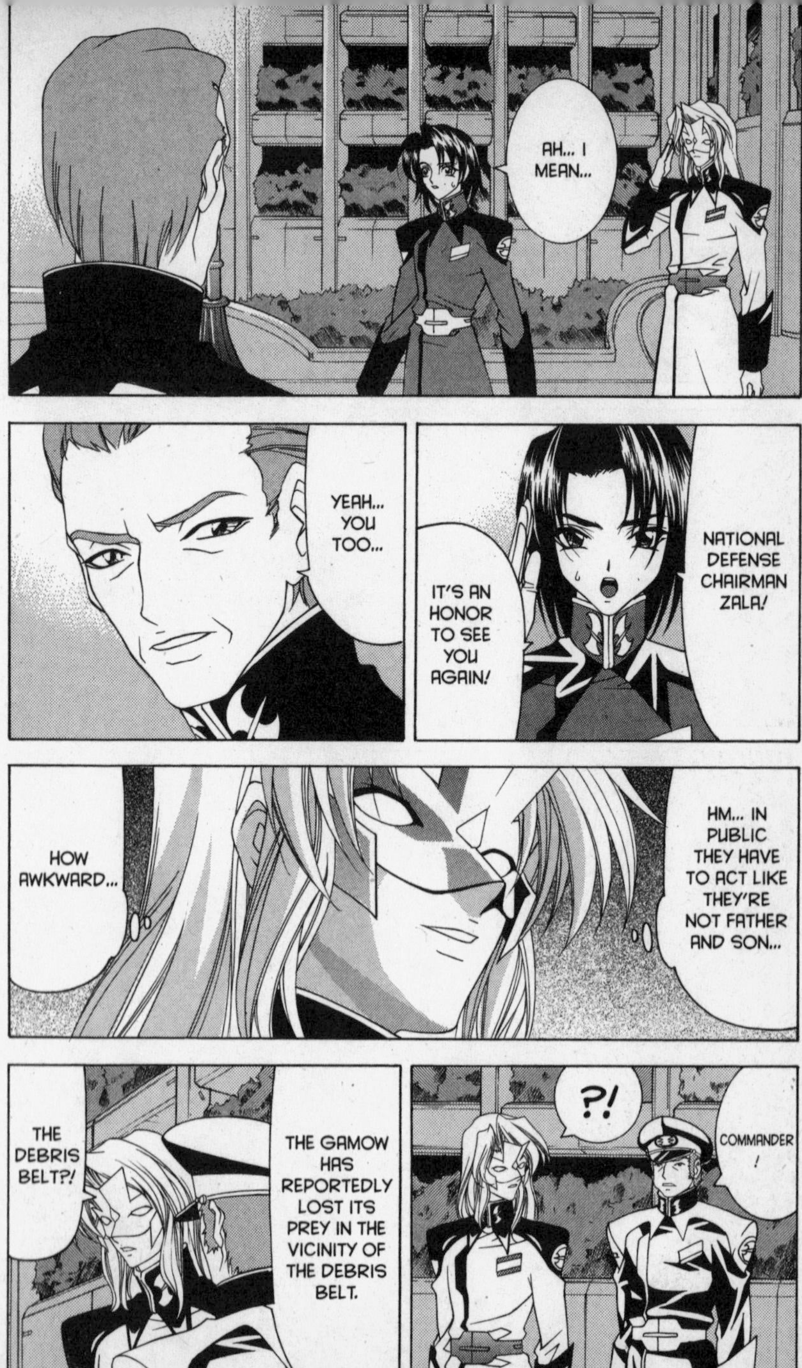
AH... I MEAN...
NATIONAL DEFENSE CHAIRMAN ZALA!
IT'S AN HONOR TO SEE YOU AGAIN!
YEAH... YOU TOO...
HM... IN PUBLIC THEY HAVE TO ACT LIKE THEY'RE NOT FATHER AND SON...
HOW AWKWARD...
COMMANDER!
?!
THE GAMOW HAS REPORTEDLY LOST ITS PREY IN THE VICINITY OF THE DEBRIS BELT.
THE DEBRIS BELT?!

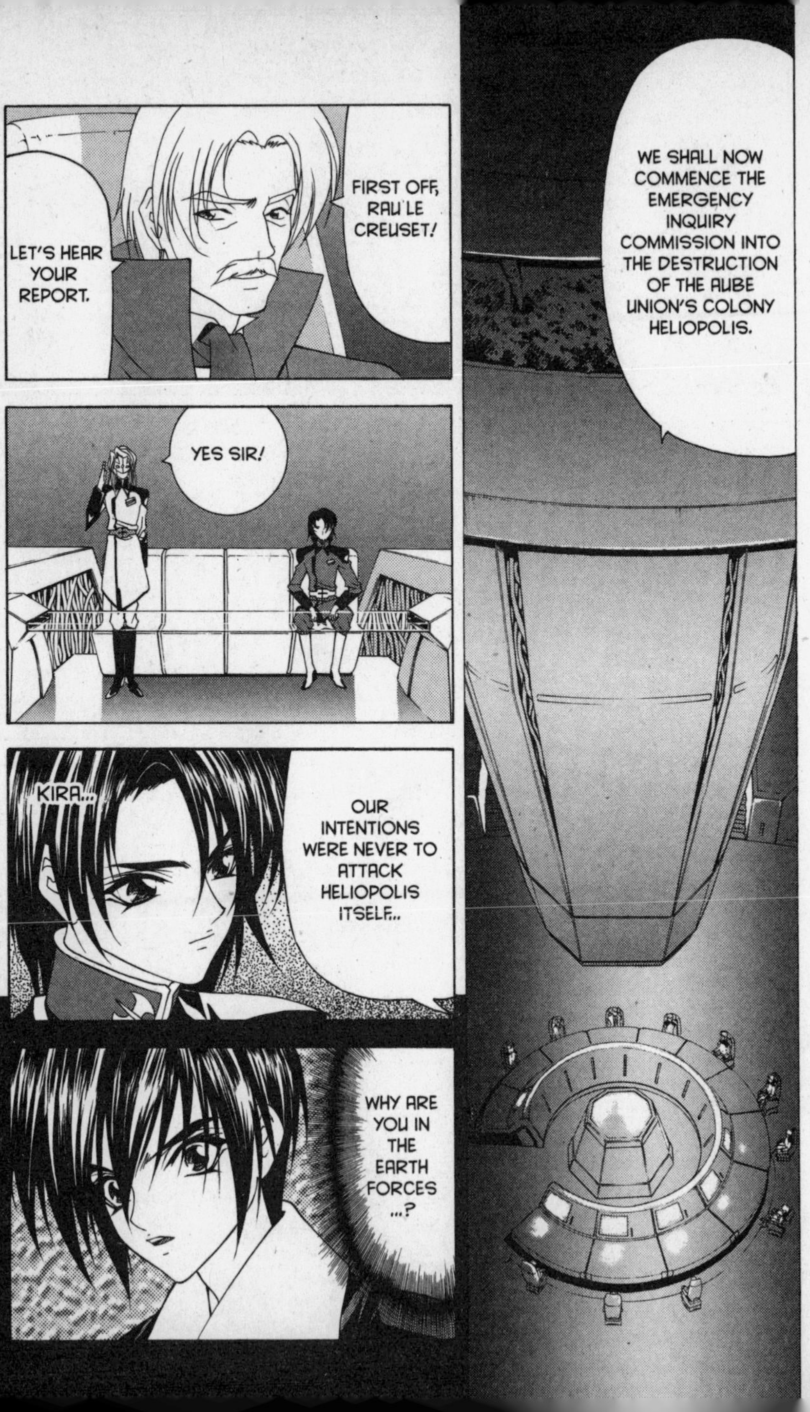
WE SHALL NOW COMMENCE THE EMERGENCY INQUIRY COMMISSION INTO THE DESTRUCTION OF THE AUBE UNION'S COLONY HELIOPOLIS.
FIRST OFF, RAU LE CREUSET!
LET'S HEAR YOUR REPORT.
YES SIR!
OUR INTENTIONS WERE NEVER TO ATTACK HELIOPOLIS ITSELF...
KIRA...
WHY ARE YOU IN THE EARTH FORCES ...?

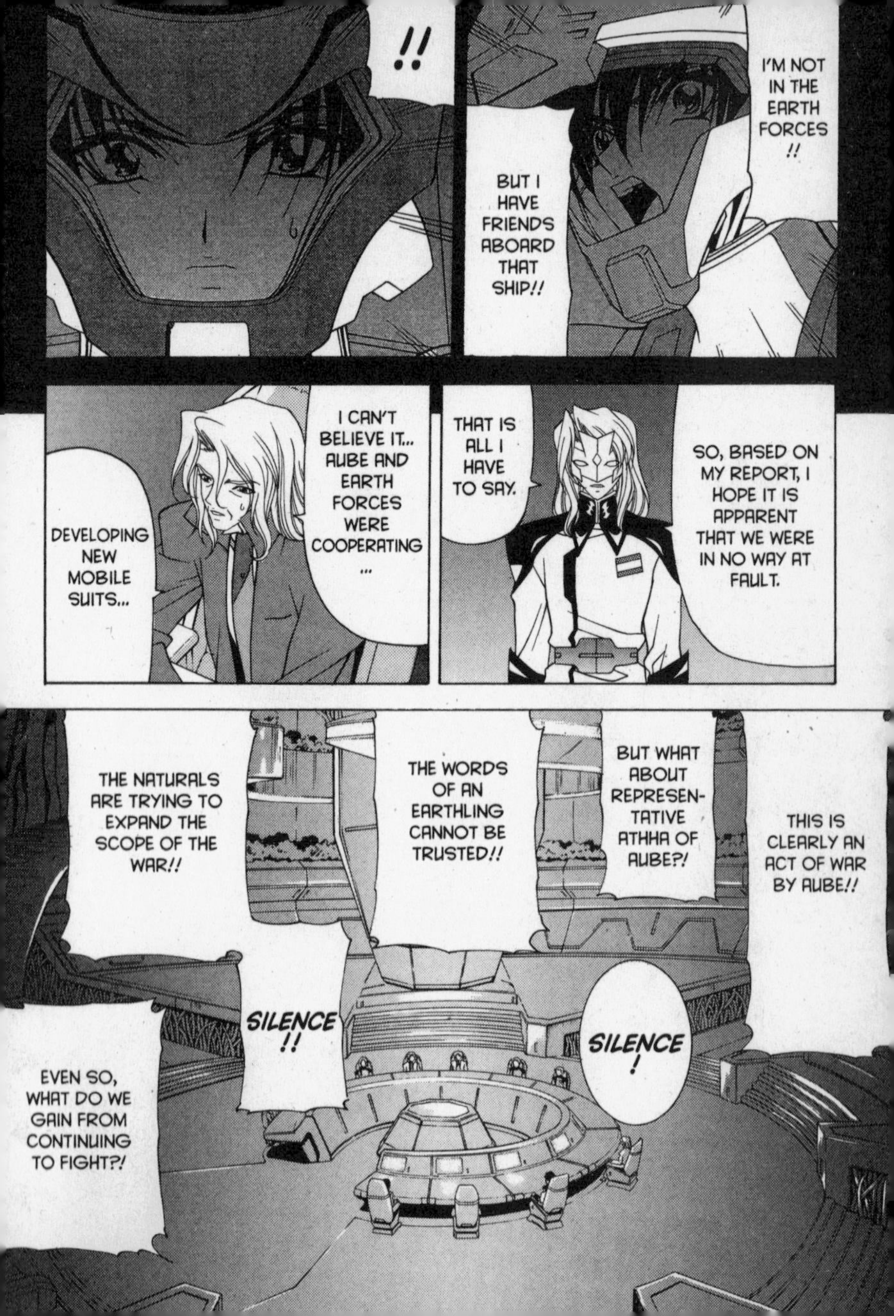
I'M NOT IN THE EARTH FORCES!!
BUT I HAVE FRIENDS ABOARD THAT SHIP!!
!!
SO, BASED ON MY REPORT, I HOPE IT IS APPARENT THAT WE WERE IN NO WAY AT FAULT.
THAT IS ALL I HAVE TO SAY.
I CAN'T BELIEVE IT... AUBE AND EARTH FORCES WERE COOPERATING...
DEVELOPING NEW MOBILE SUITS...
THIS IS CLEARLY AN ACT OF WAR BY AUBE!!
BUT WHAT ABOUT REPRESEN-TATIVE ATHHA OF AUBE?!
THE WORDS OF AN EARTHLING CANNOT BE TRUSTED!!
THE NATURALS ARE TRYING TO EXPAND THE SCOPE OF THE WAR!!
SILENCE!
SILENCE!!
EVEN SO, WHAT DO WE GAIN FROM CONTINUING TO FIGHT?!

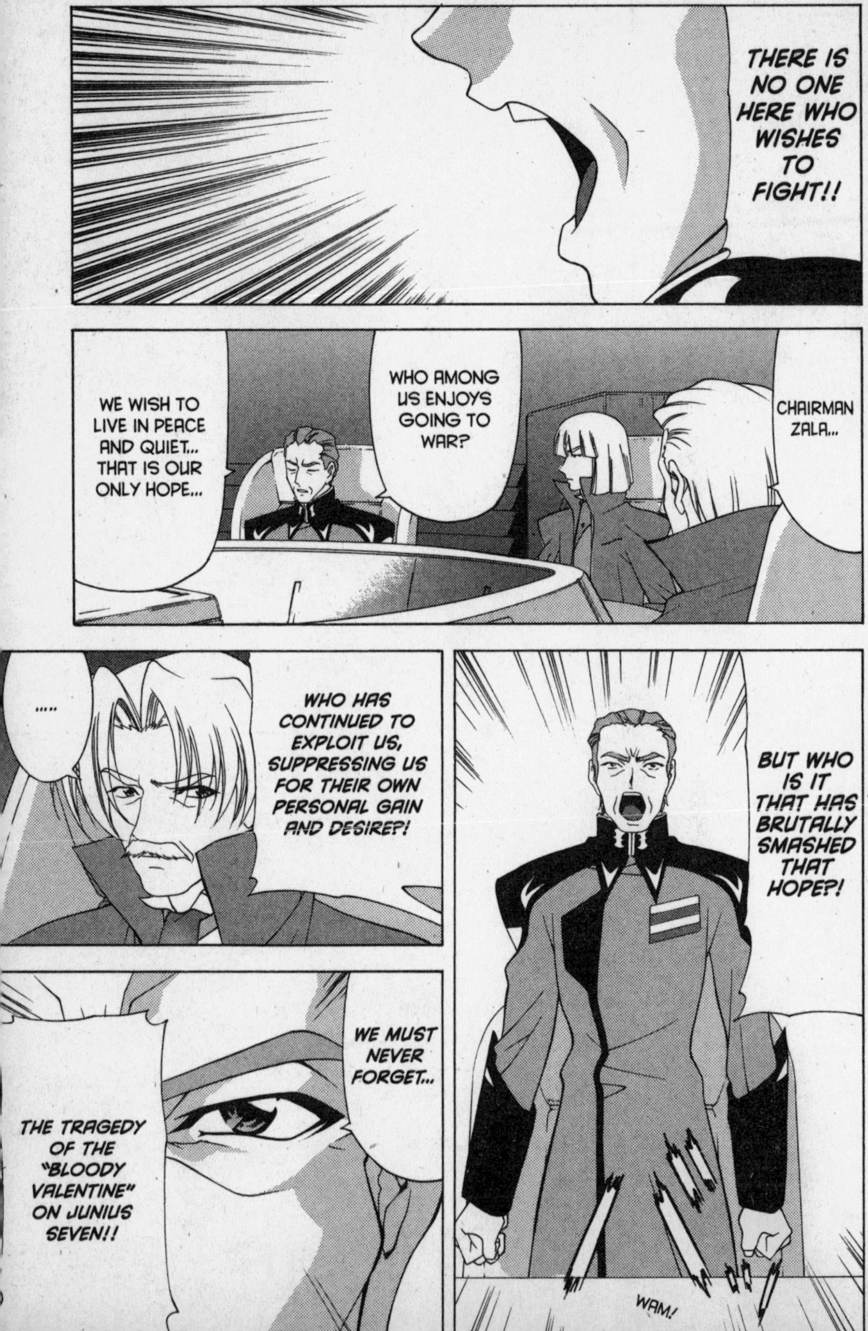
THERE IS NO ONE HERE WHO WISHES TO FIGHT!!
CHAIRMAN ZALA...
WHO AMONG US ENJOYS GOING TO WAR?
WE WISH TO LIVE IN PEACE AND QUIET... THAT IS OUR ONLY HOPE...
BUT WHO IS IT THAT HAS BRUTALLY SMASHED THAT HOPE?!
WAM!
WHO HAS CONTINUED TO EXPLOIT US, SUPPRESSING US FOR THEIR OWN PERSONAL GAIN AND DESIRE?!
.....
WE MUST NEVER FORGET...
THE TRAGEDY OF THE "BLOODY VALENTINE" ON JUNIUS SEVEN!!

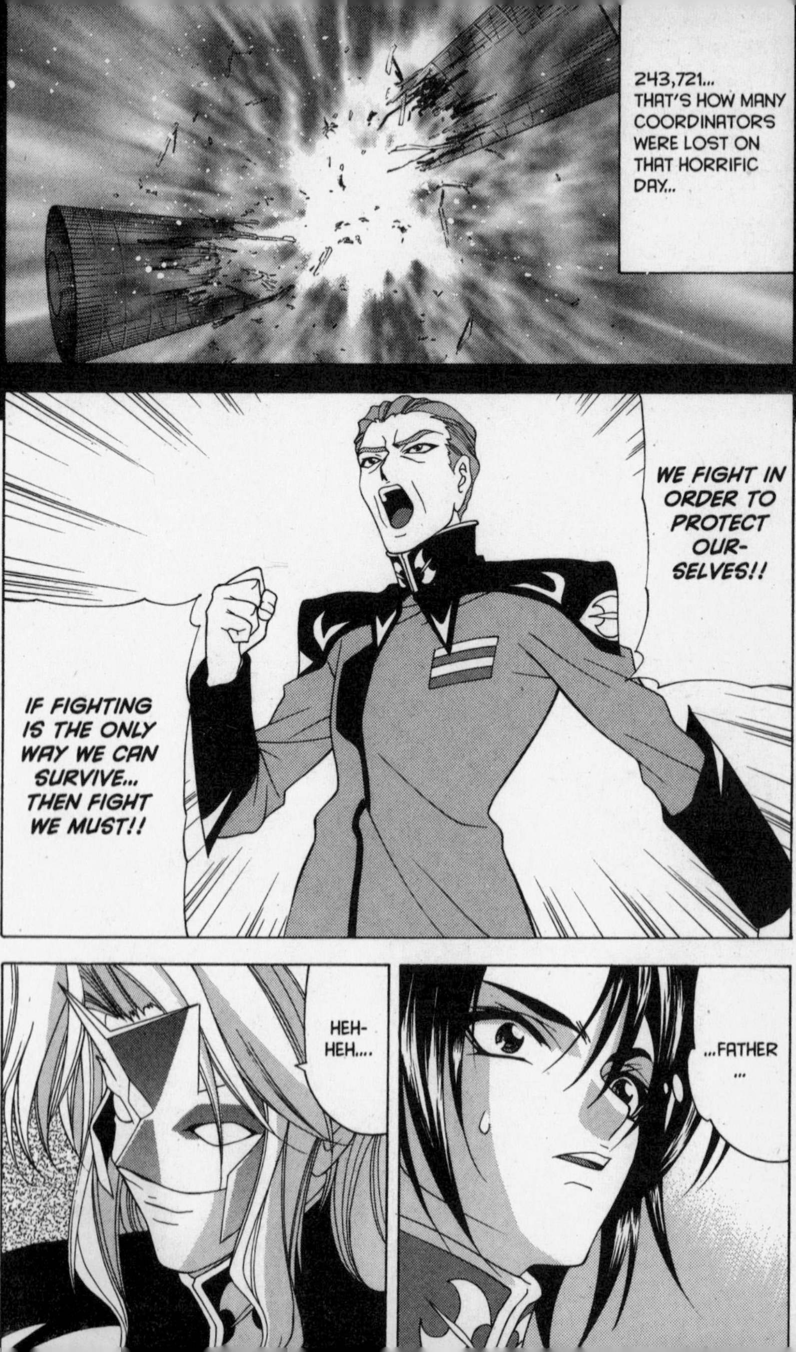
243,721... THAT'S HOW MANY COORDINATORS WERE LOST ON THAT HORRIFIC DAY...
WE FIGHT IN ORDER TO PROTECT OURSELVES!!
IF FIGHTING IS THE ONLY WAY WE CAN SURVIVE... THEN FIGHT WE MUST!!
...FATHER ...
HEH-HEH....

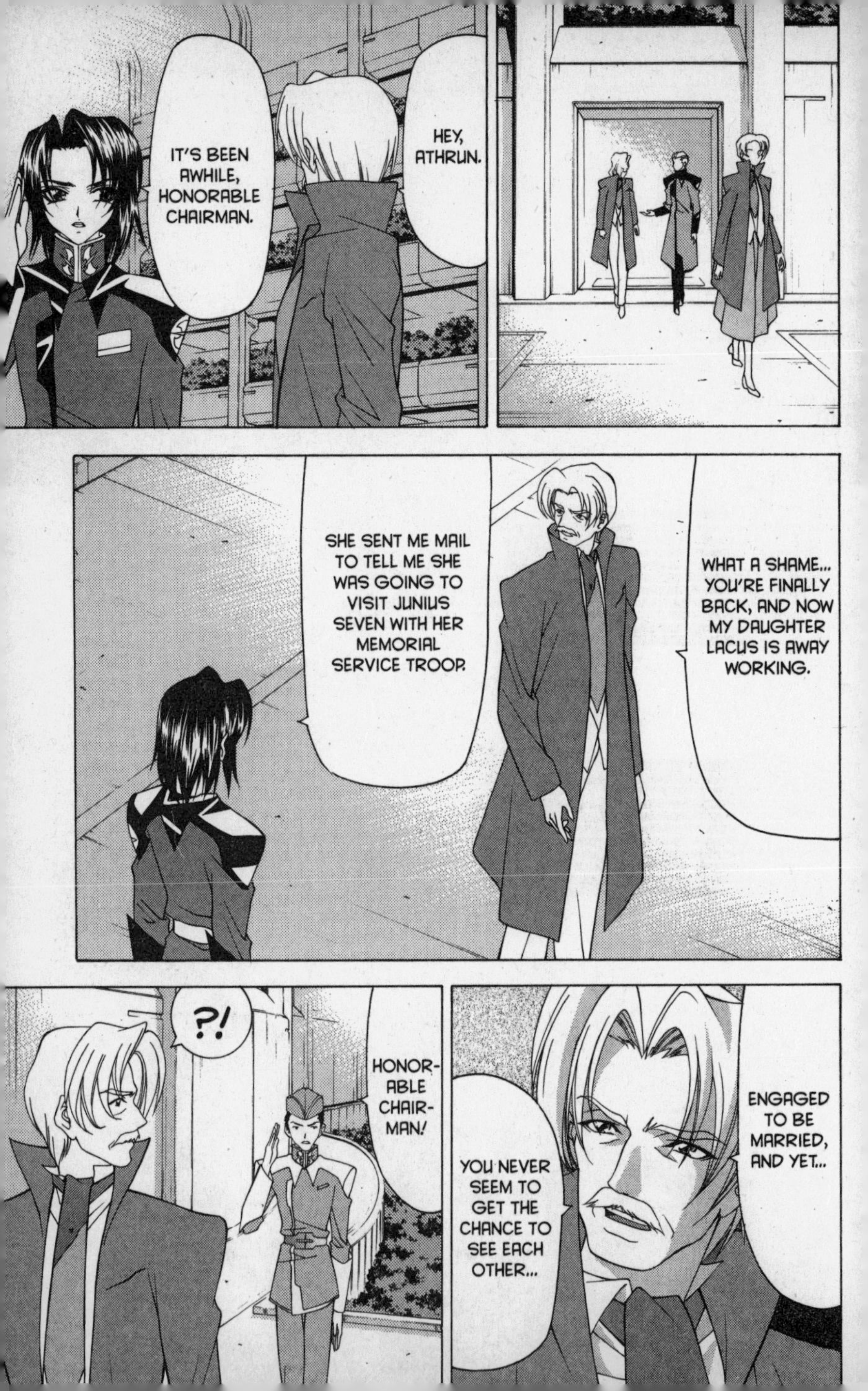
HEY, ATHRUN.
IT'S BEEN AWHILE, HONORABLE CHAIRMAN.
WHAT A SHAME... YOU'RE FINALLY BACK, AND NOW MY DAUGHTER LACUS IS AWAY WORKING.
SHE SENT ME MAIL TO TELL ME SHE WAS GOING TO VISIT JUNIUS SEVEN WITH HER MEMORIAL SERVICE TROOP.
ENGAGED TO BE MARRIED, AND YET...
YOU NEVER SEEM TO GET THE CHANCE TO SEE EACH OTHER...
HONOR-ABLE CHAIR-MAN!
?!

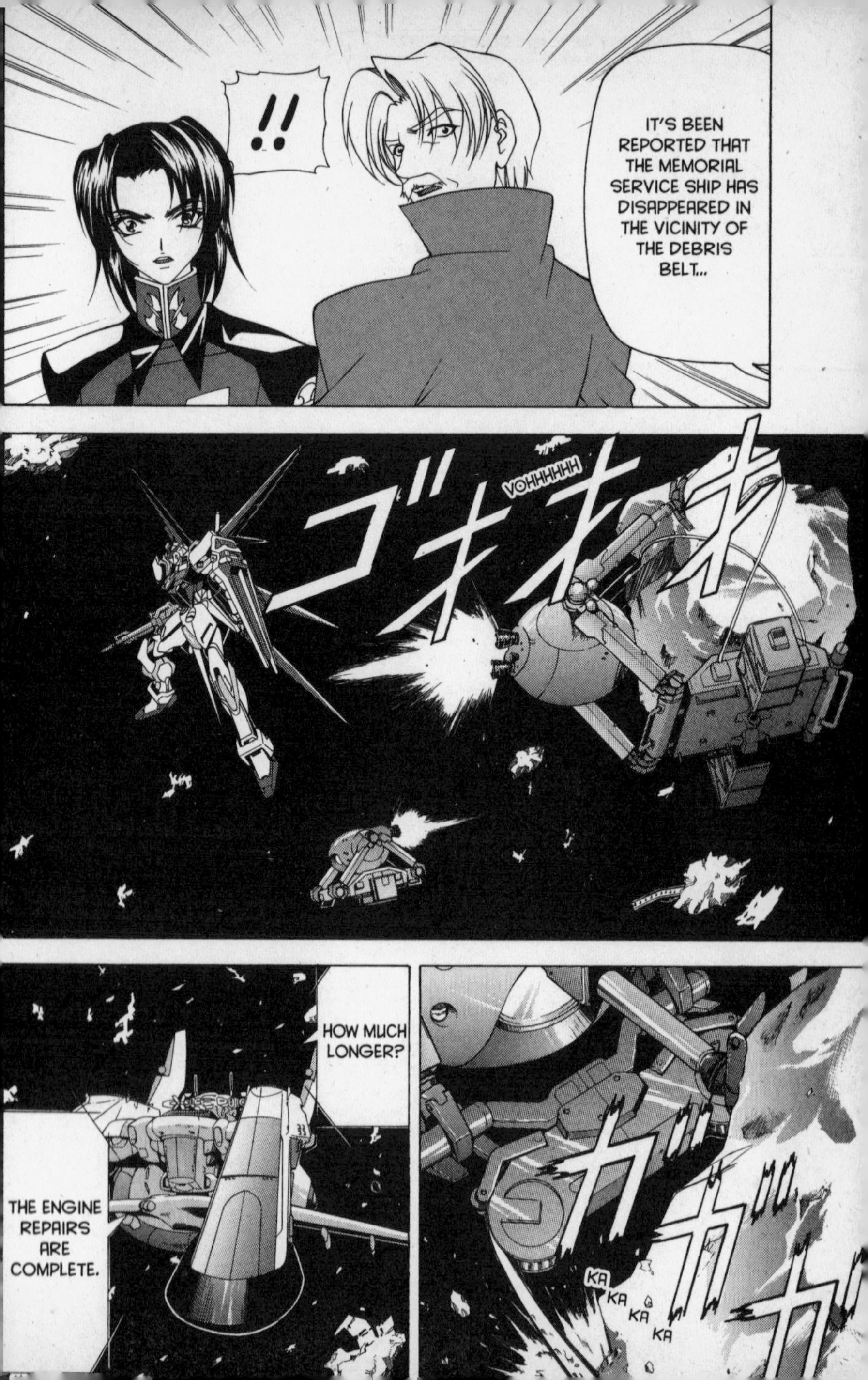
IT'S BEEN REPORTED THAT THE MEMORIAL SERVICE SHIP HAS DISAPPEARED IN THE VICINITY OF THE DEBRIS BELT...
!!
VOHHHHHH
KA KA KA KA
HOW MUCH LONGER?
THE ENGINE REPAIRS ARE COMPLETE.

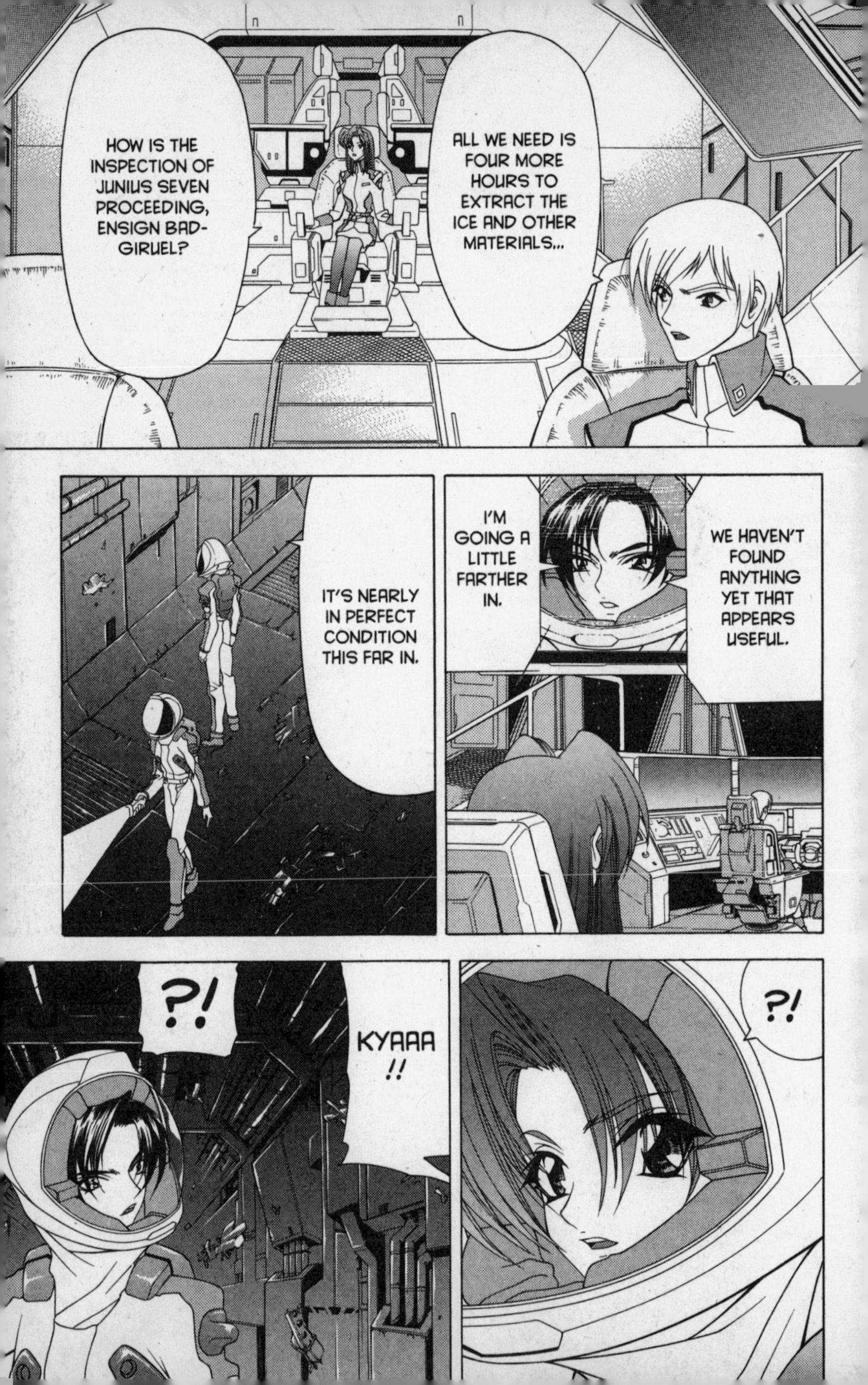
HOW IS THE INSPECTION OF JUNIUS SEVEN PROCEEDING, ENSIGN BAD-GIRUEL?
ALL WE NEED IS FOUR MORE HOURS TO EXTRACT THE ICE AND OTHER MATERIALS...
WE HAVEN'T FOUND ANYTHING YET THAT APPEARS USEFUL.
I'M GOING A LITTLE FARTHER IN.
IT'S NEARLY IN PERFECT CONDITION THIS FAR IN.
?!
?!
KYAAA !!

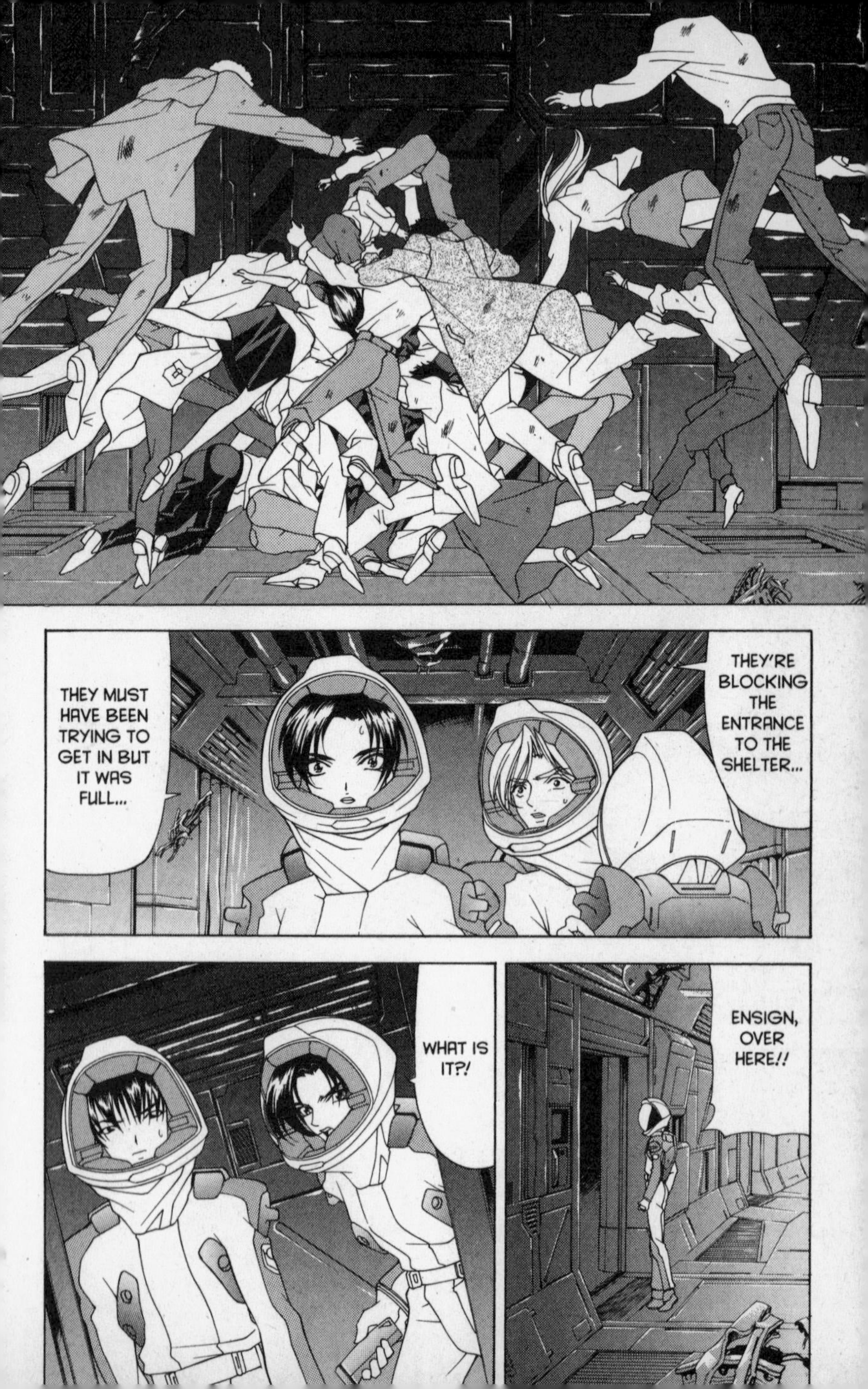
THEY'RE BLOCKING THE ENTRANCE TO THE SHELTER...
THEY MUST HAVE BEEN TRYING TO GET IN BUT IT WAS FULL...
ENSIGN, OVER HERE!!
WHAT IS IT?!

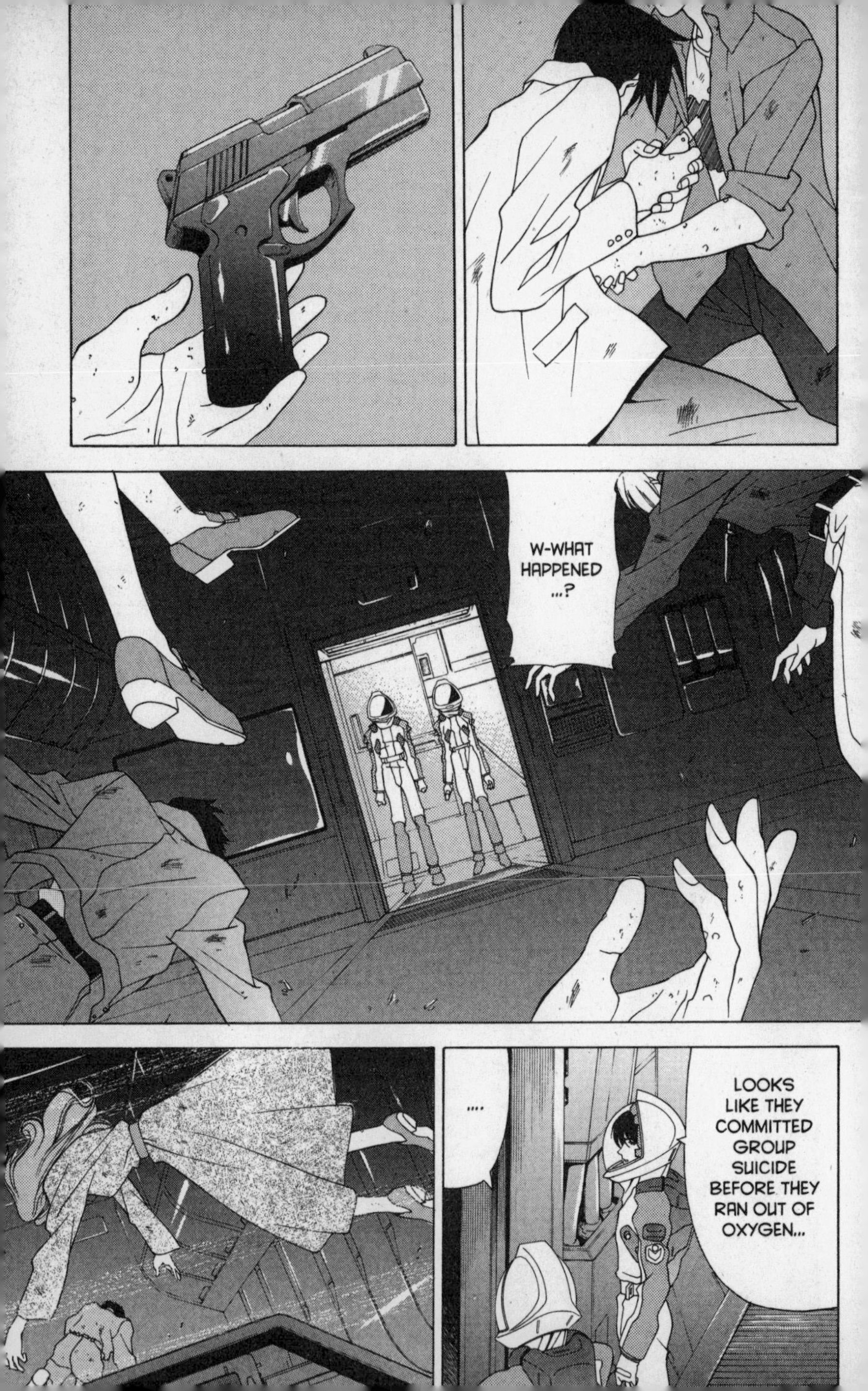
W-WHAT HAPPENED ...?
LOOKS LIKE THEY COMMITTED GROUP SUICIDE BEFORE THEY RAN OUT OF OXYGEN...
....

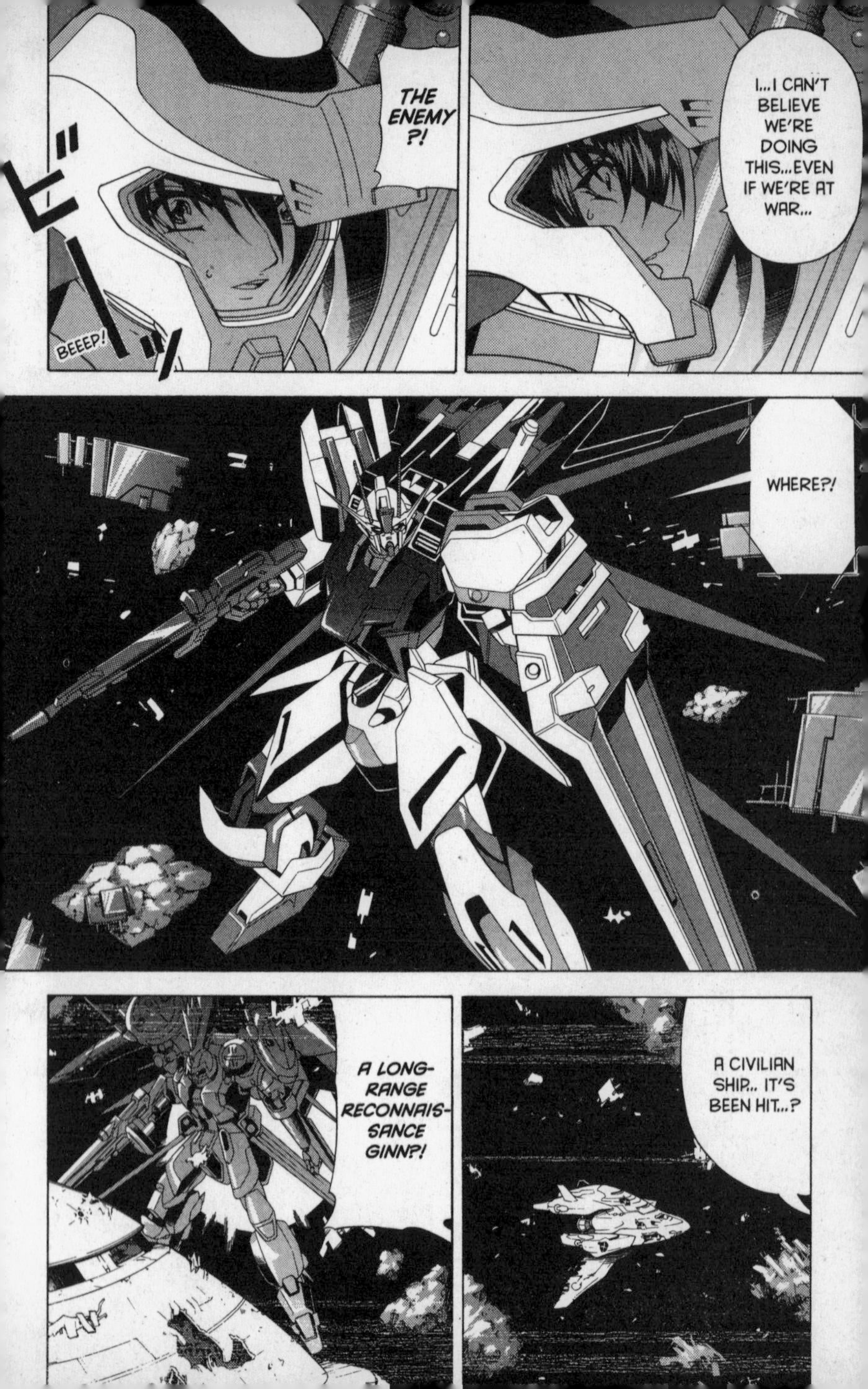
I...I CAN'T BELIEVE WE'RE DOING THIS...EVEN IF WE'RE AT WAR...
THE ENEMY?!
BEEEP!
WHERE?!
A CIVILIAN SHIP... IT'S BEEN HIT...?
A LONG-RANGE RECONNAISSANCE GINN?!

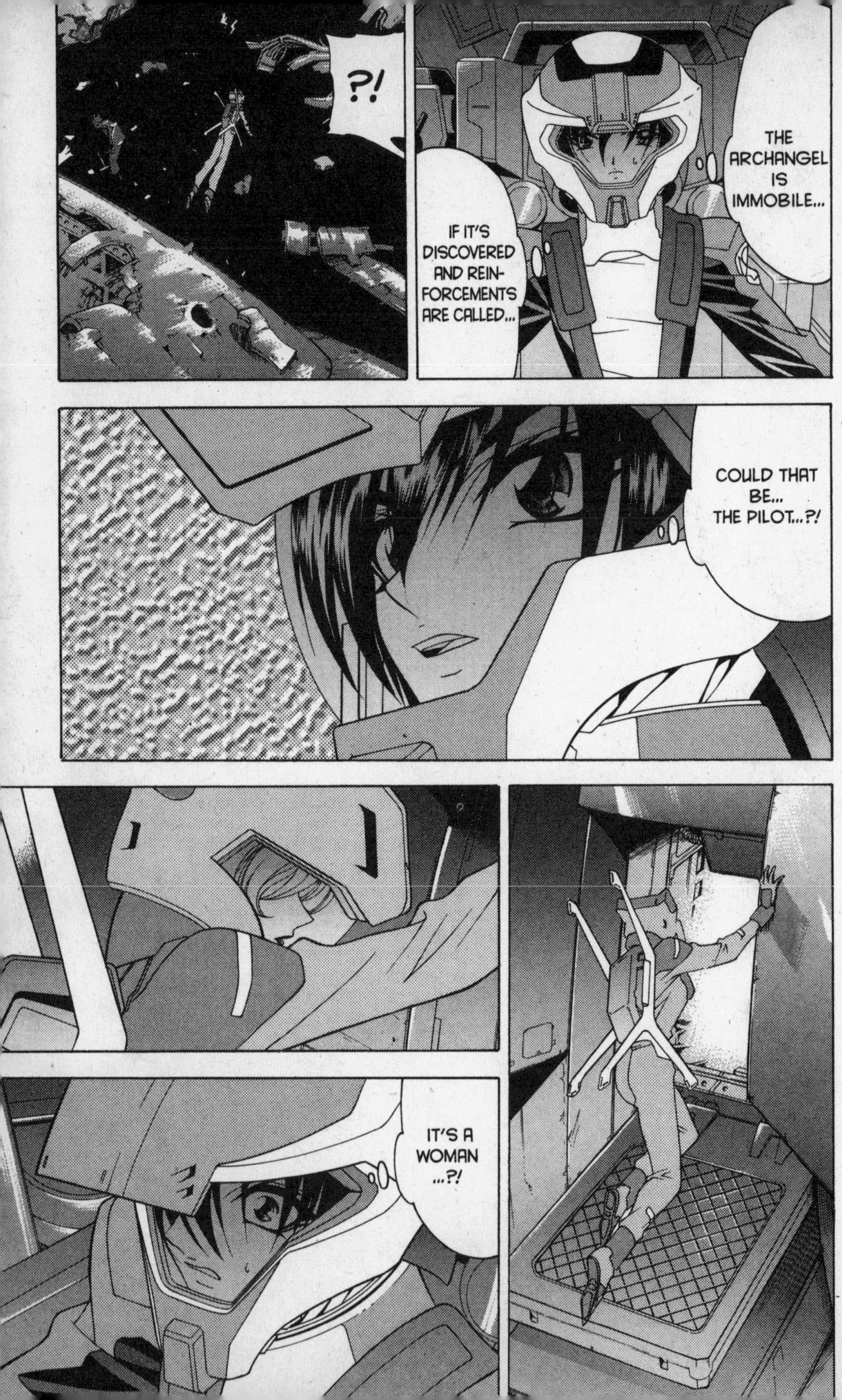
THE ARCHANGEL IS IMMOBILE...
IF IT'S DISCOVERED AND REIN-FORCEMENTS ARE CALLED...
?!
COULD THAT BE... THE PILOT...?!
IT'S A WOMAN ...?!

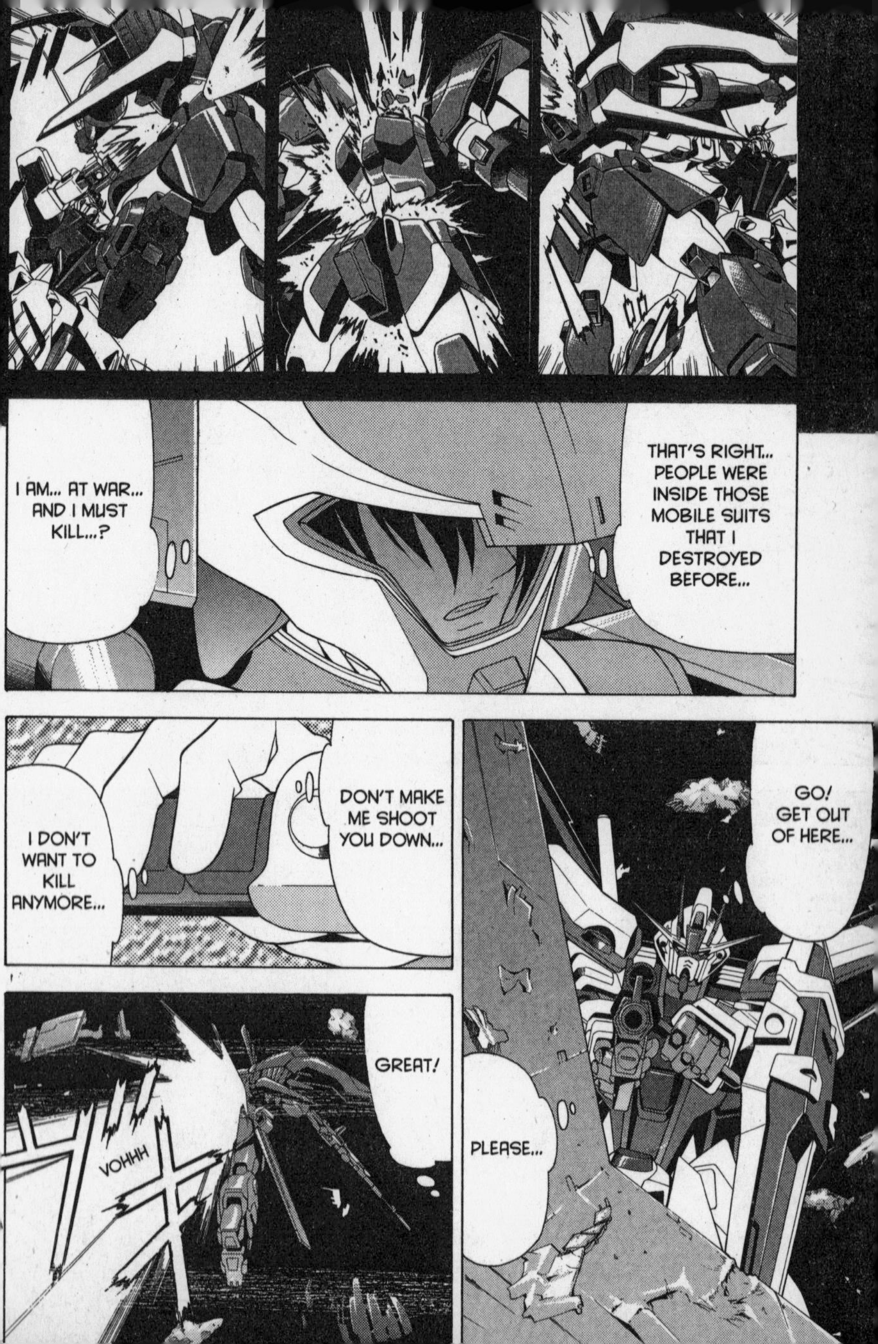
THAT'S RIGHT... PEOPLE WERE INSIDE THOSE MOBILE SUITS THAT I DESTROYED BEFORE...
I AM... AT WAR... AND I MUST KILL...?
GO! GET OUT OF HERE...
PLEASE...
DON'T MAKE ME SHOOT YOU DOWN...
I DON'T WANT TO KILL ANYMORE...
GREAT!
VOHHH

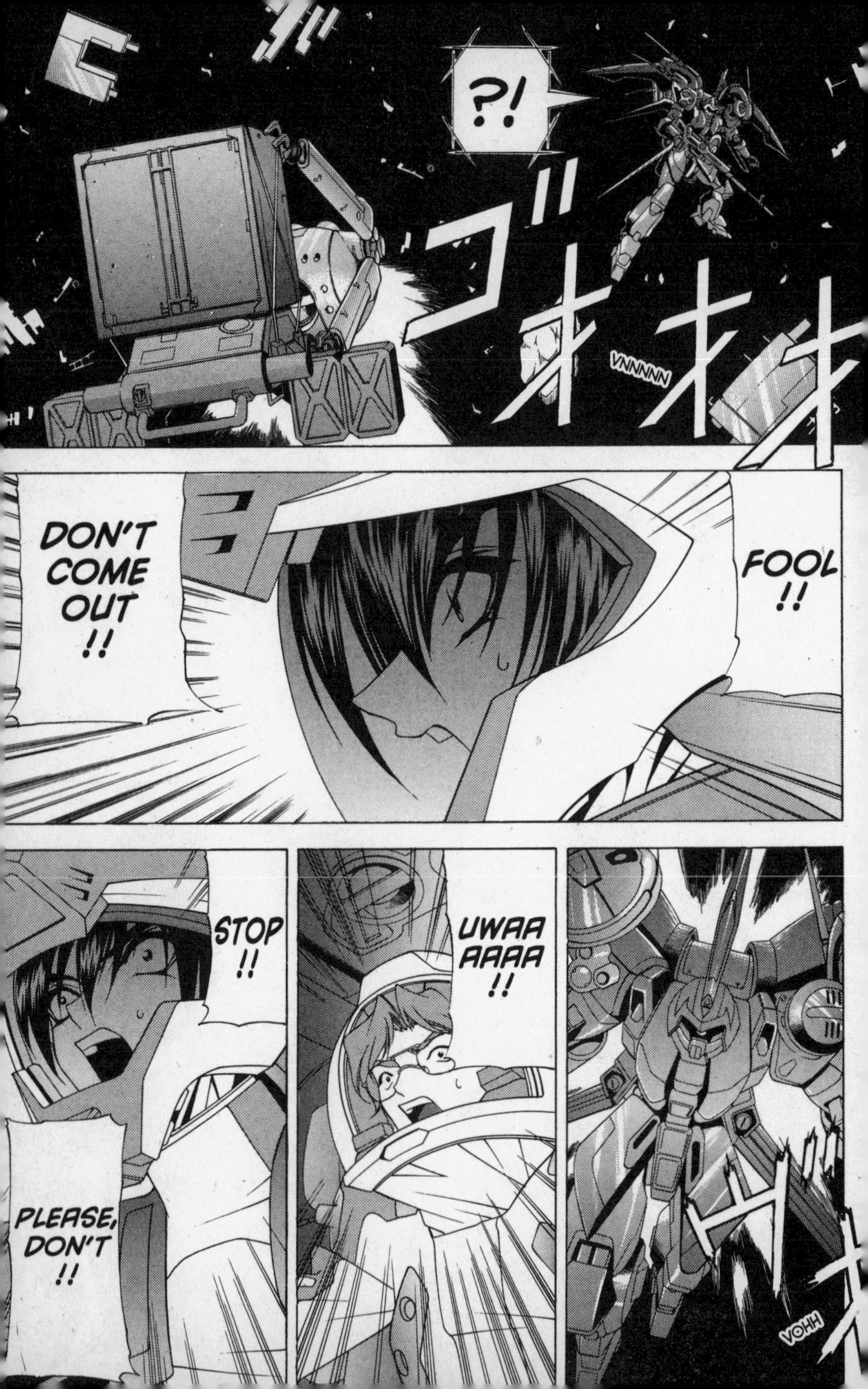
?!
ゴオオオ
VNNNNN
FOOL !!
DON'T COME OUT !!
VOHH
UWAA AAAA !!
STOP !!
PLEASE, DON'T !!

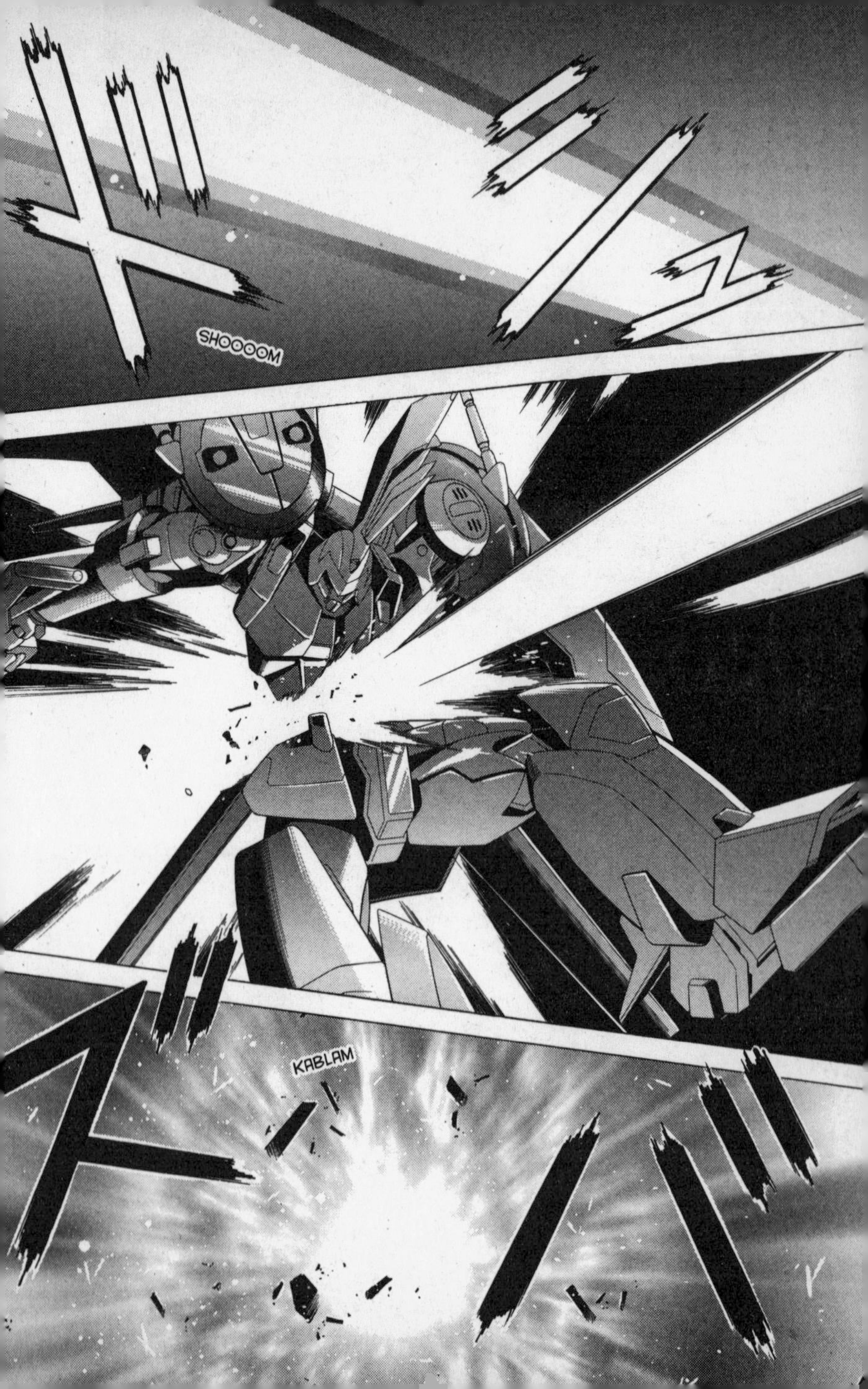
SHOOOOM
KABLAM

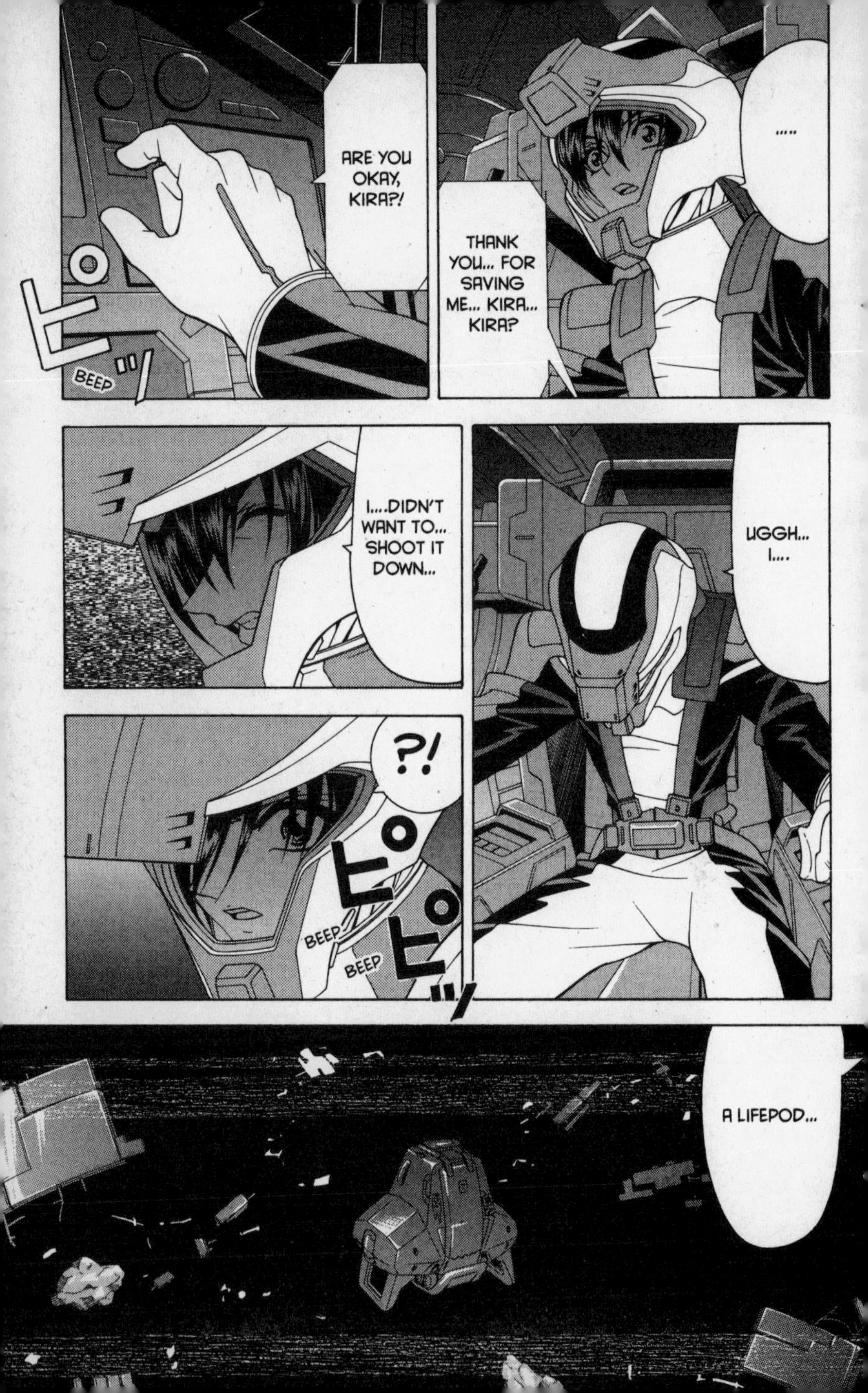
.....
THANK YOU... FOR SAVING ME... KIRA... KIRA?
ARE YOU OKAY, KIRA?!
BEEP
UGGH... I....
I....DIDN'T WANT TO... SHOOT IT DOWN...
?!
BEEP
BEEP
A LIFEPOD...

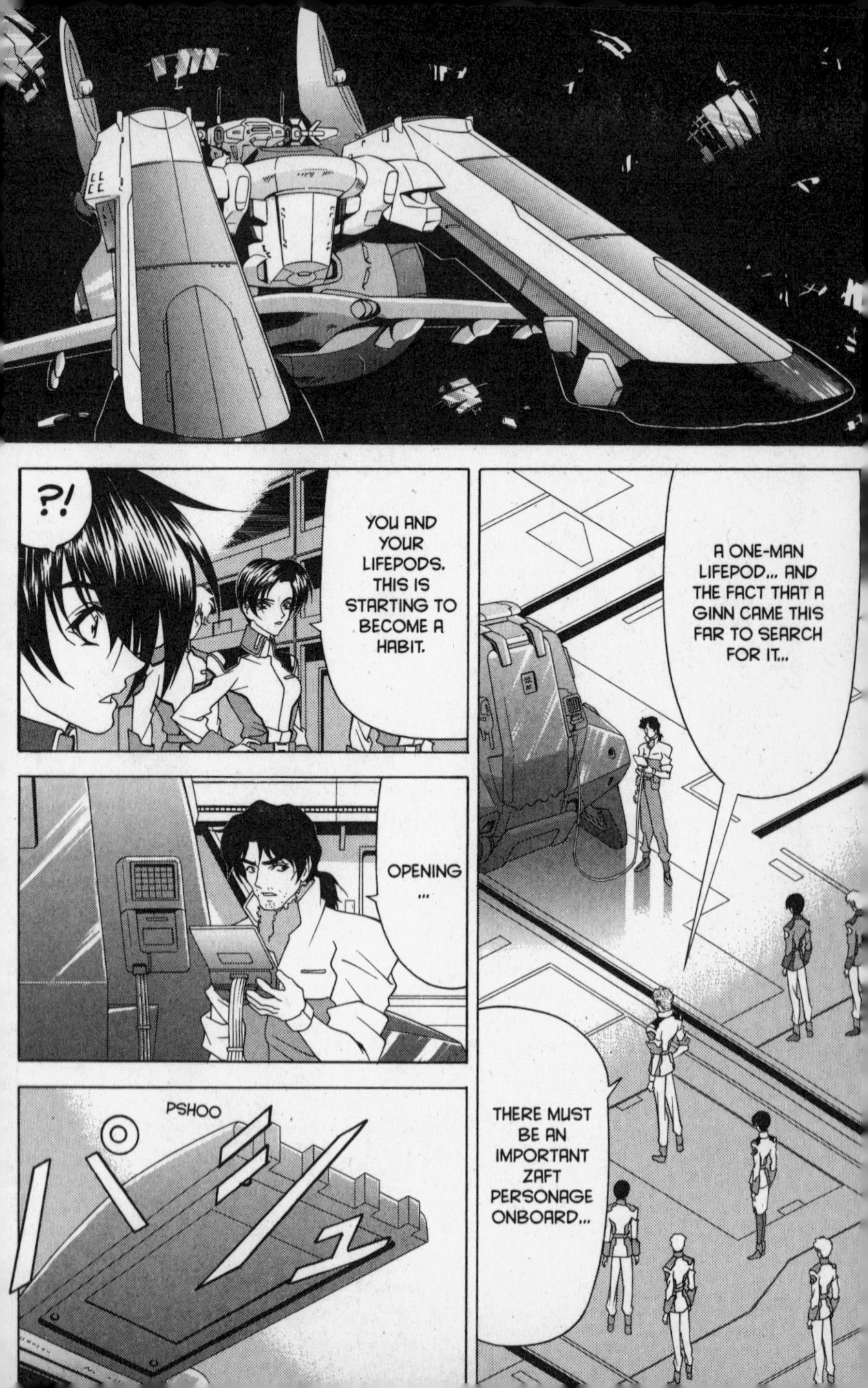
A ONE-MAN LIFEPOD... AND THE FACT THAT A GINN CAME THIS FAR TO SEARCH FOR IT...
THERE MUST BE AN IMPORTANT ZAFT PERSONAGE ONBOARD...
YOU AND YOUR LIFEPODS. THIS IS STARTING TO BECOME A HABIT.
?!
OPENING ...
PSHOO

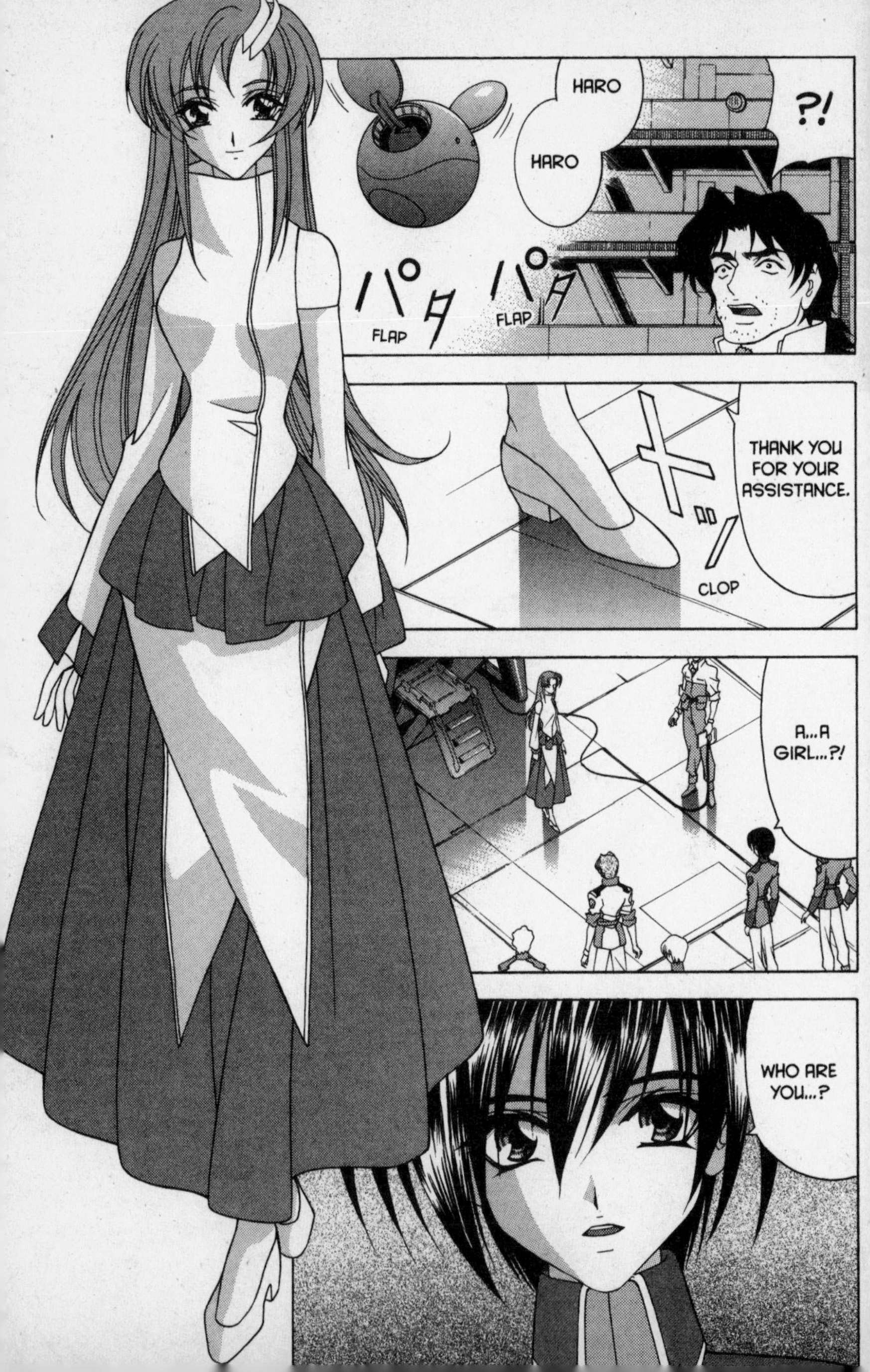
?!
HARO
HARO
パタ
FLAP
パタ
FLAP
THANK YOU FOR YOUR ASSISTANCE.
CLOP
A...A GIRL...?!
WHO ARE YOU...?

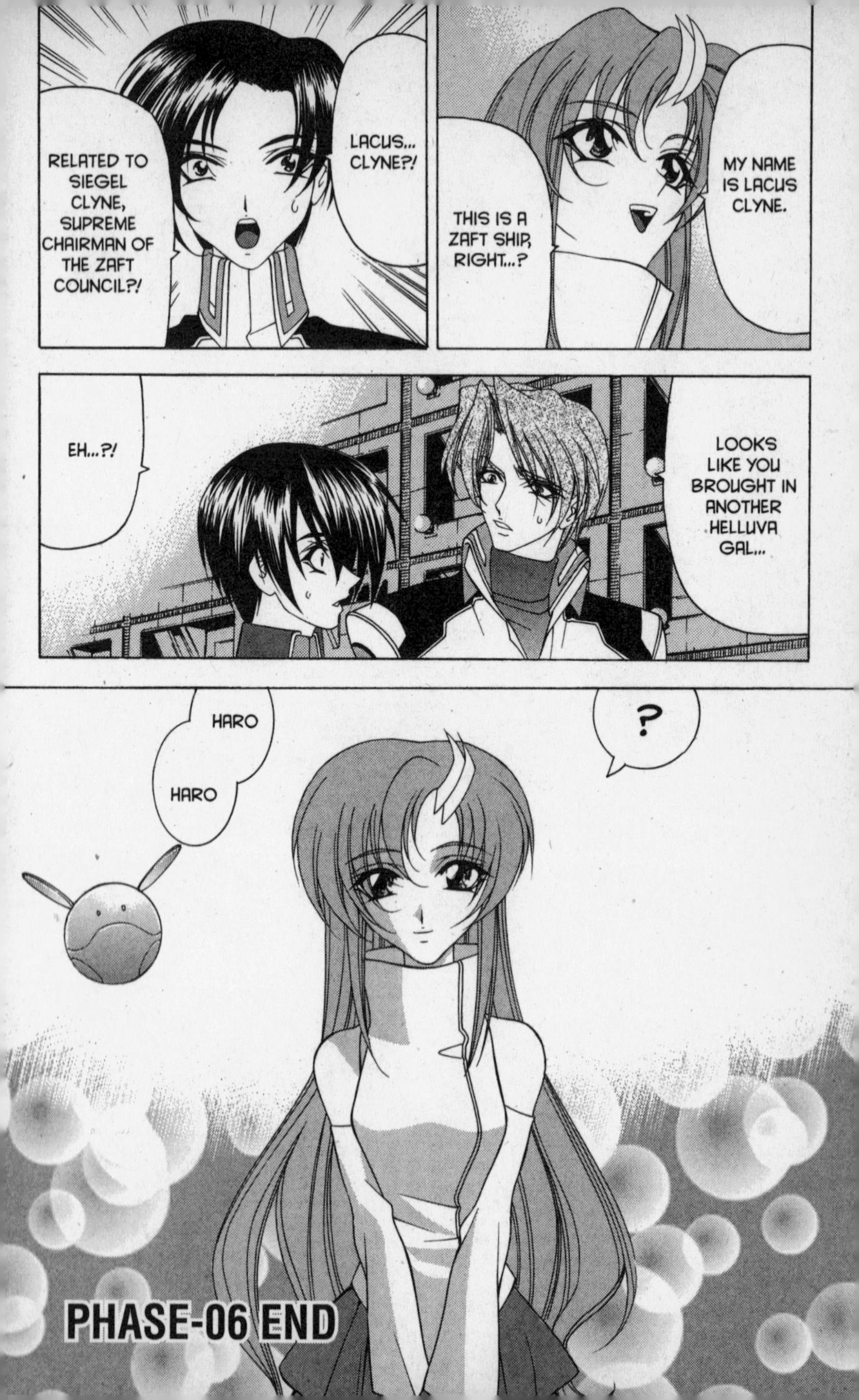
MY NAME IS LACUS CLYNE.
THIS IS A ZAFT SHIP, RIGHT...?
LACUS... CLYNE?!
RELATED TO SIEGEL CLYNE, SUPREME CHAIRMAN OF THE ZAFT COUNCIL?!
LOOKS LIKE YOU BROUGHT IN ANOTHER HELLUVA GAL...
EH...?!
?
HARO
HARO
PHASE-06 END

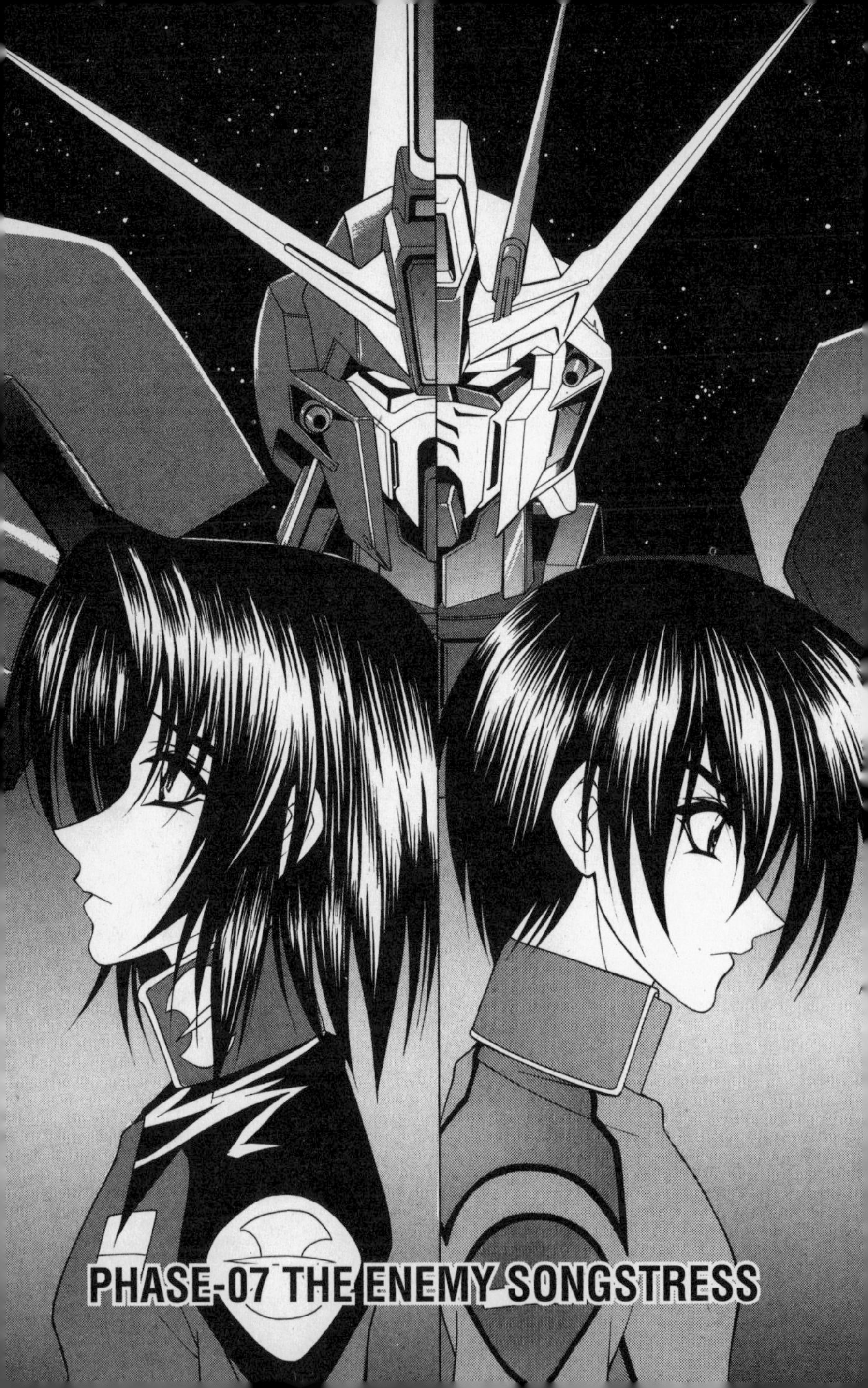
PHASE-07 THE ENEMY SONGSTRESS

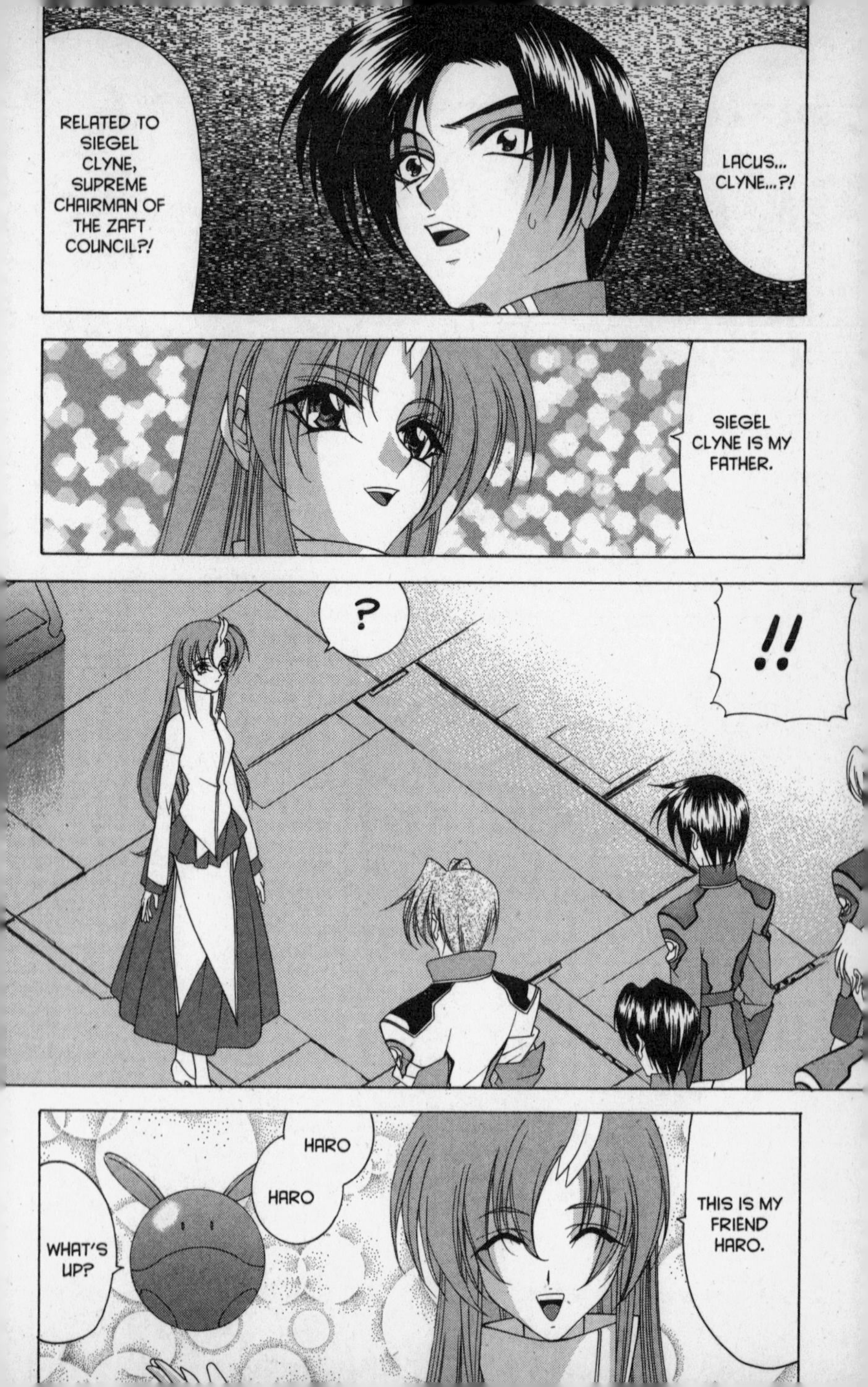
LACUS... CLYNE...?!
RELATED TO SIEGEL CLYNE, SUPREME CHAIRMAN OF THE ZAFT COUNCIL?!
SIEGEL CLYNE IS MY FATHER.
!!
?
THIS IS MY FRIEND HARO.
HARO
HARO
WHAT'S UP?

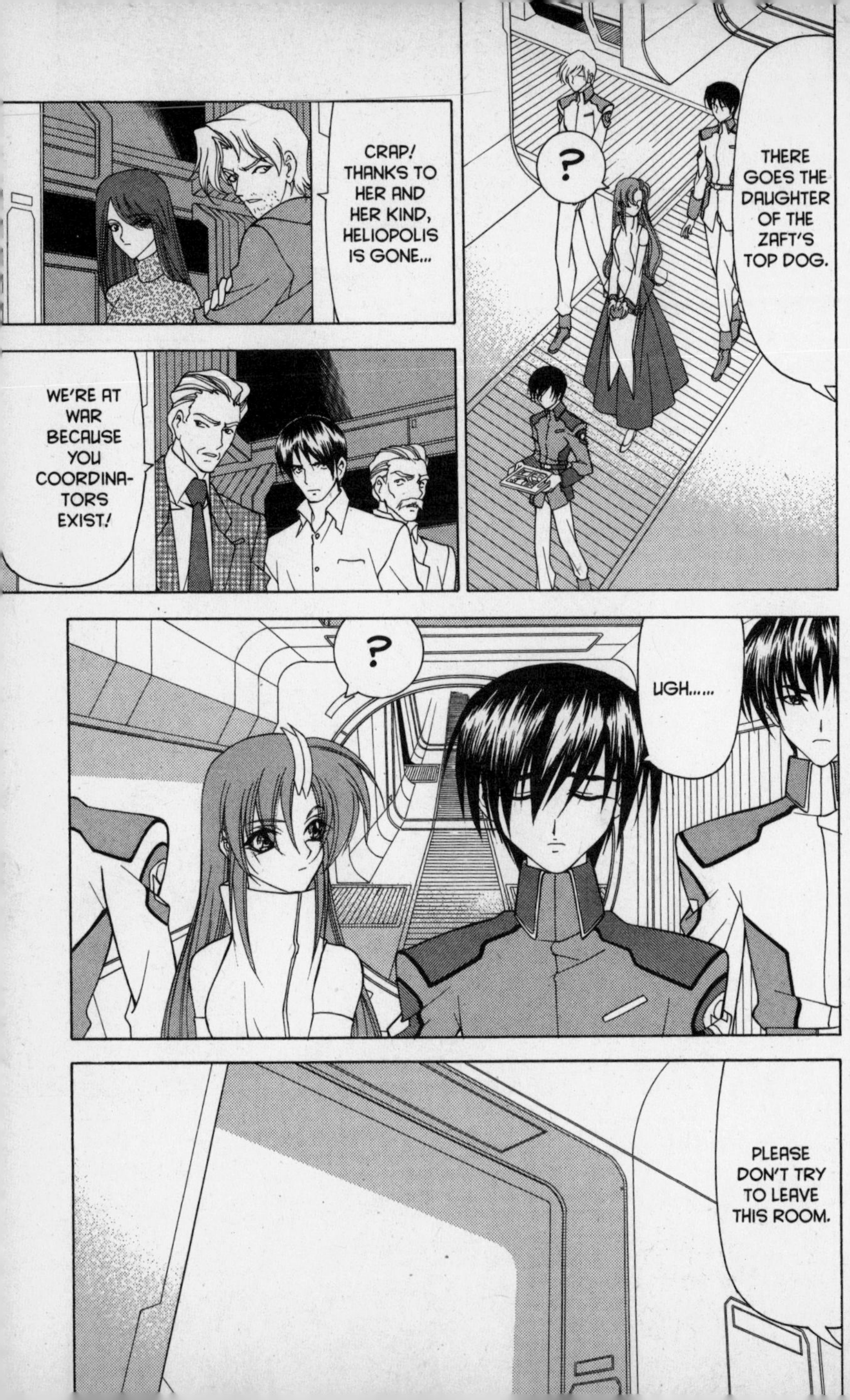
THERE GOES THE DAUGHTER OF THE ZAFT'S TOP DOG.
?
CRAP! THANKS TO HER AND HER KIND, HELIOPOLIS IS GONE...
WE'RE AT WAR BECAUSE YOU COORDINA-TORS EXIST!
UGH......
?
PLEASE DON'T TRY TO LEAVE THIS ROOM.

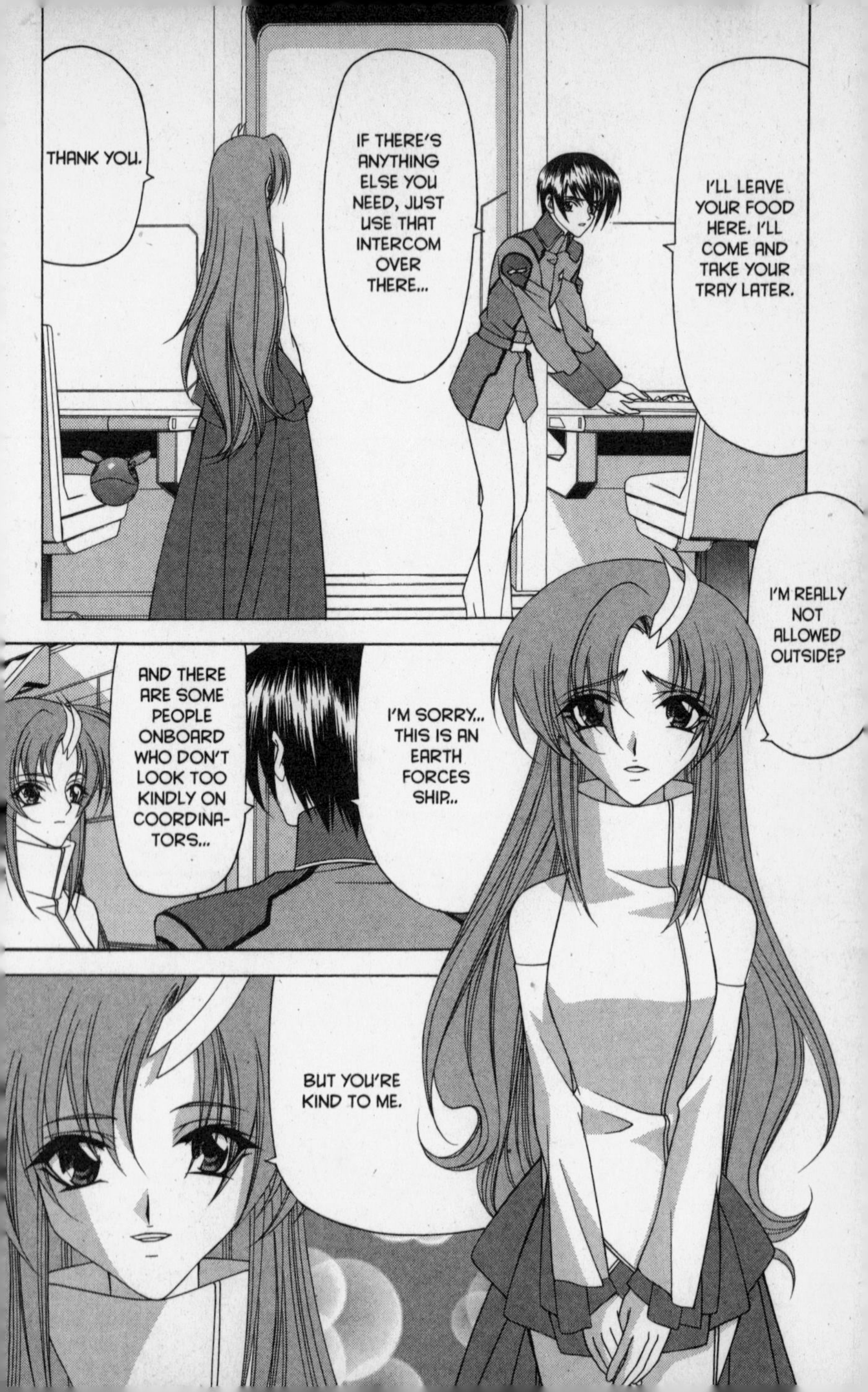
I'LL LEAVE YOUR FOOD HERE. I'LL COME AND TAKE YOUR TRAY LATER.
IF THERE'S ANYTHING ELSE YOU NEED, JUST USE THAT INTERCOM OVER THERE...
THANK YOU.
I'M REALLY NOT ALLOWED OUTSIDE?
I'M SORRY... THIS IS AN EARTH FORCES SHIP...
AND THERE ARE SOME PEOPLE ONBOARD WHO DON'T LOOK TOO KINDLY ON COORDINA-TORS...
BUT YOU'RE KIND TO ME.

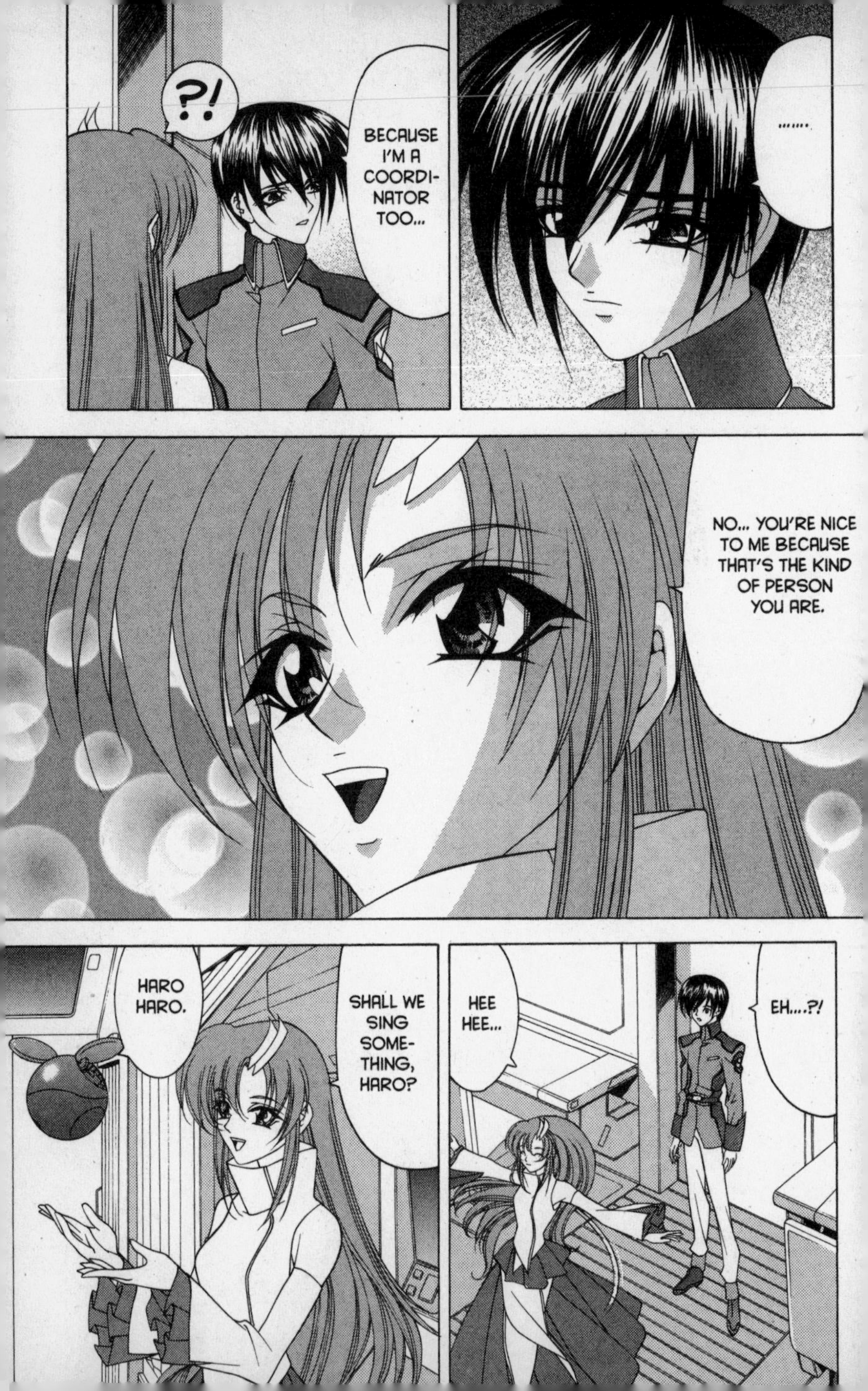
....
BECAUSE I'M A COORDINATOR TOO...
?!
NO... YOU'RE NICE TO ME BECAUSE THAT'S THE KIND OF PERSON YOU ARE.
EH....?!
HEE HEE...
SHALL WE SING SOMETHING, HARO?
HARO HARO.

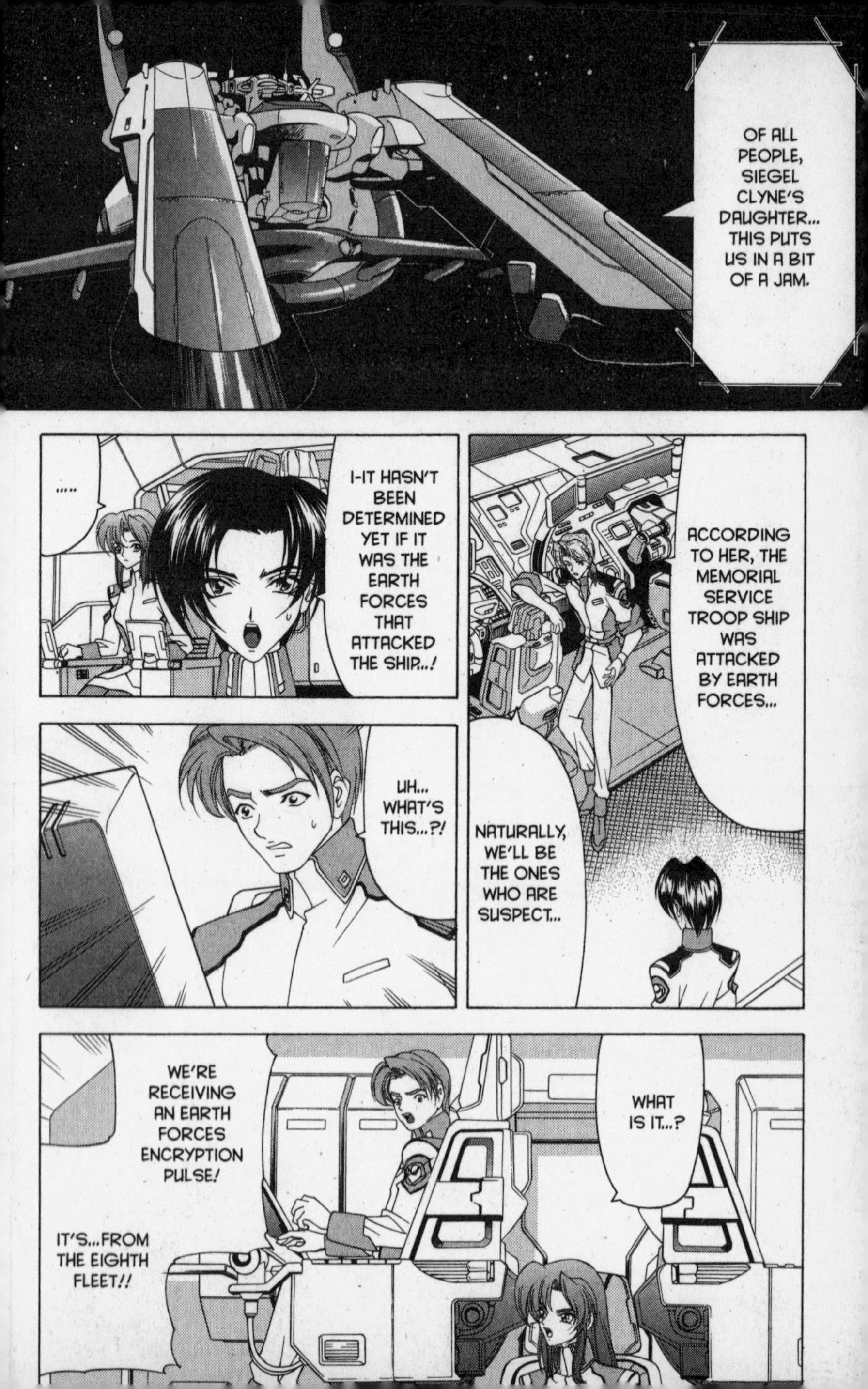
OF ALL PEOPLE, SIEGEL CLYNE'S DAUGHTER... THIS PUTS US IN A BIT OF A JAM.
ACCORDING TO HER, THE MEMORIAL SERVICE TROOP SHIP WAS ATTACKED BY EARTH FORCES...
NATURALLY, WE'LL BE THE ONES WHO ARE SUSPECT...
I-IT HASN'T BEEN DETERMINED YET IF IT WAS THE EARTH FORCES THAT ATTACKED THE SHIP...!
.....
UH... WHAT'S THIS...?!
WHAT IS IT...?
WE'RE RECEIVING AN EARTH FORCES ENCRYPTION PULSE!
IT'S...FROM THE EIGHTH FLEET!!

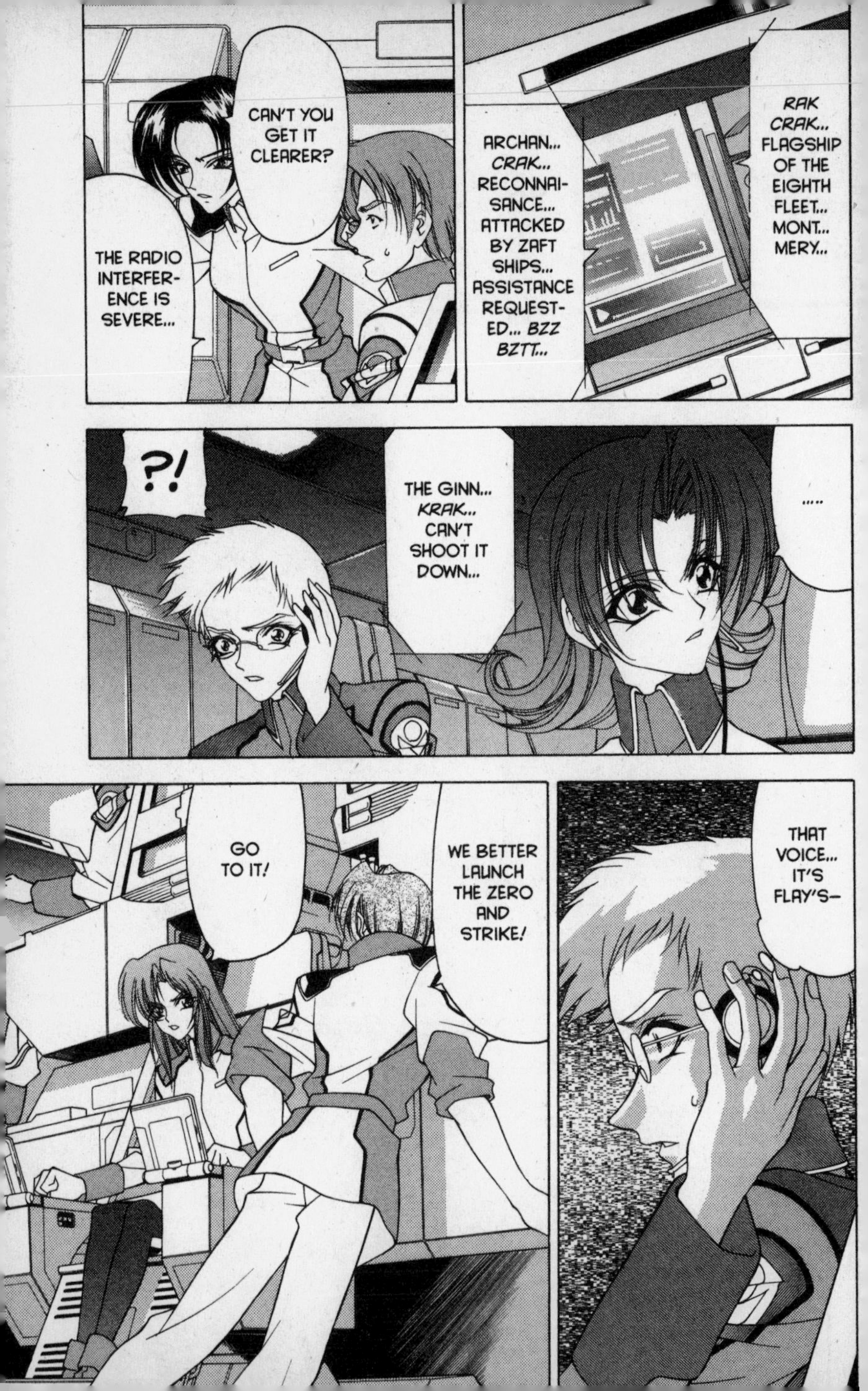
RAK CRAK... FLAGSHIP OF THE EIGHTH FLEET... MONT... MERY...
ARCHAN... CRAK... RECONNAI-SANCE... ATTACKED BY ZAFT SHIPS... ASSISTANCE REQUEST-ED... BZZ BZTT...
CAN'T YOU GET IT CLEARER?
THE RADIO INTERFER-ENCE IS SEVERE...
.....
THE GINN... KRAK... CAN'T SHOOT IT DOWN...
?!
THAT VOICE... IT'S FLAY'S—
WE BETTER LAUNCH THE ZERO AND STRIKE!
GO TO IT!

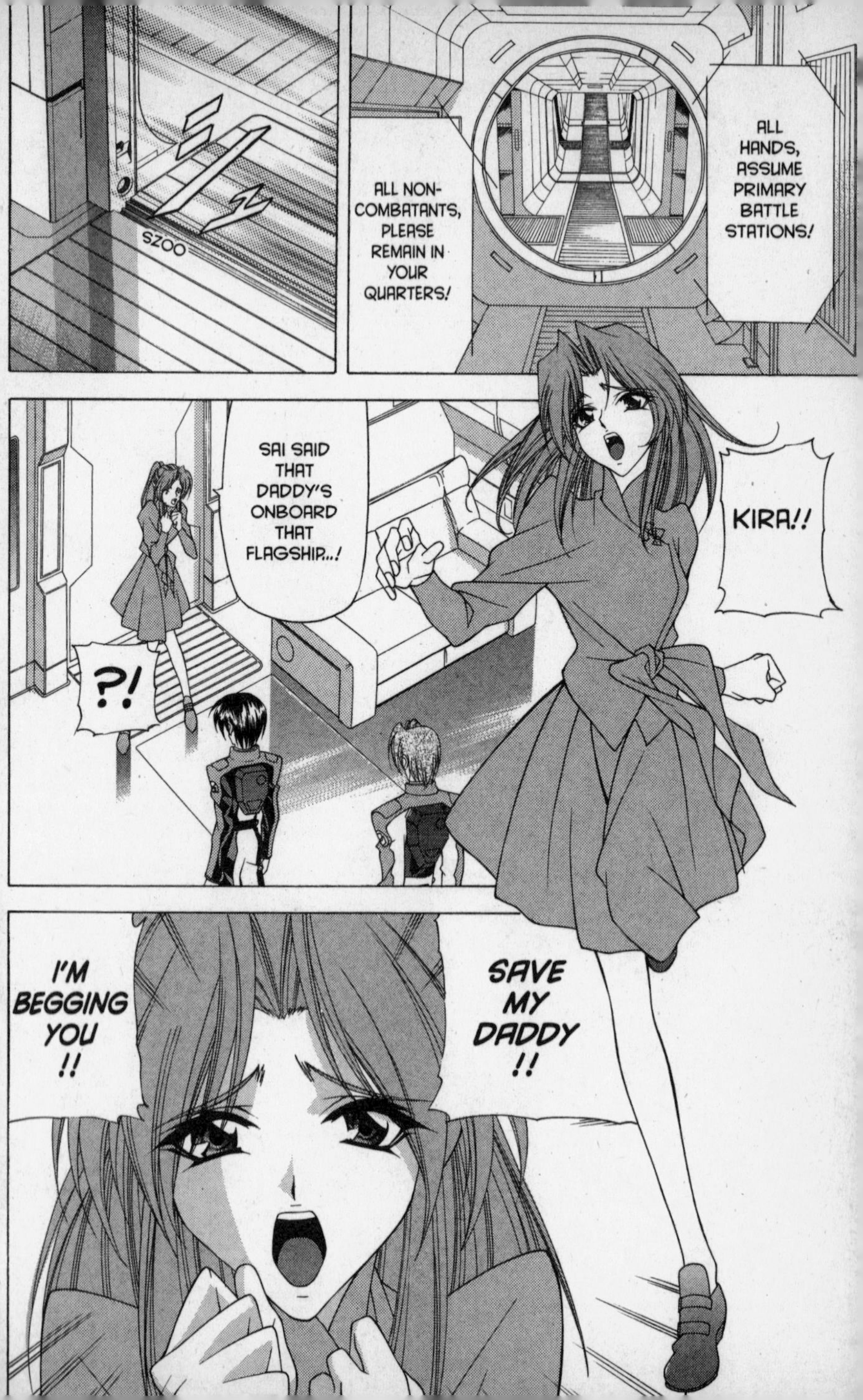
ALL HANDS, ASSUME PRIMARY BATTLE STATIONS!
ALL NON-COMBATANTS, PLEASE REMAIN IN YOUR QUARTERS!
SZOO
KIRA!!
SAI SAID THAT DADDY'S ONBOARD THAT FLAGSHIP...!
?!
SAVE MY DADDY !!
I'M BEGGING YOU !!

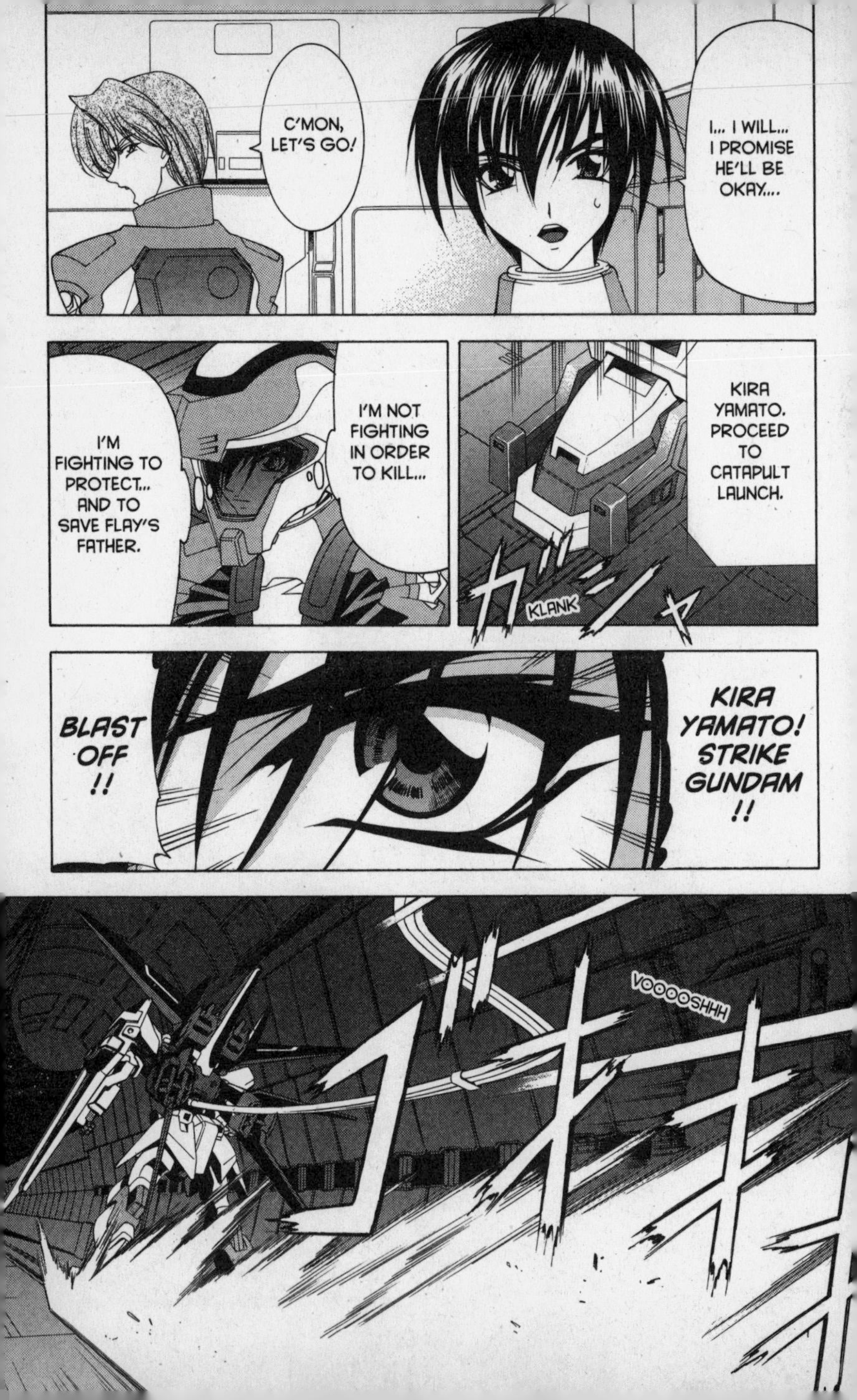
I... I WILL... I PROMISE HE'LL BE OKAY....
C'MON, LET'S GO!
KIRA YAMATO. PROCEED TO CATAPULT LAUNCH.
KLANK
I'M NOT FIGHTING IN ORDER TO KILL...
I'M FIGHTING TO PROTECT... AND TO SAVE FLAY'S FATHER.
KIRA YAMATO! STRIKE GUNDAM !!
BLAST OFF !!
VOOOOSHHH

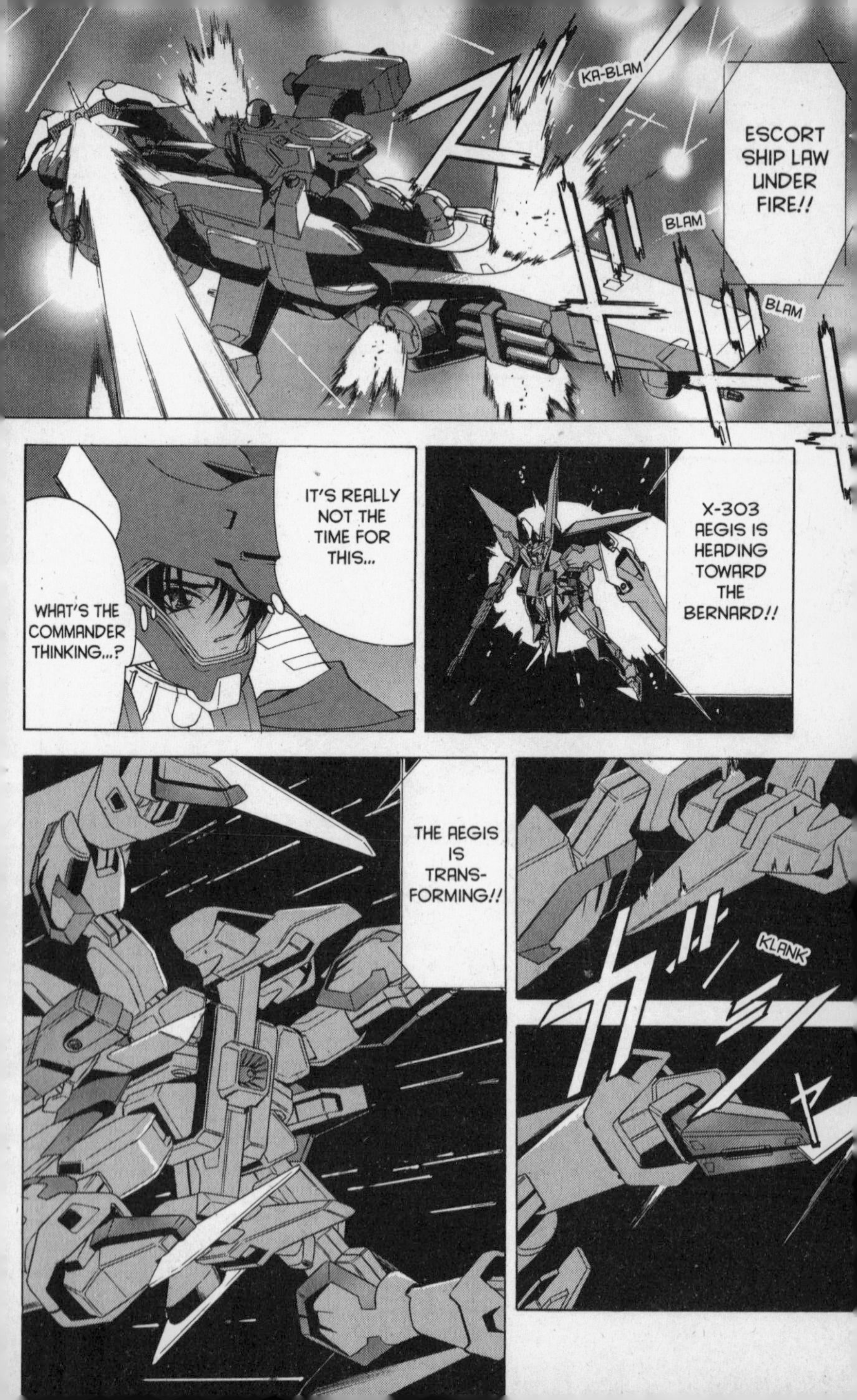
KA-BLAM
ESCORT SHIP LAW UNDER FIRE!!
BLAM
BLAM
X-303 AEGIS IS HEADING TOWARD THE BERNARD!!
IT'S REALLY NOT THE TIME FOR THIS...
WHAT'S THE COMMANDER THINKING...?
KLANK
THE AEGIS IS TRANSFORMING!!

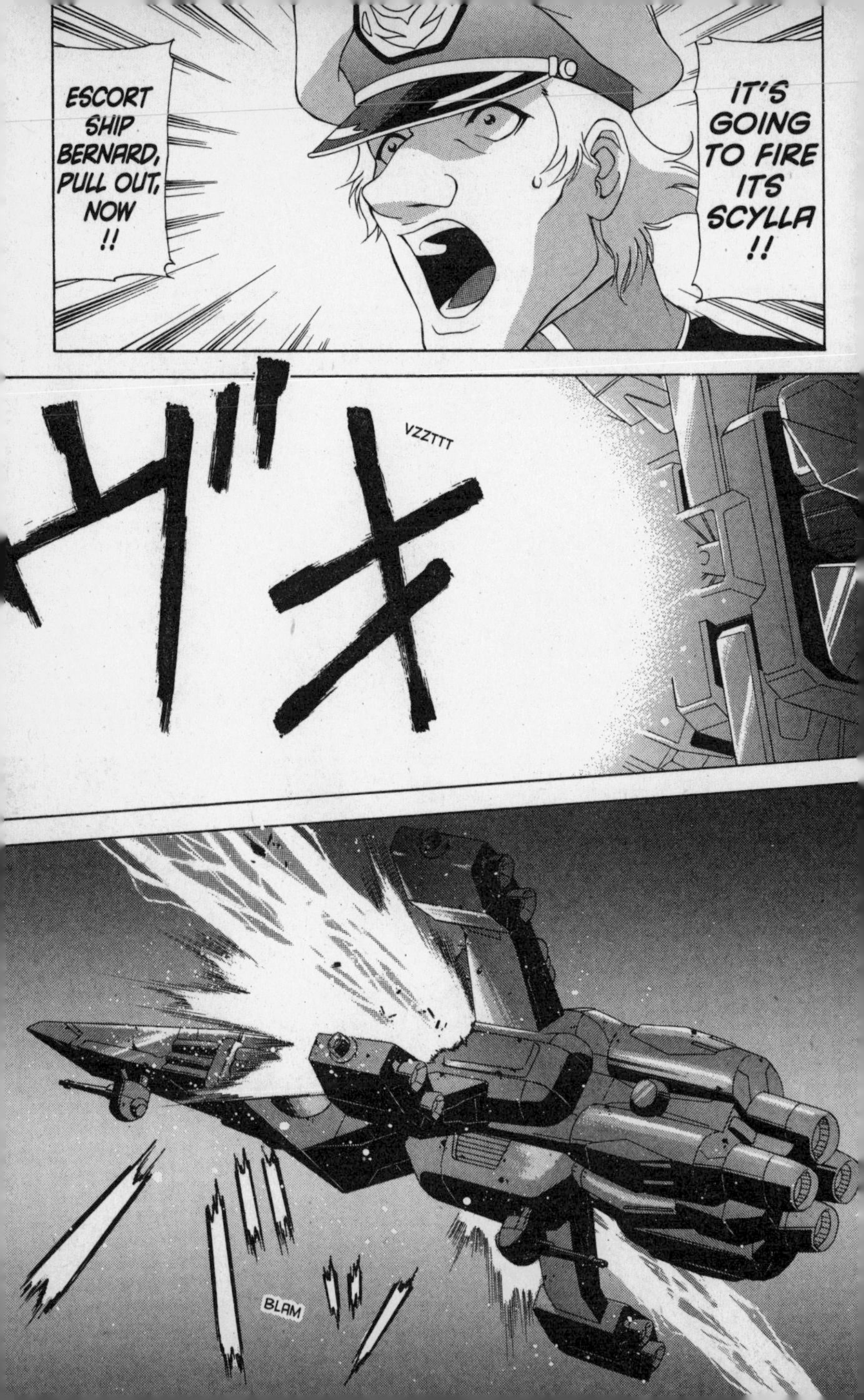
IT'S GOING TO FIRE ITS SCYLLA !!
ESCORT SHIP BERNARD, PULL OUT, NOW !!
ザキ
VZZTTT
BLAM

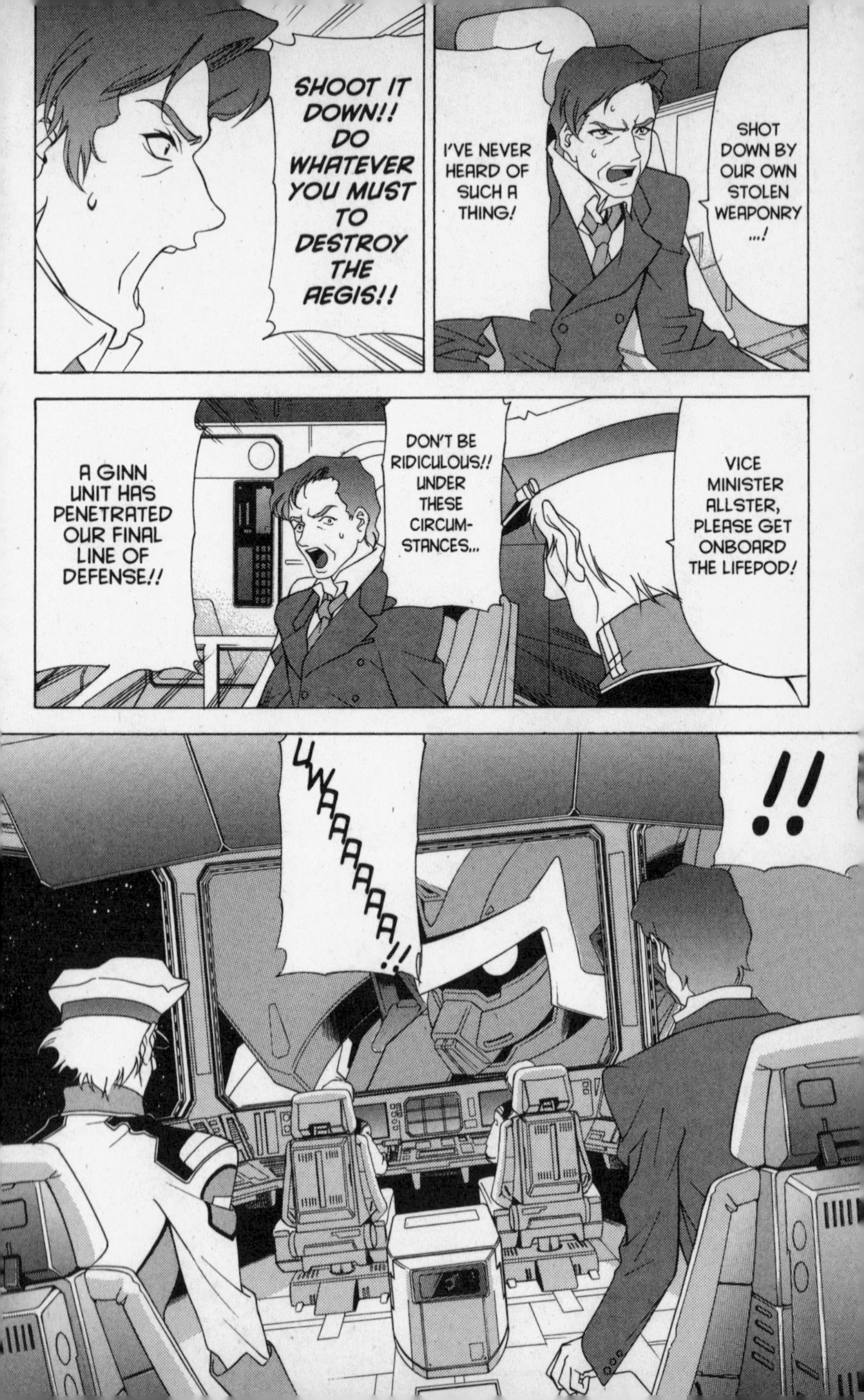
SHOT DOWN BY OUR OWN STOLEN WEAPONRY ...!
I'VE NEVER HEARD OF SUCH A THING!
SHOOT IT DOWN!! DO WHATEVER YOU MUST TO DESTROY THE AEGIS!!
VICE MINISTER ALLSTER, PLEASE GET ONBOARD THE LIFEPOD!
DON'T BE RIDICULOUS!! UNDER THESE CIRCUM-STANCES...
A GINN UNIT HAS PENETRATED OUR FINAL LINE OF DEFENSE!!
!!
UWAAAAAAAA!!

FLAY
!!

SINCE THEN ~ JUST A TINY BIT OF TIME HAS ELAPSED ~

JASRAC COPYRIGHT 0310038-301

AND THE MEMORIES ~ HAVE ONLY GOTTEN SWEETER TO THE LAST ~

SZOO

ON THIS QUIET EVENING ~ I AWAIT YOUR RETURN ~

COME BACK ~ FOR THE SMILES ~ FROM THOSE TIMES ~ NOW FORGOTTEN

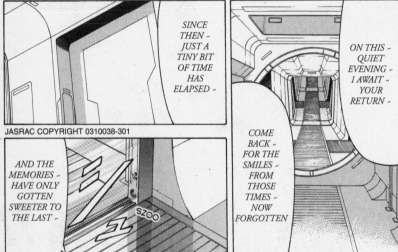

HARO?

THE STARS ~
......

?!

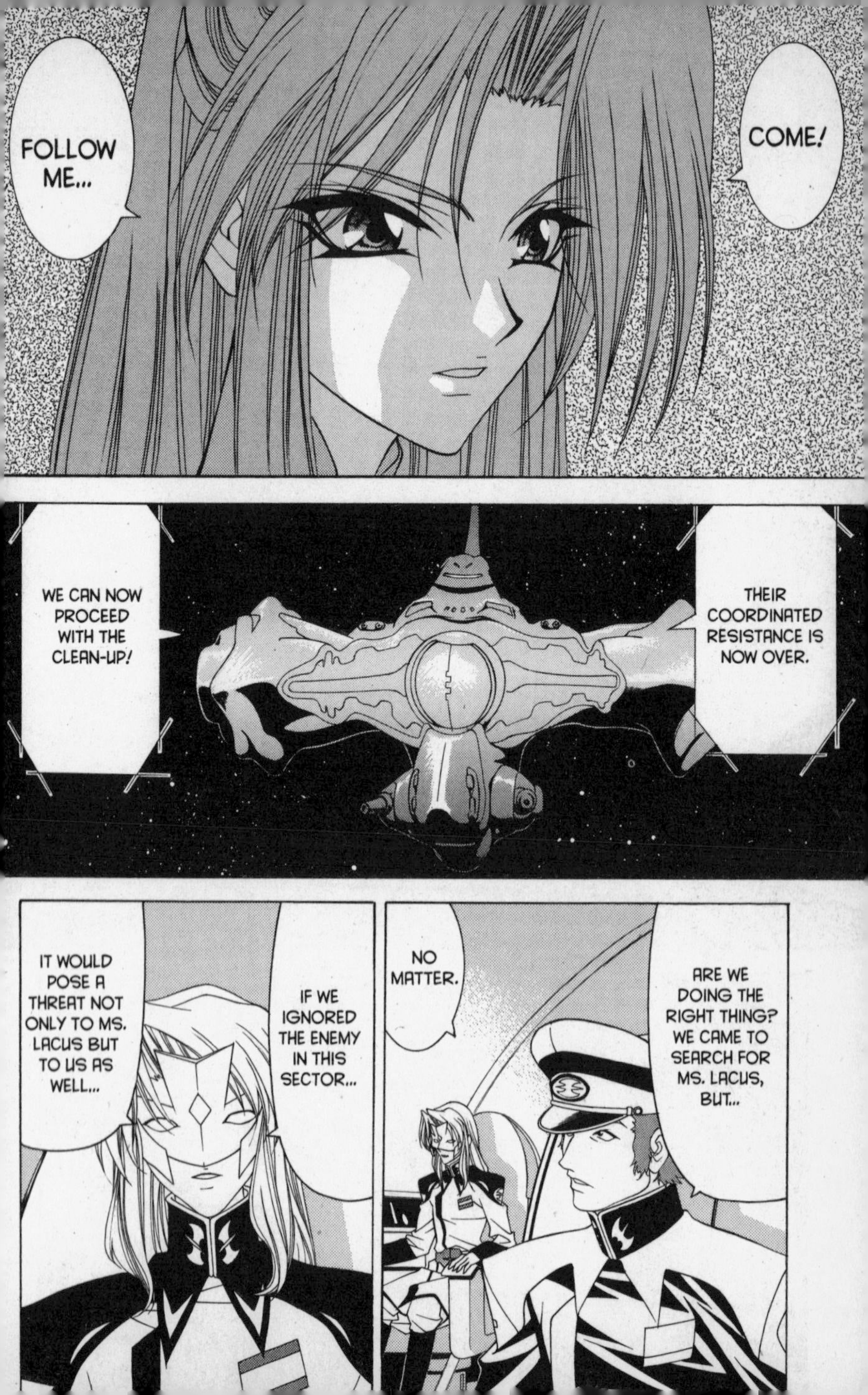
COME!
FOLLOW ME...
THEIR COORDINATED RESISTANCE IS NOW OVER.
WE CAN NOW PROCEED WITH THE CLEAN-UP!
ARE WE DOING THE RIGHT THING? WE CAME TO SEARCH FOR MS. LACUS, BUT...
NO MATTER.
IF WE IGNORED THE ENEMY IN THIS SECTOR...
IT WOULD POSE A THREAT NOT ONLY TO MS. LACUS BUT TO US AS WELL...

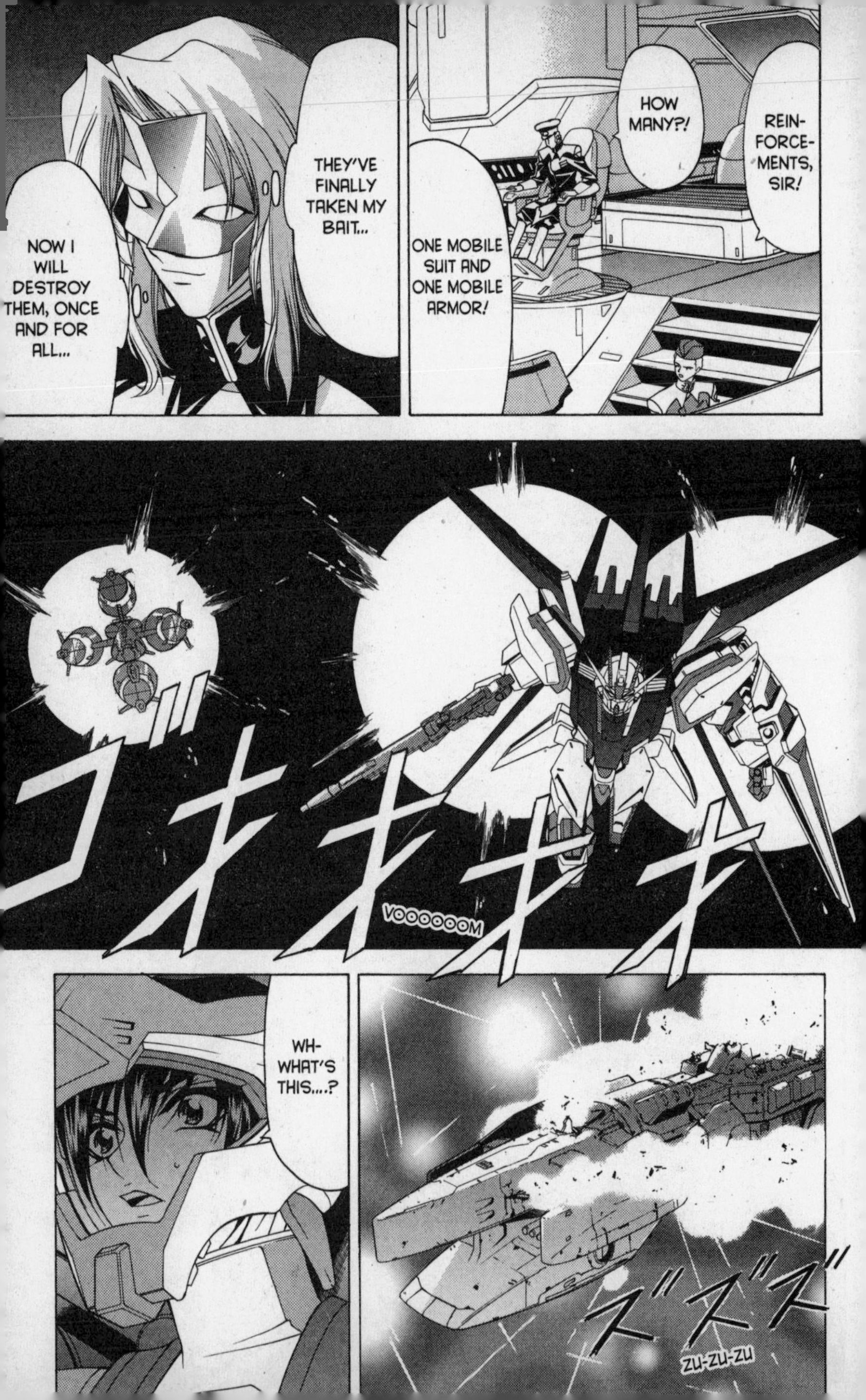
REIN-FORCEMENTS, SIR!
HOW MANY?!
ONE MOBILE SUIT AND ONE MOBILE ARMOR!
THEY'VE FINALLY TAKEN MY BAIT...
NOW I WILL DESTROY THEM, ONCE AND FOR ALL...
VOOOOOOM
ZU-ZU-ZU
WH-WHAT'S THIS....?

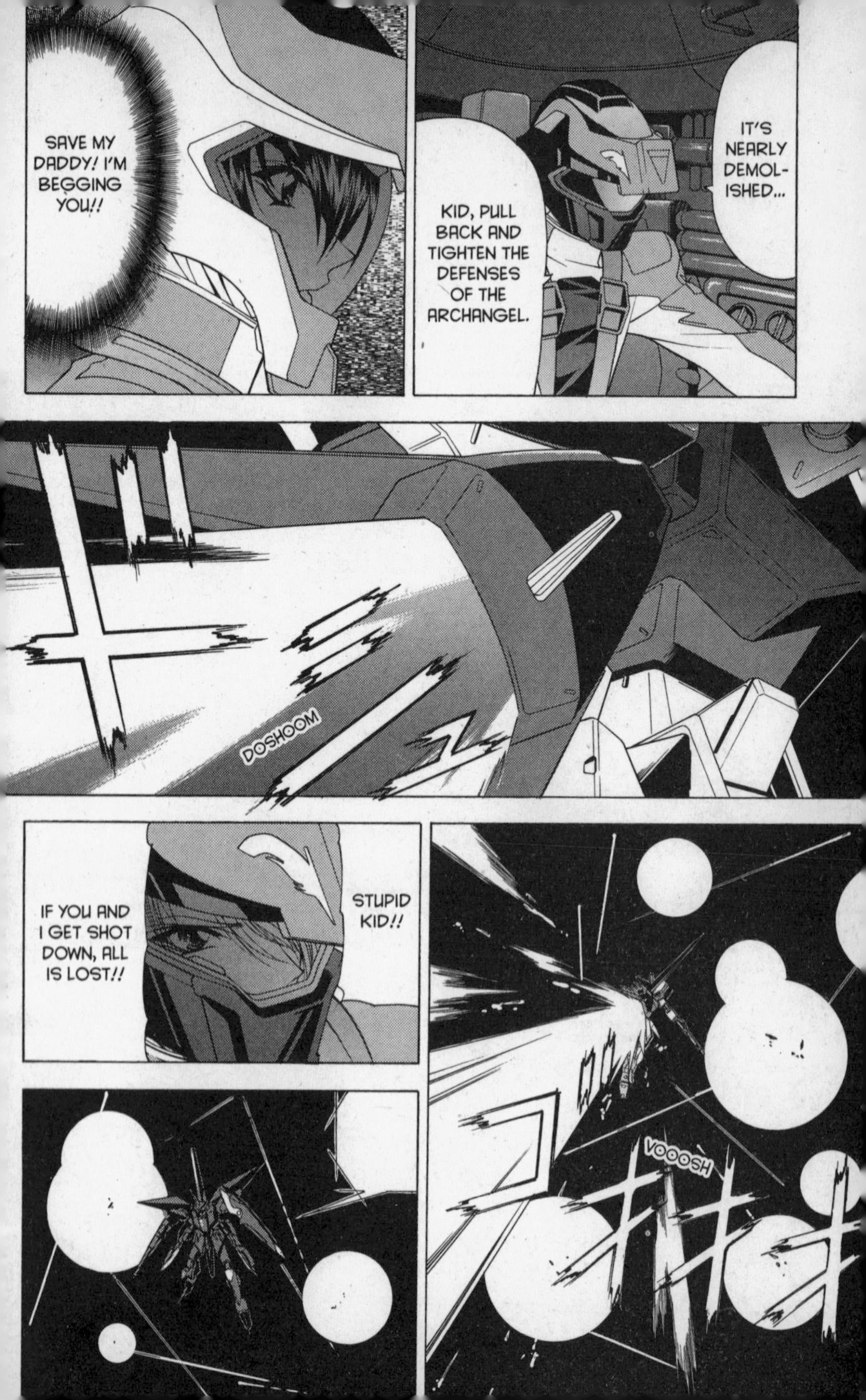
IT'S NEARLY DEMOL-ISHED...
KID, PULL BACK AND TIGHTEN THE DEFENSES OF THE ARCHANGEL.
SAVE MY DADDY! I'M BEGGING YOU!!
DOSHOOM
VOOOSH
STUPID KID!!
IF YOU AND I GET SHOT DOWN, ALL IS LOST!!

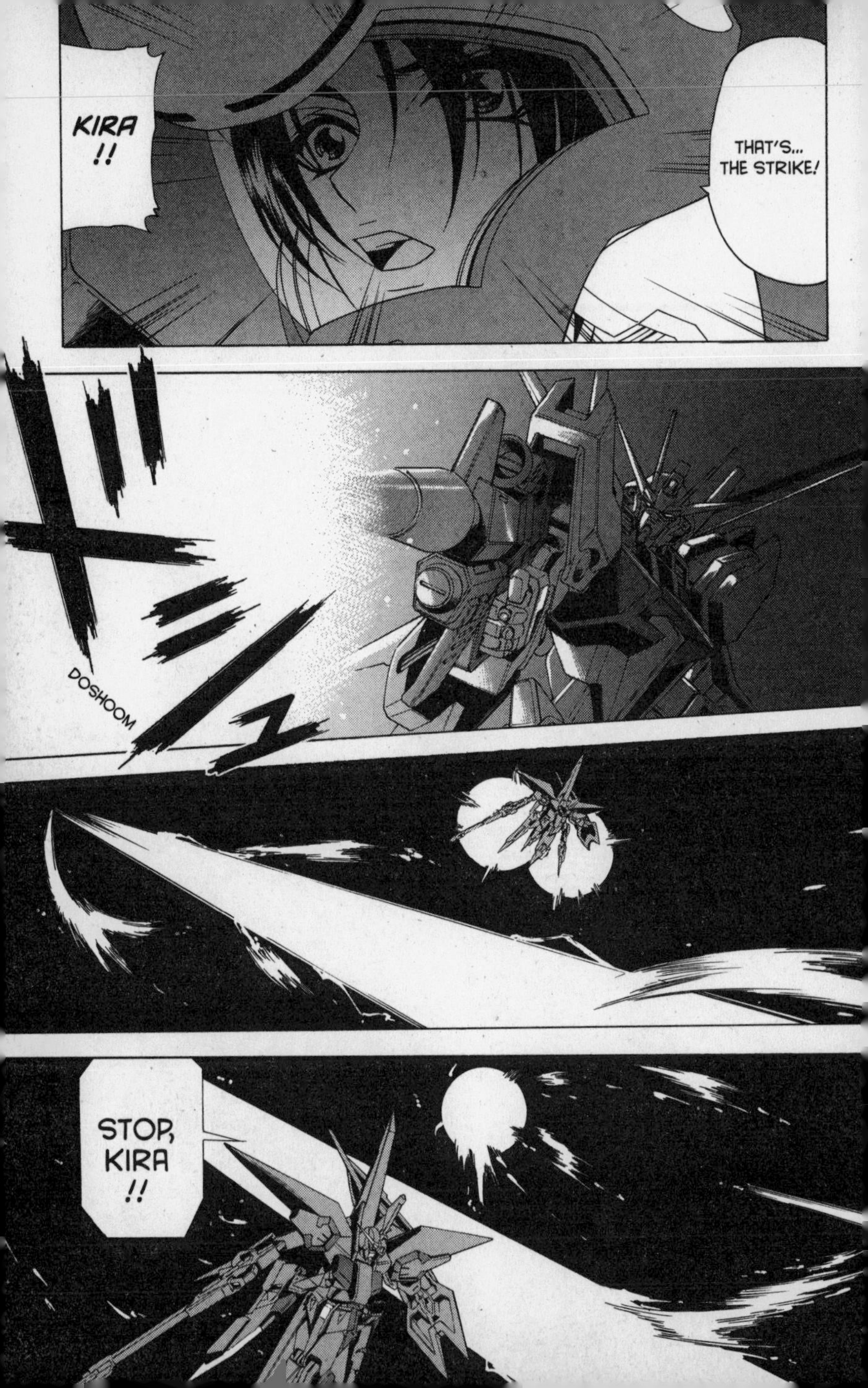
THAT'S... THE STRIKE!
KIRA !!
DOSHOOM
STOP, KIRA !!

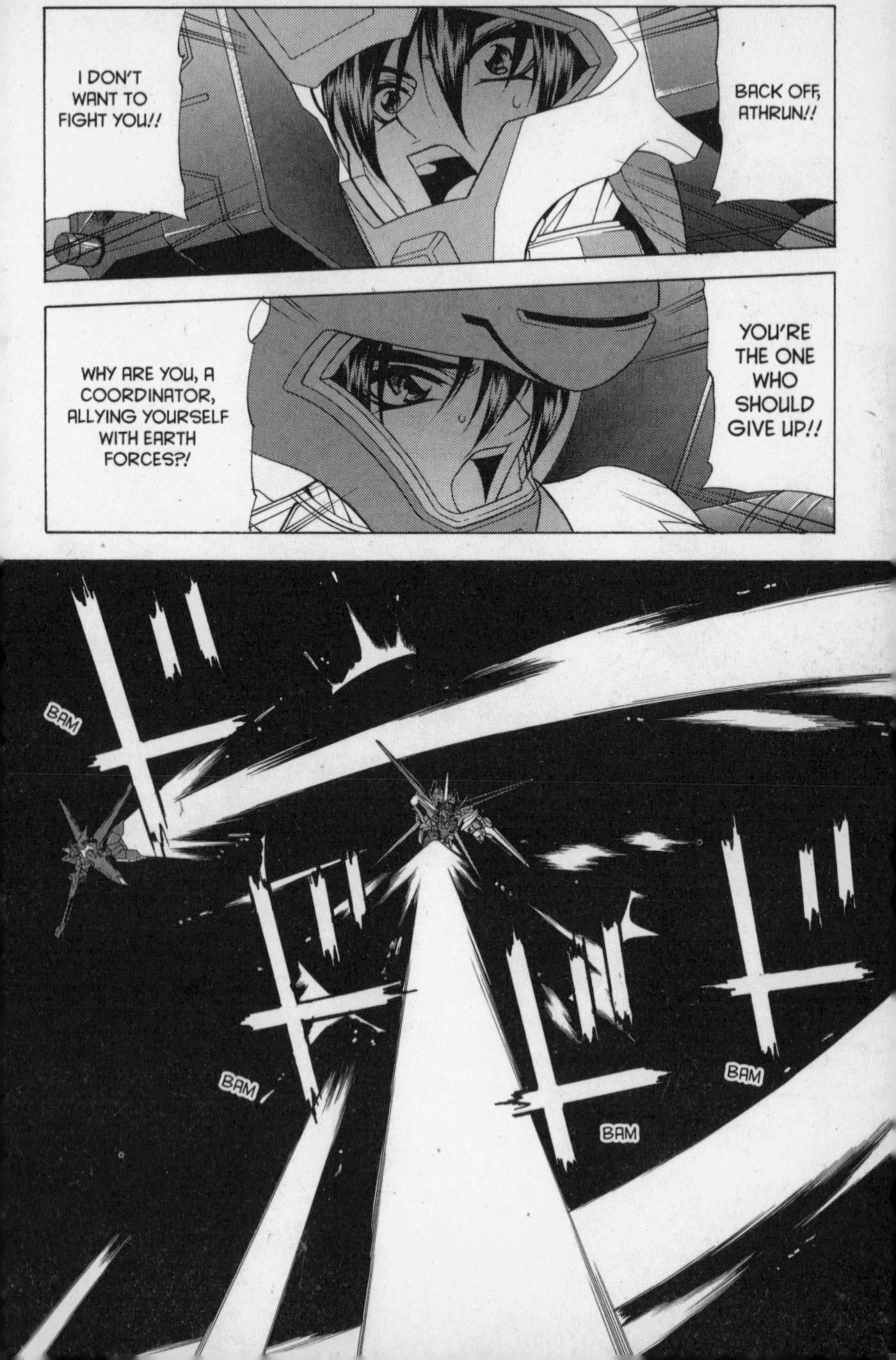
BACK OFF, ATHRUN!!
I DON'T WANT TO FIGHT YOU!!
YOU'RE THE ONE WHO SHOULD GIVE UP!!
WHY ARE YOU, A COORDINATOR, ALLYING YOURSELF WITH EARTH FORCES?!
BAM
BAM
BAM
BAM

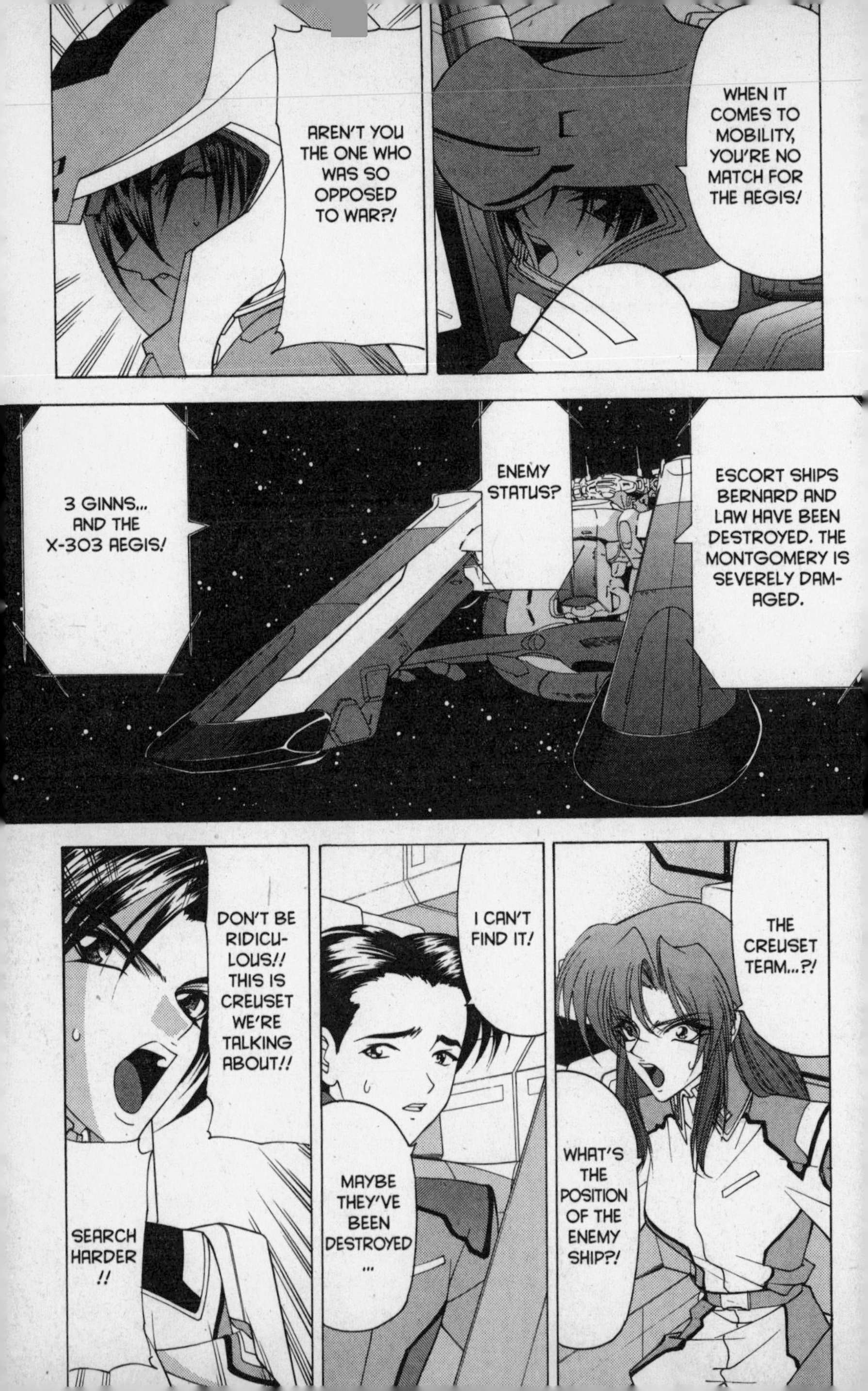
WHEN IT COMES TO MOBILITY, YOU'RE NO MATCH FOR THE AEGIS!
AREN'T YOU THE ONE WHO WAS SO OPPOSED TO WAR?!
ESCORT SHIPS BERNARD AND LAW HAVE BEEN DESTROYED. THE MONTGOMERY IS SEVERELY DAM-AGED.
ENEMY STATUS?
3 GINNS... AND THE X-303 AEGIS!
THE CREUSET TEAM...?!
WHAT'S THE POSITION OF THE ENEMY SHIP?!
I CAN'T FIND IT!
MAYBE THEY'VE BEEN DESTROYED ...
DON'T BE RIDICU-LOUS!! THIS IS CREUSET WE'RE TALKING ABOUT!!
SEARCH HARDER !!

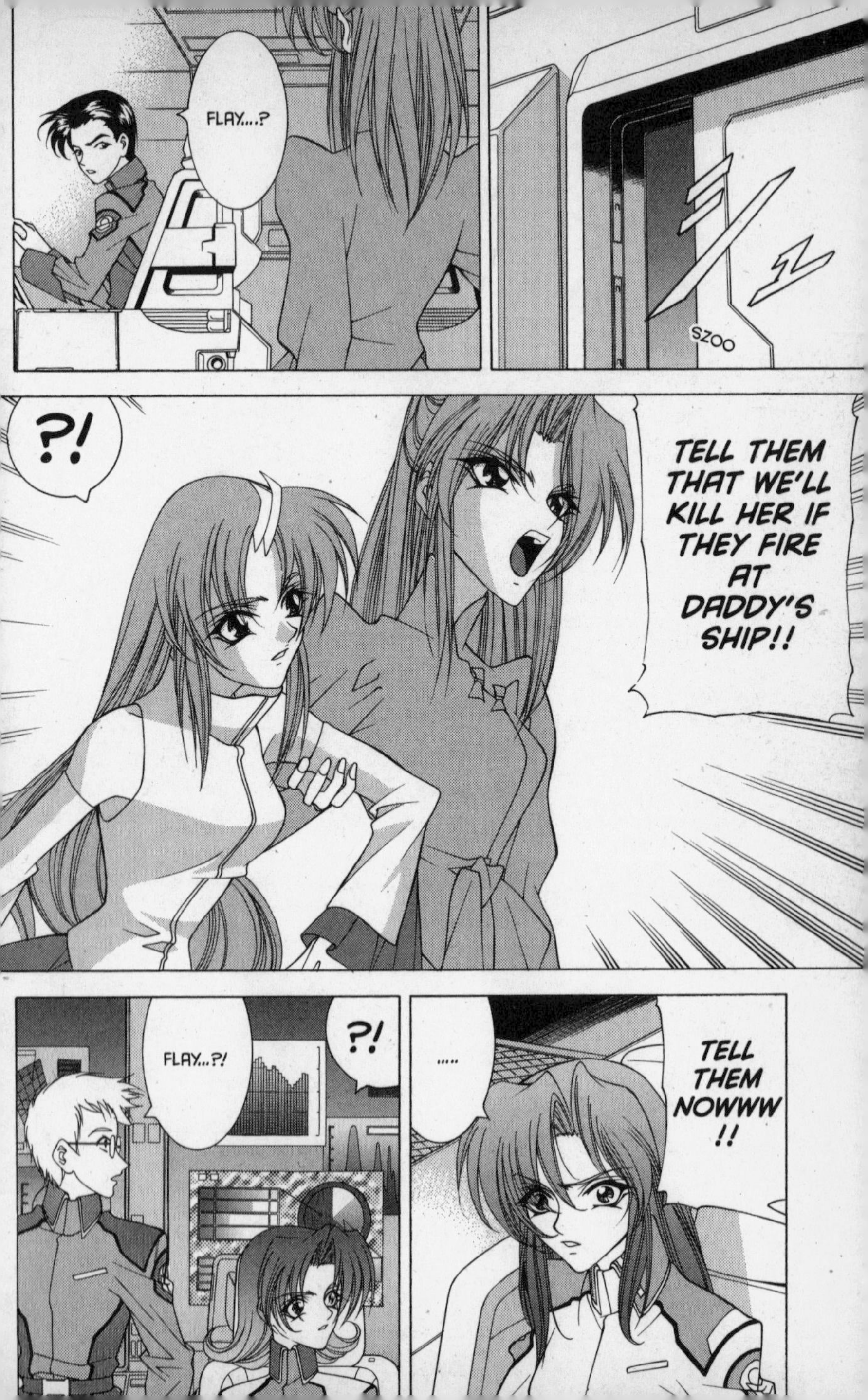
SZOO
FLAY....?
TELL THEM THAT WE'LL KILL HER IF THEY FIRE AT DADDY'S SHIP!!
?!
TELL THEM NOWWW!!
.....
?!
FLAY...?!

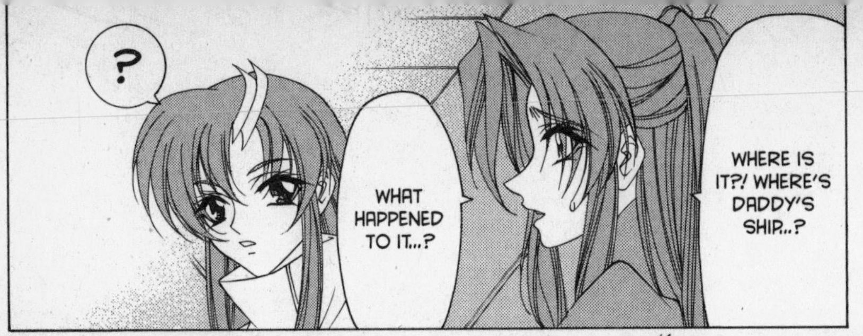
WHERE IS IT?! WHERE'S DADDY'S SHIP...?
WHAT HAPPENED TO IT...?
?
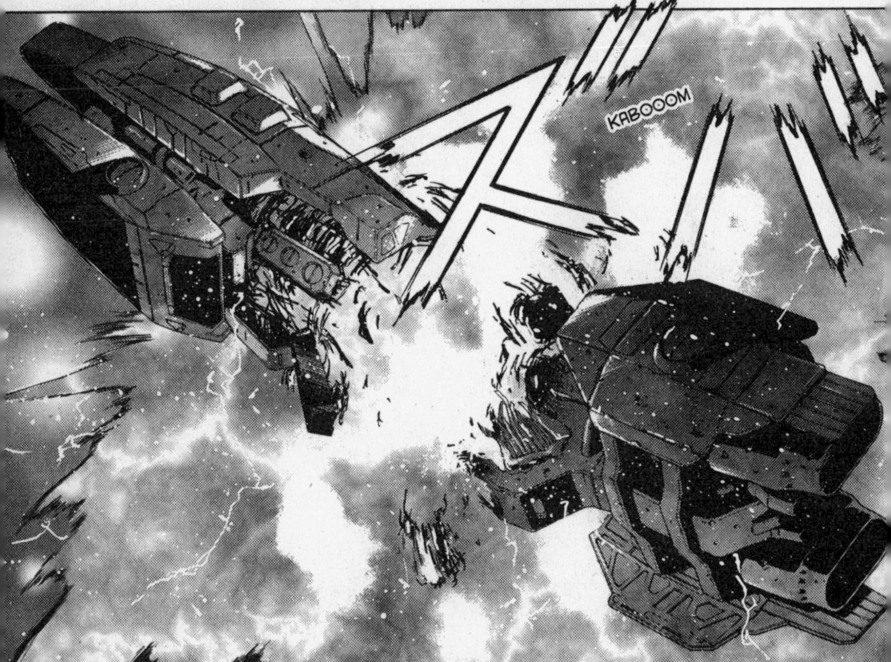
KABOOOM
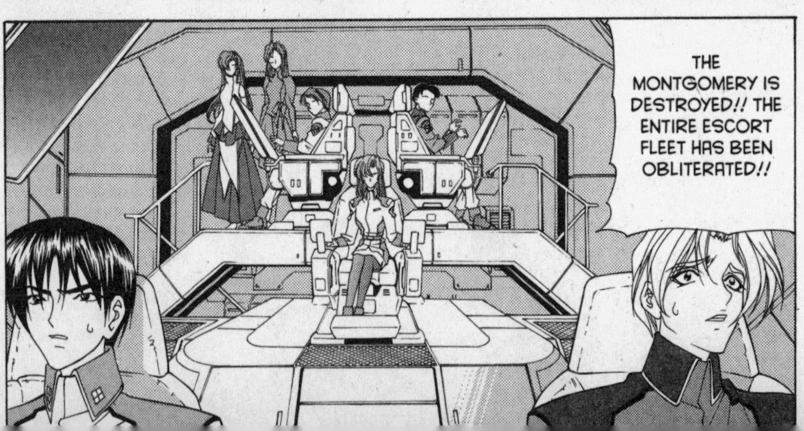
THE MONTGOMERY IS DESTROYED!! THE ENTIRE ESCORT FLEET HAS BEEN OBLITERATED!!

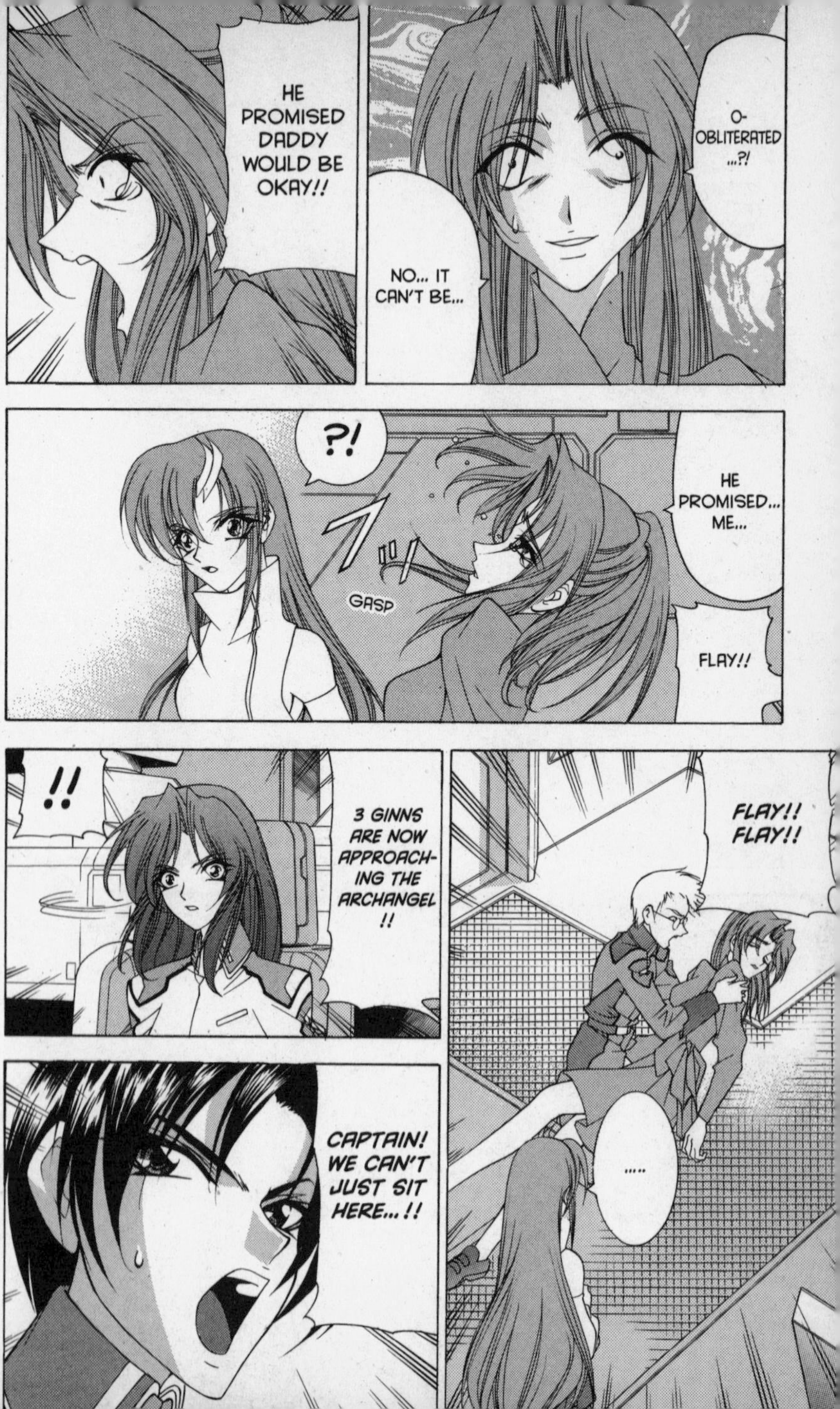

O-OBLITERATED ...?!
NO... IT CAN'T BE...
HE PROMISED DADDY WOULD BE OKAY!!
HE PROMISED... ME...
?!
FLAY!!
GASP
FLAY!! FLAY!!
.....
!!
3 GINNS ARE NOW APPROACHING THE ARCHANGEL !!
CAPTAIN! WE CAN'T JUST SIT HERE...!!

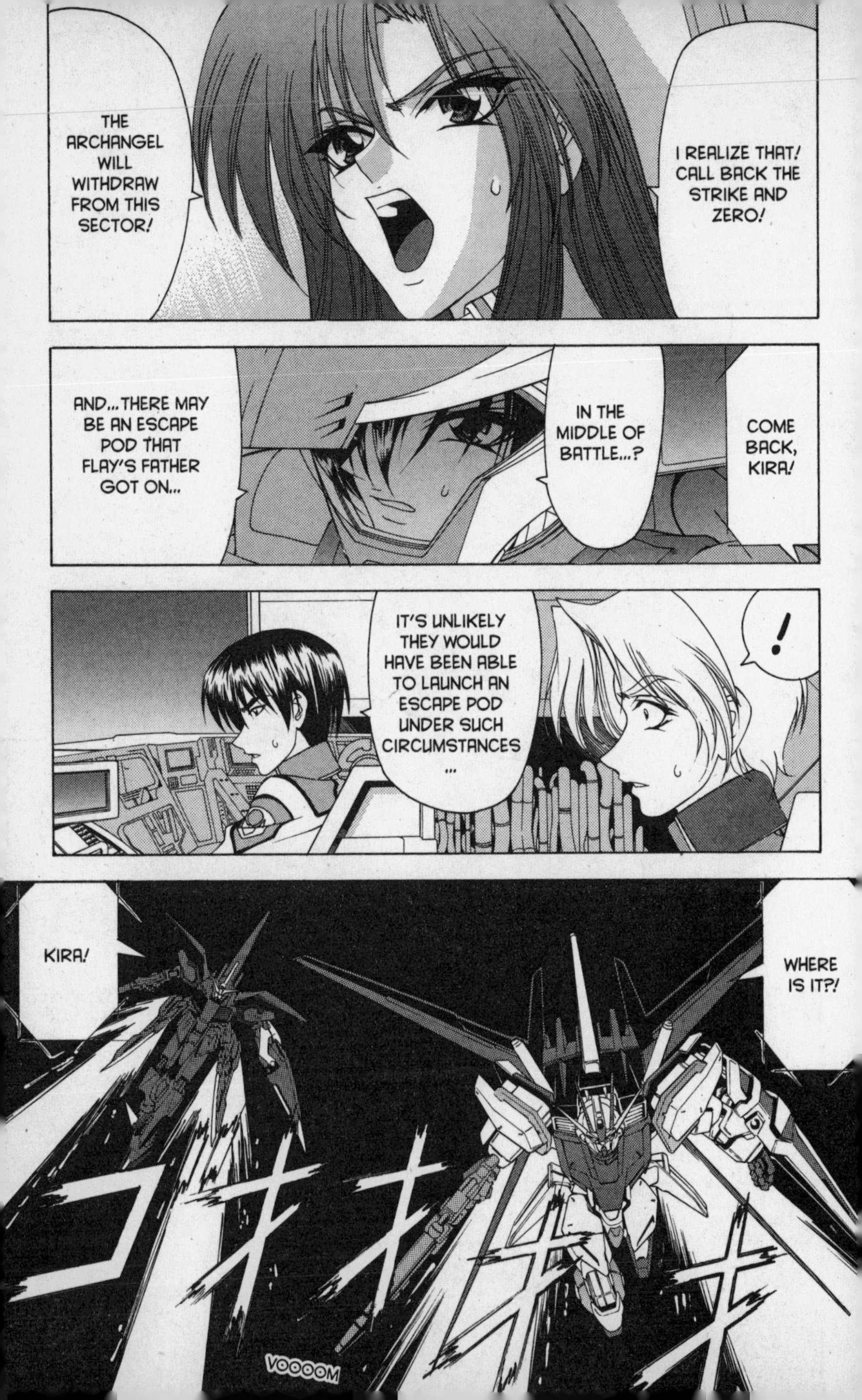
I REALIZE THAT! CALL BACK THE STRIKE AND ZERO!
THE ARCHANGEL WILL WITHDRAW FROM THIS SECTOR!
COME BACK, KIRA!
IN THE MIDDLE OF BATTLE...?
AND...THERE MAY BE AN ESCAPE POD THAT FLAY'S FATHER GOT ON...
!
IT'S UNLIKELY THEY WOULD HAVE BEEN ABLE TO LAUNCH AN ESCAPE POD UNDER SUCH CIRCUMSTANCES...
WHERE IS IT?!
KIRA!
VOOOOM

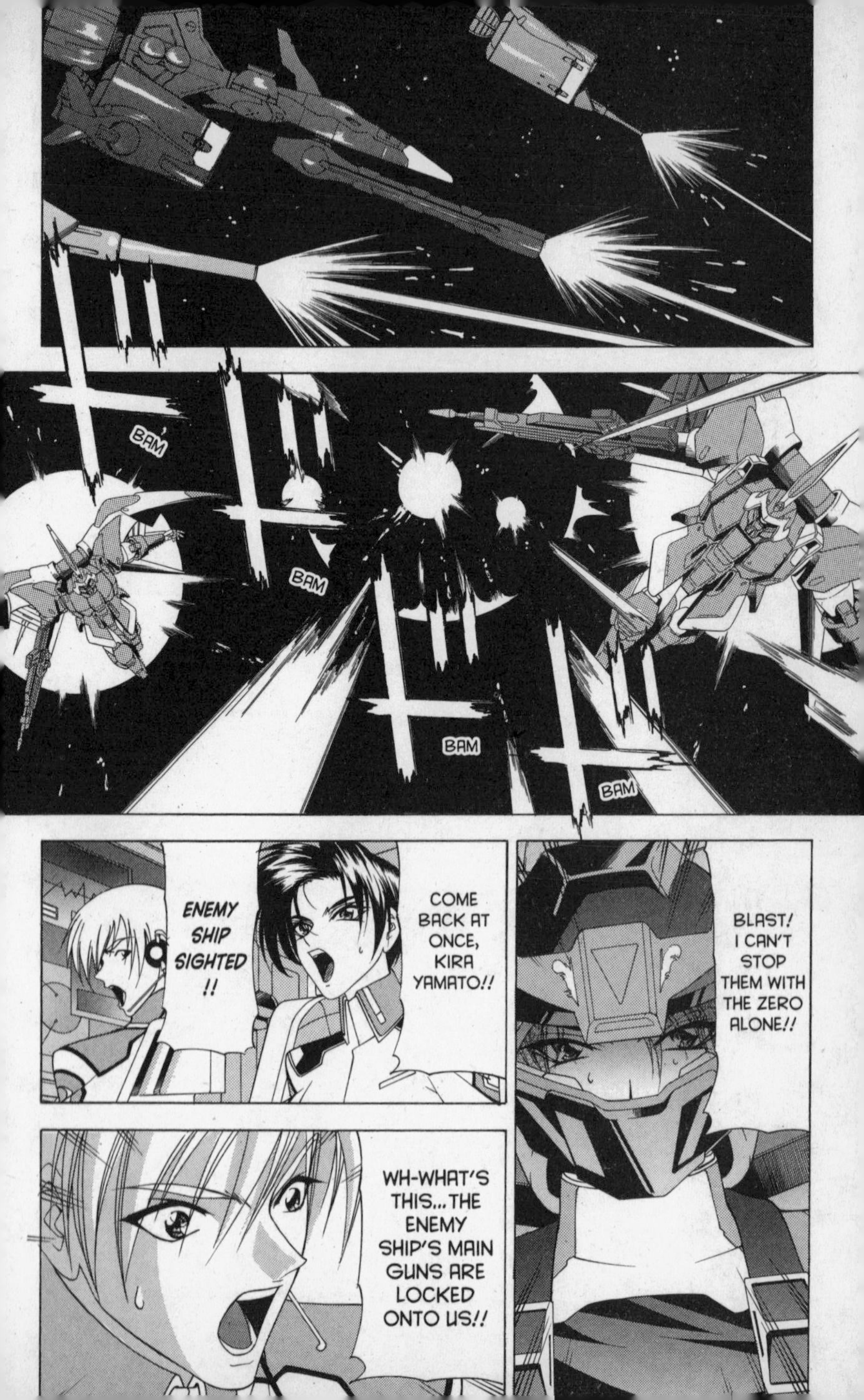
BAM
BAM
BAM
BAM
BLAST! I CAN'T STOP THEM WITH THE ZERO ALONE!!
COME BACK AT ONCE, KIRA YAMATO!!
ENEMY SHIP SIGHTED!!
WH-WHAT'S THIS...THE ENEMY SHIP'S MAIN GUNS ARE LOCKED ONTO US!!

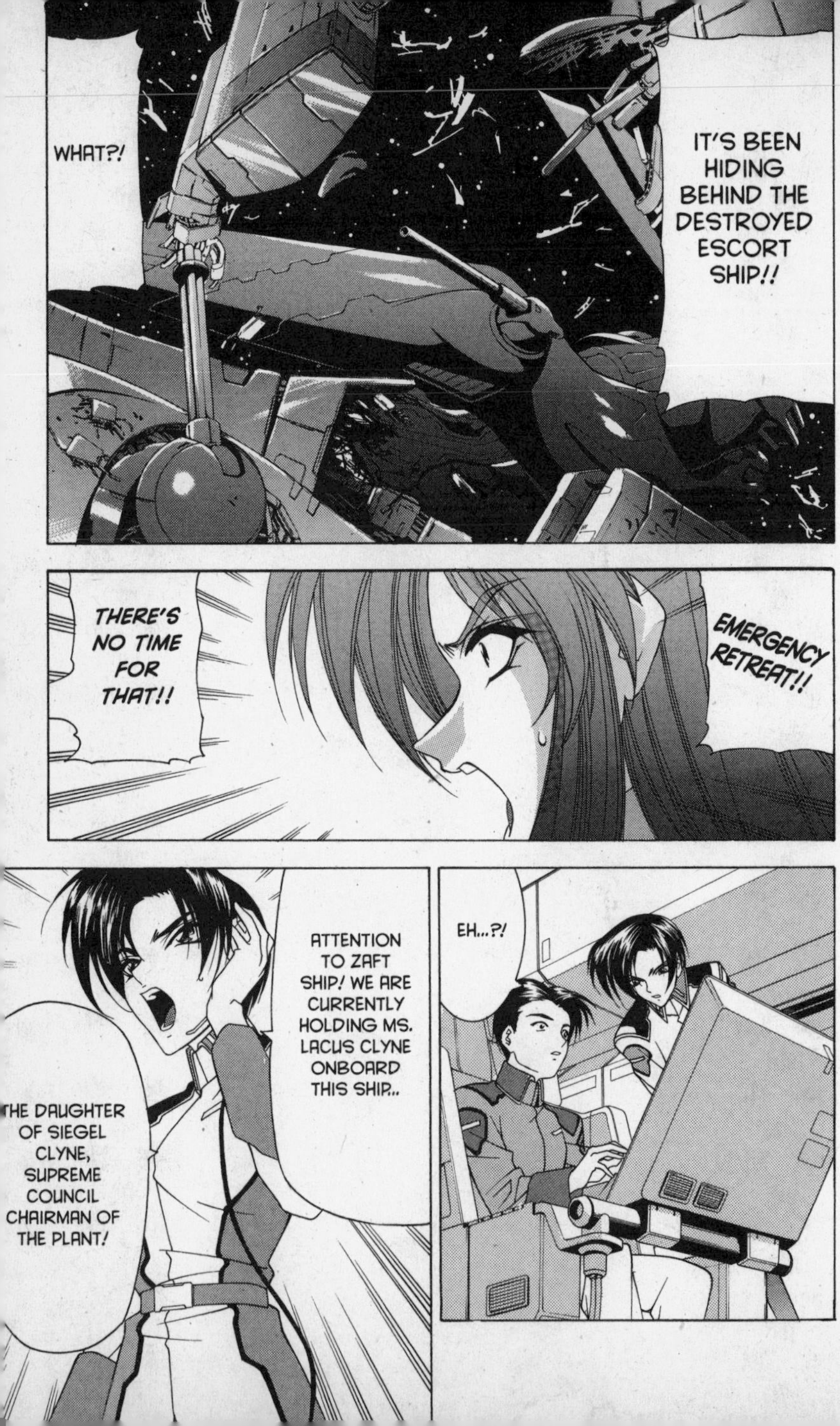
IT'S BEEN HIDING BEHIND THE DESTROYED ESCORT SHIP!!
WHAT?!
EMERGENCY RETREAT!!
THERE'S NO TIME FOR THAT!!
EH...?!
ATTENTION TO ZAFT SHIP! WE ARE CURRENTLY HOLDING MS. LACUS CLYNE ONBOARD THIS SHIP...
THE DAUGHTER OF SIEGEL CLYNE, SUPREME COUNCIL CHAIRMAN OF THE PLANT!

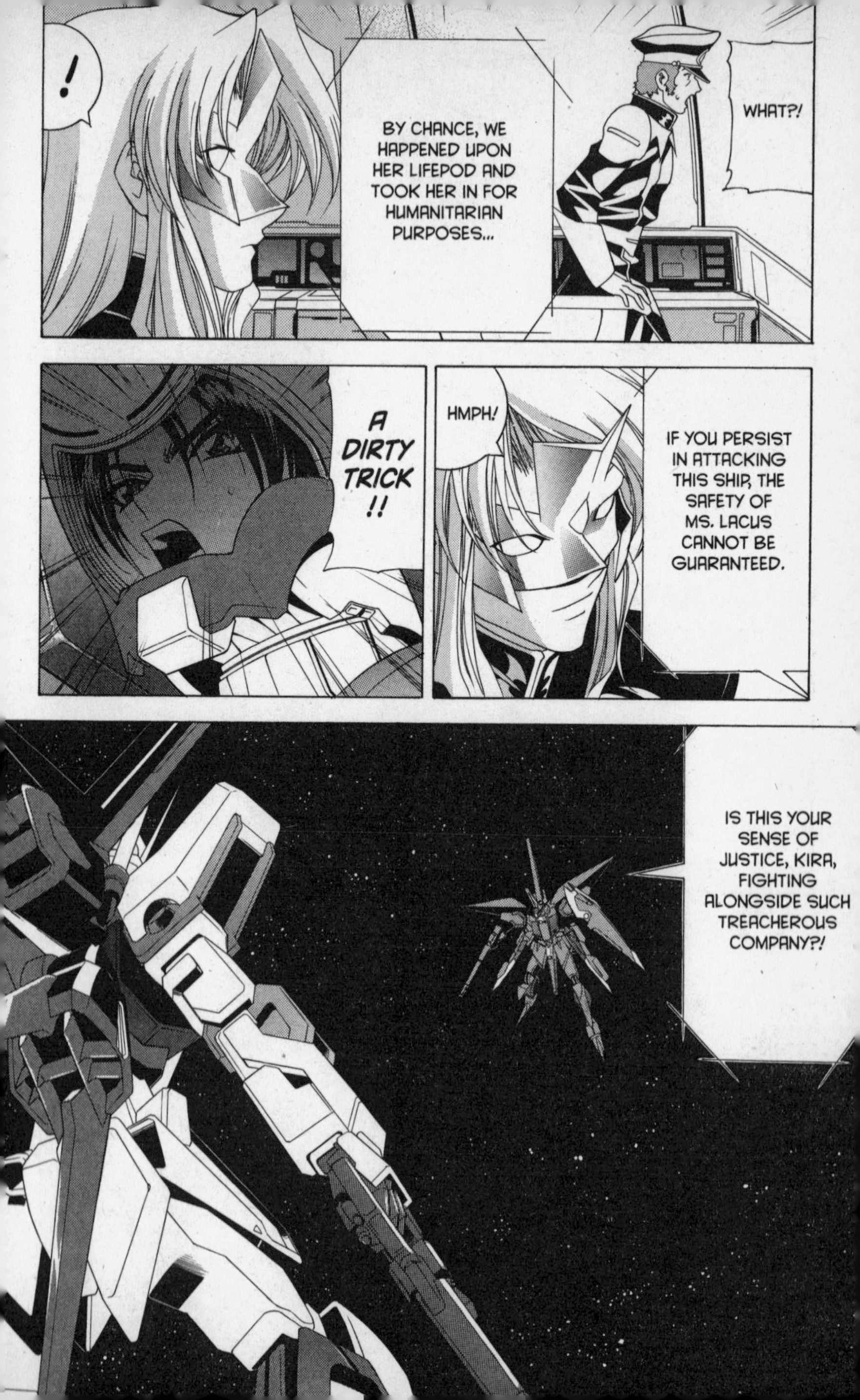
WHAT?!
BY CHANCE, WE HAPPENED UPON HER LIFEPOD AND TOOK HER IN FOR HUMANITARIAN PURPOSES...
!
IF YOU PERSIST IN ATTACKING THIS SHIP, THE SAFETY OF MS. LACUS CANNOT BE GUARANTEED.
HMPH!
A DIRTY TRICK !!
IS THIS YOUR SENSE OF JUSTICE, KIRA, FIGHTING ALONGSIDE SUCH TREACHEROUS COMPANY?!

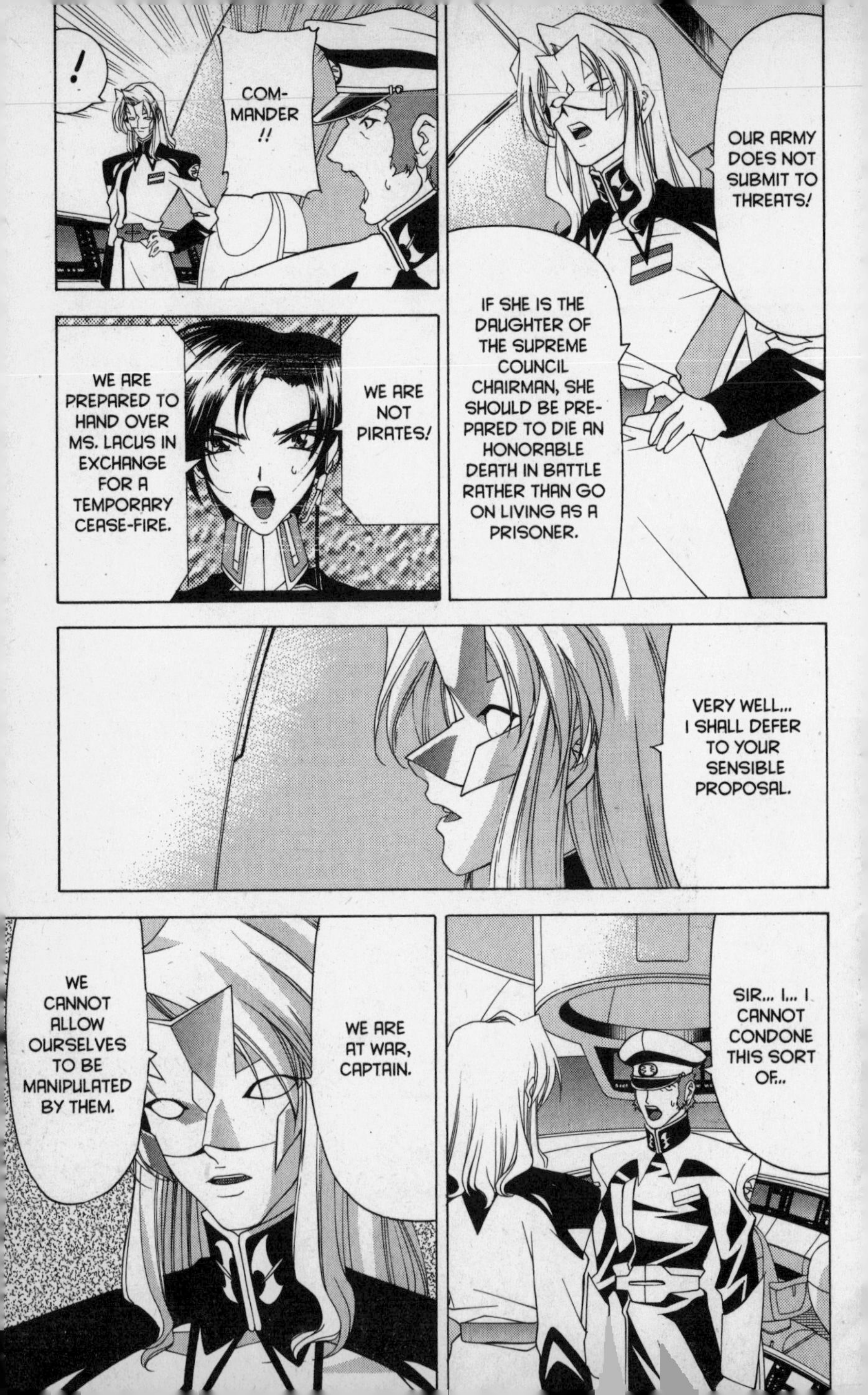

OUR ARMY DOES NOT SUBMIT TO THREATS!
IF SHE IS THE DAUGHTER OF THE SUPREME COUNCIL CHAIRMAN, SHE SHOULD BE PRE-PARED TO DIE AN HONORABLE DEATH IN BATTLE RATHER THAN GO ON LIVING AS A PRISONER.
COM-MANDER !!
!
WE ARE NOT PIRATES!
WE ARE PREPARED TO HAND OVER MS. LACUS IN EXCHANGE FOR A TEMPORARY CEASE-FIRE.
VERY WELL... I SHALL DEFER TO YOUR SENSIBLE PROPOSAL.
SIR... I... I CANNOT CONDONE THIS SORT OF...
WE ARE AT WAR, CAPTAIN.
WE CANNOT ALLOW OURSELVES TO BE MANIPULATED BY THEM.

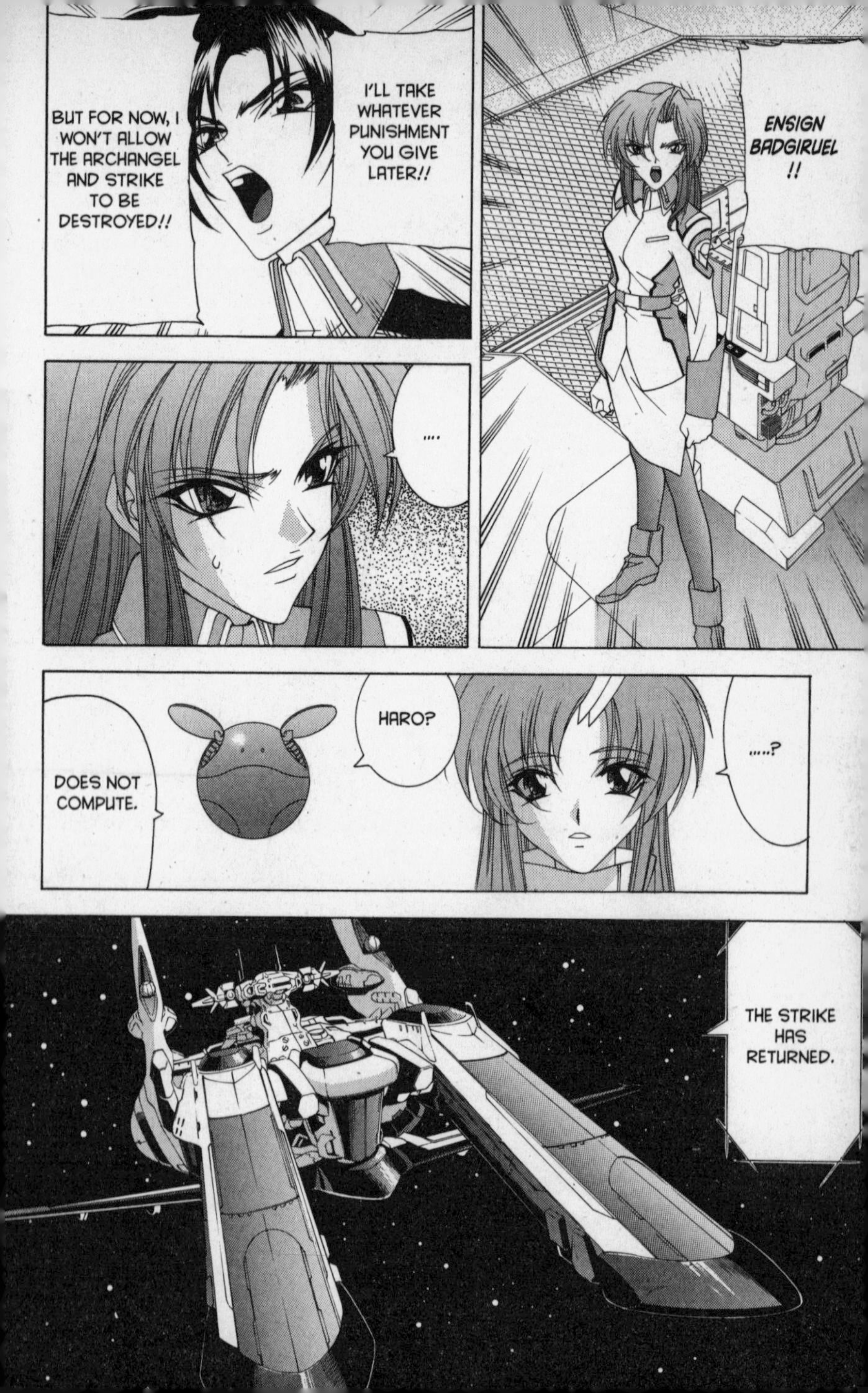
ENSIGN BADGIRUEL !!
I'LL TAKE WHATEVER PUNISHMENT YOU GIVE LATER!!
BUT FOR NOW, I WON'T ALLOW THE ARCHANGEL AND STRIKE TO BE DESTROYED!!
....
.....?
HARO?
DOES NOT COMPUTE.
THE STRIKE HAS RETURNED.

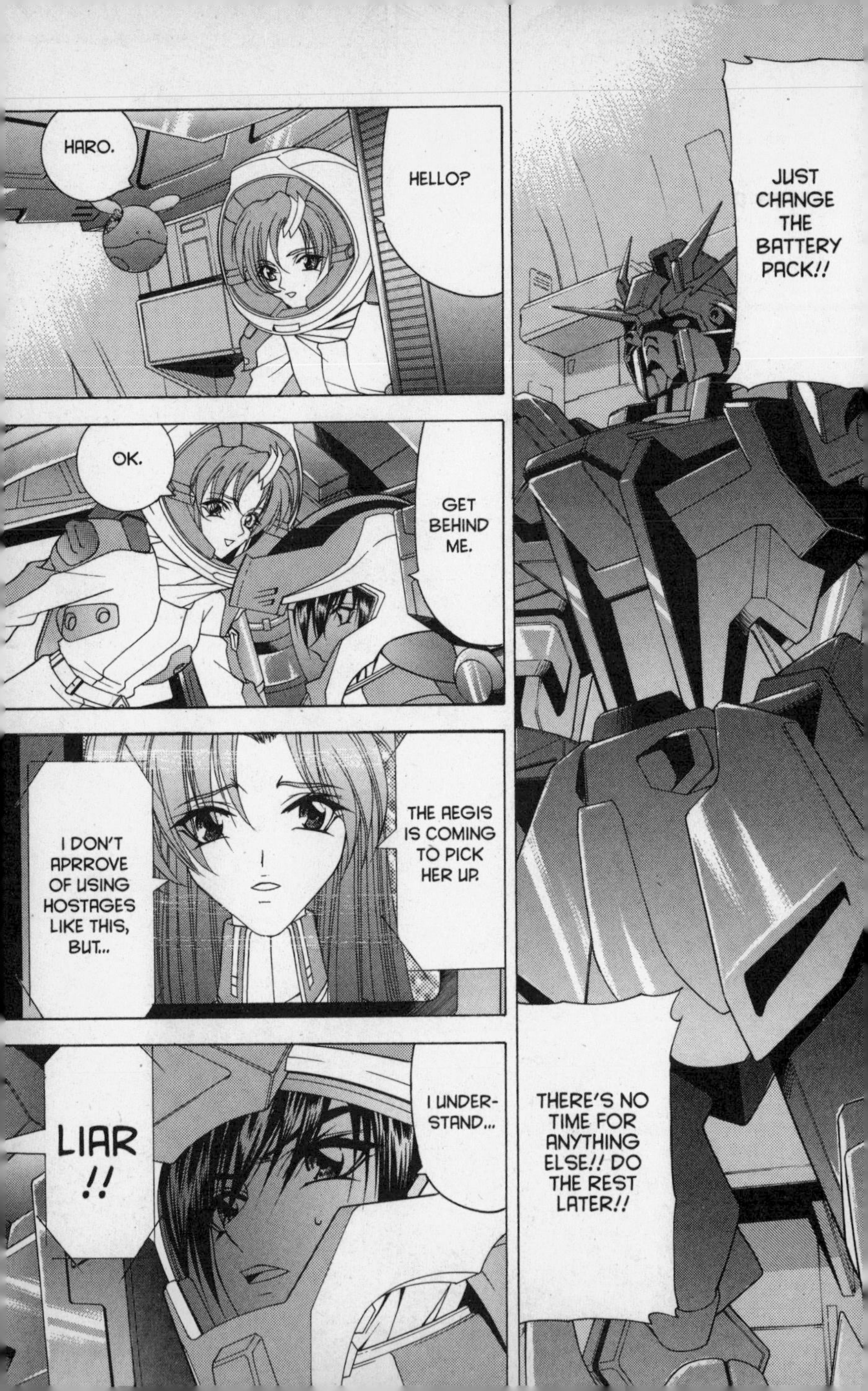
JUST CHANGE THE BATTERY PACK!!
THERE'S NO TIME FOR ANYTHING ELSE!! DO THE REST LATER!!
HELLO?
HARO.
GET BEHIND ME.
OK.
THE AEGIS IS COMING TO PICK HER UP.
I DON'T APRROVE OF USING HOSTAGES LIKE THIS, BUT...
I UNDER-STAND...
LIAR!!

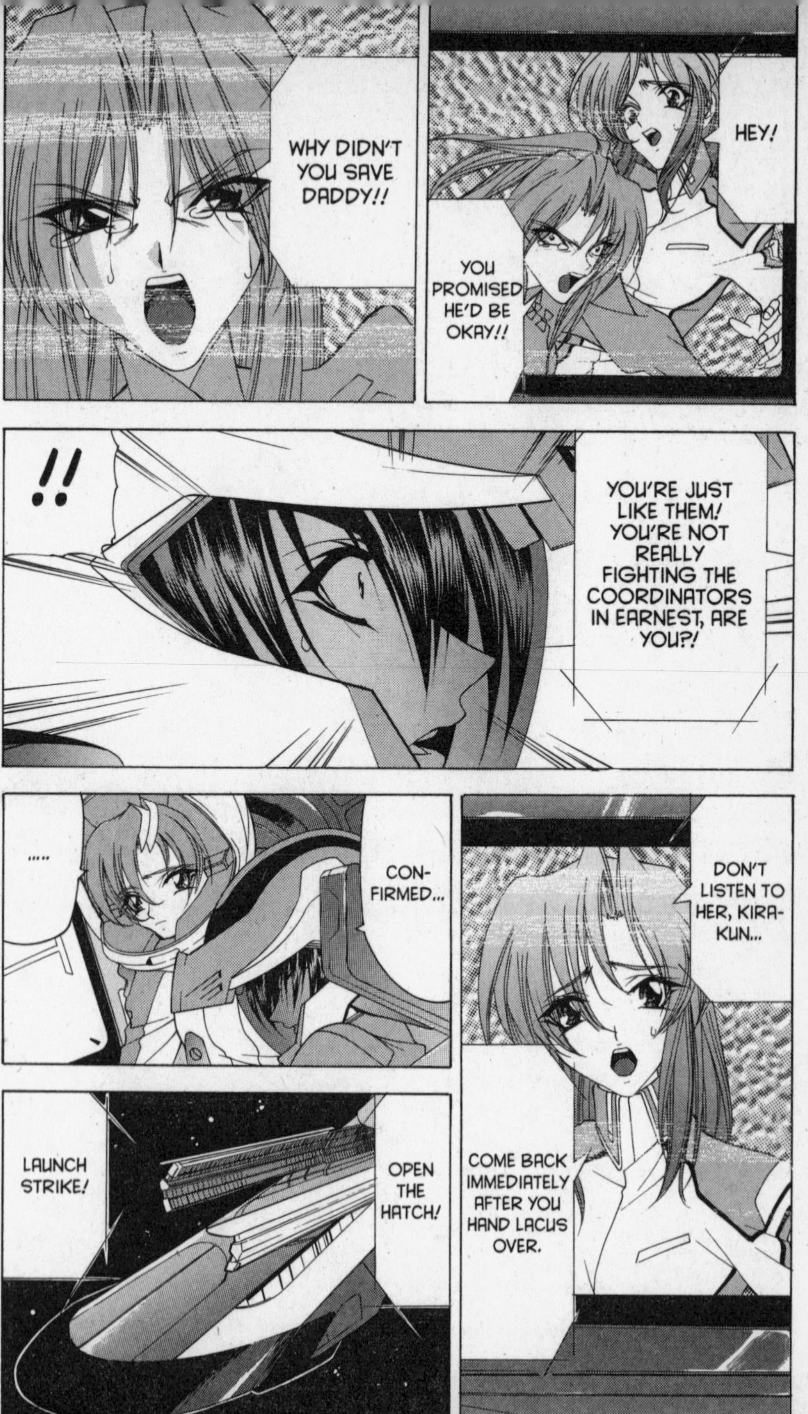
HEY!
YOU PROMISED HE'D BE OKAY!!
WHY DIDN'T YOU SAVE DADDY!!
YOU'RE JUST LIKE THEM! YOU'RE NOT REALLY FIGHTING THE COORDINATORS IN EARNEST, ARE YOU?!
!!
DON'T LISTEN TO HER, KIRA-KUN...
COME BACK IMMEDIATELY AFTER YOU HAND LACUS OVER.
CON-FIRMED...
.....
OPEN THE HATCH!
LAUNCH STRIKE!

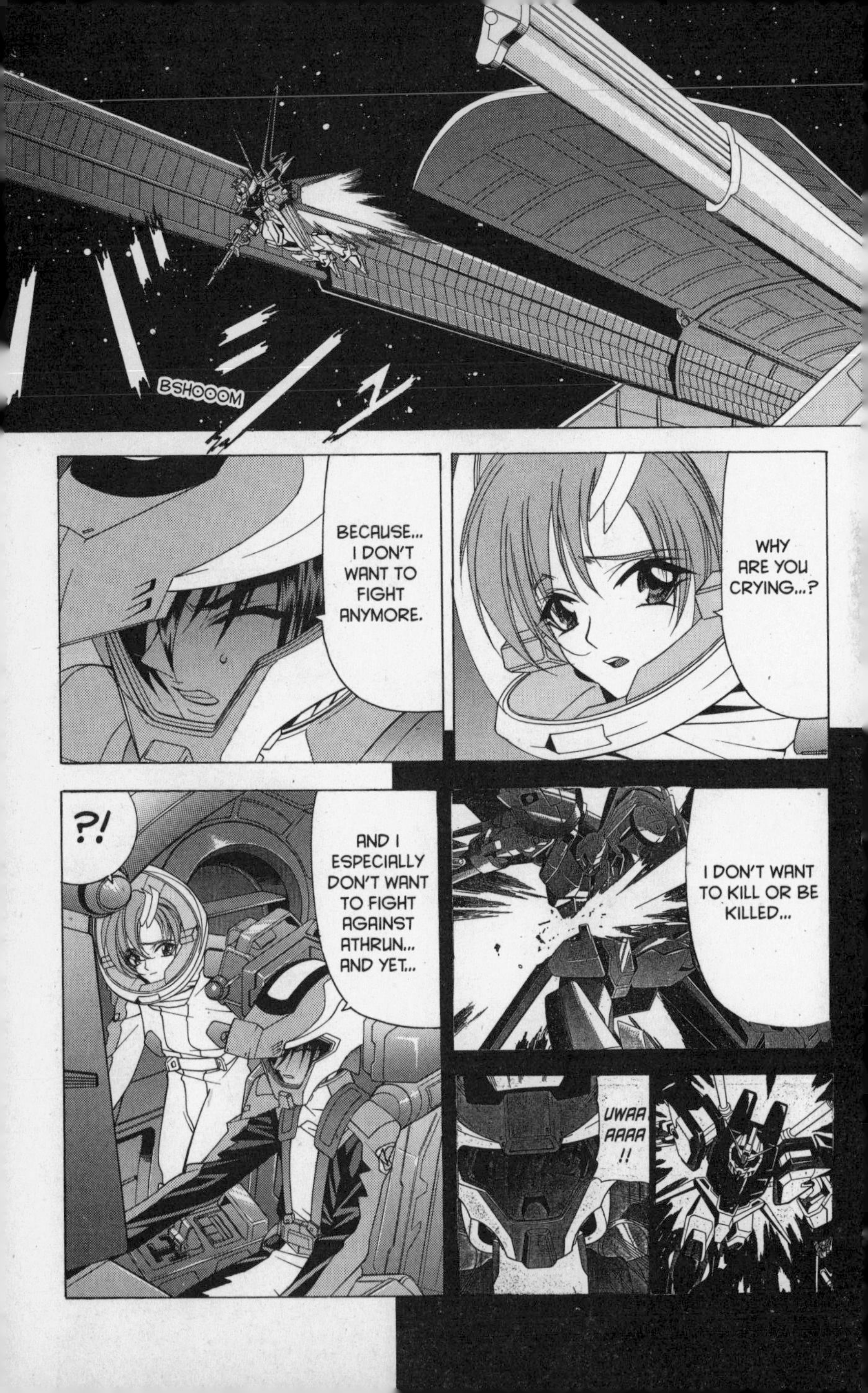
BSHOOOM
WHY ARE YOU CRYING...?
BECAUSE... I DON'T WANT TO FIGHT ANYMORE.
I DON'T WANT TO KILL OR BE KILLED...
UWAA AAAA !!
AND I ESPECIALLY DON'T WANT TO FIGHT AGAINST ATHRUN... AND YET...
?!

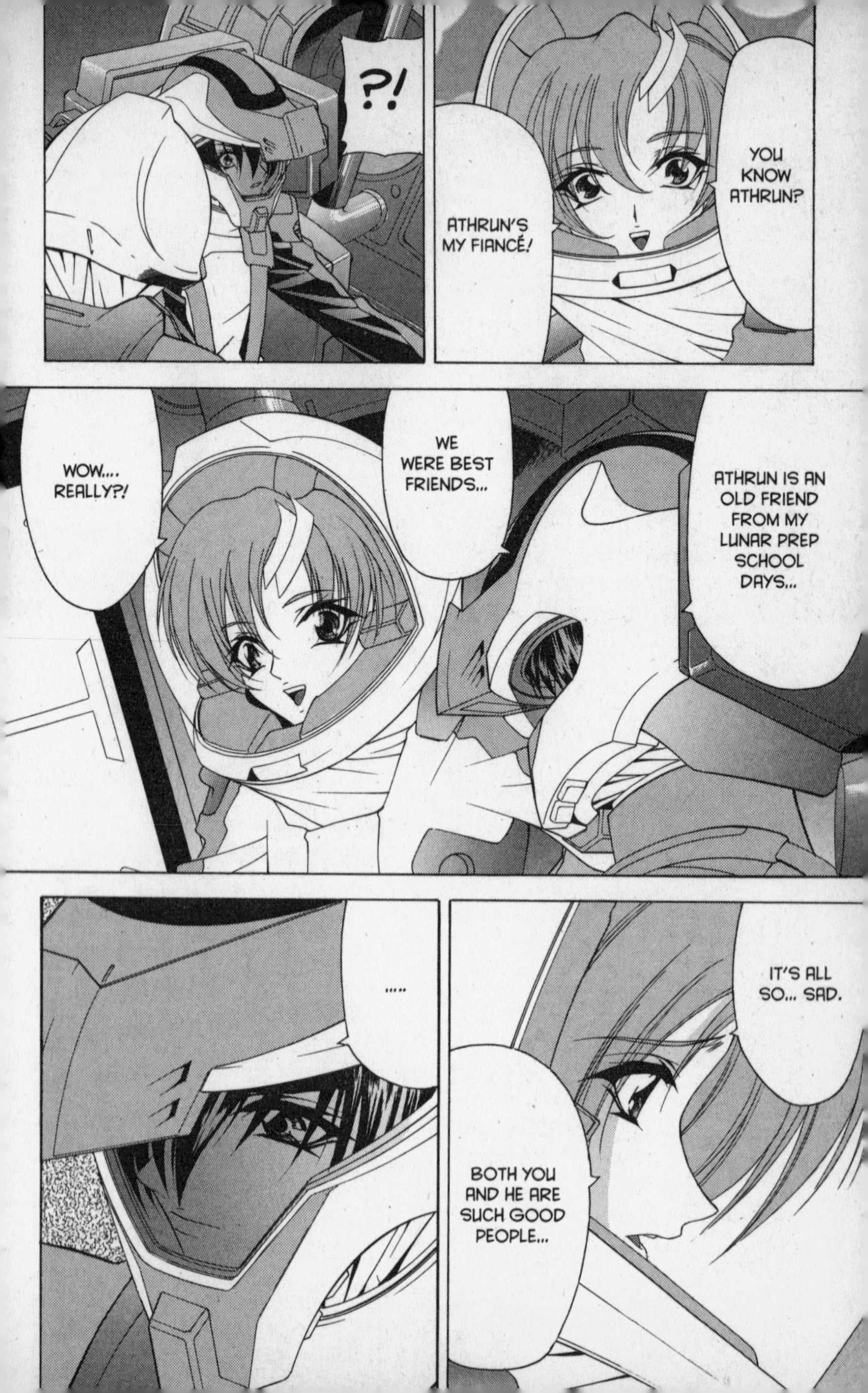

YOU KNOW ATHRUN?
ATHRUN'S MY FIANCÉ!
?!
ATHRUN IS AN OLD FRIEND FROM MY LUNAR PREP SCHOOL DAYS...
WE WERE BEST FRIENDS...
WOW.... REALLY?!
IT'S ALL SO... SAD.
BOTH YOU AND HE ARE SUCH GOOD PEOPLE...
.....

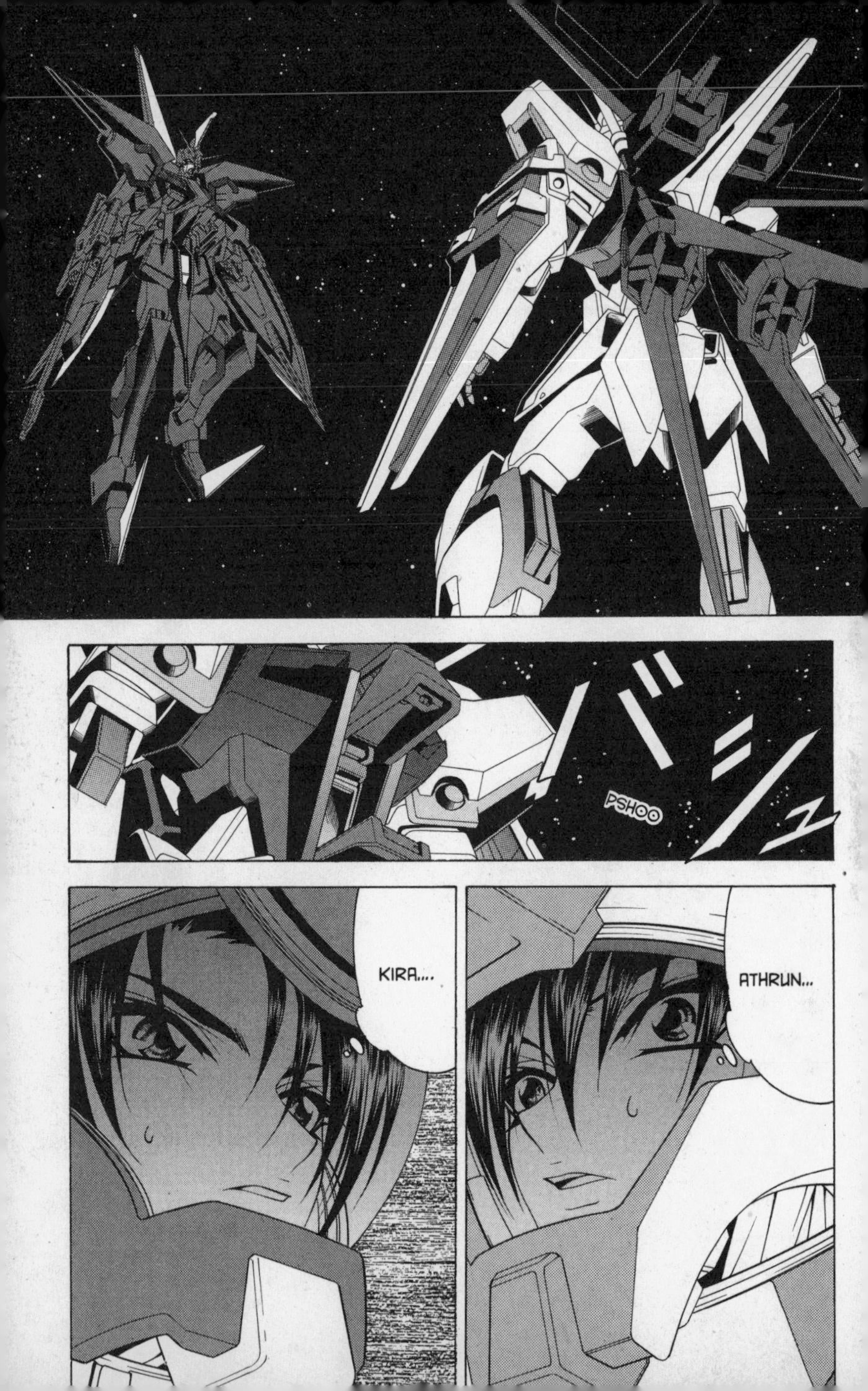
PSHOO
ATHRUN...
KIRA....

KIRA.... KIRA YAMATO.

SORRY FOR THE TROUBLE I CAUSED...

...UM...

TAKE IT EASY...

THANK YOU, KIRA-SAMA... AND TAKE CARE.

LACUS... YOU MEAN SO MUCH TO ME...

I MISSED YOU SO MUCH!

I'M SO HAPPY TO SEE YOU, ATHRUN!

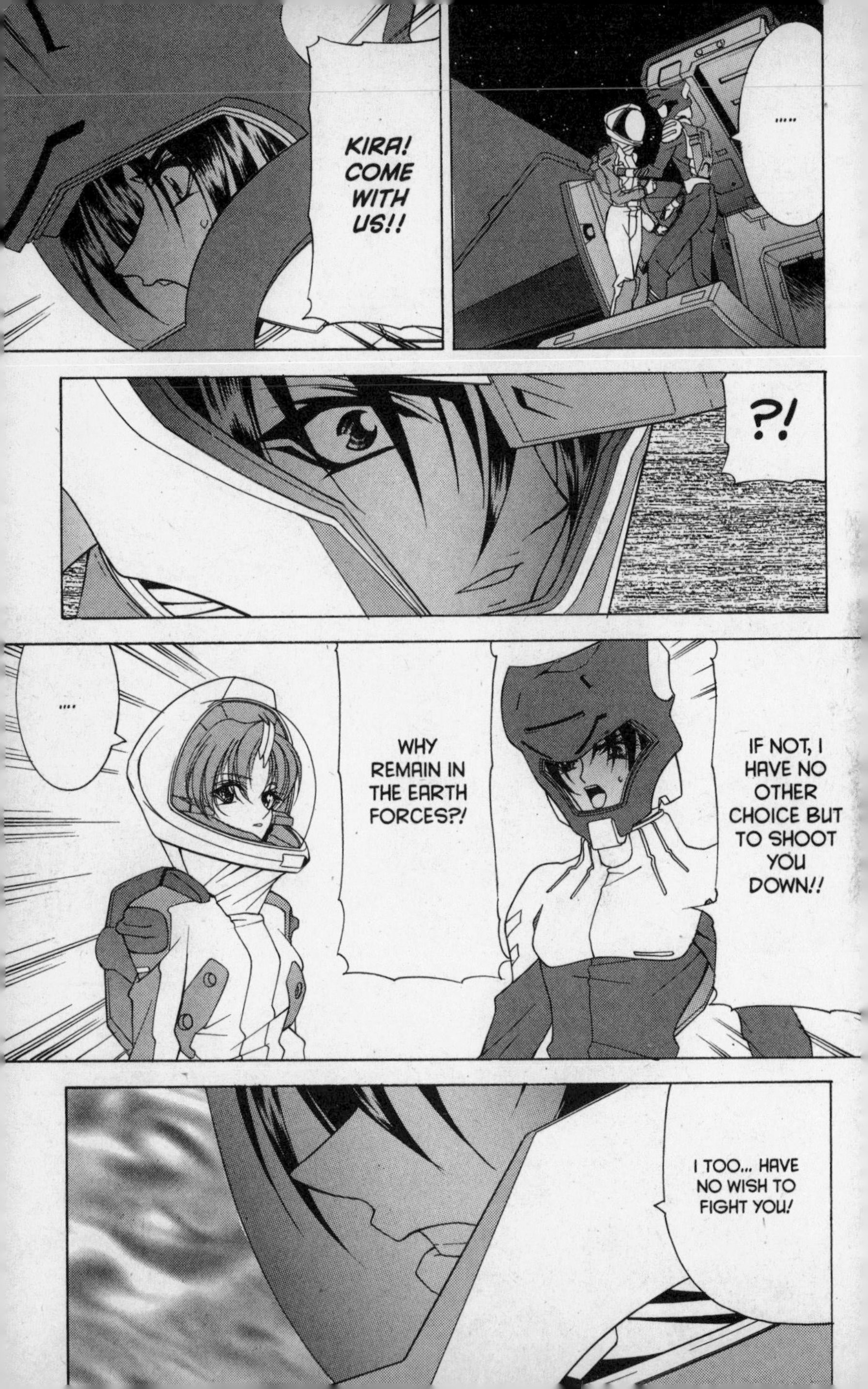
.....
KIRA! COME WITH US!!
?!
IF NOT, I HAVE NO OTHER CHOICE BUT TO SHOOT YOU DOWN!!
WHY REMAIN IN THE EARTH FORCES?!
....
I TOO... HAVE NO WISH TO FIGHT YOU!

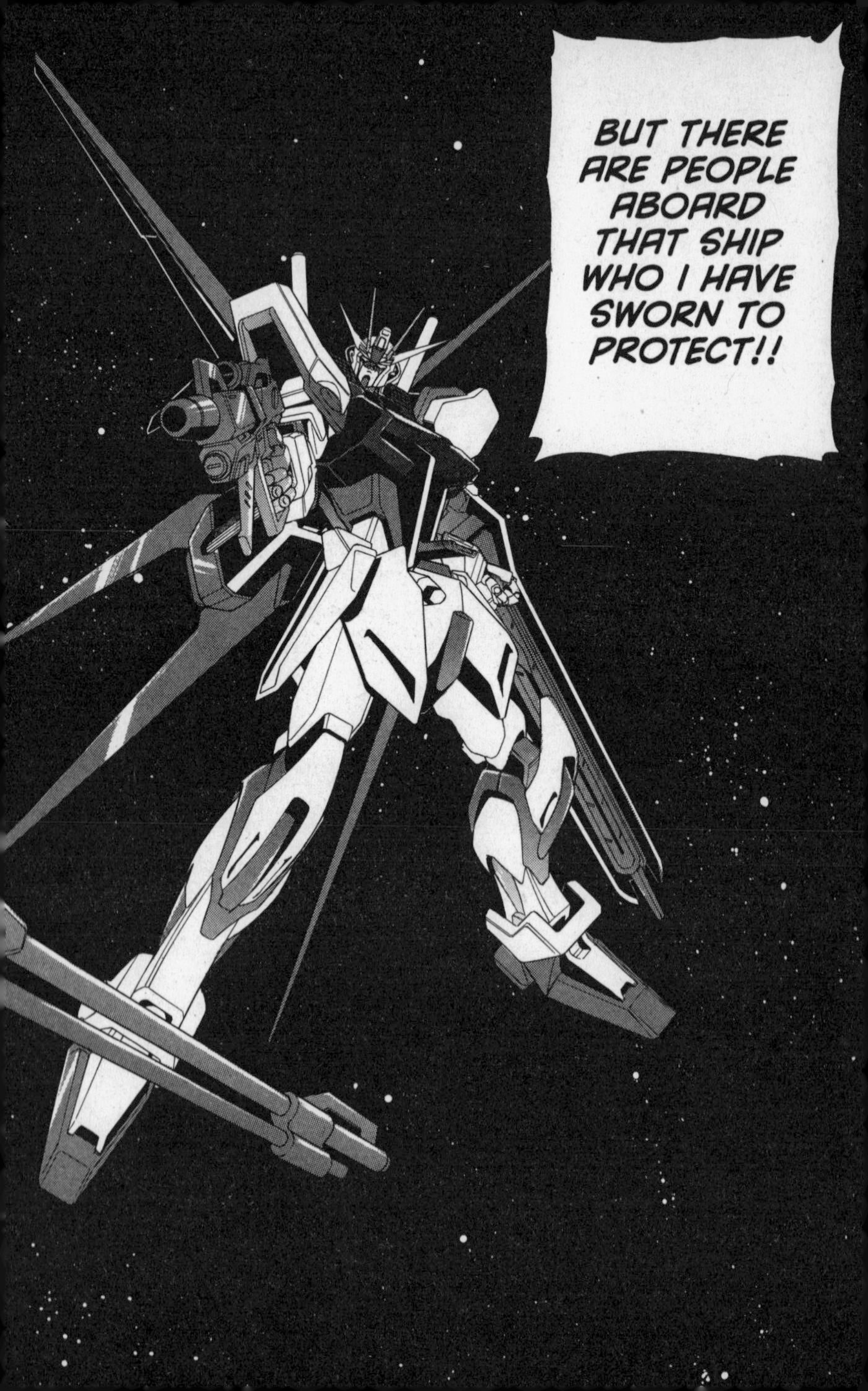
BUT THERE ARE PEOPLE ABOARD THAT SHIP WHO I HAVE SWORN TO PROTECT!!

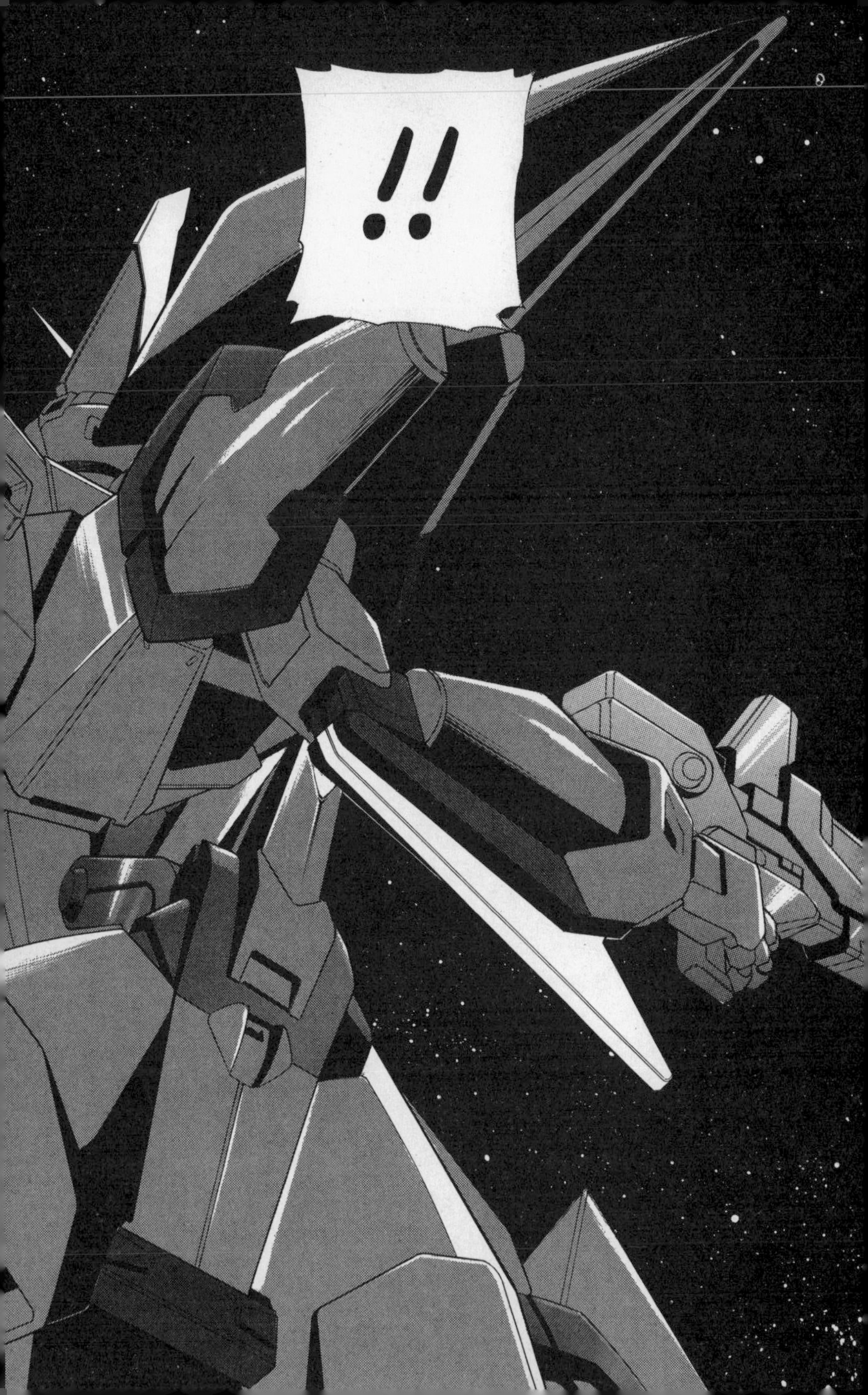
!!

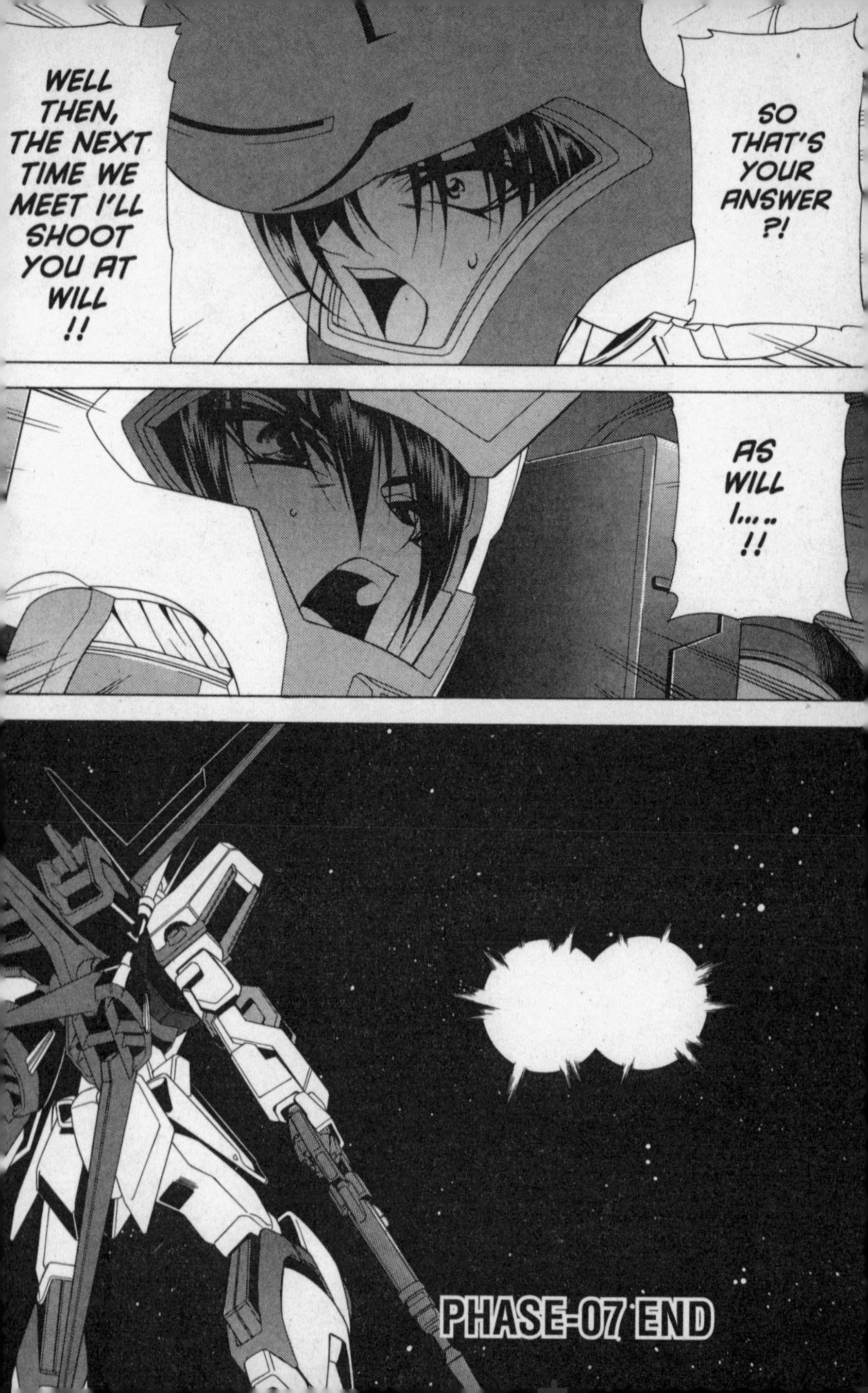
SO THAT'S YOUR ANSWER ?!
WELL THEN, THE NEXT TIME WE MEET I'LL SHOOT YOU AT WILL !!
AS WILL I..... !!
PHASE-07 END

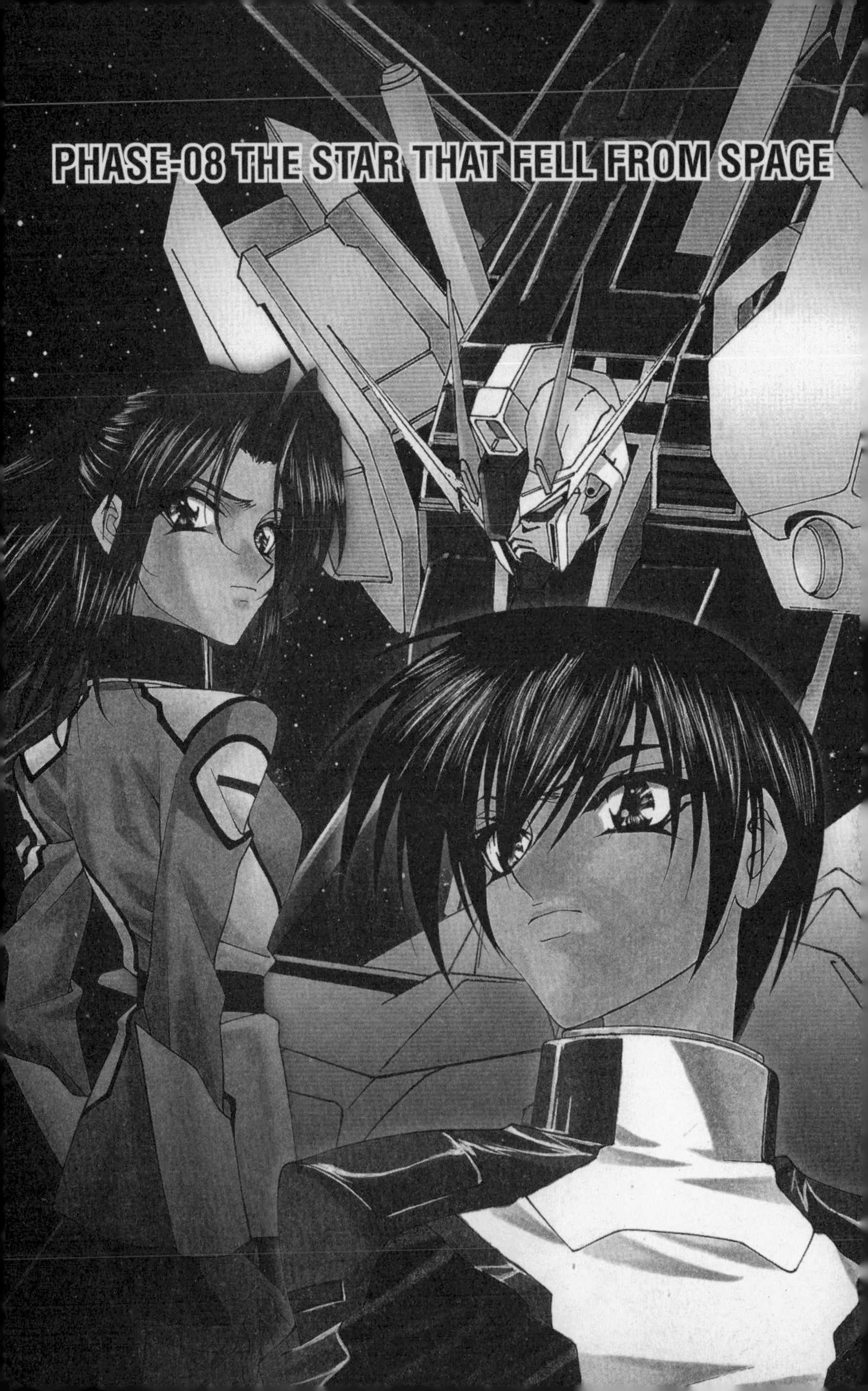
PHASE-08 THE STAR THAT FELL FROM SPACE

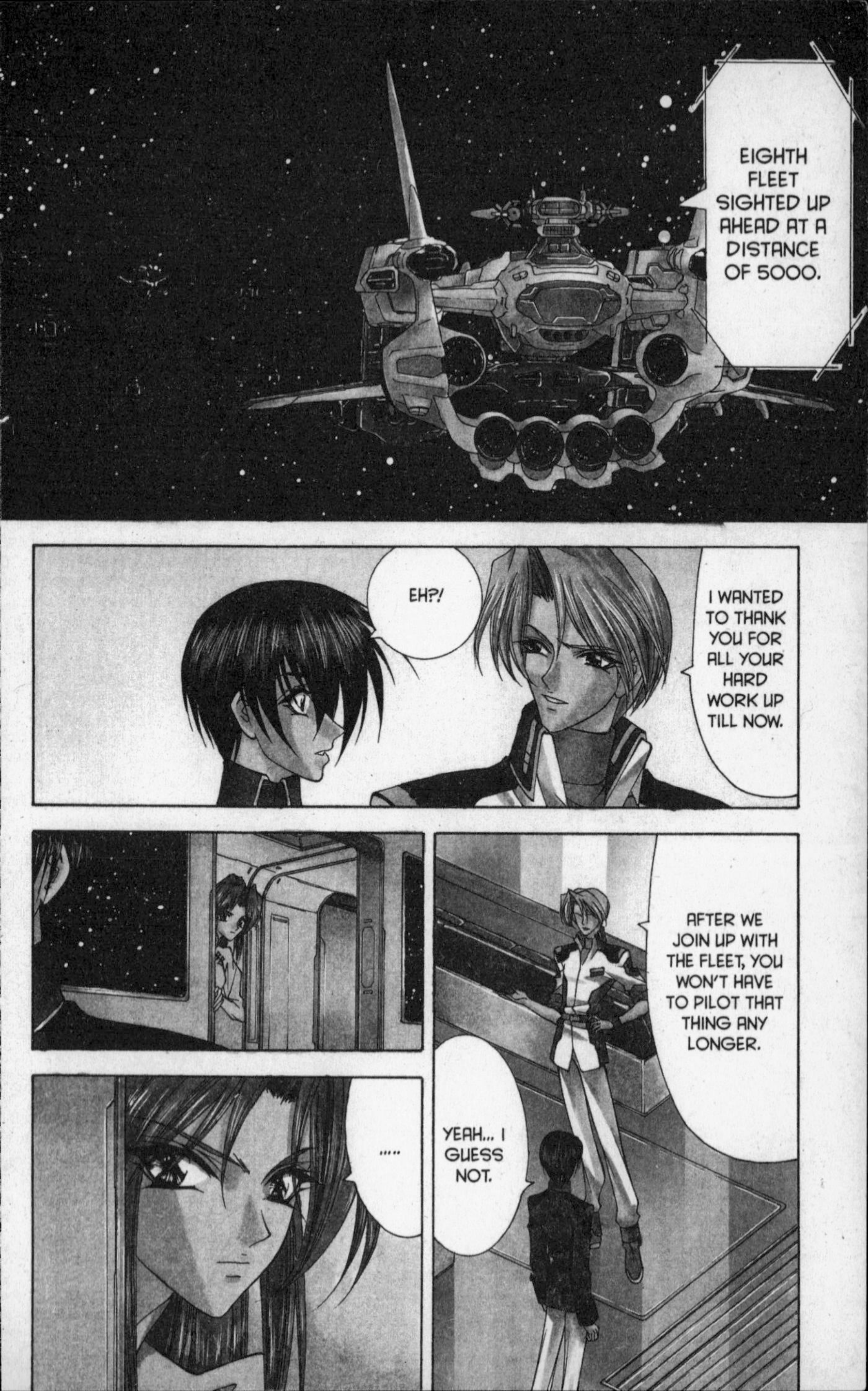
EIGHTH FLEET SIGHTED UP AHEAD AT A DISTANCE OF 5000.
I WANTED TO THANK YOU FOR ALL YOUR HARD WORK UP TILL NOW.
EH?!
AFTER WE JOIN UP WITH THE FLEET, YOU WON'T HAVE TO PILOT THAT THING ANY LONGER.
YEAH... I GUESS NOT.
.....

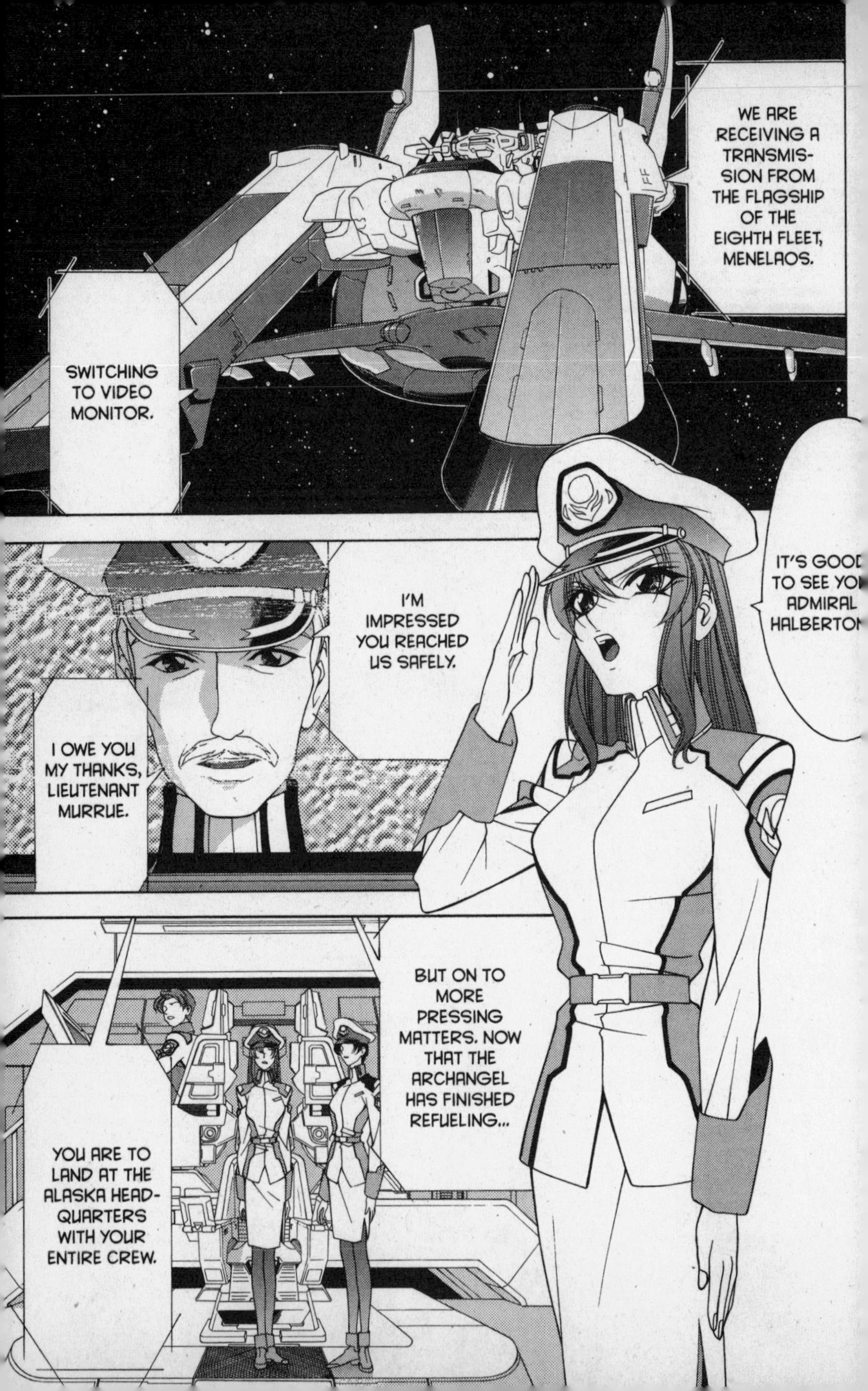
WE ARE RECEIVING A TRANSMISSION FROM THE FLAGSHIP OF THE EIGHTH FLEET, MENELAOS.
SWITCHING TO VIDEO MONITOR.
IT'S GOOD TO SEE YO ADMIRAL HALBERTO
I'M IMPRESSED YOU REACHED US SAFELY.
I OWE YOU MY THANKS, LIEUTENANT MURRUE.
BUT ON TO MORE PRESSING MATTERS. NOW THAT THE ARCHANGEL HAS FINISHED REFUELING...
YOU ARE TO LAND AT THE ALASKA HEADQUARTERS WITH YOUR ENTIRE CREW.

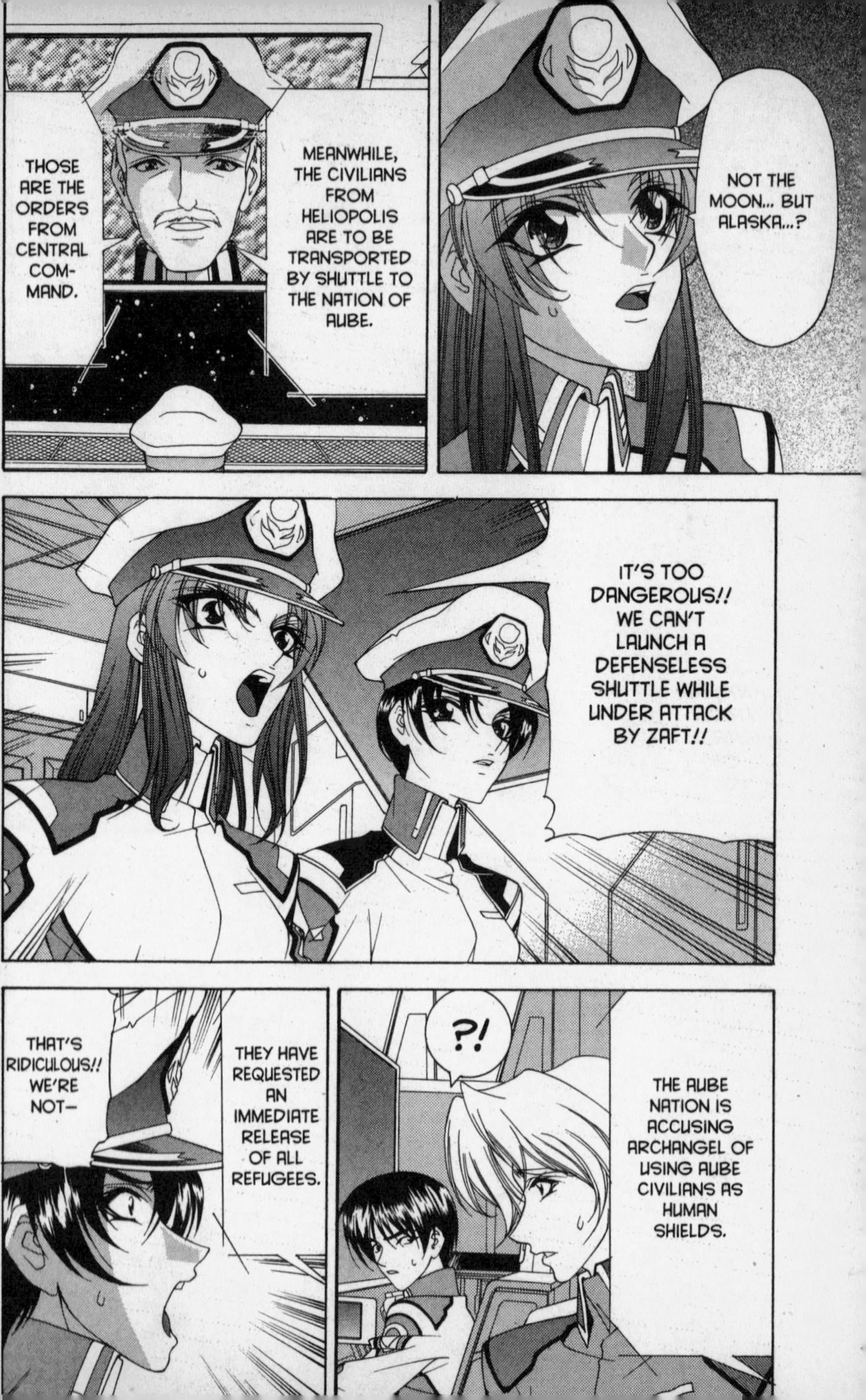
NOT THE MOON... BUT ALASKA...?
MEANWHILE, THE CIVILIANS FROM HELIOPOLIS ARE TO BE TRANSPORTED BY SHUTTLE TO THE NATION OF AUBE.
THOSE ARE THE ORDERS FROM CENTRAL COM-MAND.
IT'S TOO DANGEROUS!! WE CAN'T LAUNCH A DEFENSELESS SHUTTLE WHILE UNDER ATTACK BY ZAFT!!
?!
THE AUBE NATION IS ACCUSING ARCHANGEL OF USING AUBE CIVILIANS AS HUMAN SHIELDS.
THEY HAVE REQUESTED AN IMMEDIATE RELEASE OF ALL REFUGEES.
THAT'S RIDICULOUS!! WE'RE NOT—

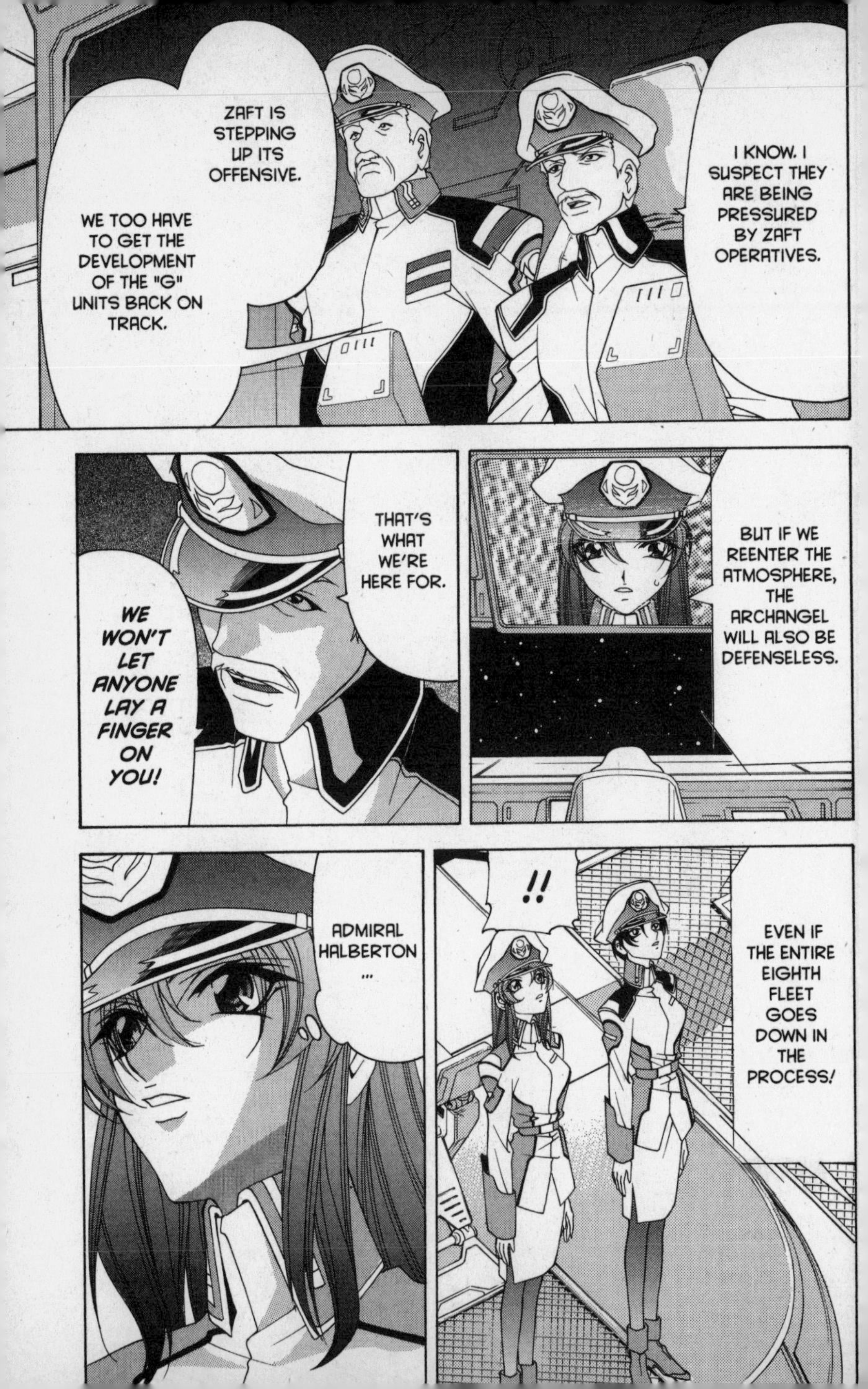
I KNOW. I SUSPECT THEY ARE BEING PRESSURED BY ZAFT OPERATIVES.
ZAFT IS STEPPING UP ITS OFFENSIVE.
WE TOO HAVE TO GET THE DEVELOPMENT OF THE "G" UNITS BACK ON TRACK.
BUT IF WE REENTER THE ATMOSPHERE, THE ARCHANGEL WILL ALSO BE DEFENSELESS.
THAT'S WHAT WE'RE HERE FOR.
WE WON'T LET ANYONE LAY A FINGER ON YOU!
!!
EVEN IF THE ENTIRE EIGHTH FLEET GOES DOWN IN THE PROCESS!
ADMIRAL HALBERTON ...

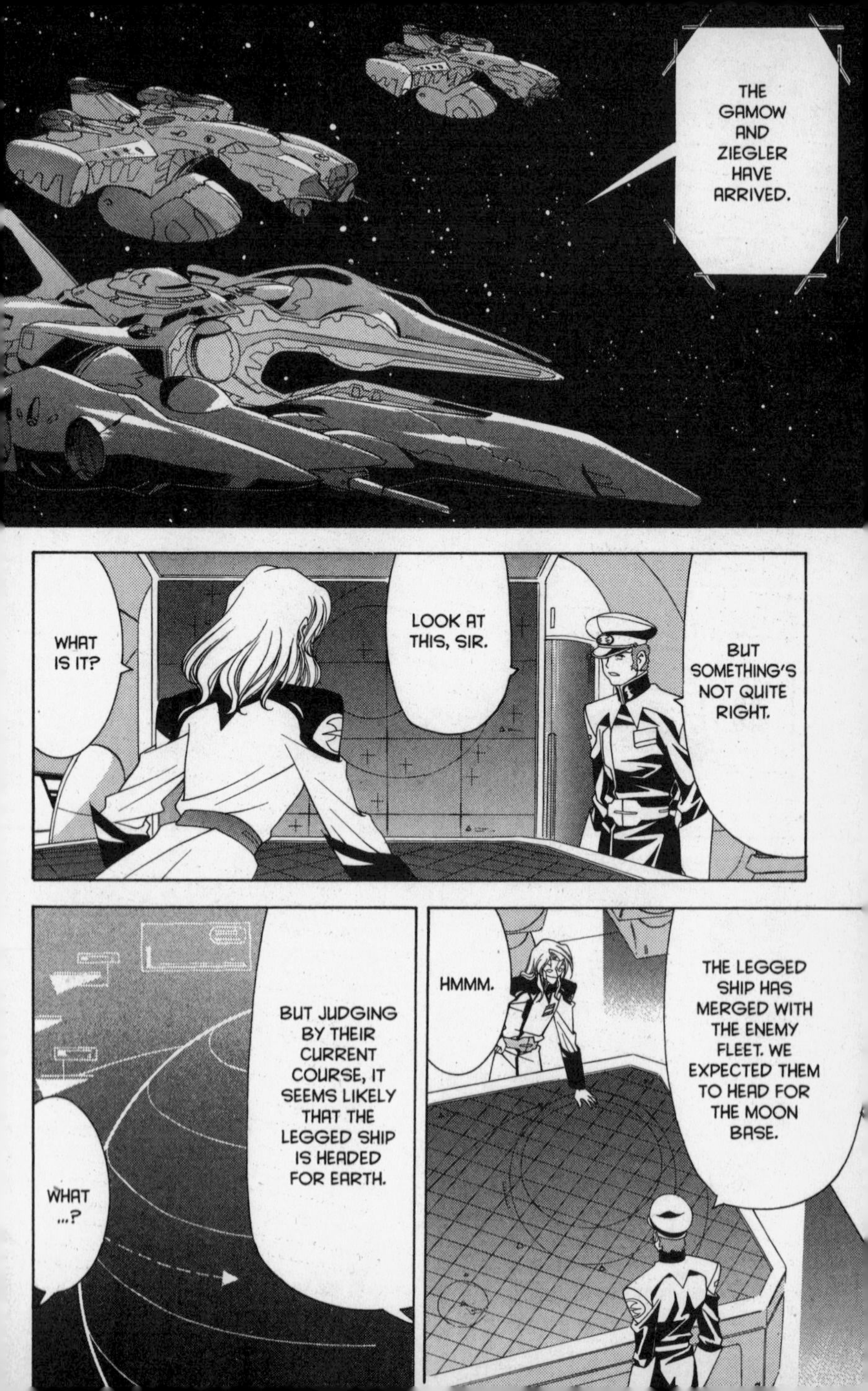
THE GAMOW AND ZIEGLER HAVE ARRIVED.
BUT SOMETHING'S NOT QUITE RIGHT.
LOOK AT THIS, SIR.
WHAT IS IT?
THE LEGGED SHIP HAS MERGED WITH THE ENEMY FLEET. WE EXPECTED THEM TO HEAD FOR THE MOON BASE.
HMMM.
BUT JUDGING BY THEIR CURRENT COURSE, IT SEEMS LIKELY THAT THE LEGGED SHIP IS HEADED FOR EARTH.
WHAT ...?

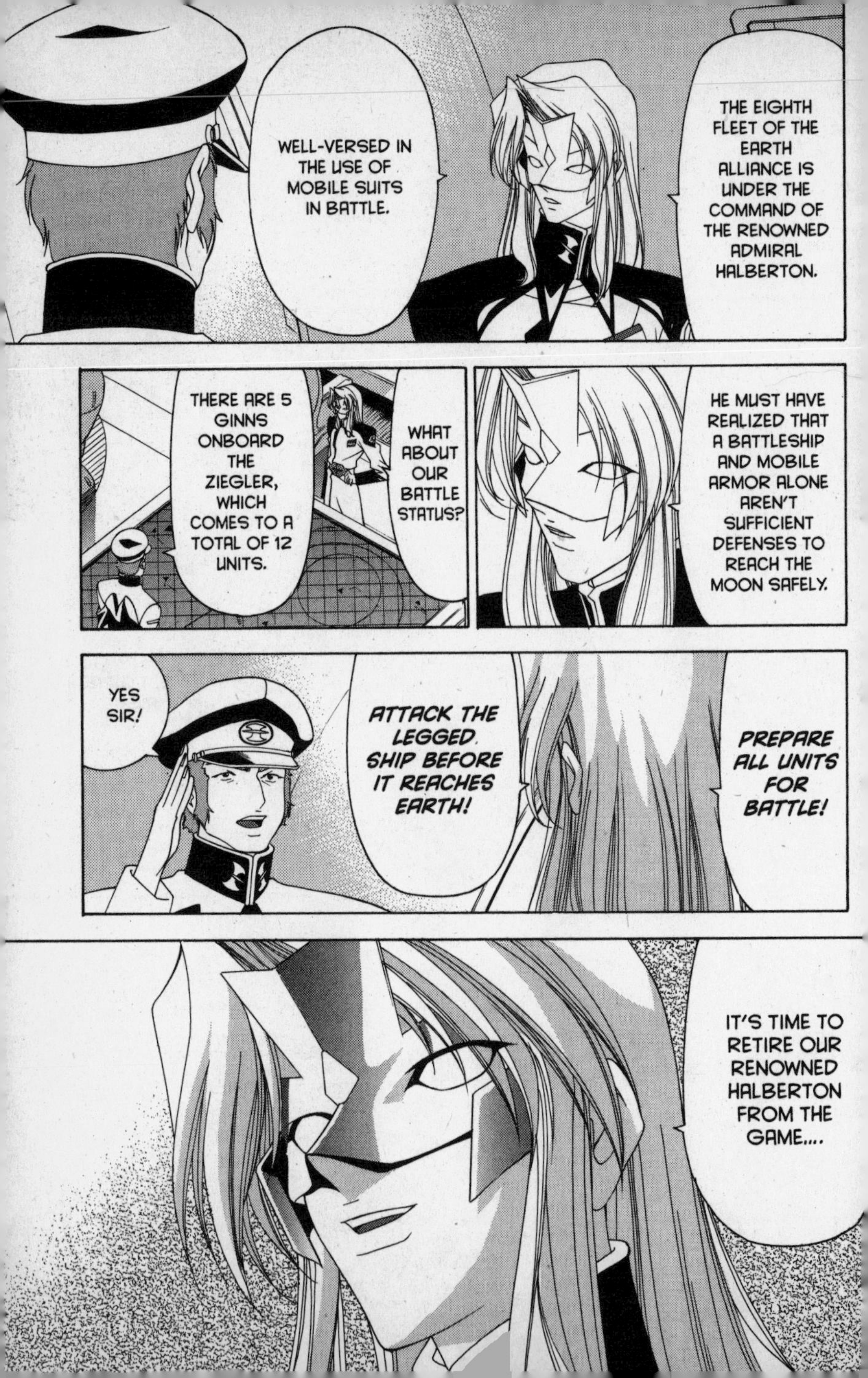
THE EIGHTH FLEET OF THE EARTH ALLIANCE IS UNDER THE COMMAND OF THE RENOWNED ADMIRAL HALBERTON.
WELL-VERSED IN THE USE OF MOBILE SUITS IN BATTLE.
HE MUST HAVE REALIZED THAT A BATTLESHIP AND MOBILE ARMOR ALONE AREN'T SUFFICIENT DEFENSES TO REACH THE MOON SAFELY.
WHAT ABOUT OUR BATTLE STATUS?
THERE ARE 5 GINNS ONBOARD THE ZIEGLER, WHICH COMES TO A TOTAL OF 12 UNITS.
PREPARE ALL UNITS FOR BATTLE!
ATTACK THE LEGGED SHIP BEFORE IT REACHES EARTH!
YES SIR!
IT'S TIME TO RETIRE OUR RENOWNED HALBERTON FROM THE GAME....

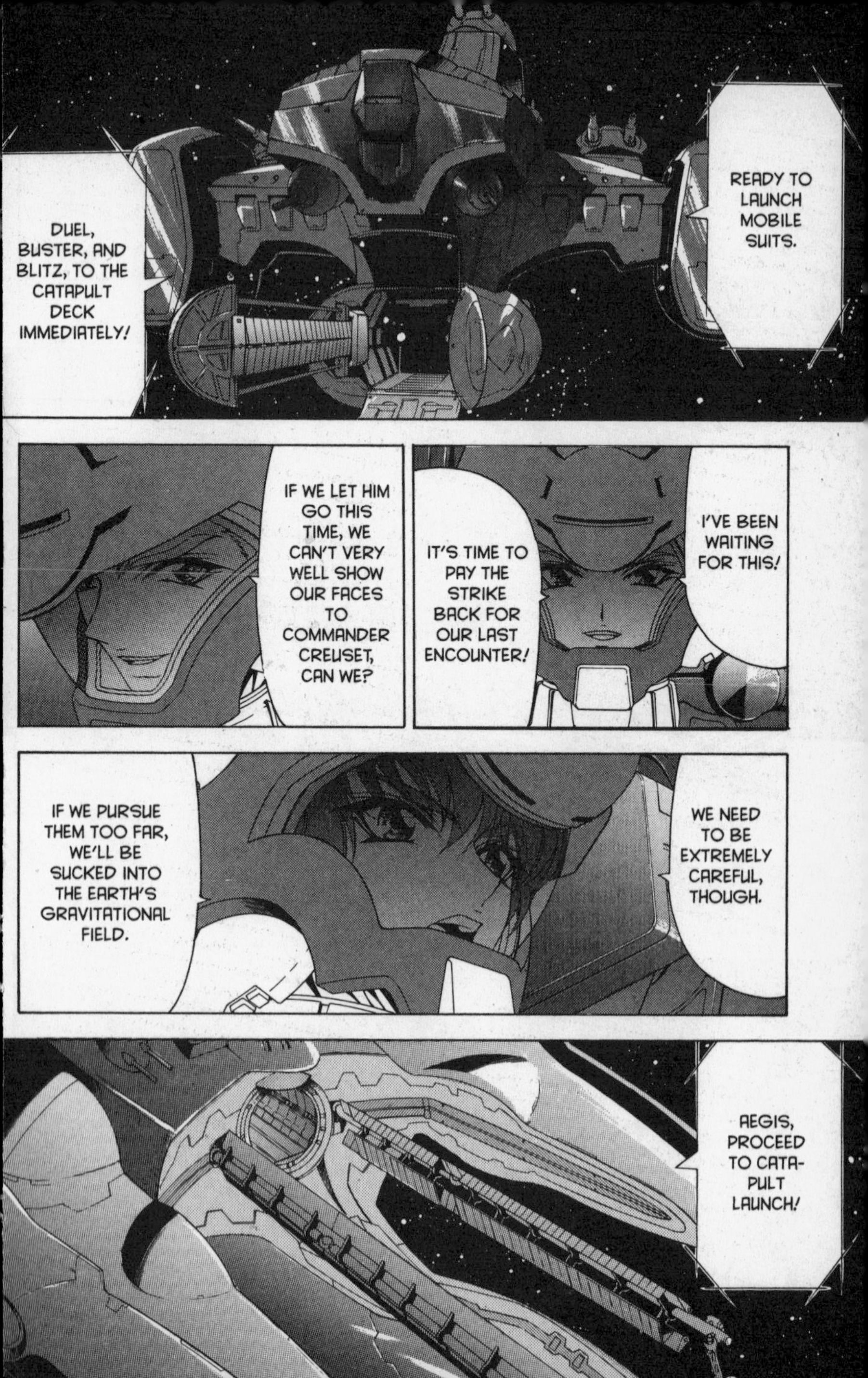
READY TO LAUNCH MOBILE SUITS.
DUEL, BUSTER, AND BLITZ, TO THE CATAPULT DECK IMMEDIATELY!
I'VE BEEN WAITING FOR THIS!
IT'S TIME TO PAY THE STRIKE BACK FOR OUR LAST ENCOUNTER!
IF WE LET HIM GO THIS TIME, WE CAN'T VERY WELL SHOW OUR FACES TO COMMANDER CREUSET, CAN WE?
WE NEED TO BE EXTREMELY CAREFUL, THOUGH.
IF WE PURSUE THEM TOO FAR, WE'LL BE SUCKED INTO THE EARTH'S GRAVITATIONAL FIELD.
AEGIS, PROCEED TO CATA-PULT LAUNCH!

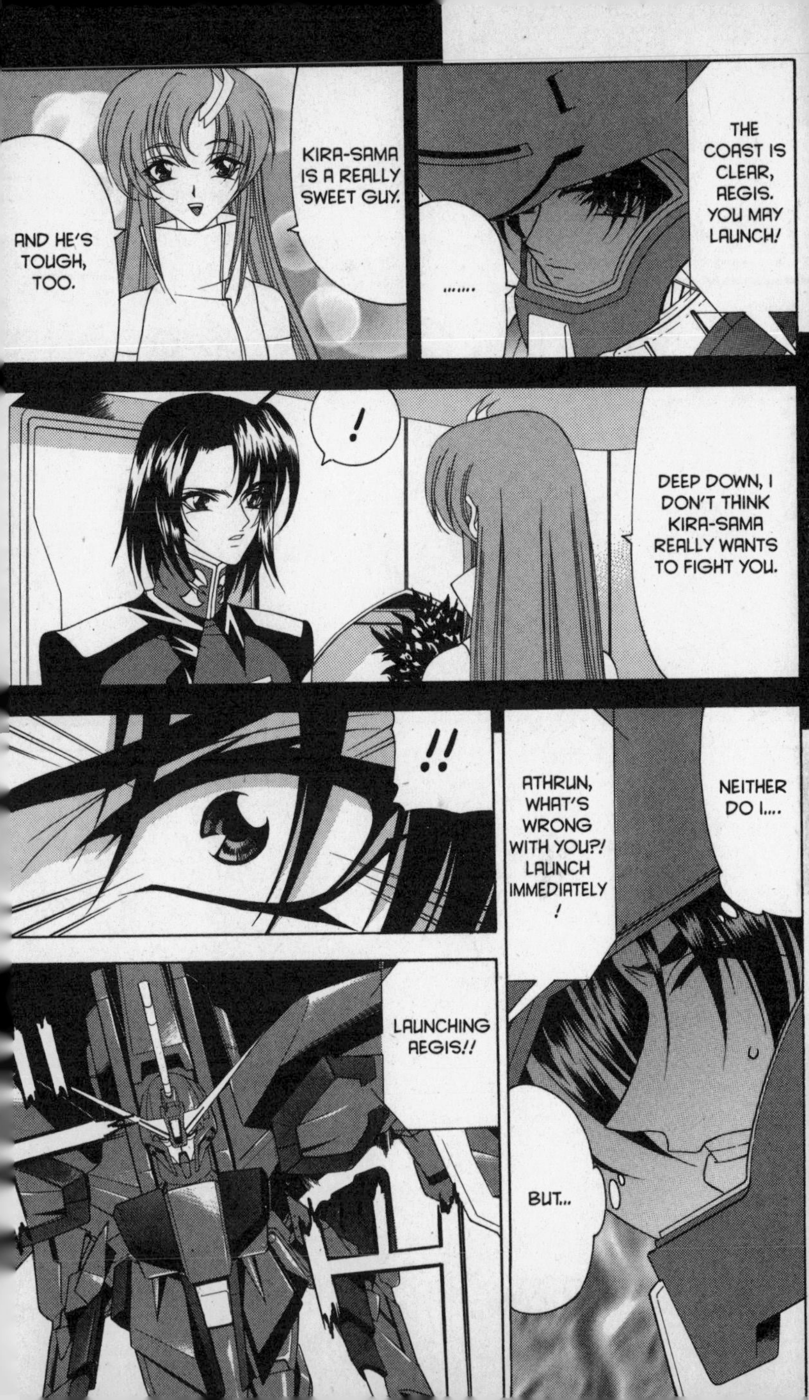
THE COAST IS CLEAR, AEGIS. YOU MAY LAUNCH!
......
KIRA-SAMA IS A REALLY SWEET GUY.
AND HE'S TOUGH, TOO.
DEEP DOWN, I DON'T THINK KIRA-SAMA REALLY WANTS TO FIGHT YOU.
!
NEITHER DO I....
ATHRUN, WHAT'S WRONG WITH YOU?! LAUNCH IMMEDIATELY!
BUT...
!!
LAUNCHING AEGIS!!

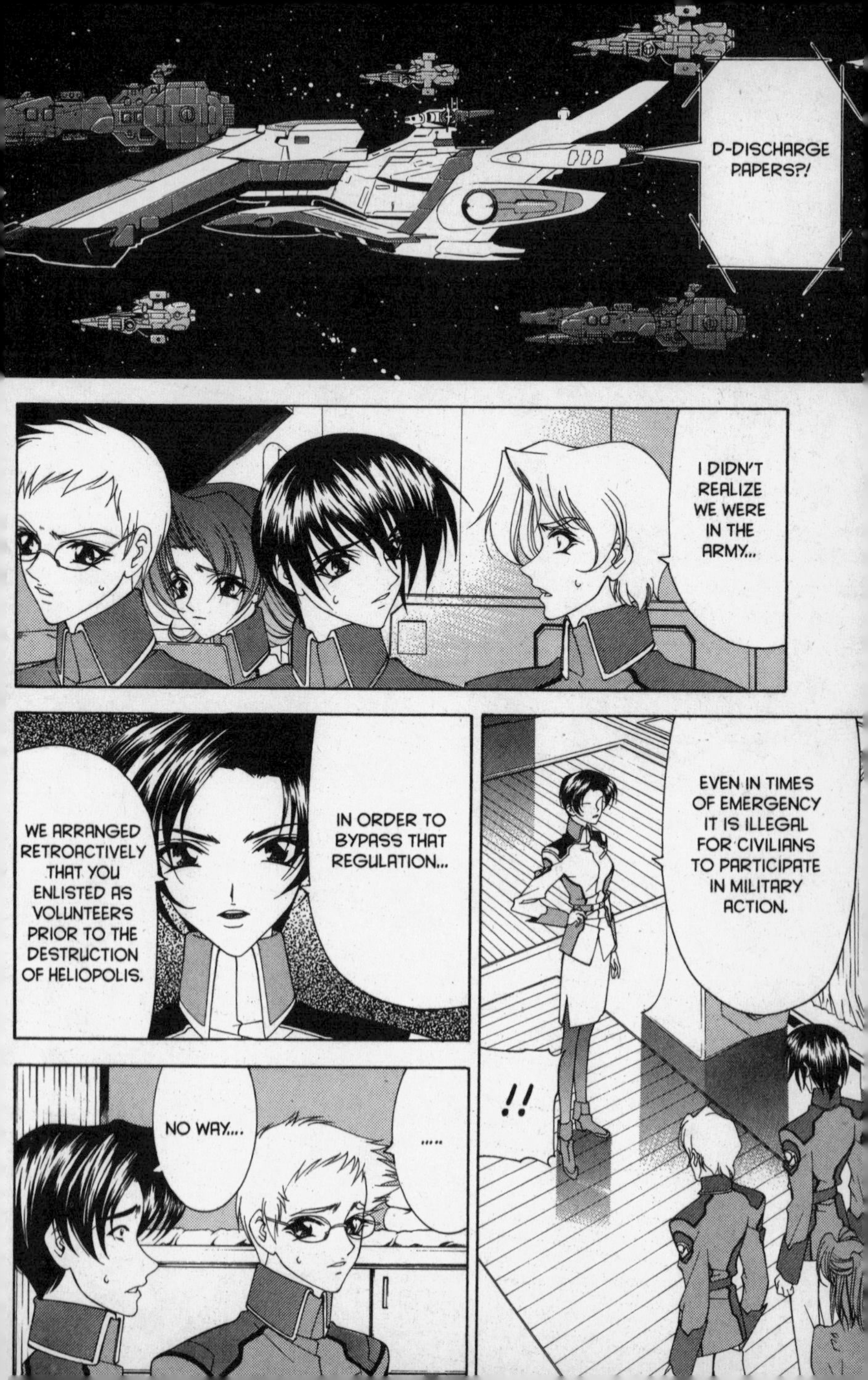
D-DISCHARGE PAPERS?!
I DIDN'T REALIZE WE WERE IN THE ARMY...
EVEN IN TIMES OF EMERGENCY IT IS ILLEGAL FOR CIVILIANS TO PARTICIPATE IN MILITARY ACTION.
!!
IN ORDER TO BYPASS THAT REGULATION...
WE ARRANGED RETROACTIVELY THAT YOU ENLISTED AS VOLUNTEERS PRIOR TO THE DESTRUCTION OF HELIOPOLIS.
.....
NO WAY....

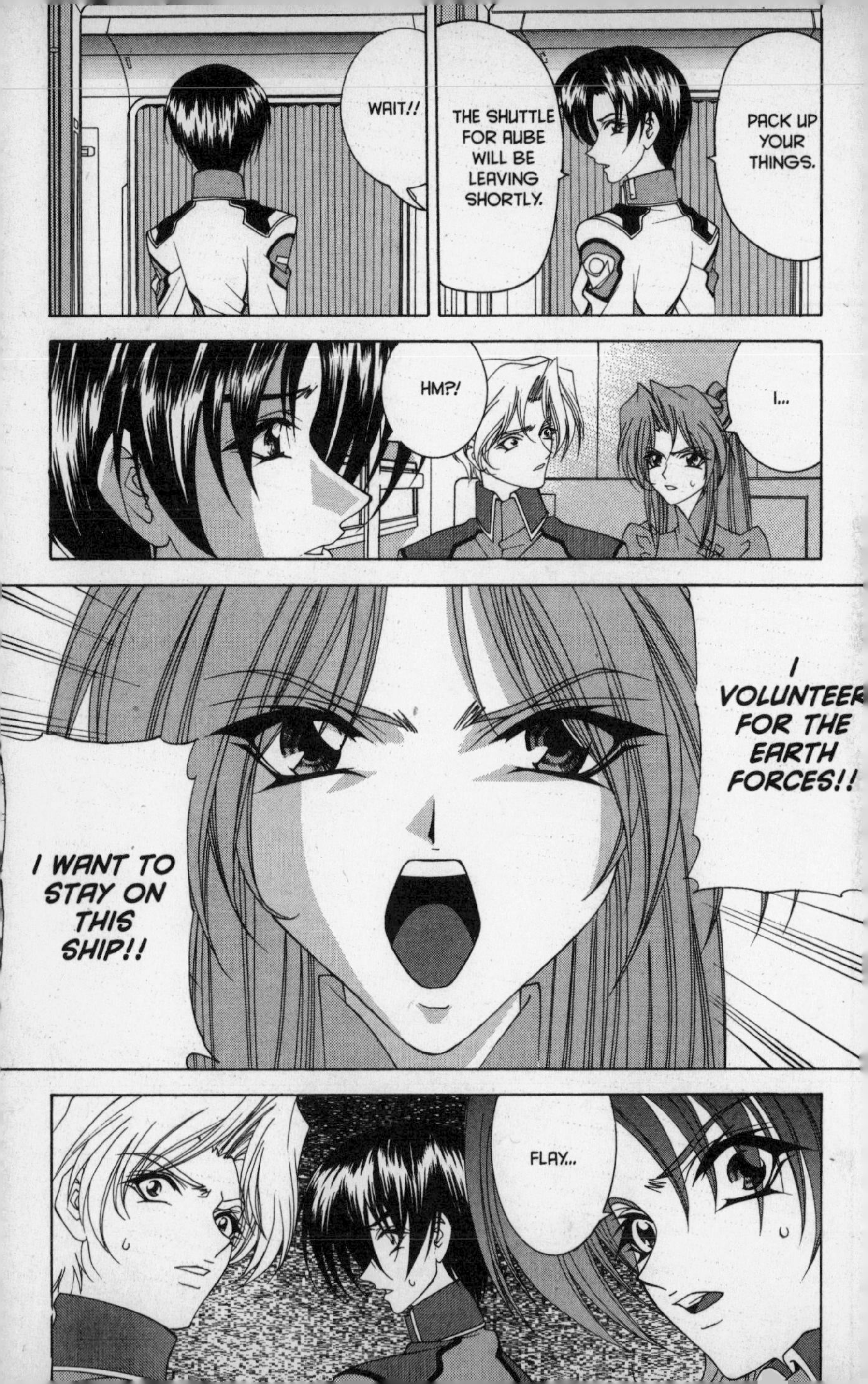
PACK UP YOUR THINGS.
THE SHUTTLE FOR AUBE WILL BE LEAVING SHORTLY.
WAIT!!
I...
HM?!
I VOLUNTEER FOR THE EARTH FORCES!!
I WANT TO STAY ON THIS SHIP!!
FLAY...

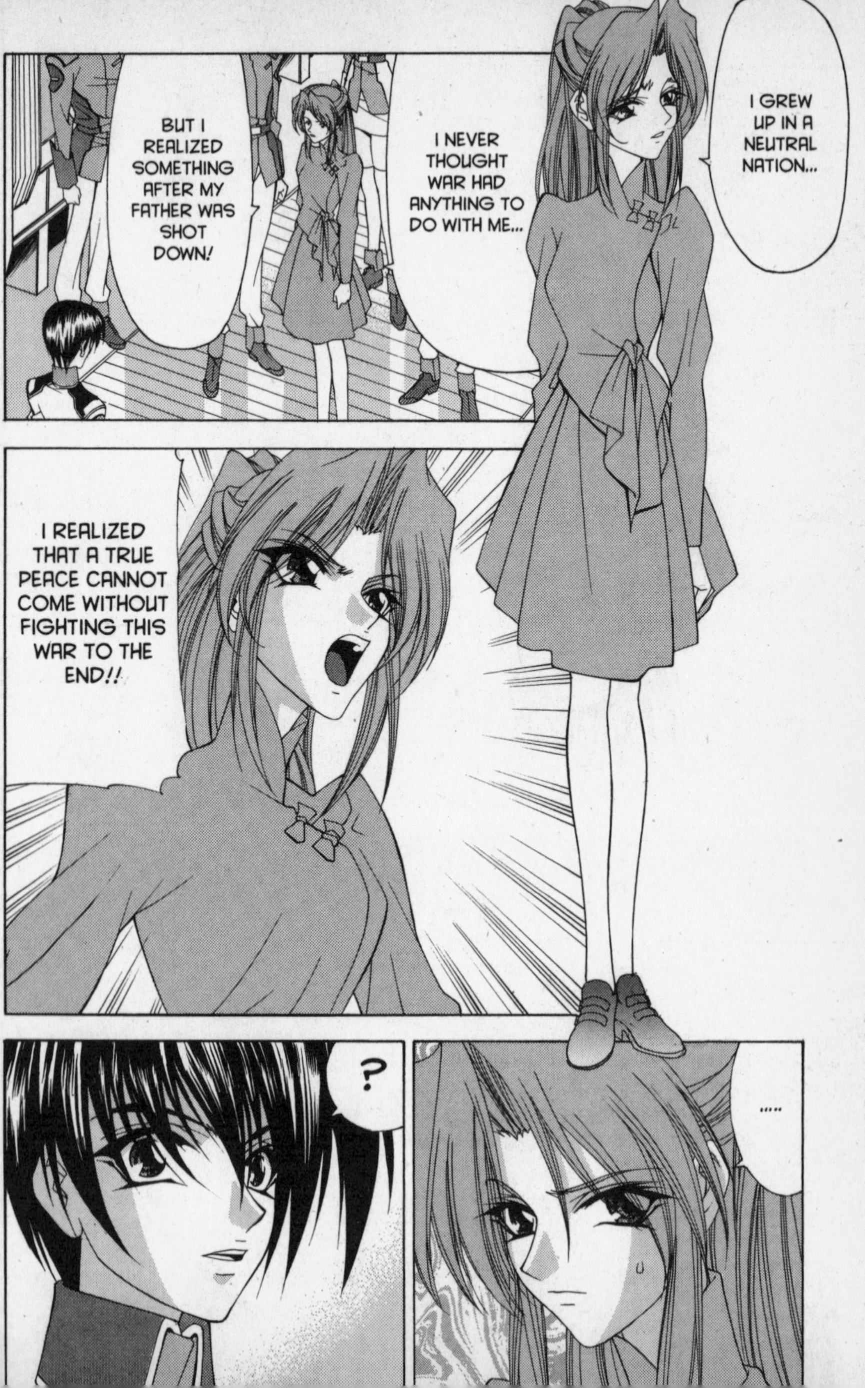
I GREW UP IN A NEUTRAL NATION...
I NEVER THOUGHT WAR HAD ANYTHING TO DO WITH ME...
BUT I REALIZED SOMETHING AFTER MY FATHER WAS SHOT DOWN!
I REALIZED THAT A TRUE PEACE CANNOT COME WITHOUT FIGHTING THIS WAR TO THE END!!
.....
?

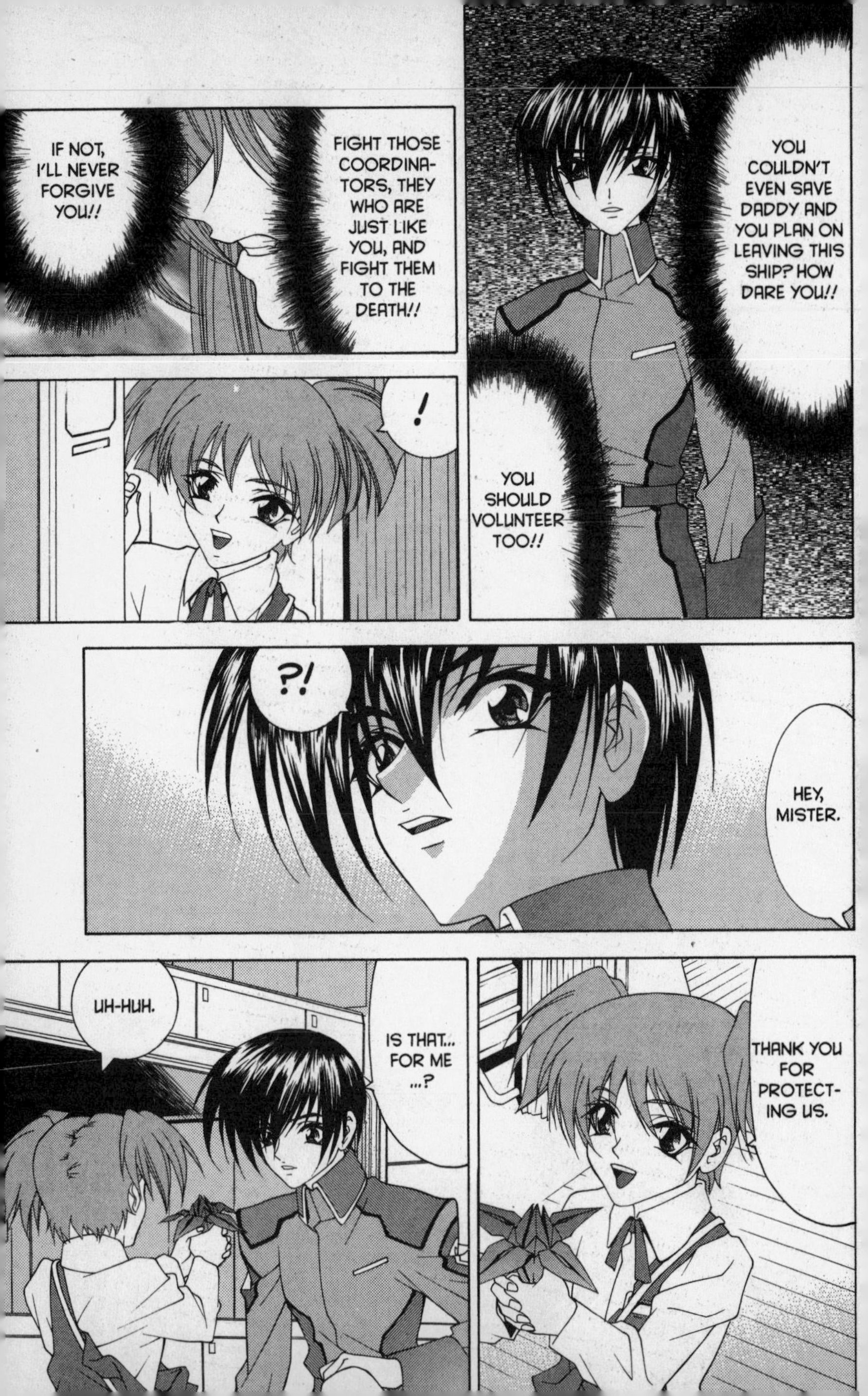
YOU COULDN'T EVEN SAVE DADDY AND YOU PLAN ON LEAVING THIS SHIP? HOW DARE YOU!!
YOU SHOULD VOLUNTEER TOO!!
FIGHT THOSE COORDINATORS, THEY WHO ARE JUST LIKE YOU, AND FIGHT THEM TO THE DEATH!!
IF NOT, I'LL NEVER FORGIVE YOU!!
!
HEY, MISTER.
?!
THANK YOU FOR PROTECTING US.
IS THAT... FOR ME ...?
UH-HUH.

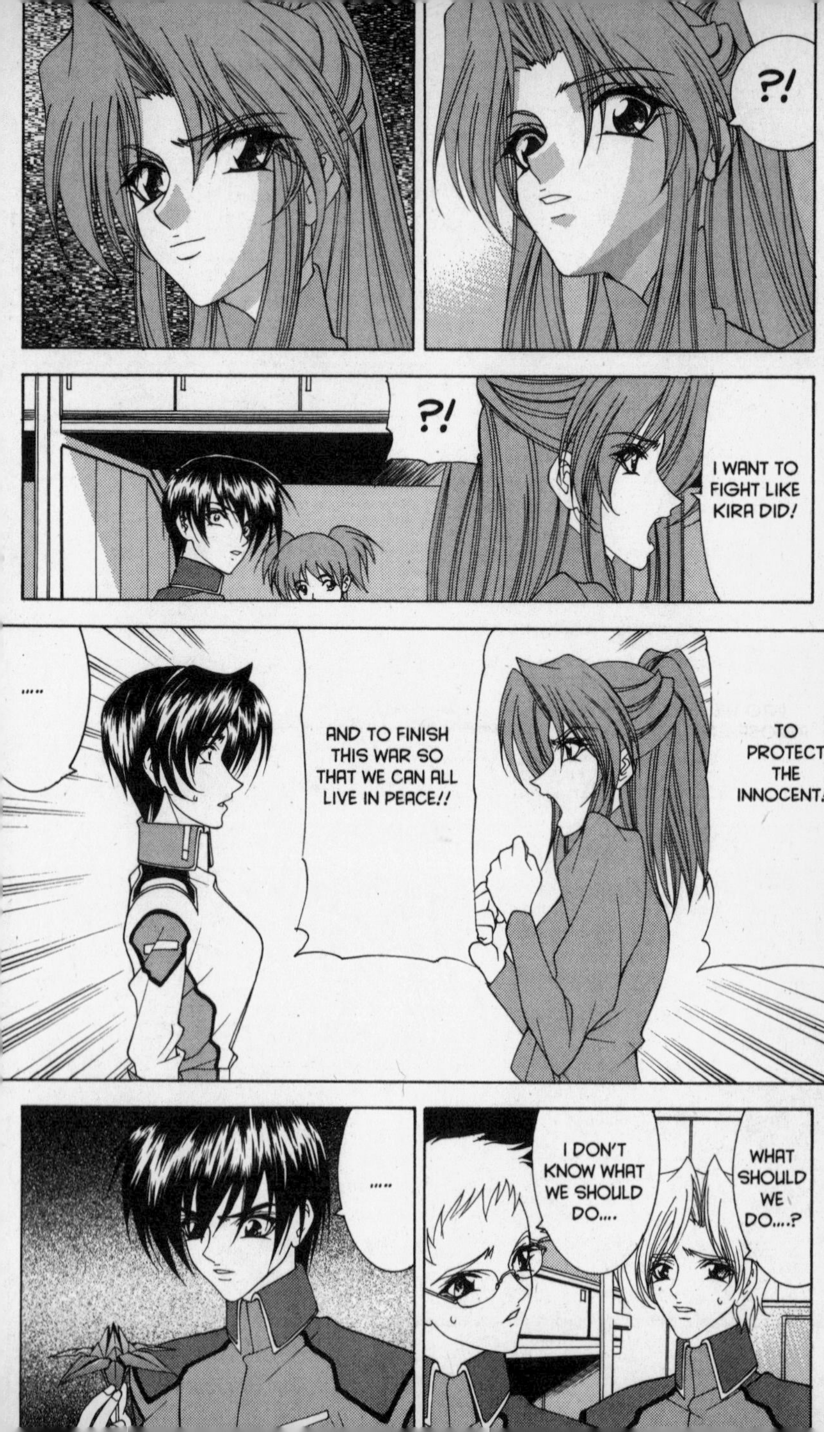
?!
I WANT TO FIGHT LIKE KIRA DID!
?!
TO PROTECT THE INNOCENT!!
AND TO FINISH THIS WAR SO THAT WE CAN ALL LIVE IN PEACE!!
.....
WHAT SHOULD WE DO....?
I DON'T KNOW WHAT WE SHOULD DO....
.....

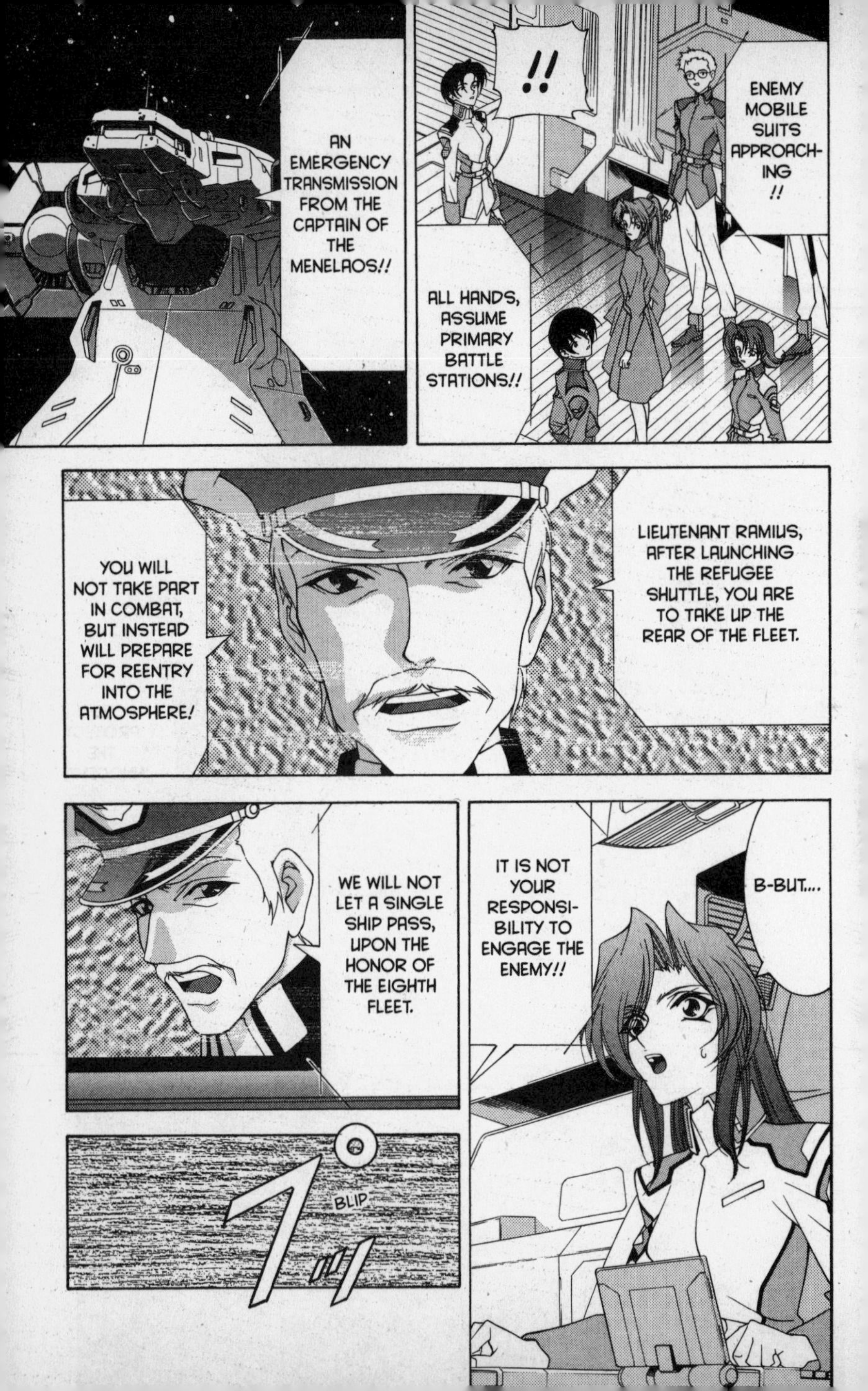
ENEMY MOBILE SUITS APPROACHING!!
!!
ALL HANDS, ASSUME PRIMARY BATTLE STATIONS!!
AN EMERGENCY TRANSMISSION FROM THE CAPTAIN OF THE MENELAOS!!
LIEUTENANT RAMIUS, AFTER LAUNCHING THE REFUGEE SHUTTLE, YOU ARE TO TAKE UP THE REAR OF THE FLEET.
YOU WILL NOT TAKE PART IN COMBAT, BUT INSTEAD WILL PREPARE FOR REENTRY INTO THE ATMOSPHERE!
B-BUT....
IT IS NOT YOUR RESPONSIBILITY TO ENGAGE THE ENEMY!!
WE WILL NOT LET A SINGLE SHIP PASS, UPON THE HONOR OF THE EIGHTH FLEET.
BLIP

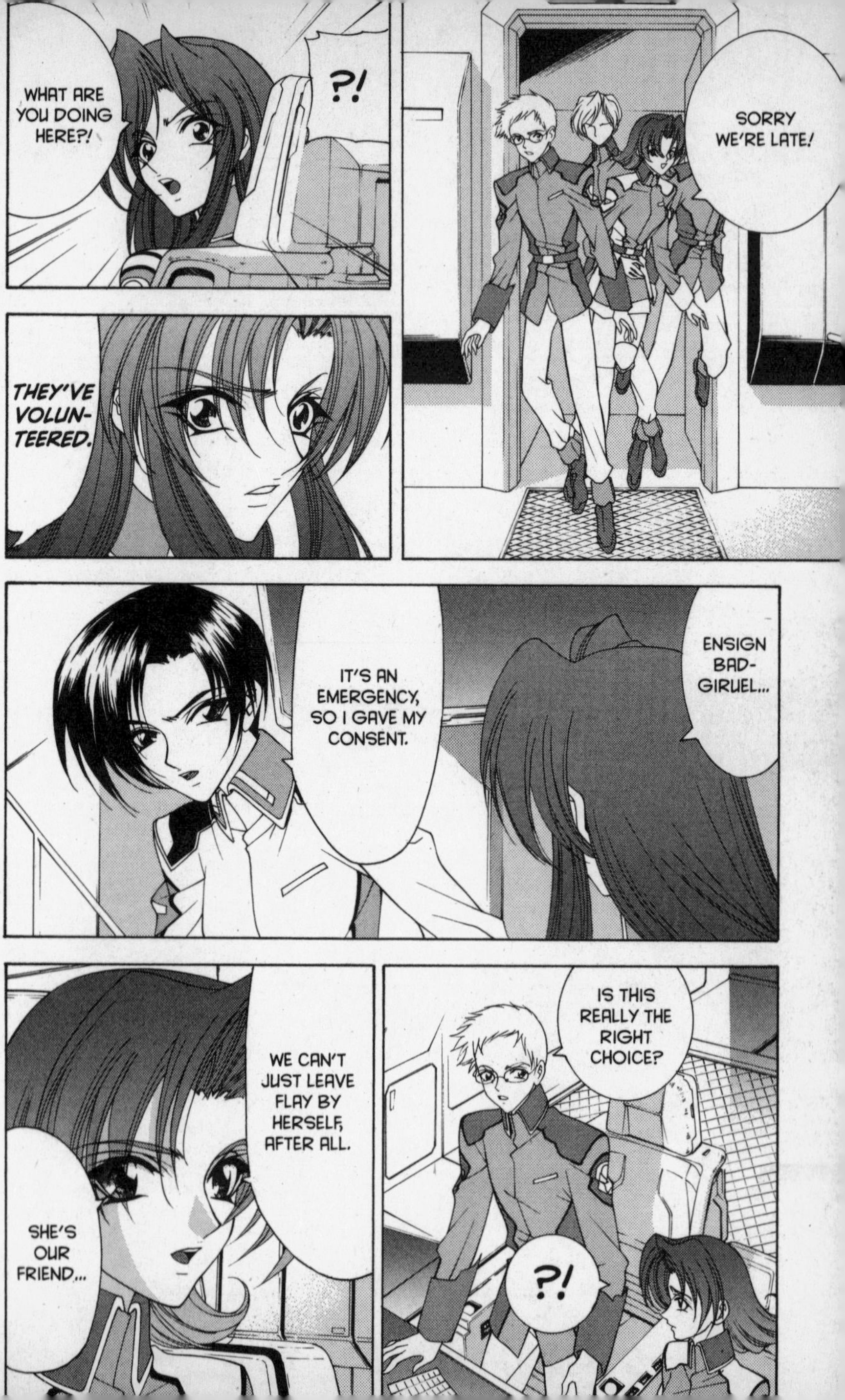
SORRY WE'RE LATE!
?!
WHAT ARE YOU DOING HERE?!
THEY'VE VOLUN-TEERED.
ENSIGN BAD-GIRUEL...
IT'S AN EMERGENCY, SO I GAVE MY CONSENT.
IS THIS REALLY THE RIGHT CHOICE?
?!
WE CAN'T JUST LEAVE FLAY BY HERSELF, AFTER ALL.
SHE'S OUR FRIEND...

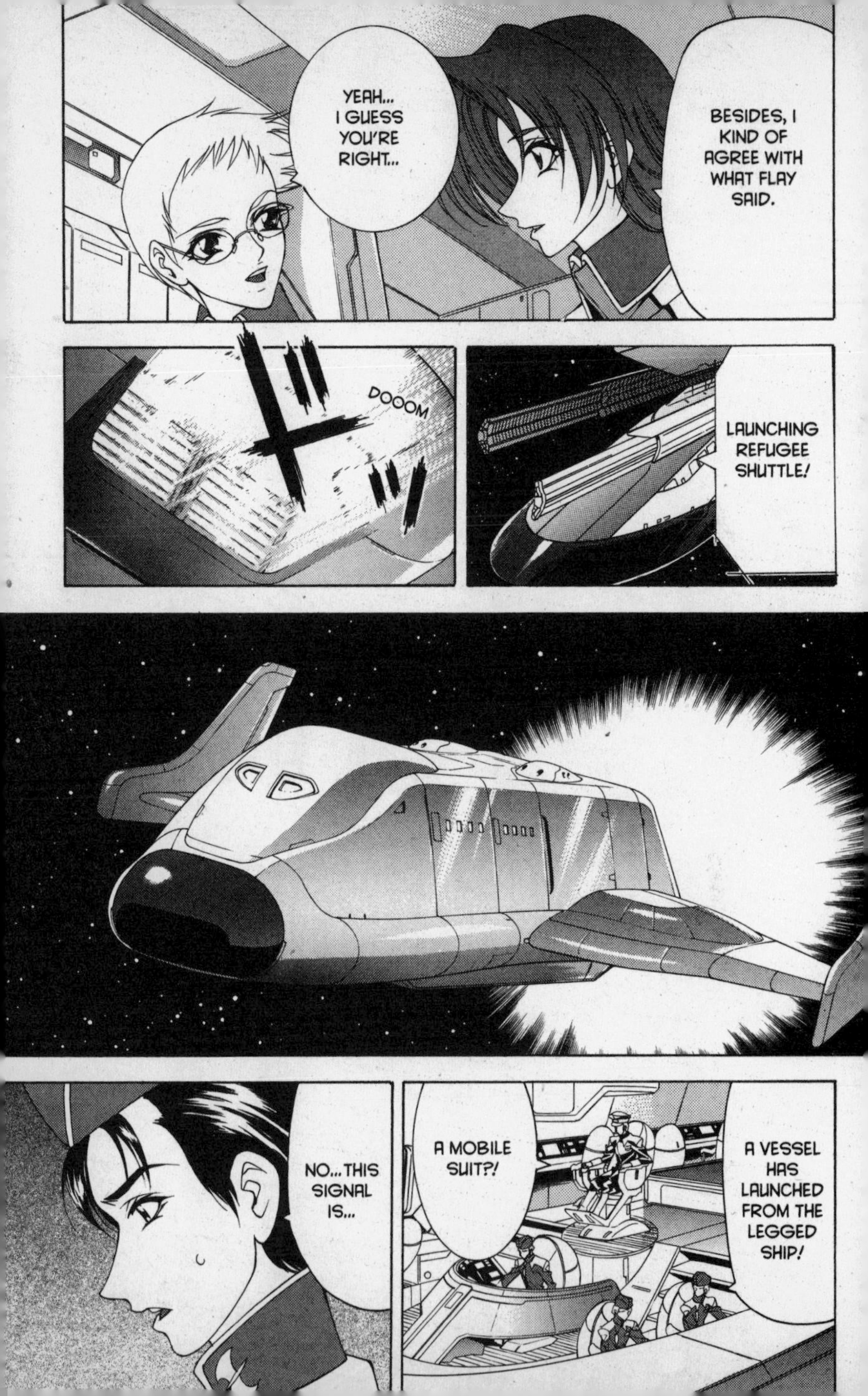
BESIDES, I KIND OF AGREE WITH WHAT FLAY SAID.
YEAH... I GUESS YOU'RE RIGHT...
LAUNCHING REFUGEE SHUTTLE!
DOOOM
A VESSEL HAS LAUNCHED FROM THE LEGGED SHIP!
A MOBILE SUIT?!
NO... THIS SIGNAL IS...

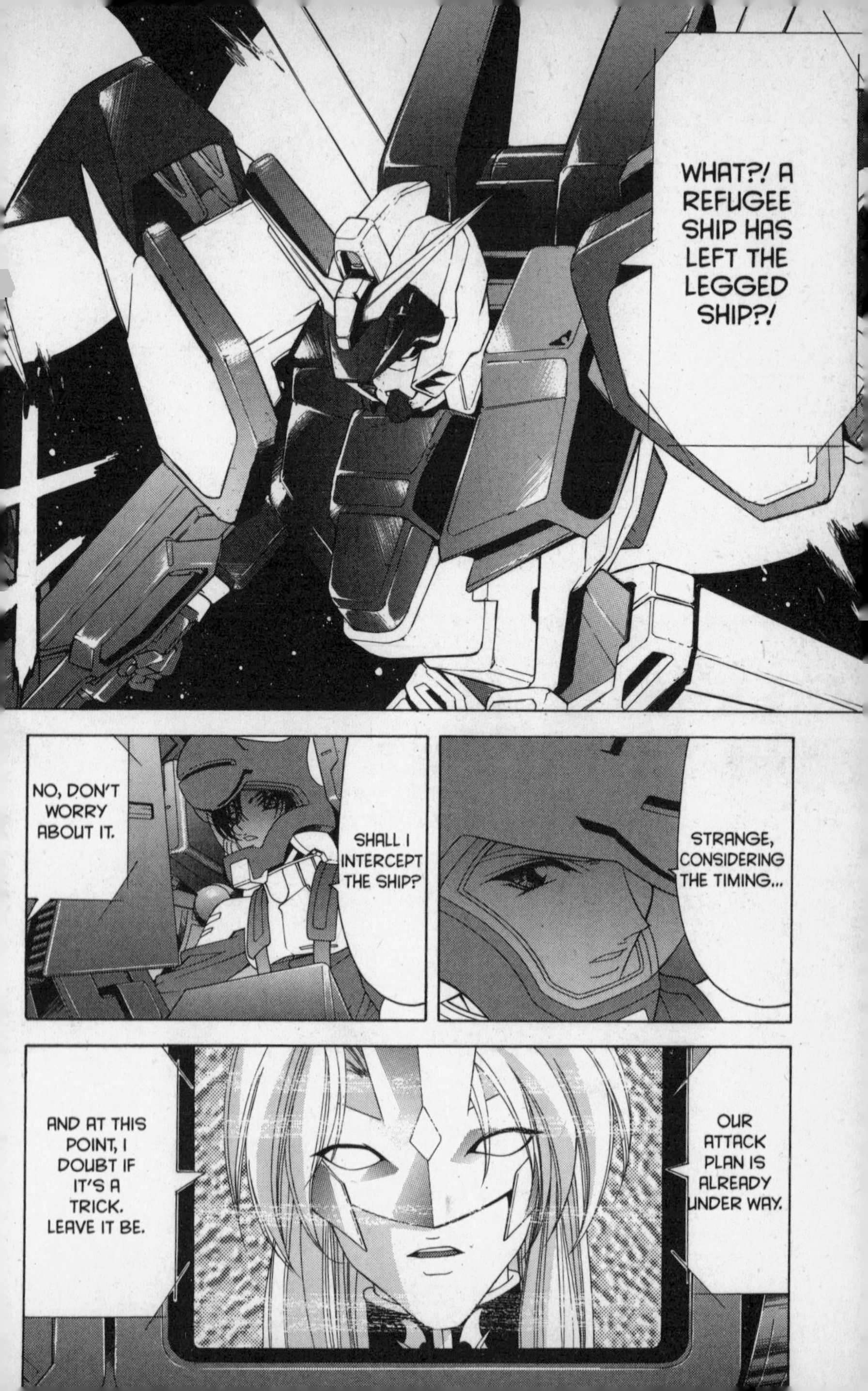
WHAT?! A REFUGEE SHIP HAS LEFT THE LEGGED SHIP?!
STRANGE, CONSIDERING THE TIMING...
SHALL I INTERCEPT THE SHIP?
NO, DON'T WORRY ABOUT IT.
OUR ATTACK PLAN IS ALREADY UNDER WAY.
AND AT THIS POINT, I DOUBT IF IT'S A TRICK. LEAVE IT BE.

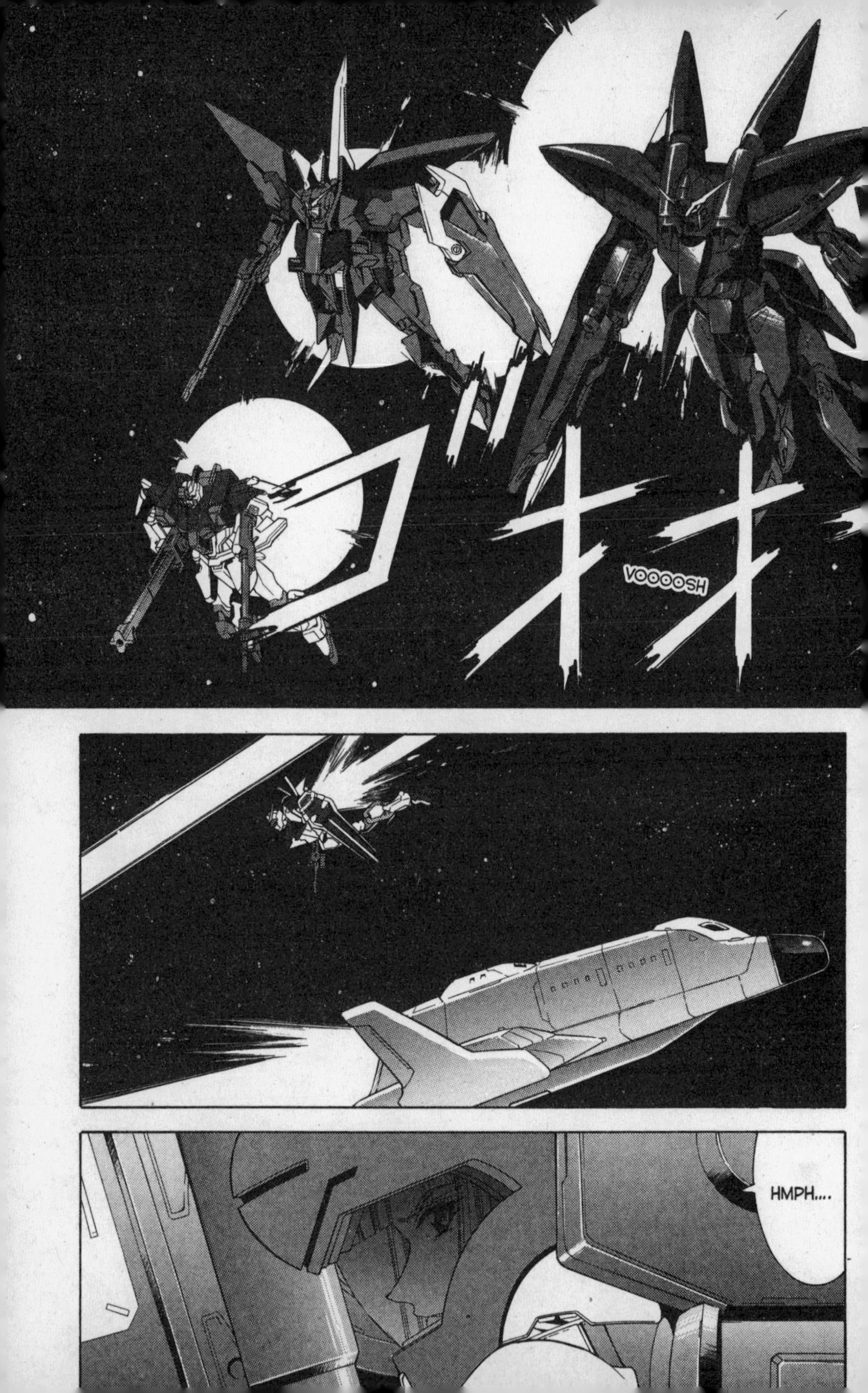
VOOOOSH
HMPH....

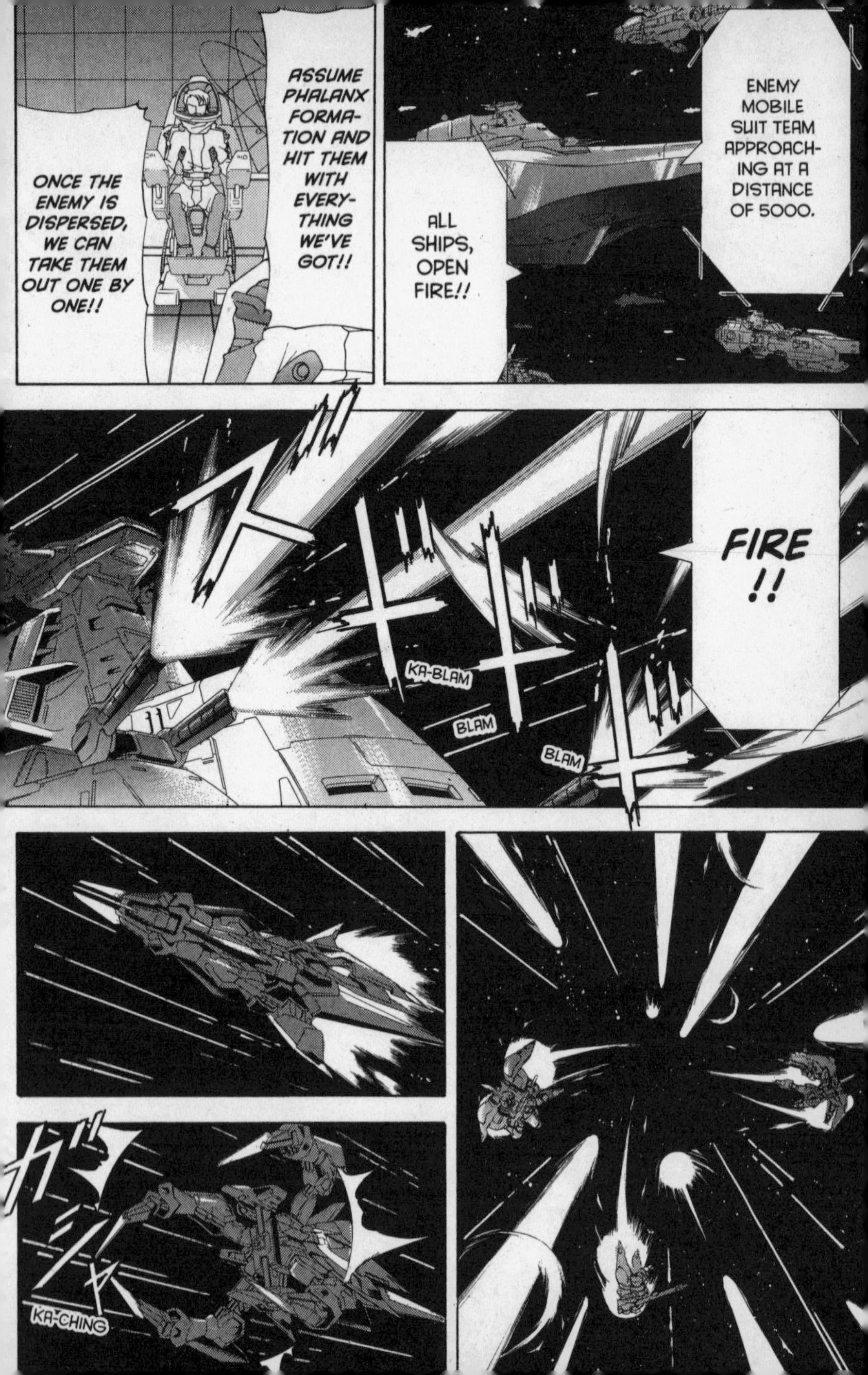
ENEMY MOBILE SUIT TEAM APPROACHING AT A DISTANCE OF 5000.
ALL SHIPS, OPEN FIRE!!
ASSUME PHALANX FORMATION AND HIT THEM WITH EVERYTHING WE'VE GOT!!
ONCE THE ENEMY IS DISPERSED, WE CAN TAKE THEM OUT ONE BY ONE!!
FIRE !!
KA-BLAM
BLAM
BLAM
KA-CHING

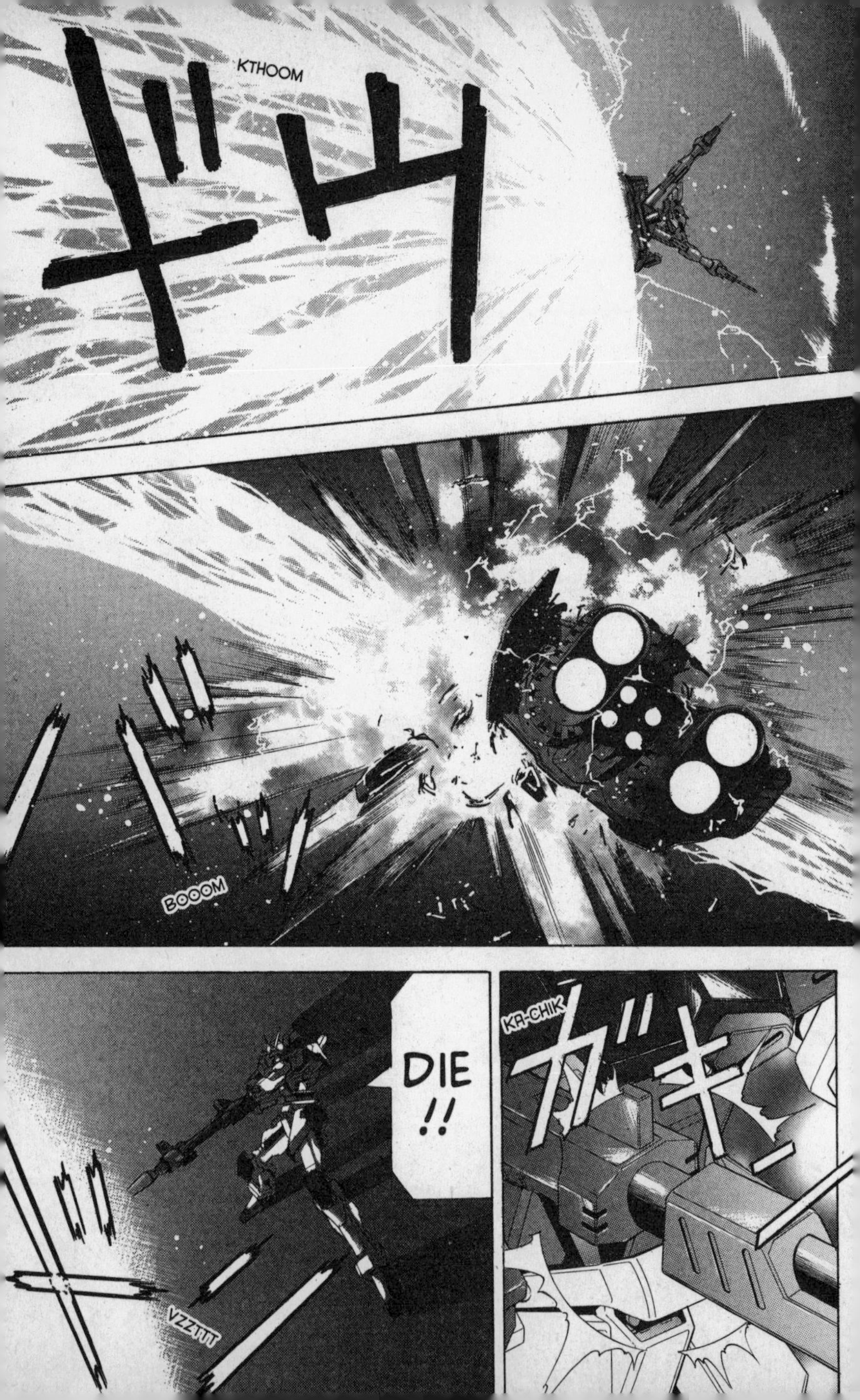
KTHOOM
ドッ
BOOOM
KA-CHIK
ガキー
DIE !!
VZZTTT

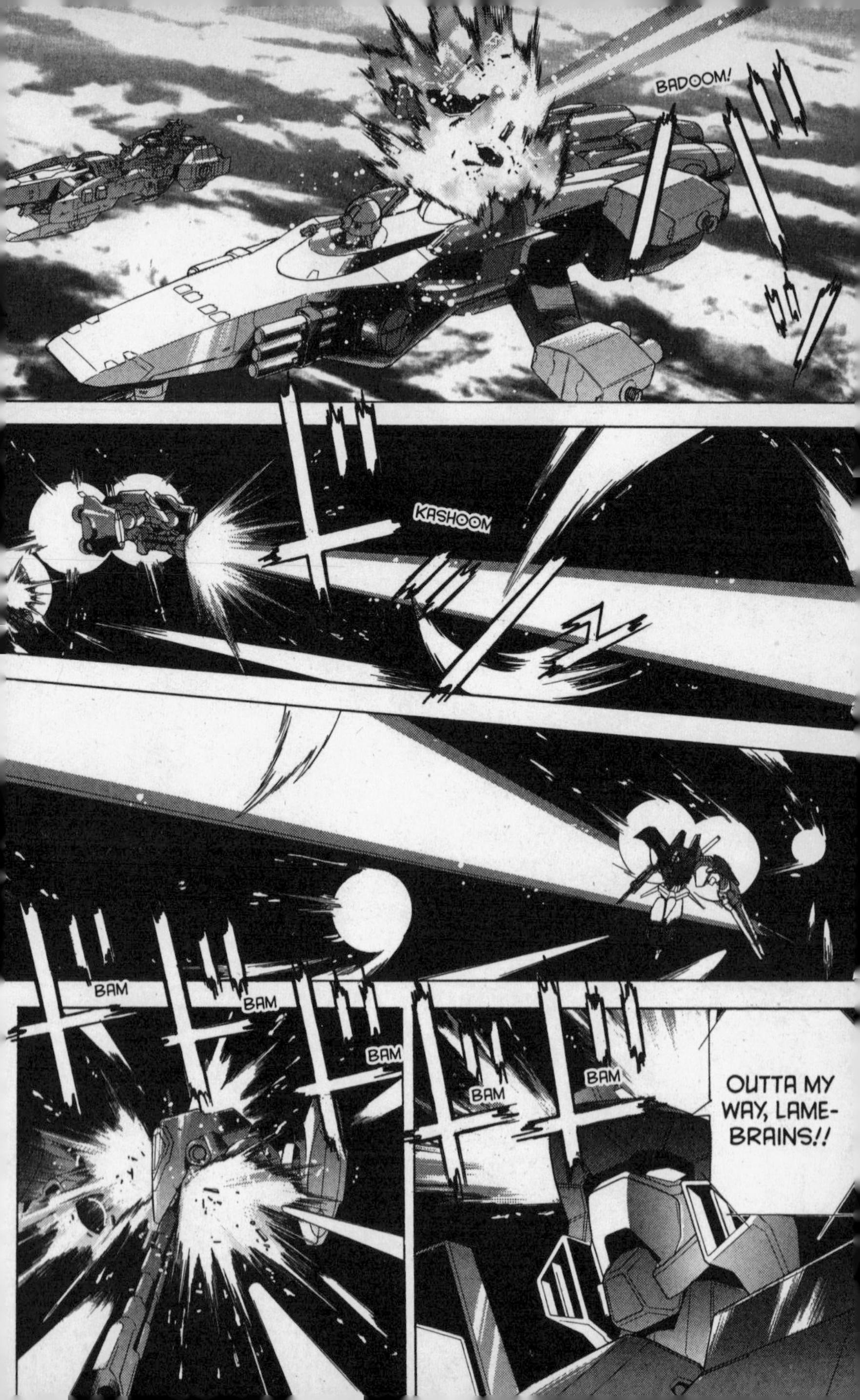
BADOOM!
KASHOOM
OUTTA MY WAY, LAME-BRAINS!!
BAM
BAM
BAM
BAM
BAM
BAM

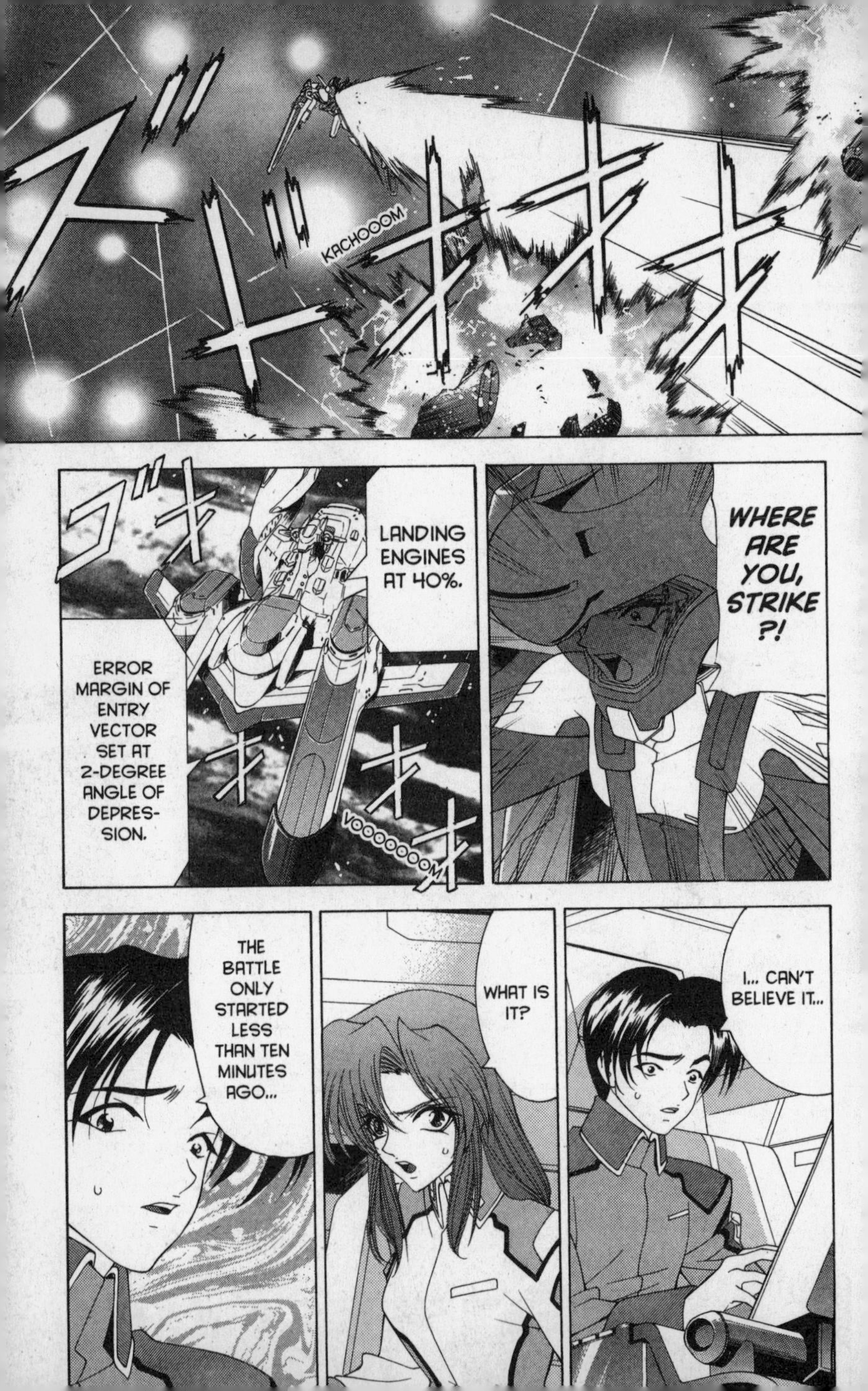
KACHOOOM
WHERE ARE YOU, STRIKE?!
LANDING ENGINES AT 40%.
ERROR MARGIN OF ENTRY VECTOR SET AT 2-DEGREE ANGLE OF DEPRESSION.
VOOOOOOOOM
I... CAN'T BELIEVE IT...
WHAT IS IT?
THE BATTLE ONLY STARTED LESS THAN TEN MINUTES AGO...

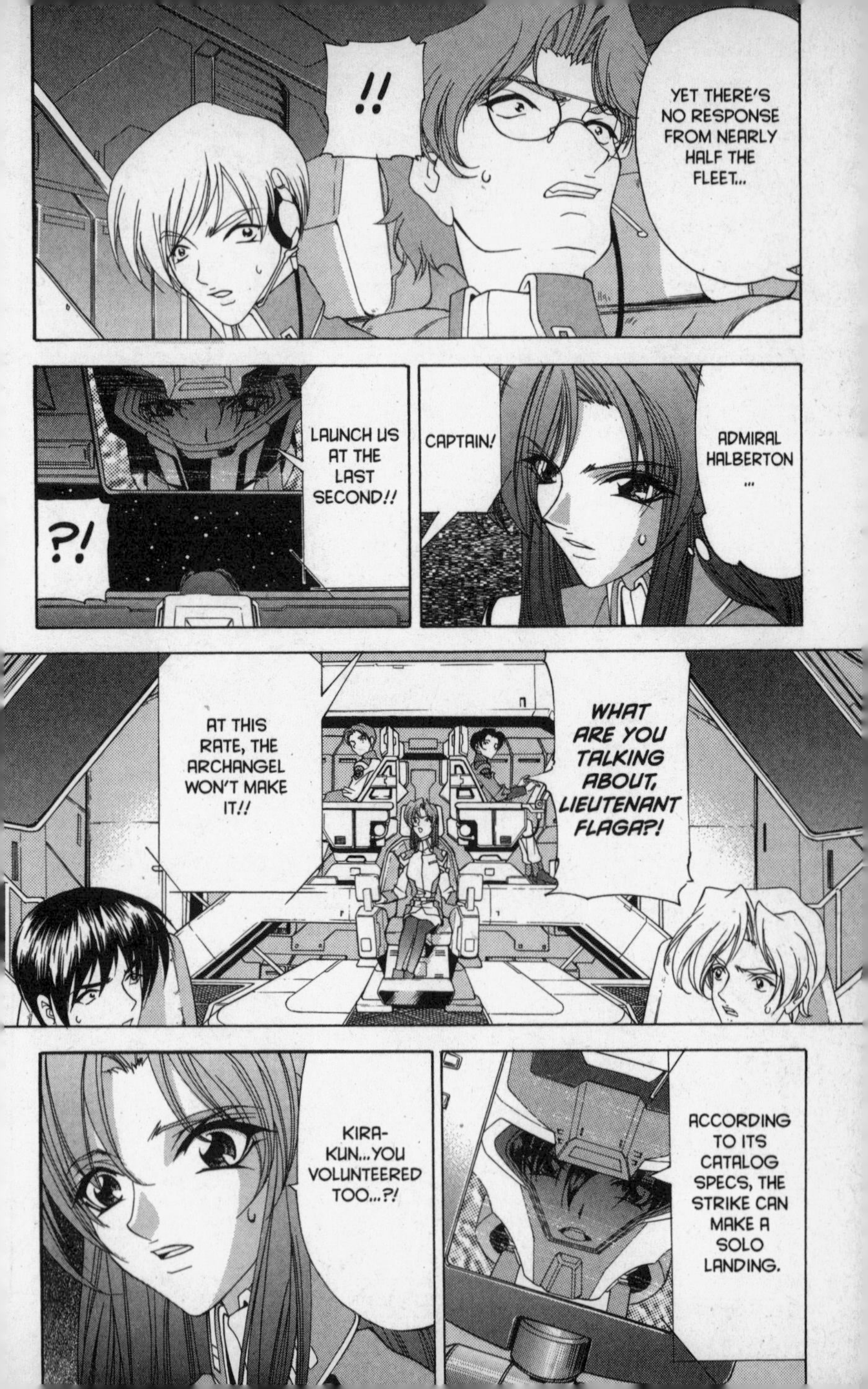
YET THERE'S NO RESPONSE FROM NEARLY HALF THE FLEET...
!!
ADMIRAL HALBERTON ...
CAPTAIN!
LAUNCH US AT THE LAST SECOND!!
?!
WHAT ARE YOU TALKING ABOUT, LIEUTENANT FLAGA?!
AT THIS RATE, THE ARCHANGEL WON'T MAKE IT!!
ACCORDING TO ITS CATALOG SPECS, THE STRIKE CAN MAKE A SOLO LANDING.
KIRA-KUN...YOU VOLUNTEERED TOO...?!

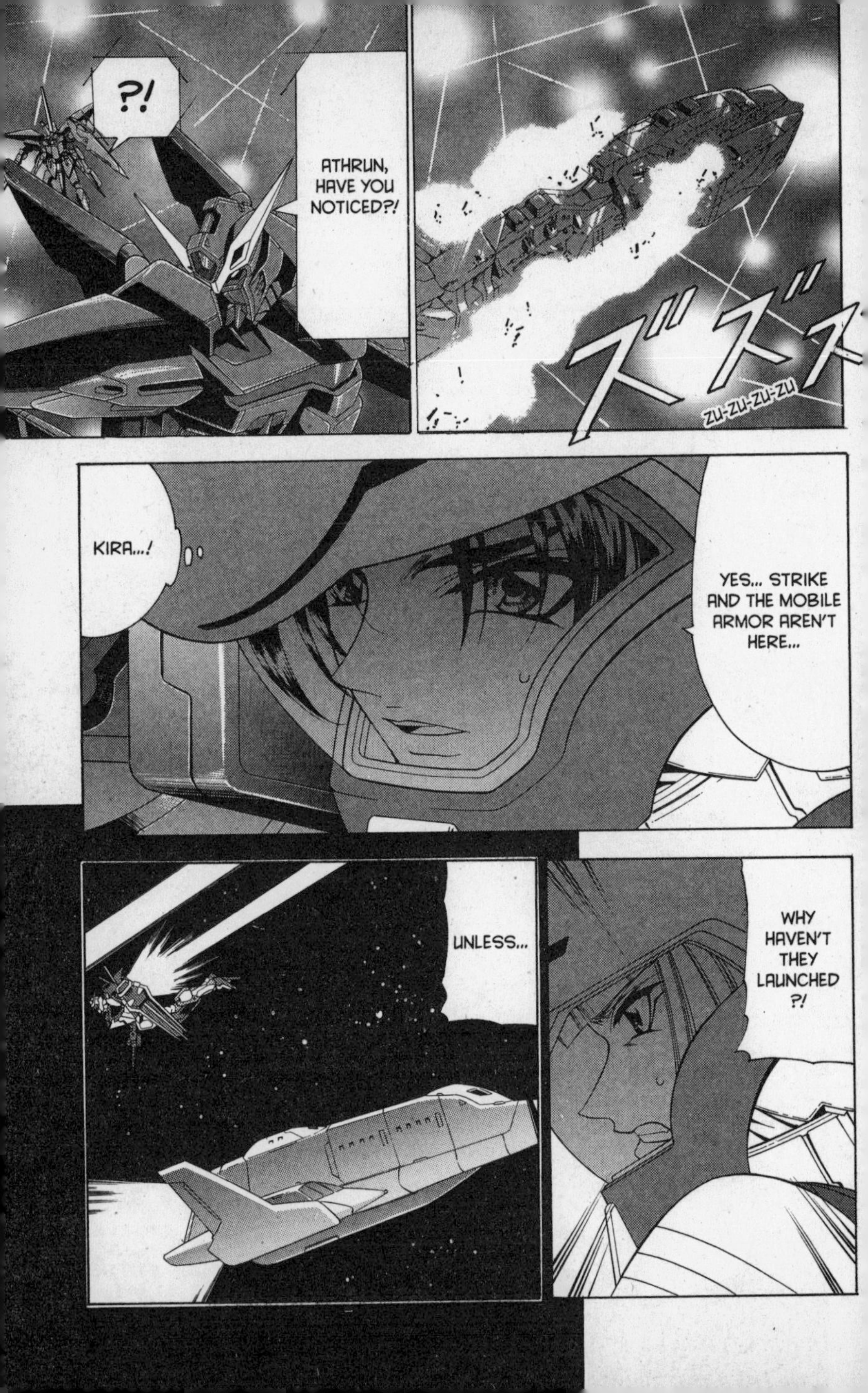
ZU-ZU-ZU-ZU
ATHRUN, HAVE YOU NOTICED?!
?!
YES... STRIKE AND THE MOBILE ARMOR AREN'T HERE...
KIRA...!
WHY HAVEN'T THEY LAUNCHED ?!
UNLESS...

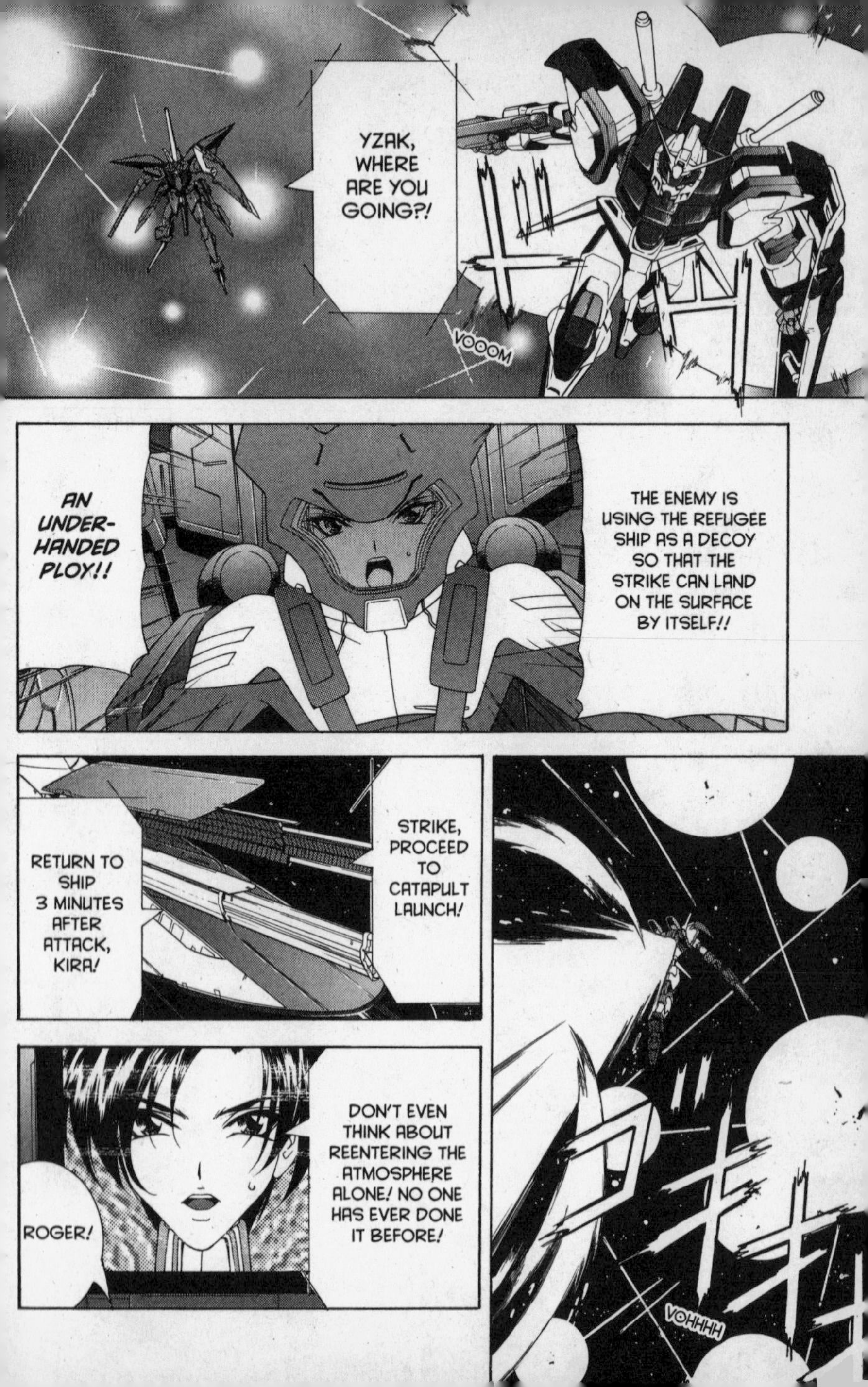
YZAK, WHERE ARE YOU GOING?!
VOOOM
THE ENEMY IS USING THE REFUGEE SHIP AS A DECOY SO THAT THE STRIKE CAN LAND ON THE SURFACE BY ITSELF!!
AN UNDER-HANDED PLOY!!
VOHHHH
STRIKE, PROCEED TO CATAPULT LAUNCH!
RETURN TO SHIP 3 MINUTES AFTER ATTACK, KIRA!
DON'T EVEN THINK ABOUT REENTERING THE ATMOSPHERE ALONE! NO ONE HAS EVER DONE IT BEFORE!
ROGER!

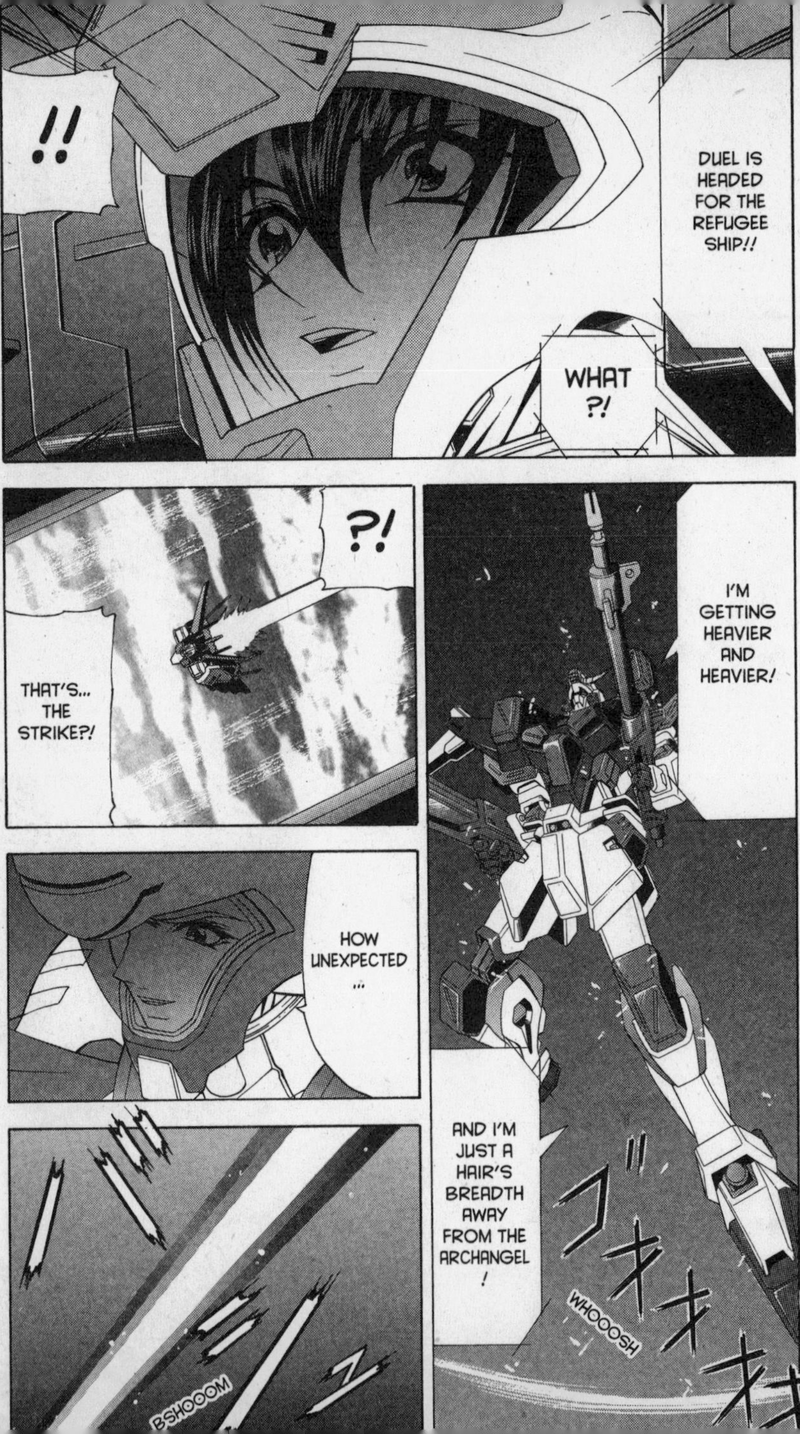
DUEL IS HEADED FOR THE REFUGEE SHIP!!
WHAT?!
!!
I'M GETTING HEAVIER AND HEAVIER!
AND I'M JUST A HAIR'S BREADTH AWAY FROM THE ARCHANGEL!
WHOOOSH
?!
THAT'S... THE STRIKE?!
HOW UNEXPECTED...
BSHOOOM

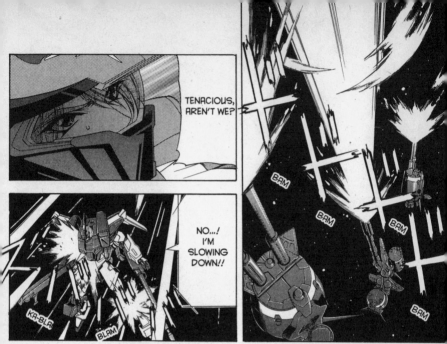

TENACIOUS, AREN'T WE?

NO...!
I'M
SLOWING
DOWN!!

BAM

BAM

BAM

BAM

KA-BLAM

BLAM

!!

VOOOOSHH

STOP HIDING
AND COME
OUT AND PLAY,
STRIKE!!

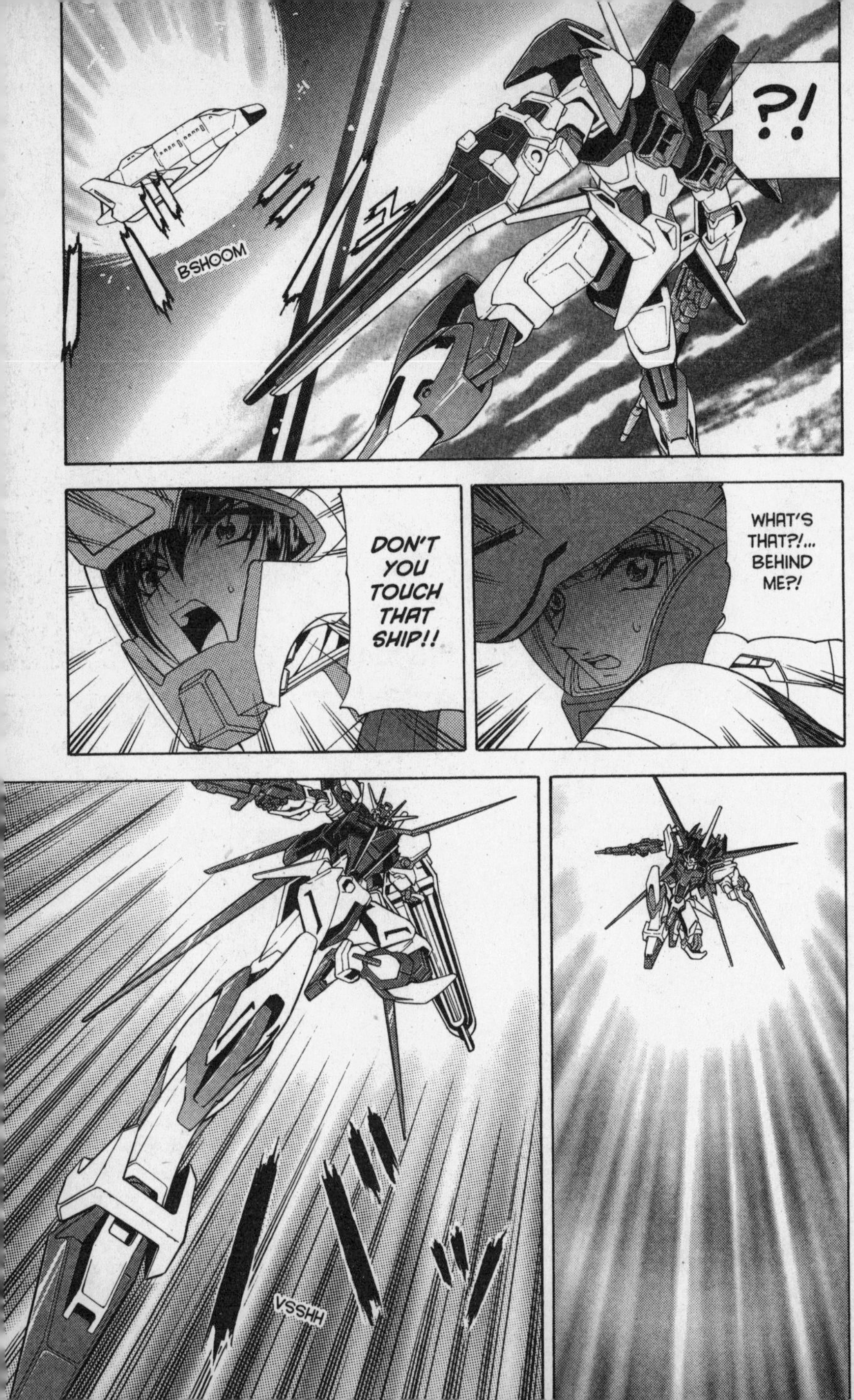
?!
BSHOOM
WHAT'S THAT?!... BEHIND ME?!
DON'T YOU TOUCH THAT SHIP!!
VSSHH

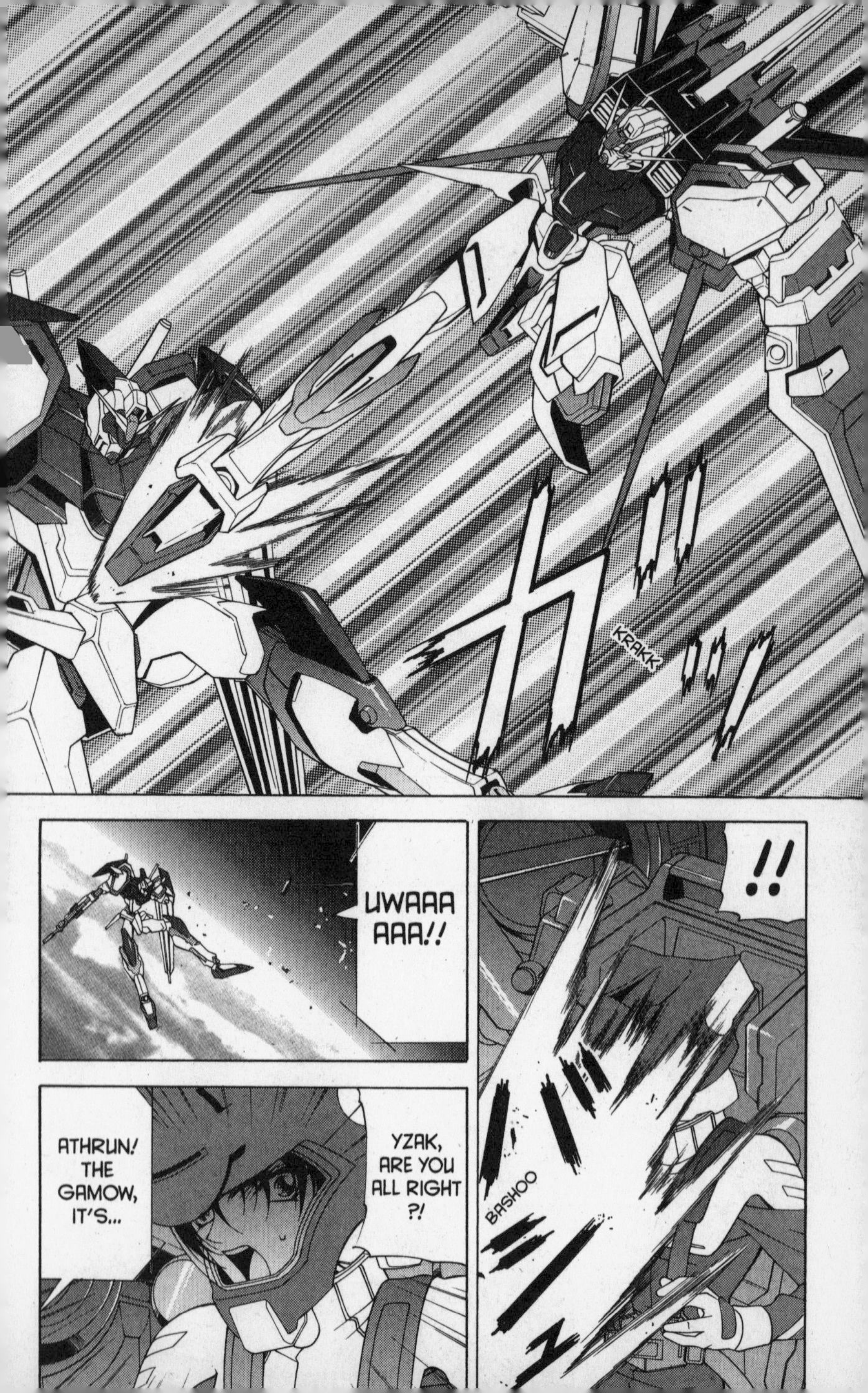
KRAKK
!!
BASHOO
UWAAAAAA!!
YZAK, ARE YOU ALL RIGHT?!
ATHRUN! THE GAMOW, IT'S...

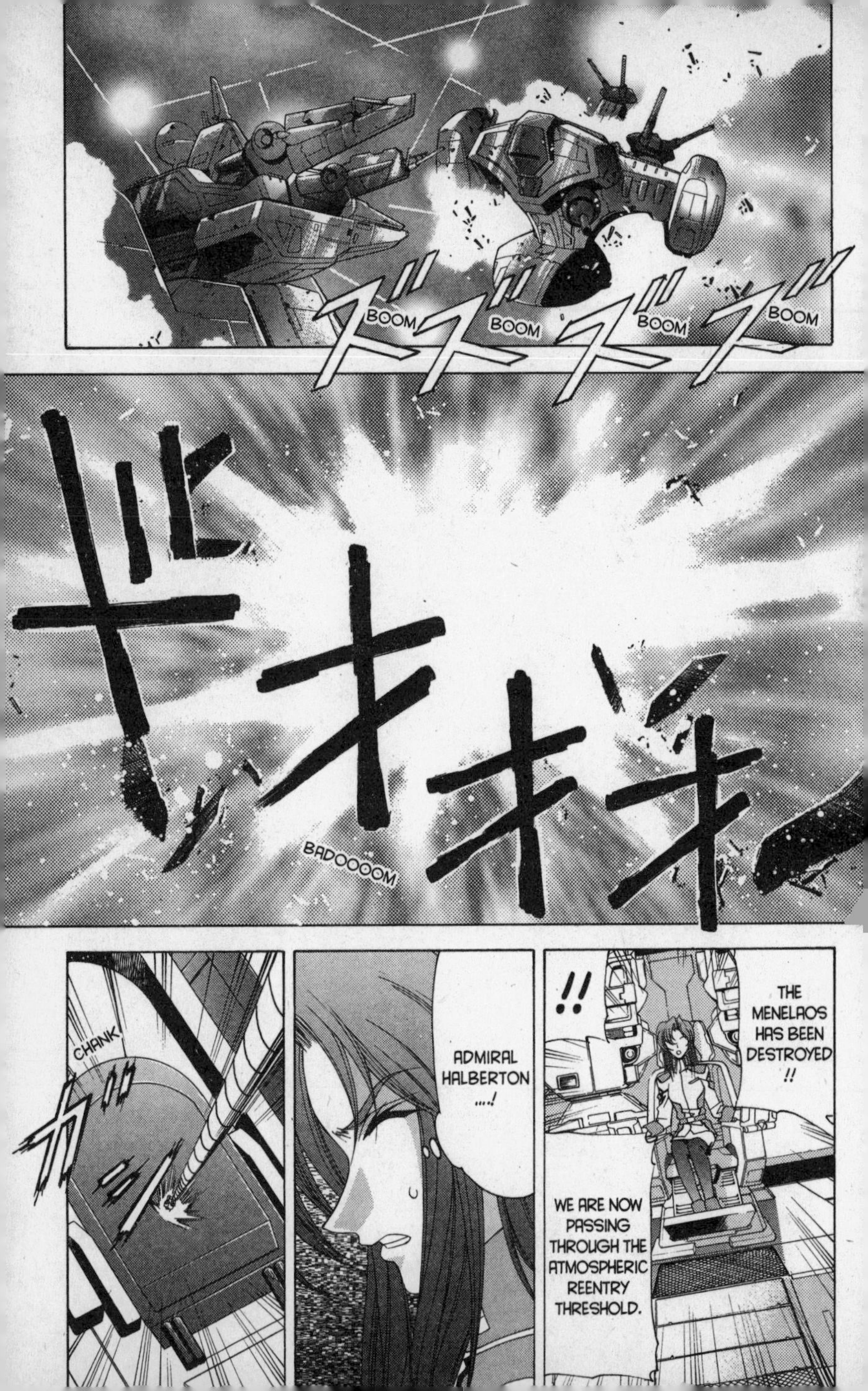
BOOM
BOOM
BOOM
BOOM
BADOOOOM
!!
THE MENELAOS HAS BEEN DESTROYED !!
WE ARE NOW PASSING THROUGH THE ATMOSPHERIC REENTRY THRESHOLD.
ADMIRAL HALBERTON ....!
CHANK

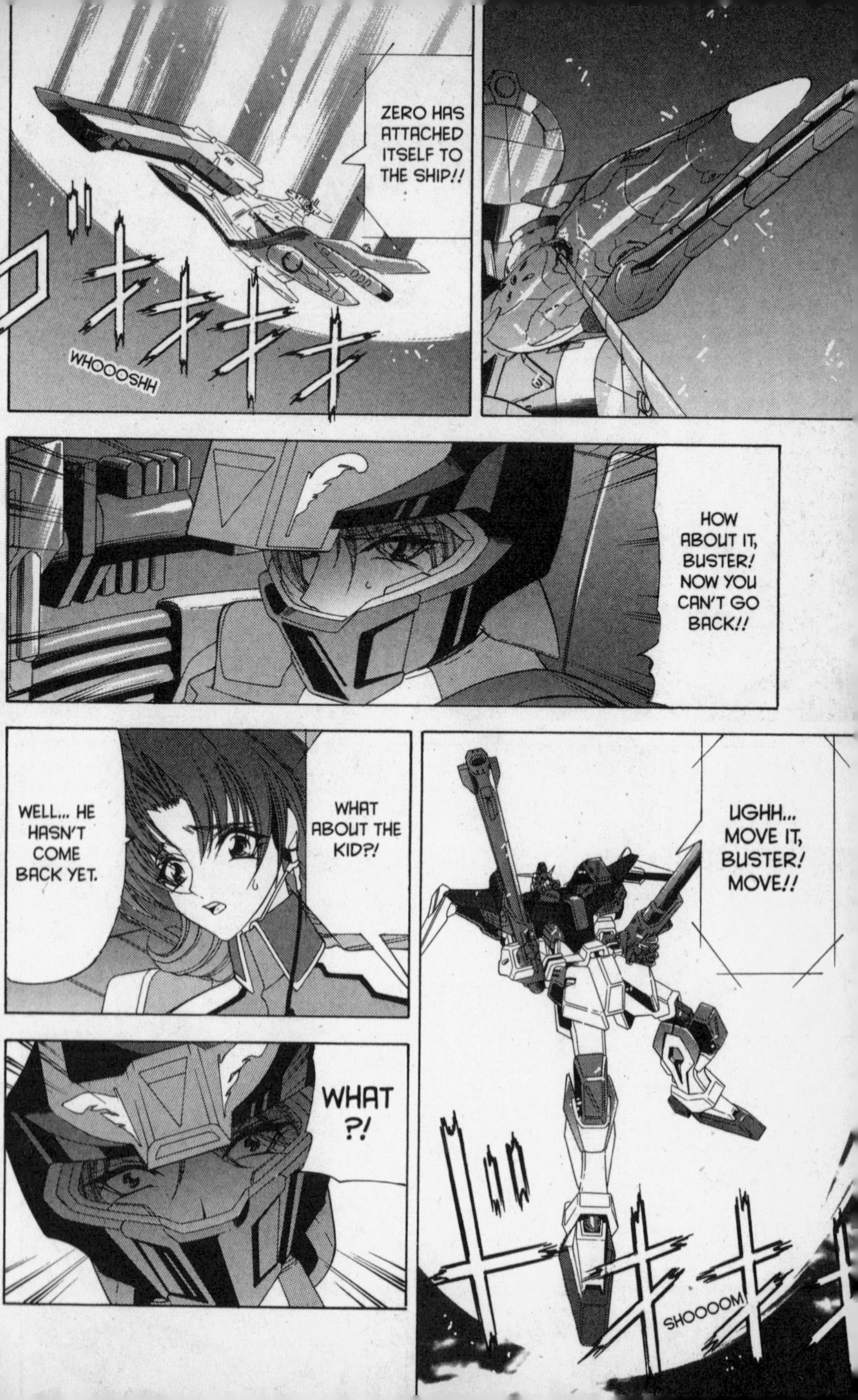
ZERO HAS ATTACHED ITSELF TO THE SHIP!!
WHOOOSHH
HOW ABOUT IT, BUSTER! NOW YOU CAN'T GO BACK!!
UGHH... MOVE IT, BUSTER! MOVE!!
SHOOOOM
WHAT ABOUT THE KID?!
WELL... HE HASN'T COME BACK YET.
WHAT ?!

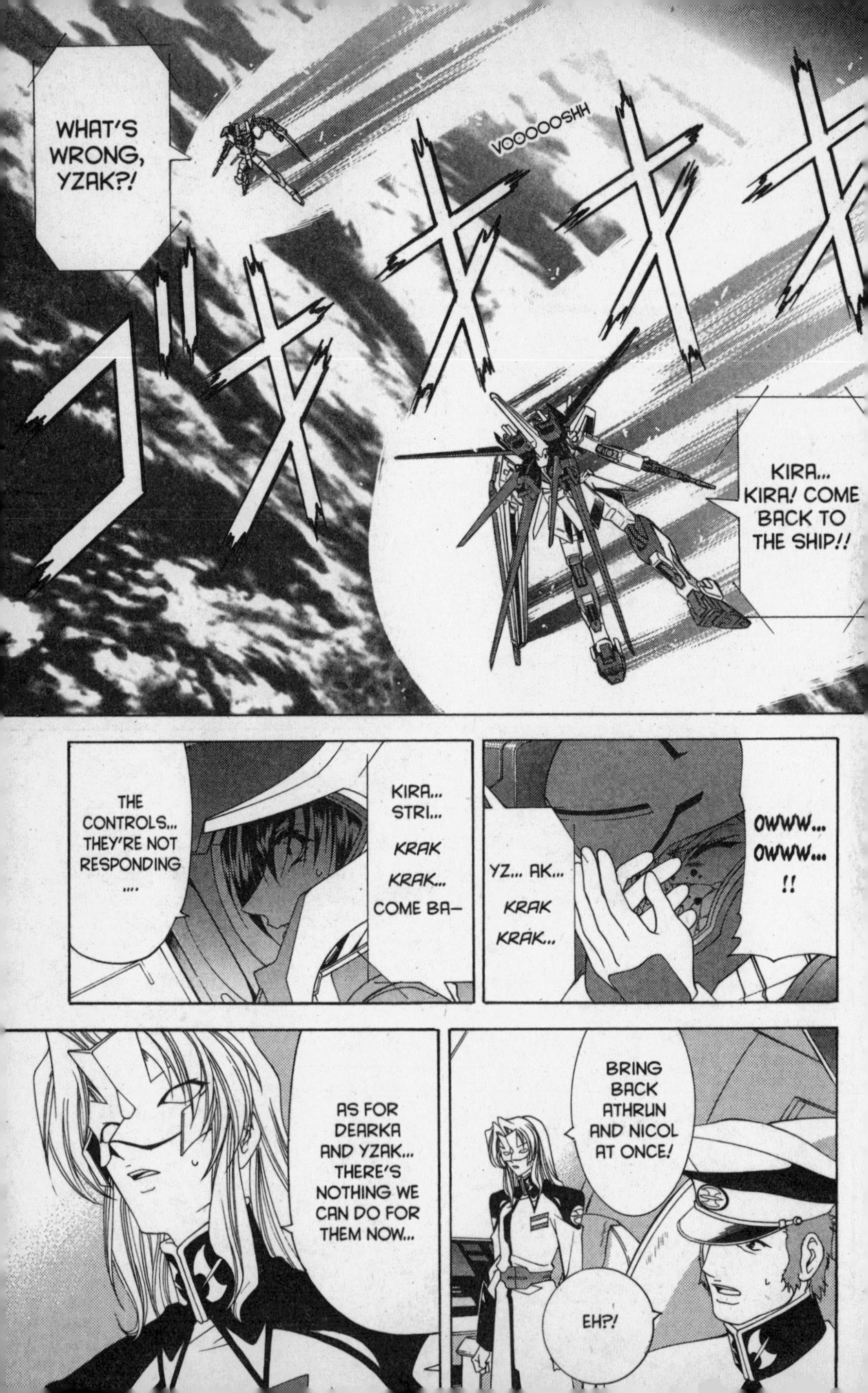
KIRA... KIRA! COME BACK TO THE SHIP!!
VOOOOOSHH
WHAT'S WRONG, YZAK?!
OWWW... OWWW... !!
YZ... AK... KRAK KRAK...
KIRA... STRI... KRAK KRAK... COME BA–
THE CONTROLS... THEY'RE NOT RESPONDING ....
BRING BACK ATHRUN AND NICOL AT ONCE!
EH?!
AS FOR DEARKA AND YZAK... THERE'S NOTHING WE CAN DO FOR THEM NOW...

?!

CURSE YOU, STRIKE !!

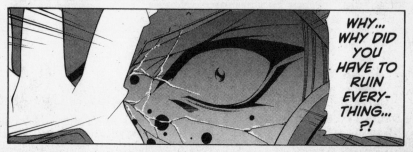

WHY... WHY DID YOU HAVE TO RUIN EVERY- THING... ?!

ZZZN

NOOO OOO !!

VOOHH

!!

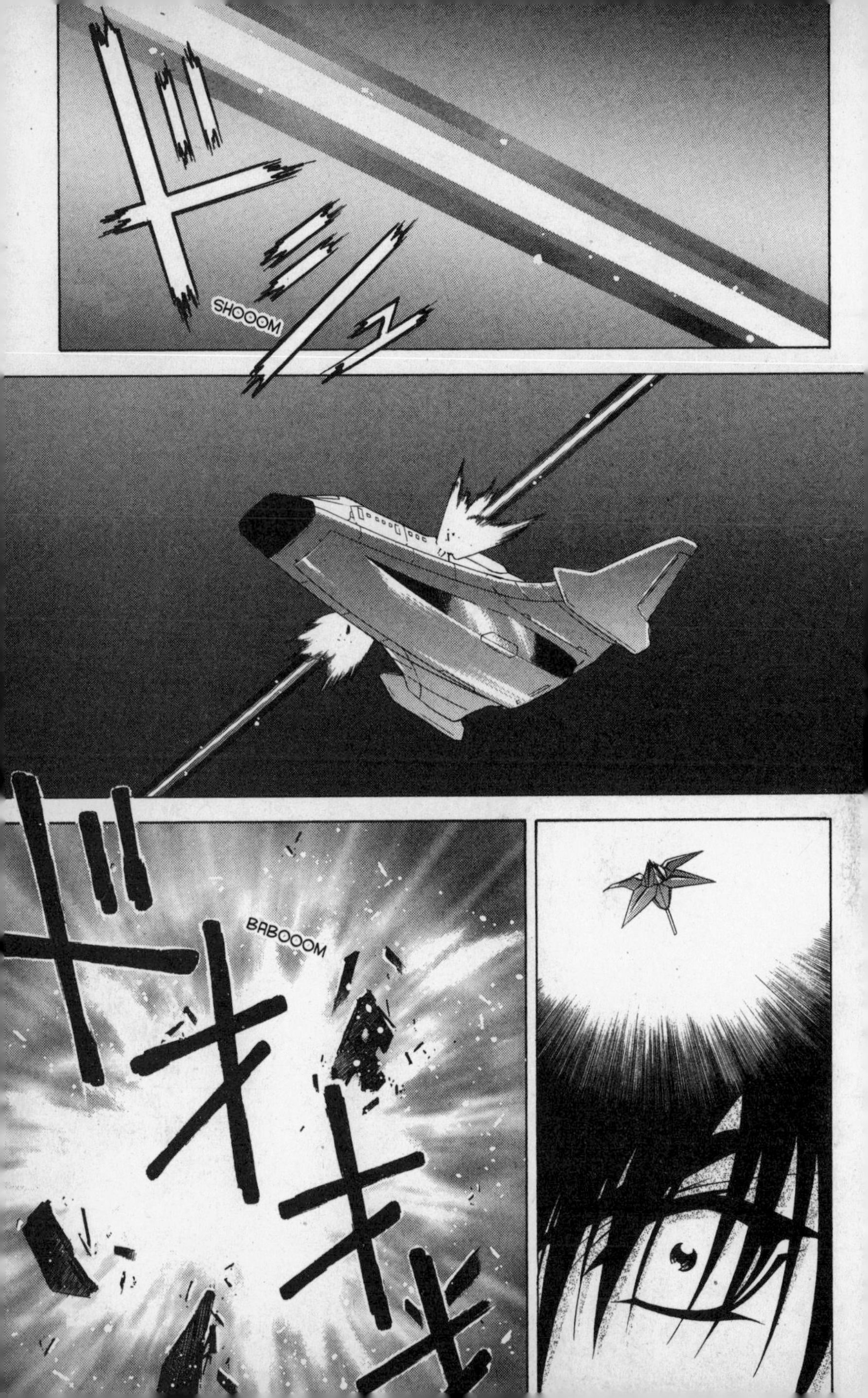
SHOOOM
BABOOOM

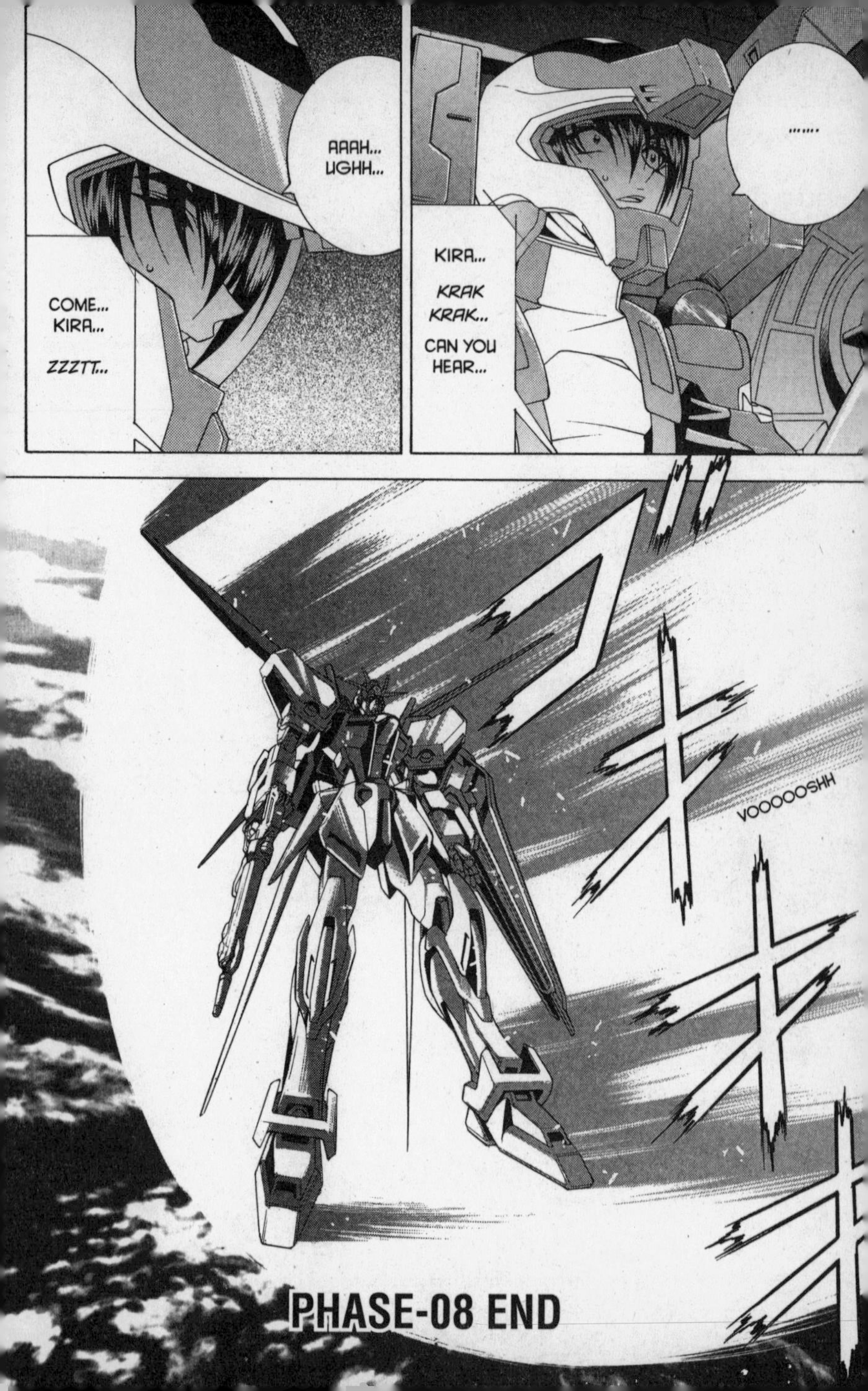
......
KIRA...
KRAK KRAK...
CAN YOU HEAR...
AAAH... UGHH...
COME... KIRA...
ZZZTT...
VOOOOOSHH
PHASE-08 END

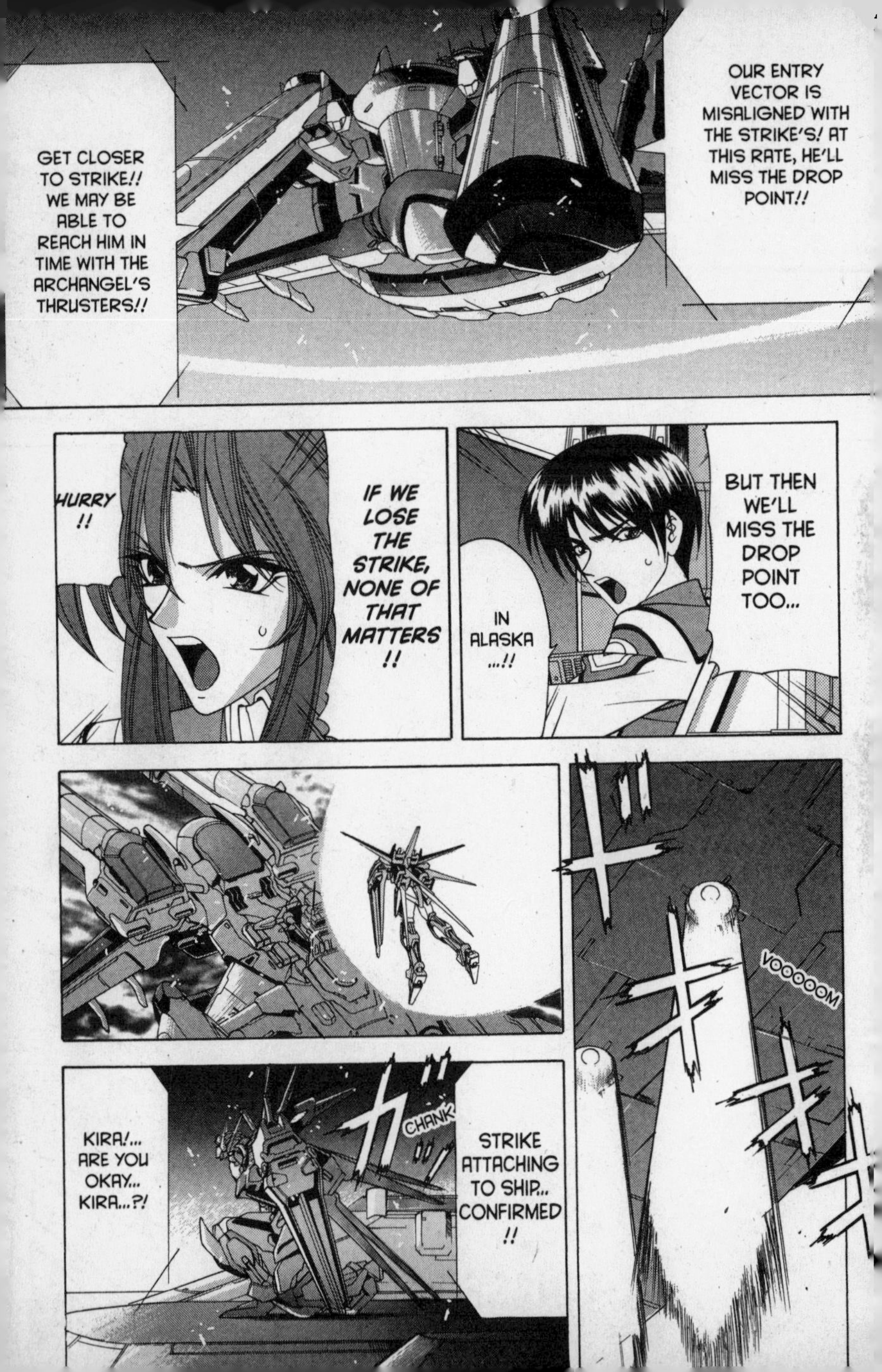
OUR ENTRY VECTOR IS MISALIGNED WITH THE STRIKE'S! AT THIS RATE, HE'LL MISS THE DROP POINT!!
GET CLOSER TO STRIKE!! WE MAY BE ABLE TO REACH HIM IN TIME WITH THE ARCHANGEL'S THRUSTERS!!
BUT THEN WE'LL MISS THE DROP POINT TOO...
IN ALASKA ...!!
IF WE LOSE THE STRIKE, NONE OF THAT MATTERS !!
HURRY !!
VOOOOOM
CHANK
STRIKE ATTACHING TO SHIP... CONFIRMED !!
KIRA!... ARE YOU OKAY... KIRA...?!

PHASE-09 THE BURNING DESERT SANDS

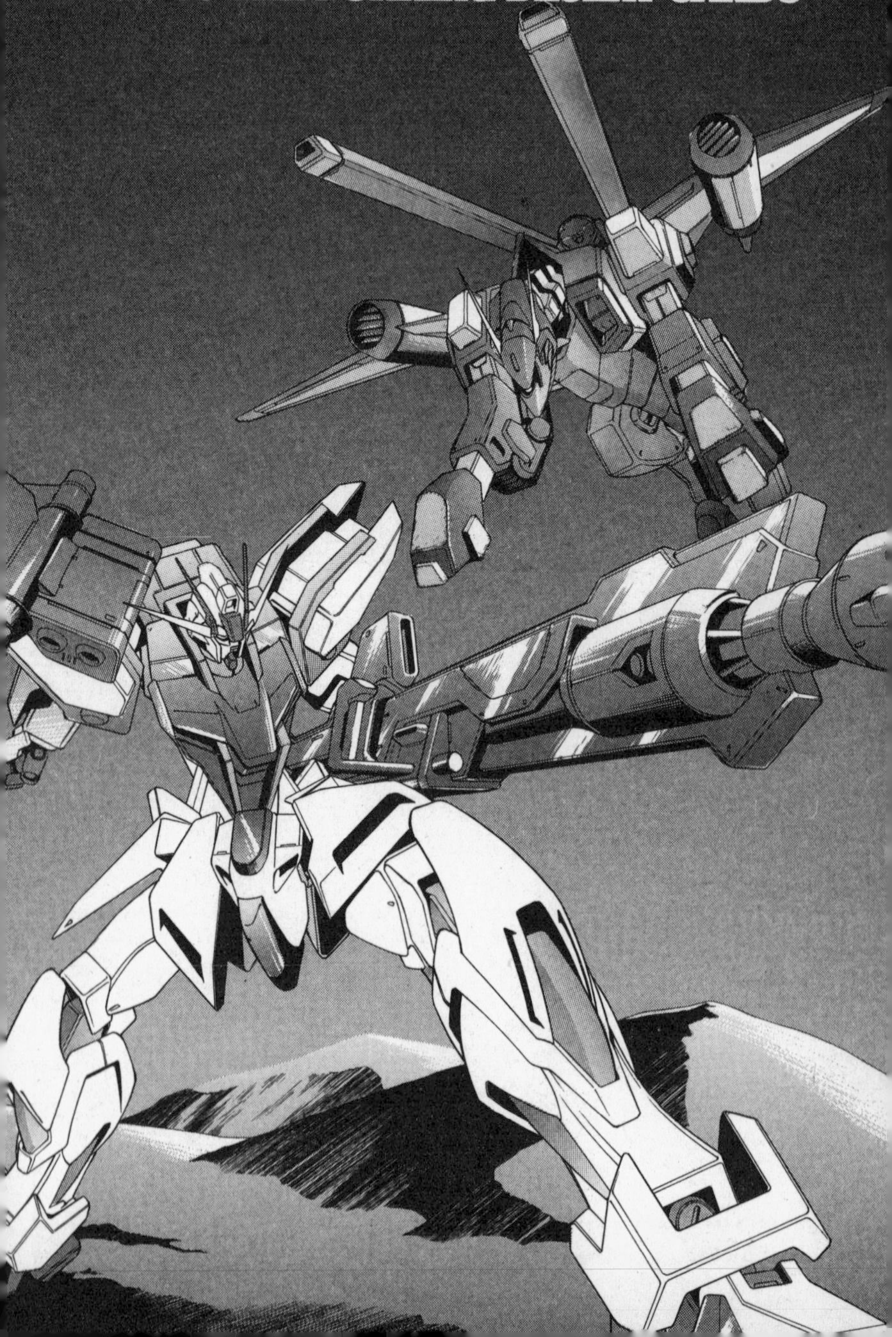

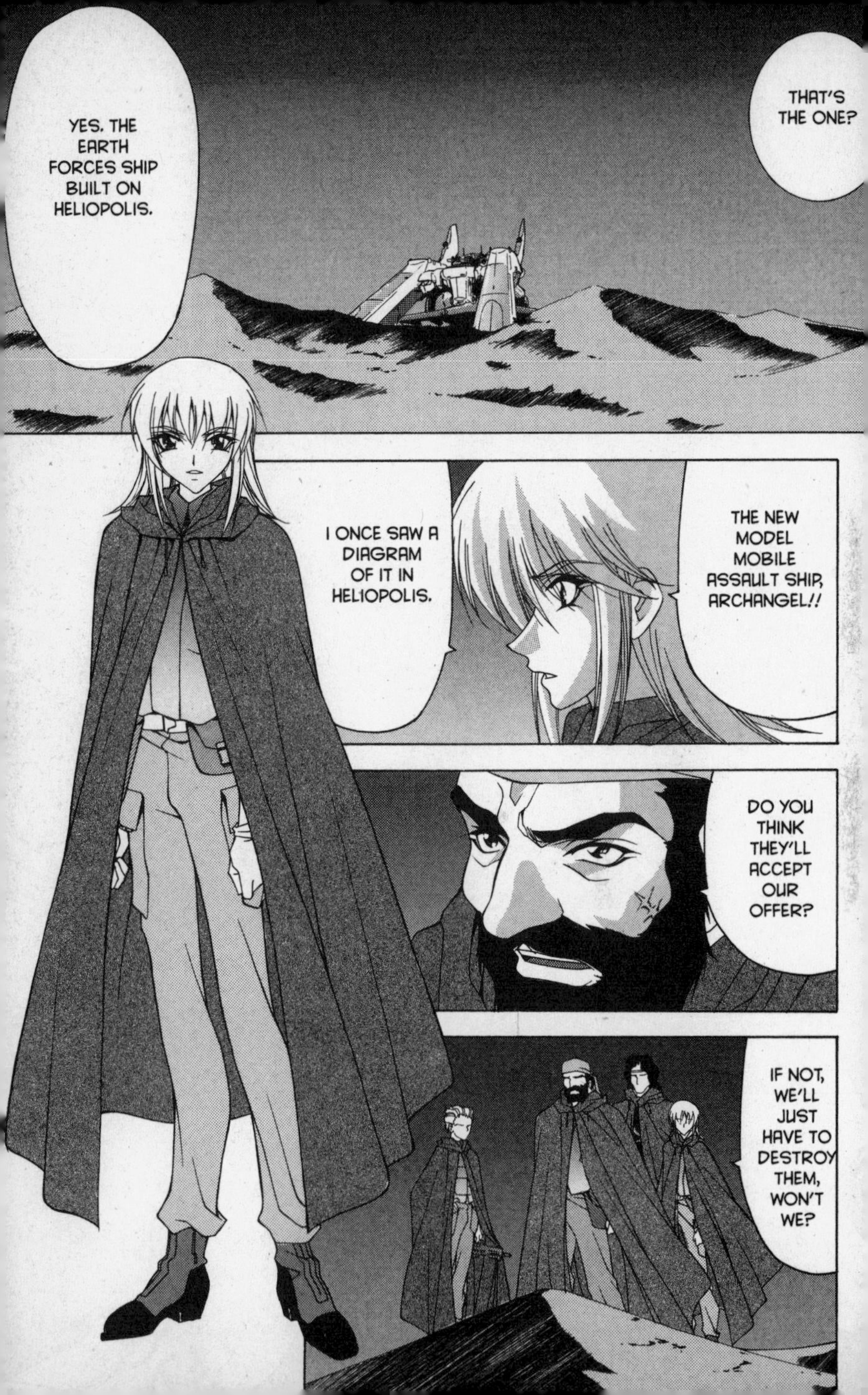
THAT'S THE ONE?
YES. THE EARTH FORCES SHIP BUILT ON HELIOPOLIS.
THE NEW MODEL MOBILE ASSAULT SHIP, ARCHANGEL!!
I ONCE SAW A DIAGRAM OF IT IN HELIOPOLIS.
DO YOU THINK THEY'LL ACCEPT OUR OFFER?
IF NOT, WE'LL JUST HAVE TO DESTROY THEM, WON'T WE?

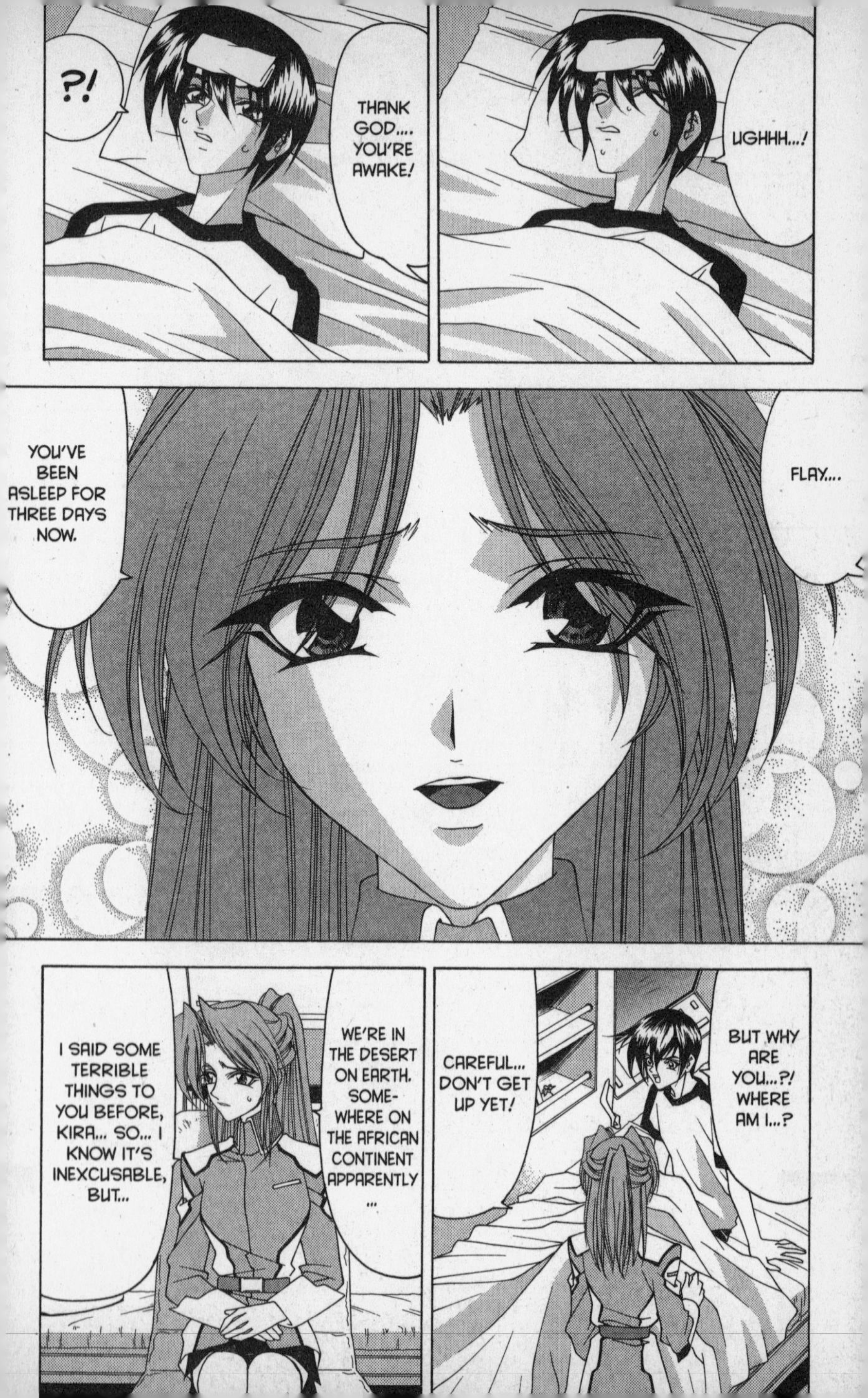
UGHHH...!
THANK GOD.... YOU'RE AWAKE!
?!
FLAY....
YOU'VE BEEN ASLEEP FOR THREE DAYS NOW.
BUT WHY ARE YOU...?! WHERE AM I...?
CAREFUL... DON'T GET UP YET!
WE'RE IN THE DESERT ON EARTH. SOME-WHERE ON THE AFRICAN CONTINENT APPARENTLY ...
I SAID SOME TERRIBLE THINGS TO YOU BEFORE, KIRA... SO... I KNOW IT'S INEXCUSABLE, BUT...

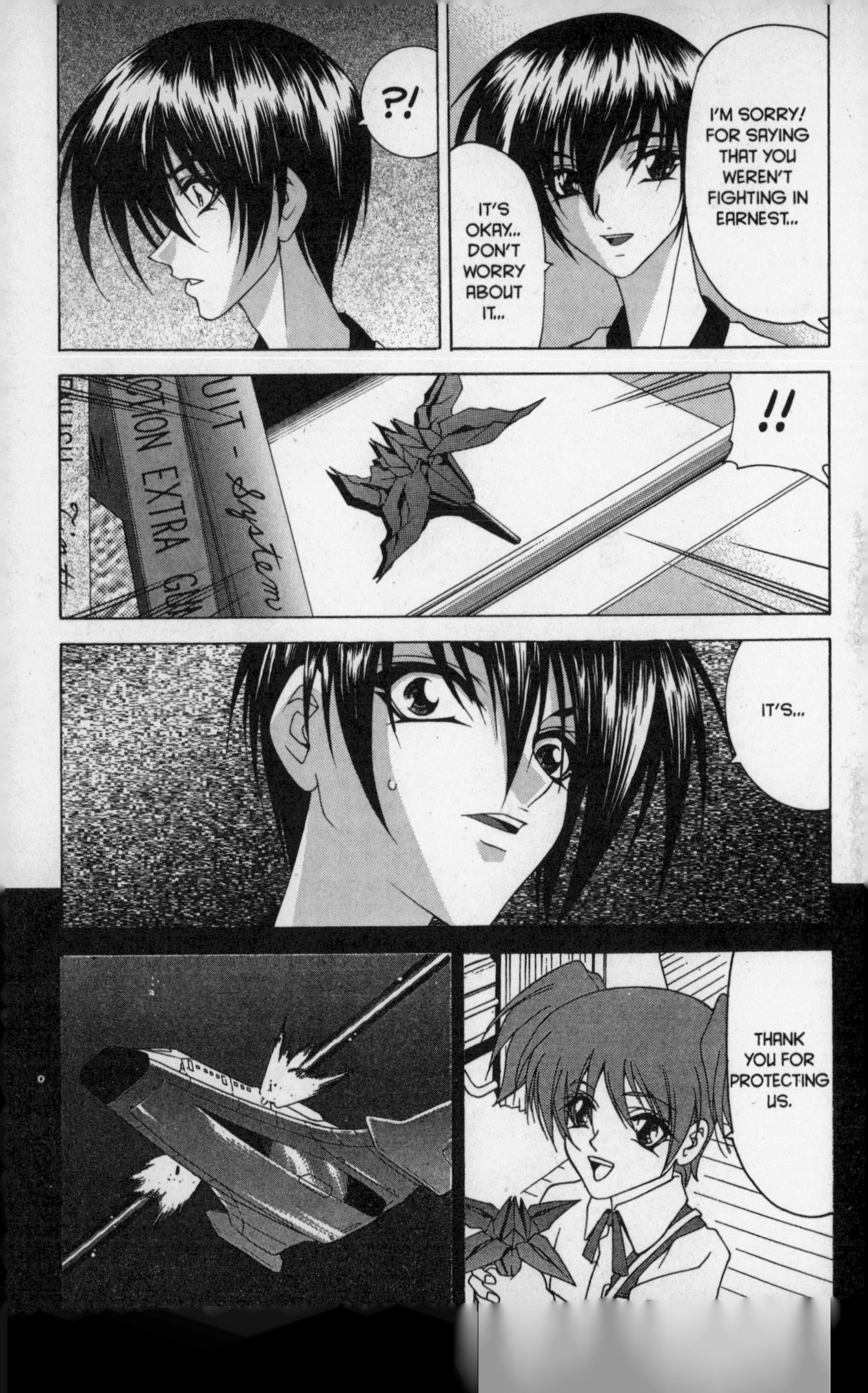
I'M SORRY! FOR SAYING THAT YOU WEREN'T FIGHTING IN EARNEST...
IT'S OKAY... DON'T WORRY ABOUT IT...
?!
!!
IT'S...
THANK YOU FOR PROTECTING US.

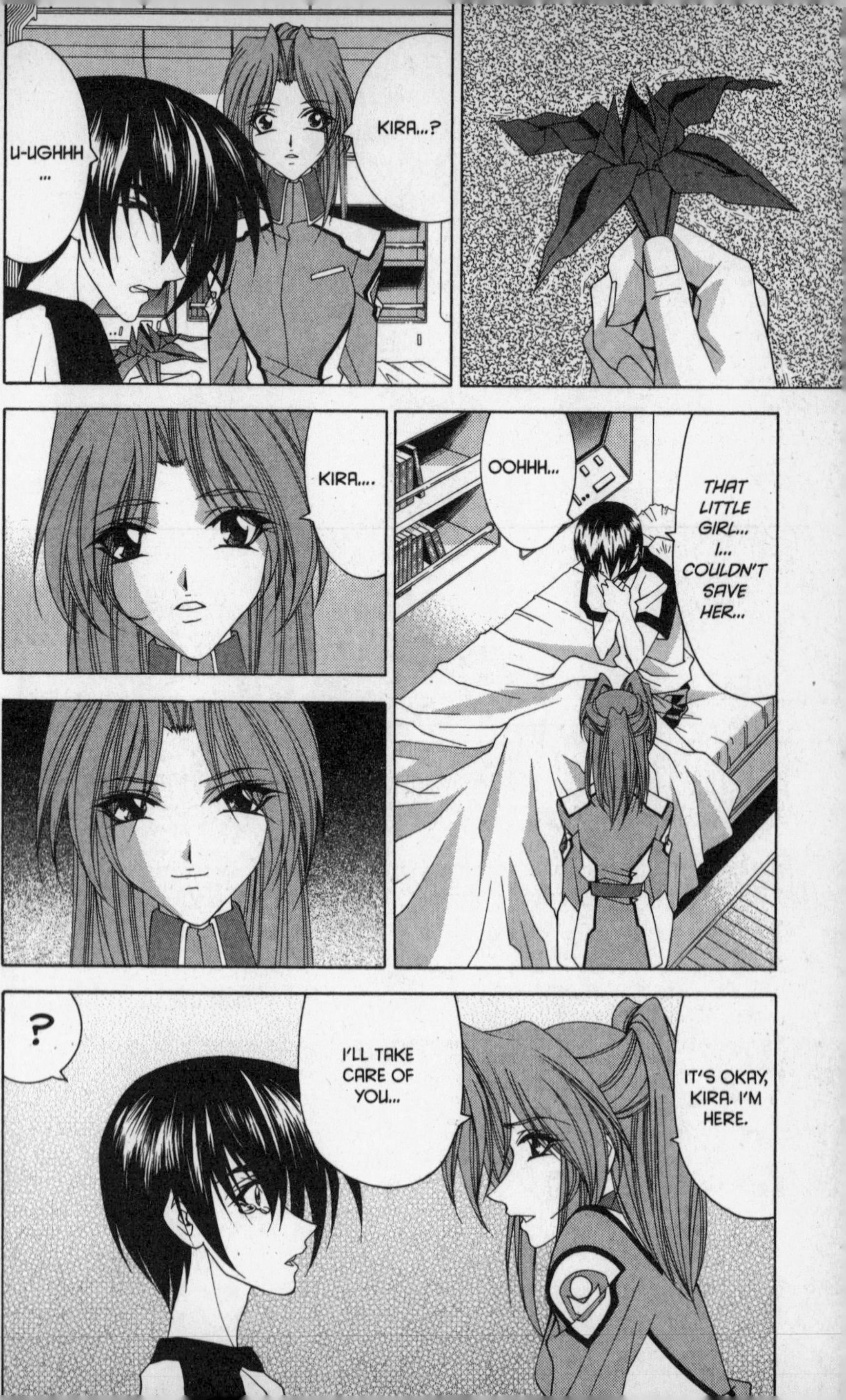
KIRA...?
U-UGHHH ...
THAT LITTLE GIRL... I... COULDN'T SAVE HER...
OOHHH...
KIRA....
IT'S OKAY, KIRA. I'M HERE.
I'LL TAKE CARE OF YOU...
?

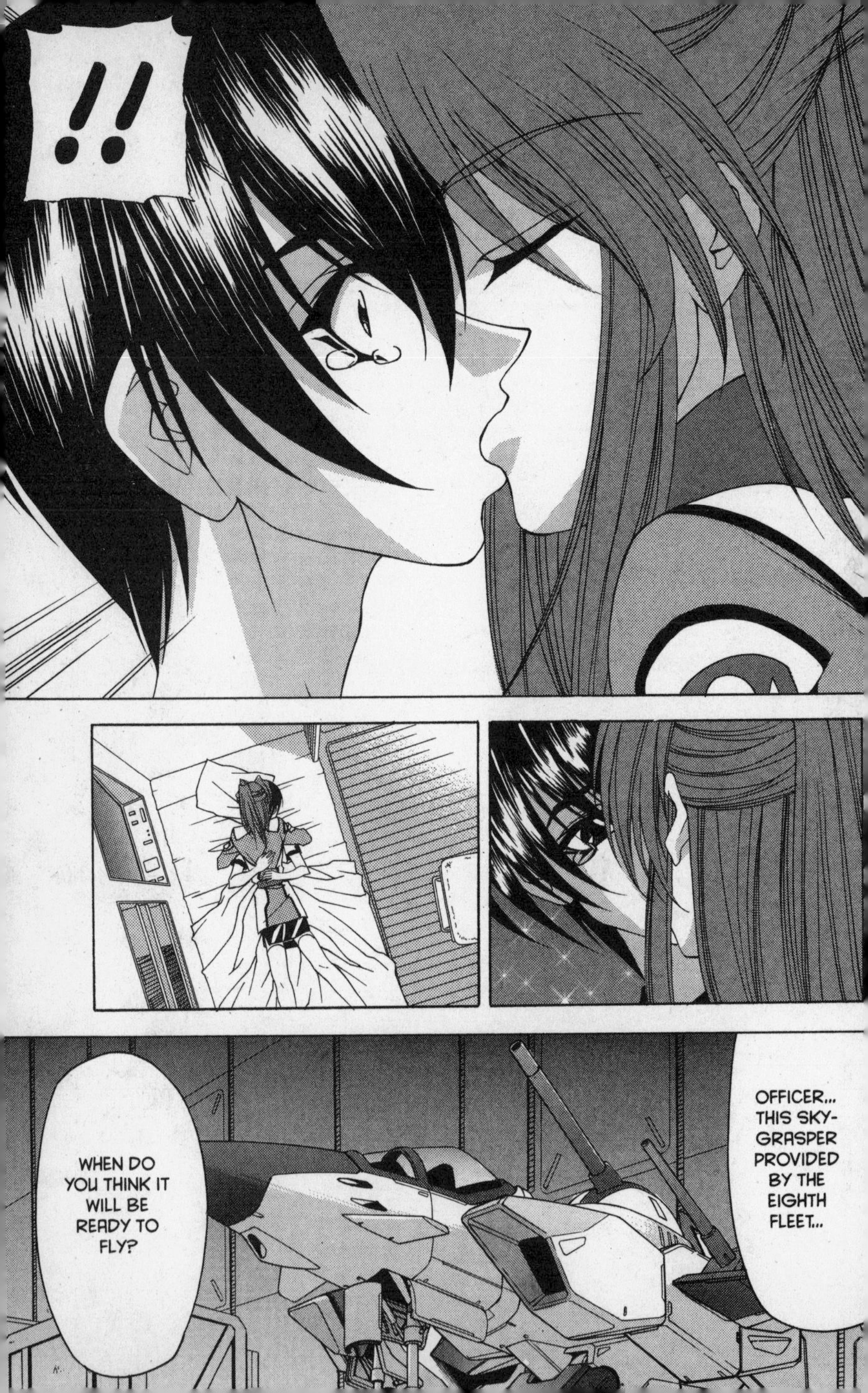
!!
OFFICER... THIS SKY-GRASPER PROVIDED BY THE EIGHTH FLEET...
WHEN DO YOU THINK IT WILL BE READY TO FLY?

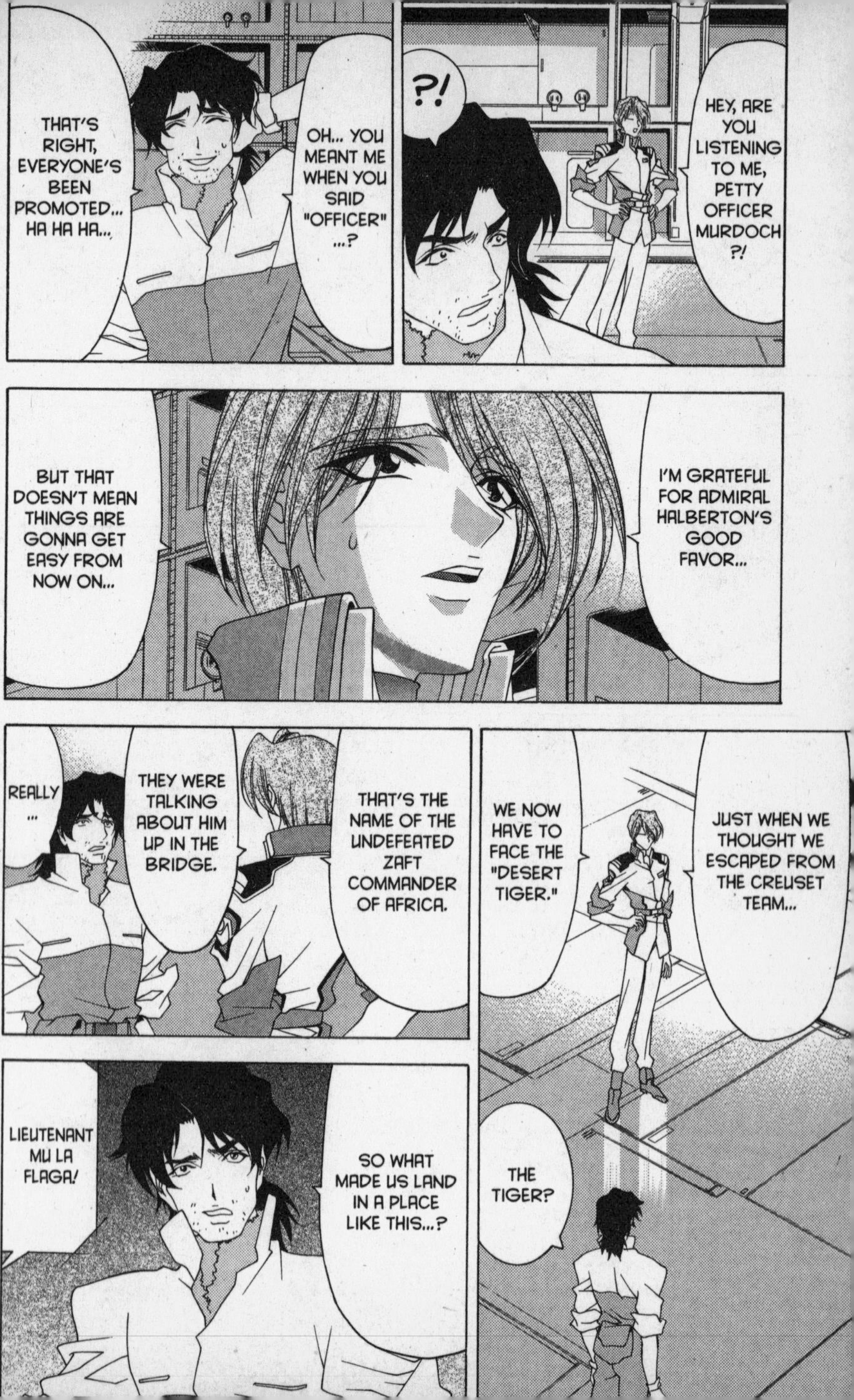
HEY, ARE YOU LISTENING TO ME, PETTY OFFICER MURDOCH?!
?!
OH... YOU MEANT ME WHEN YOU SAID "OFFICER"...?
THAT'S RIGHT, EVERYONE'S BEEN PROMOTED... HA HA HA...
I'M GRATEFUL FOR ADMIRAL HALBERTON'S GOOD FAVOR...
BUT THAT DOESN'T MEAN THINGS ARE GONNA GET EASY FROM NOW ON...
JUST WHEN WE THOUGHT WE ESCAPED FROM THE CREUSET TEAM...
WE NOW HAVE TO FACE THE "DESERT TIGER."
THE TIGER?
THAT'S THE NAME OF THE UNDEFEATED ZAFT COMMANDER OF AFRICA.
THEY WERE TALKING ABOUT HIM UP IN THE BRIDGE.
REALLY...
SO WHAT MADE US LAND IN A PLACE LIKE THIS...?
LIEUTENANT MU LA FLAGA!

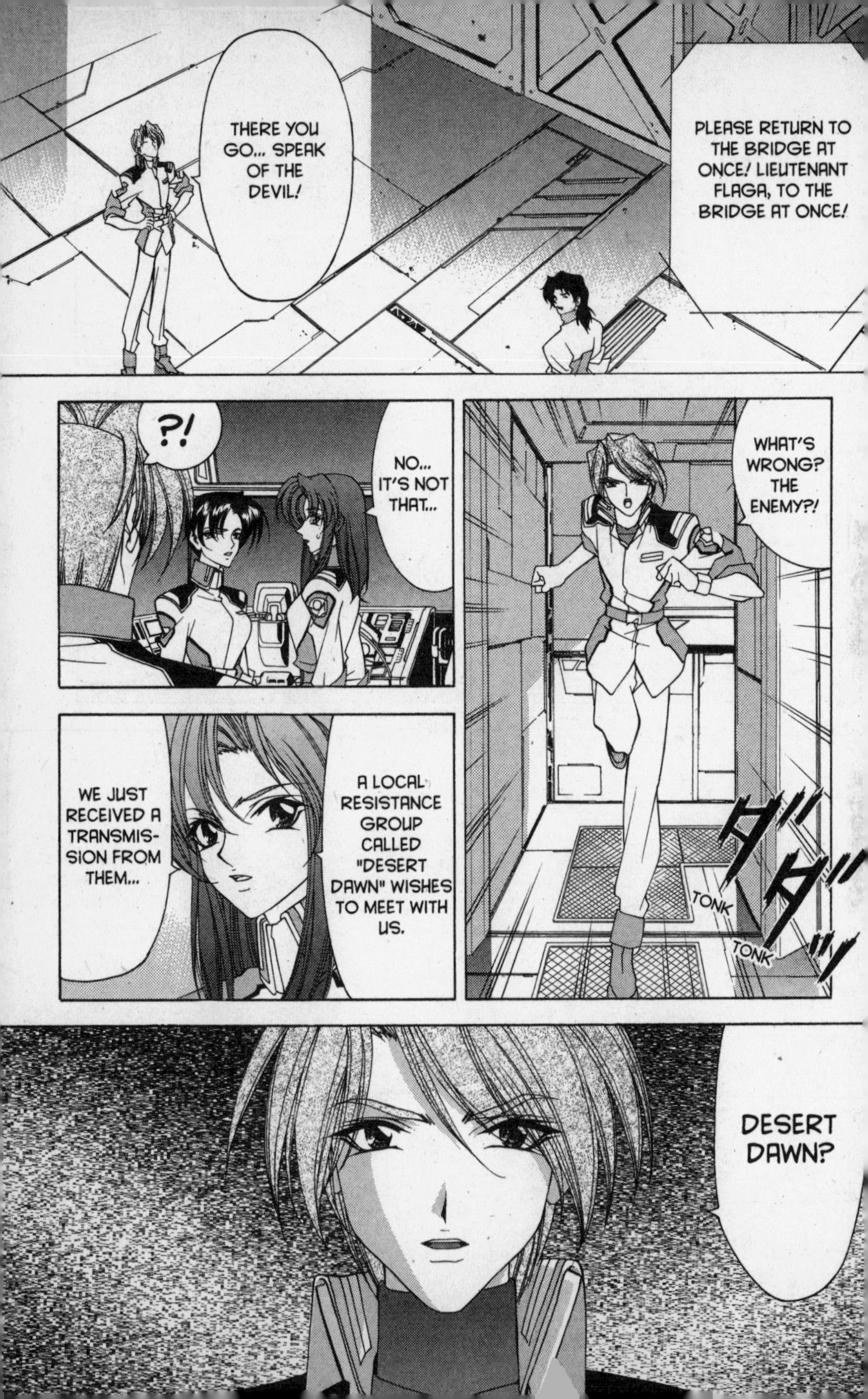
PLEASE RETURN TO THE BRIDGE AT ONCE! LIEUTENANT FLAGA, TO THE BRIDGE AT ONCE!
THERE YOU GO... SPEAK OF THE DEVIL!
WHAT'S WRONG? THE ENEMY?!
ダダッ
TONK
TONK
NO... IT'S NOT THAT...
?!
A LOCAL RESISTANCE GROUP CALLED "DESERT DAWN" WISHES TO MEET WITH US.
WE JUST RECEIVED A TRANSMISSION FROM THEM...
DESERT DAWN?

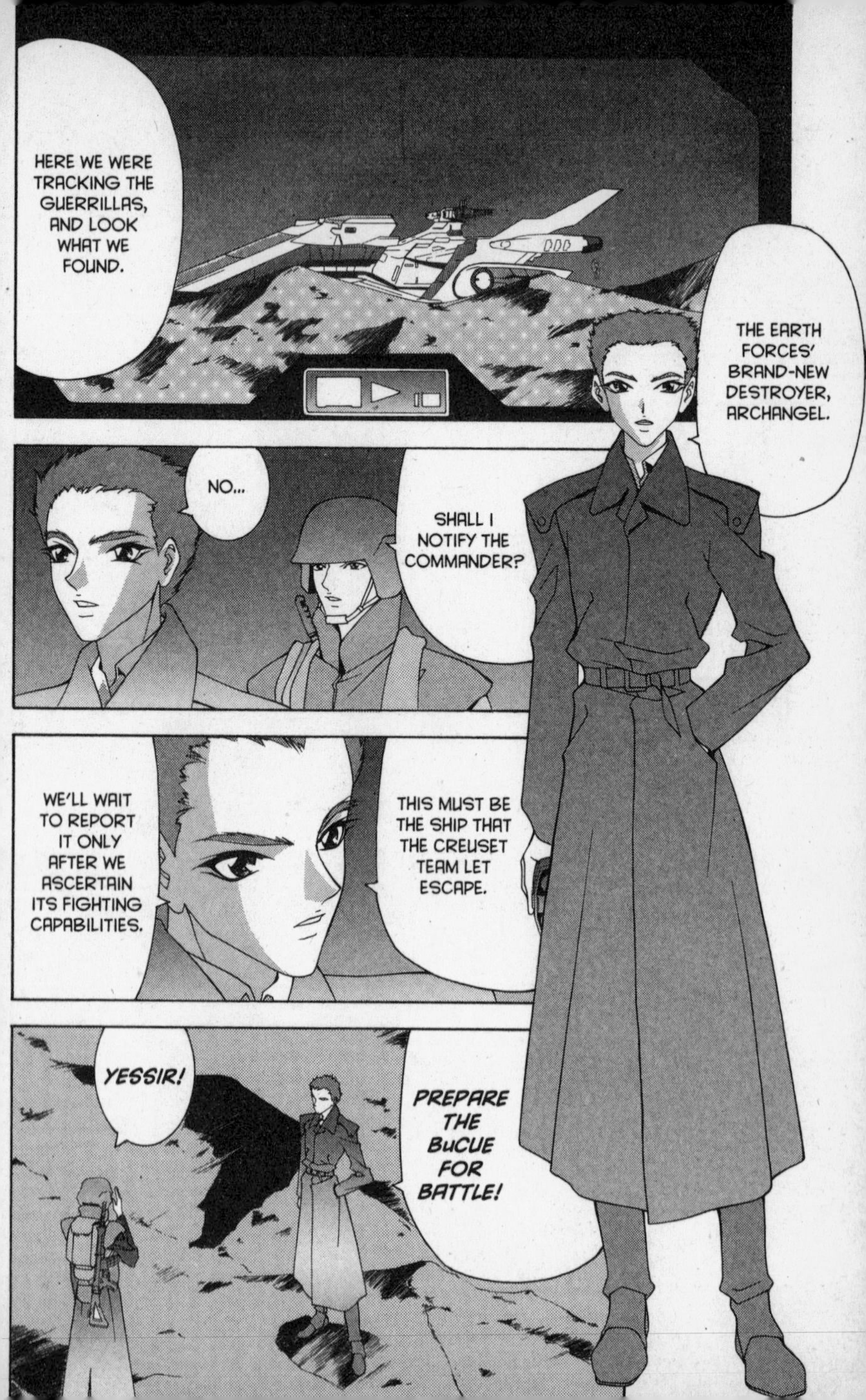
HERE WE WERE TRACKING THE GUERRILLAS, AND LOOK WHAT WE FOUND.
THE EARTH FORCES' BRAND-NEW DESTROYER, ARCHANGEL.
SHALL I NOTIFY THE COMMANDER?
NO...
THIS MUST BE THE SHIP THAT THE CREUSET TEAM LET ESCAPE.
WE'LL WAIT TO REPORT IT ONLY AFTER WE ASCERTAIN ITS FIGHTING CAPABILITIES.
PREPARE THE BuCUE FOR BATTLE!
YESSIR!

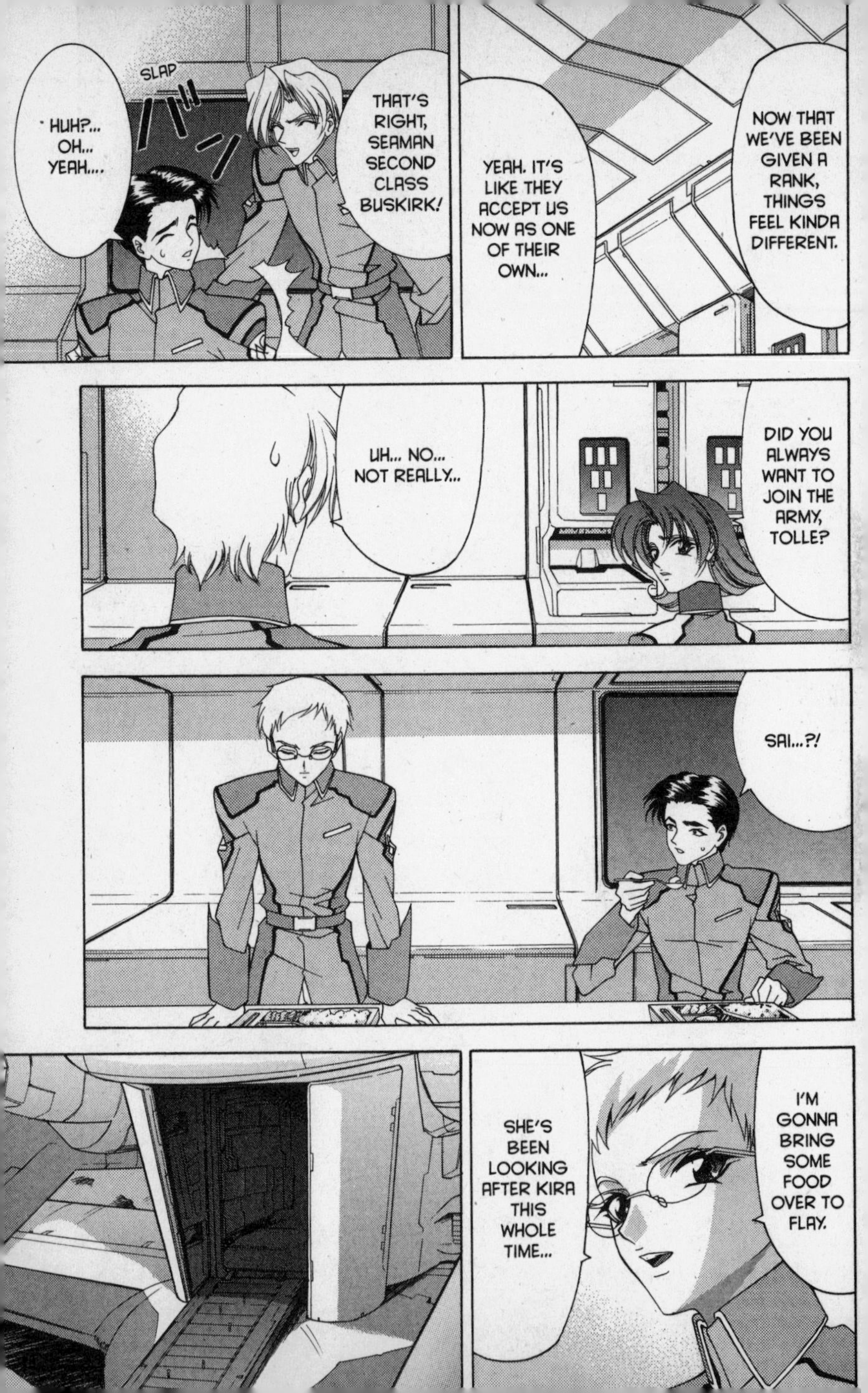
NOW THAT WE'VE BEEN GIVEN A RANK, THINGS FEEL KINDA DIFFERENT.
YEAH. IT'S LIKE THEY ACCEPT US NOW AS ONE OF THEIR OWN...
THAT'S RIGHT, SEAMAN SECOND CLASS BUSKIRK!
SLAP
HUH?... OH... YEAH....
DID YOU ALWAYS WANT TO JOIN THE ARMY, TOLLE?
UH... NO... NOT REALLY...
SAI...?!
I'M GONNA BRING SOME FOOD OVER TO FLAY.
SHE'S BEEN LOOKING AFTER KIRA THIS WHOLE TIME...

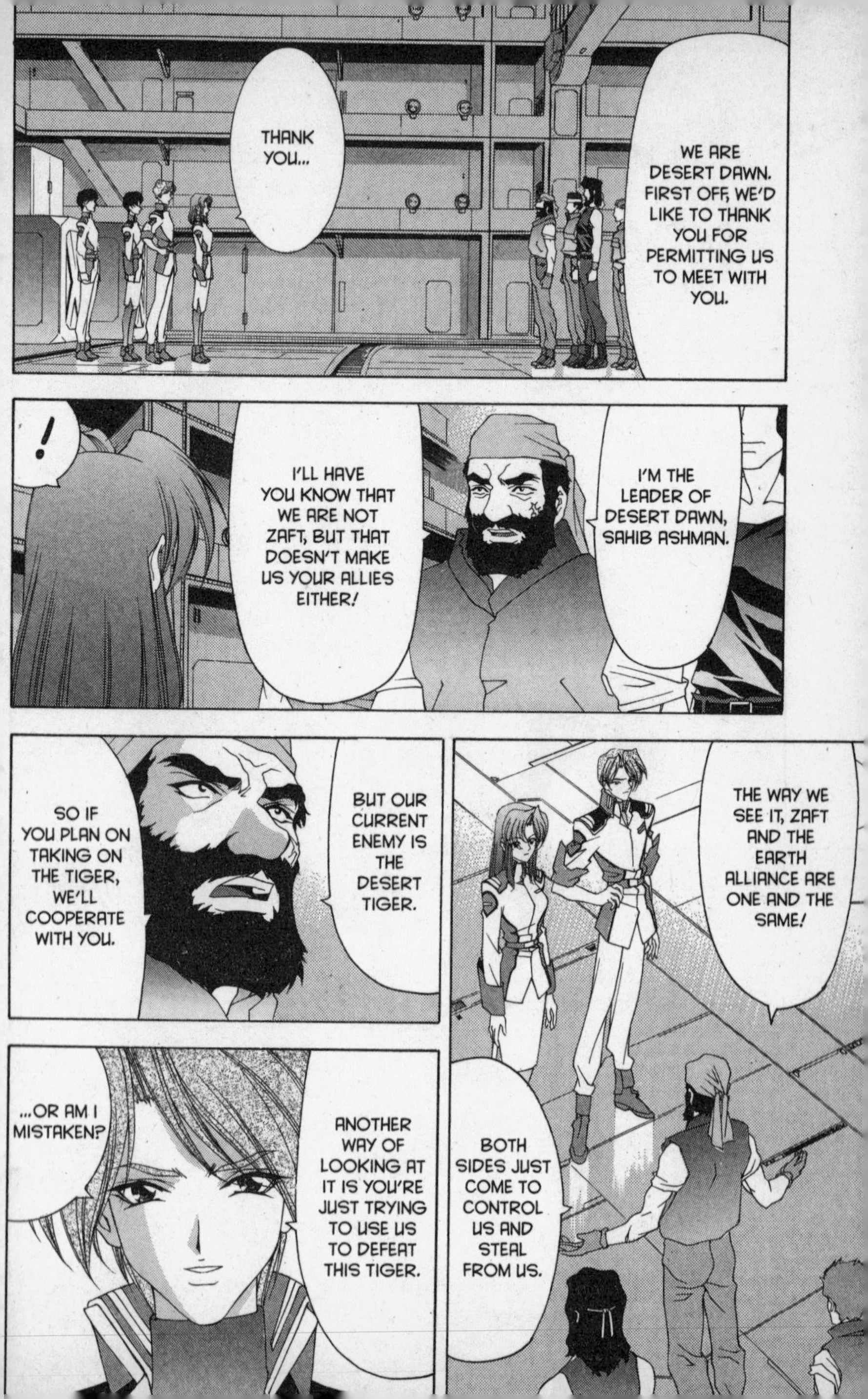
WE ARE DESERT DAWN. FIRST OFF, WE'D LIKE TO THANK YOU FOR PERMITTING US TO MEET WITH YOU.
THANK YOU...
I'M THE LEADER OF DESERT DAWN, SAHIB ASHMAN.
I'LL HAVE YOU KNOW THAT WE ARE NOT ZAFT, BUT THAT DOESN'T MAKE US YOUR ALLIES EITHER!
!
THE WAY WE SEE IT, ZAFT AND THE EARTH ALLIANCE ARE ONE AND THE SAME!
BOTH SIDES JUST COME TO CONTROL US AND STEAL FROM US.
BUT OUR CURRENT ENEMY IS THE DESERT TIGER.
SO IF YOU PLAN ON TAKING ON THE TIGER, WE'LL COOPERATE WITH YOU.
ANOTHER WAY OF LOOKING AT IT IS YOU'RE JUST TRYING TO USE US TO DEFEAT THIS TIGER.
...OR AM I MISTAKEN?

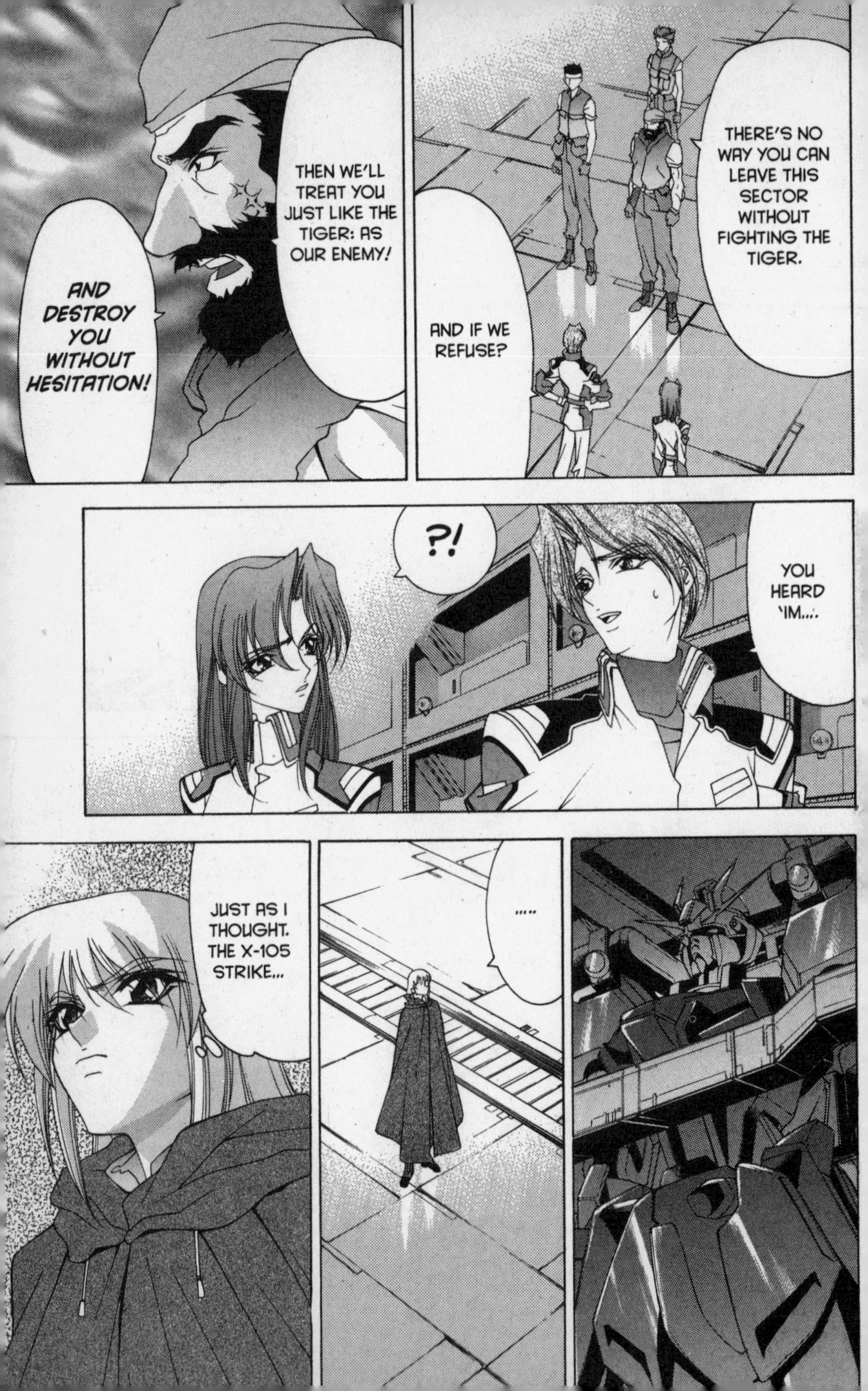
THERE'S NO WAY YOU CAN LEAVE THIS SECTOR WITHOUT FIGHTING THE TIGER.
AND IF WE REFUSE?
THEN WE'LL TREAT YOU JUST LIKE THE TIGER: AS OUR ENEMY!
AND DESTROY YOU WITHOUT HESITATION!
YOU HEARD 'IM....
?!
....
JUST AS I THOUGHT. THE X-105 STRIKE...

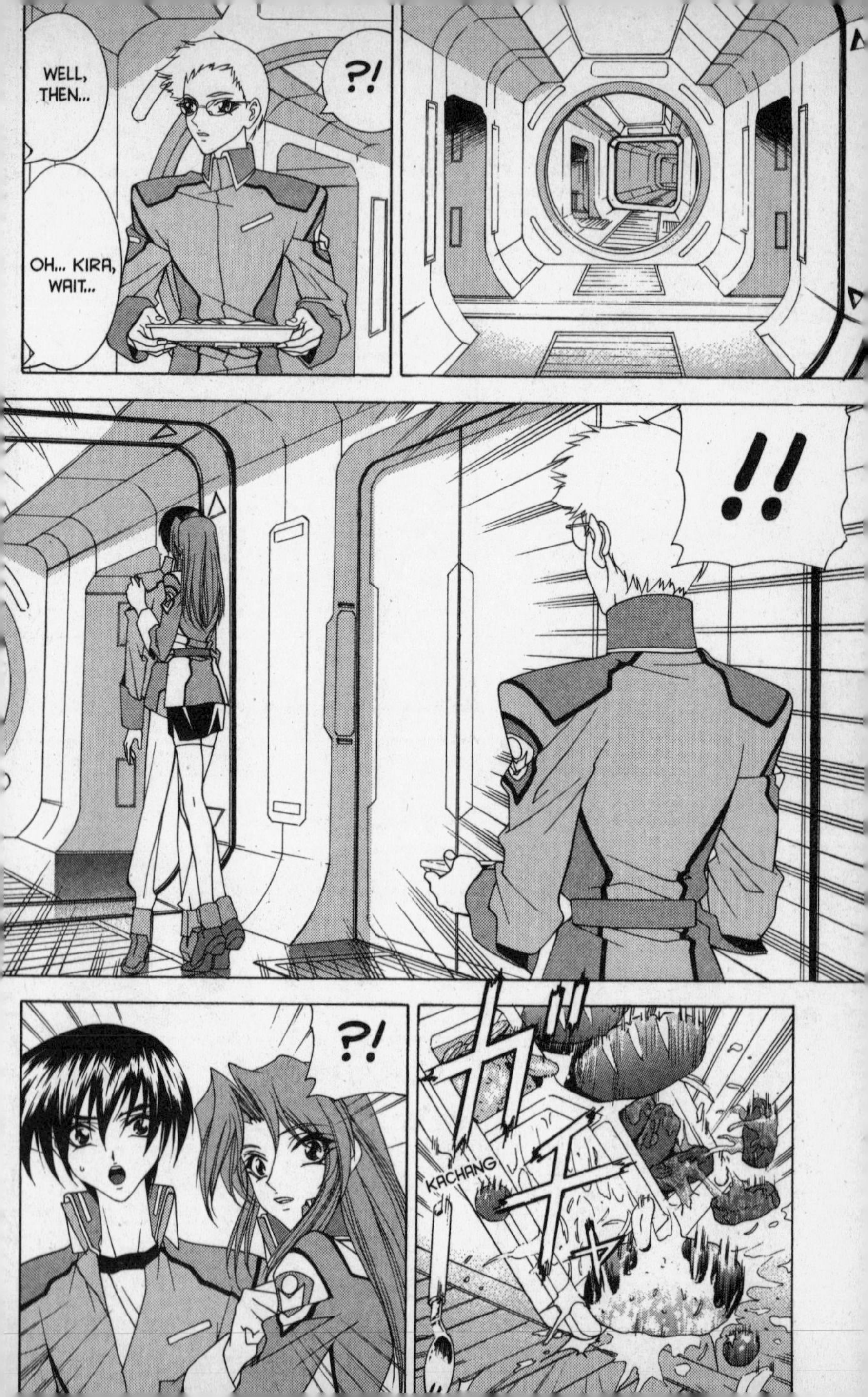
?!
WELL, THEN...
OH... KIRA, WAIT...
!!
KACHANG
?!

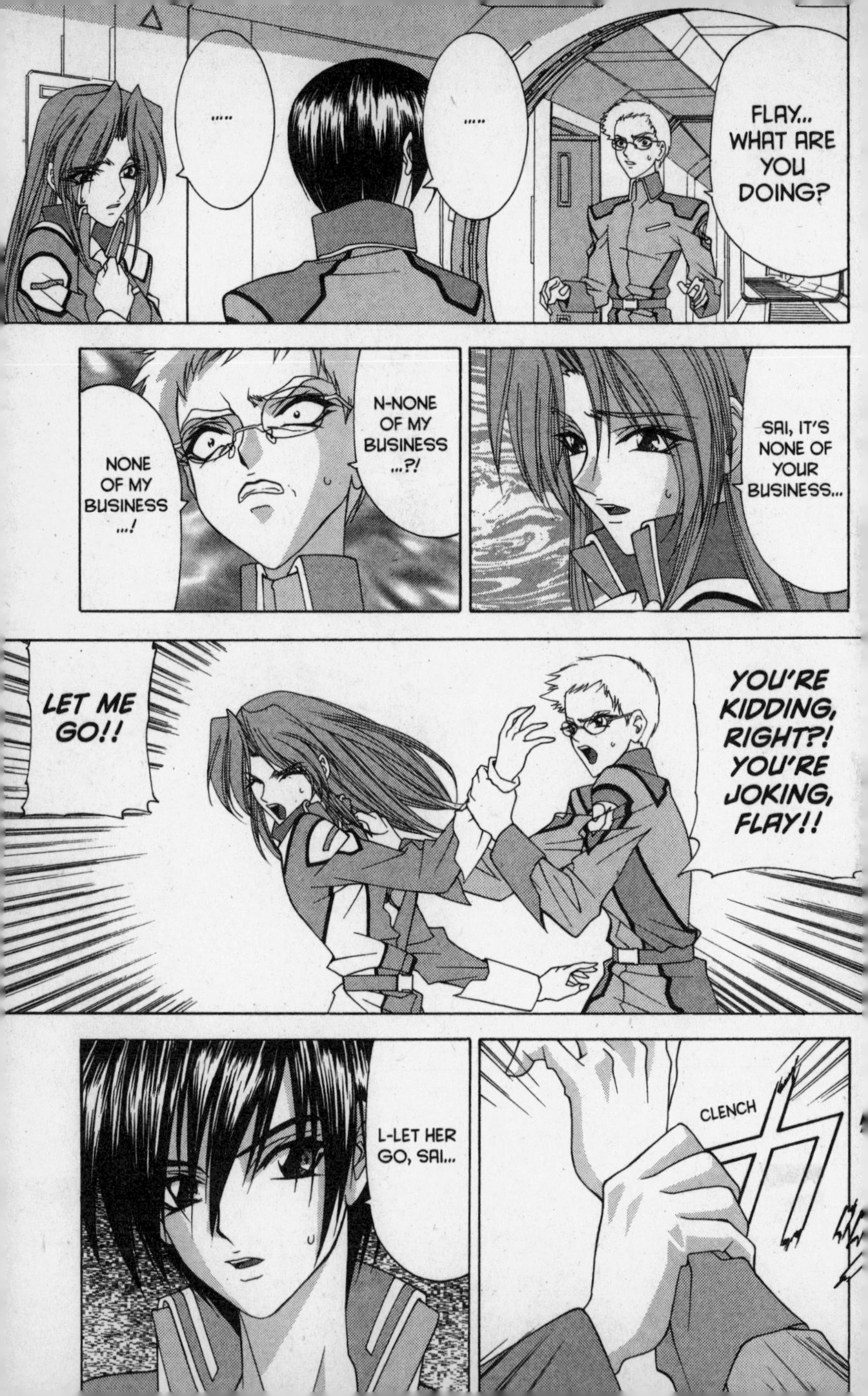
FLAY... WHAT ARE YOU DOING?
.....
.....
SAI, IT'S NONE OF YOUR BUSINESS...
N-NONE OF MY BUSINESS ...?!
NONE OF MY BUSINESS ...!
YOU'RE KIDDING, RIGHT?! YOU'RE JOKING, FLAY!!
LET ME GO!!
CLENCH
L-LET HER GO, SAI...

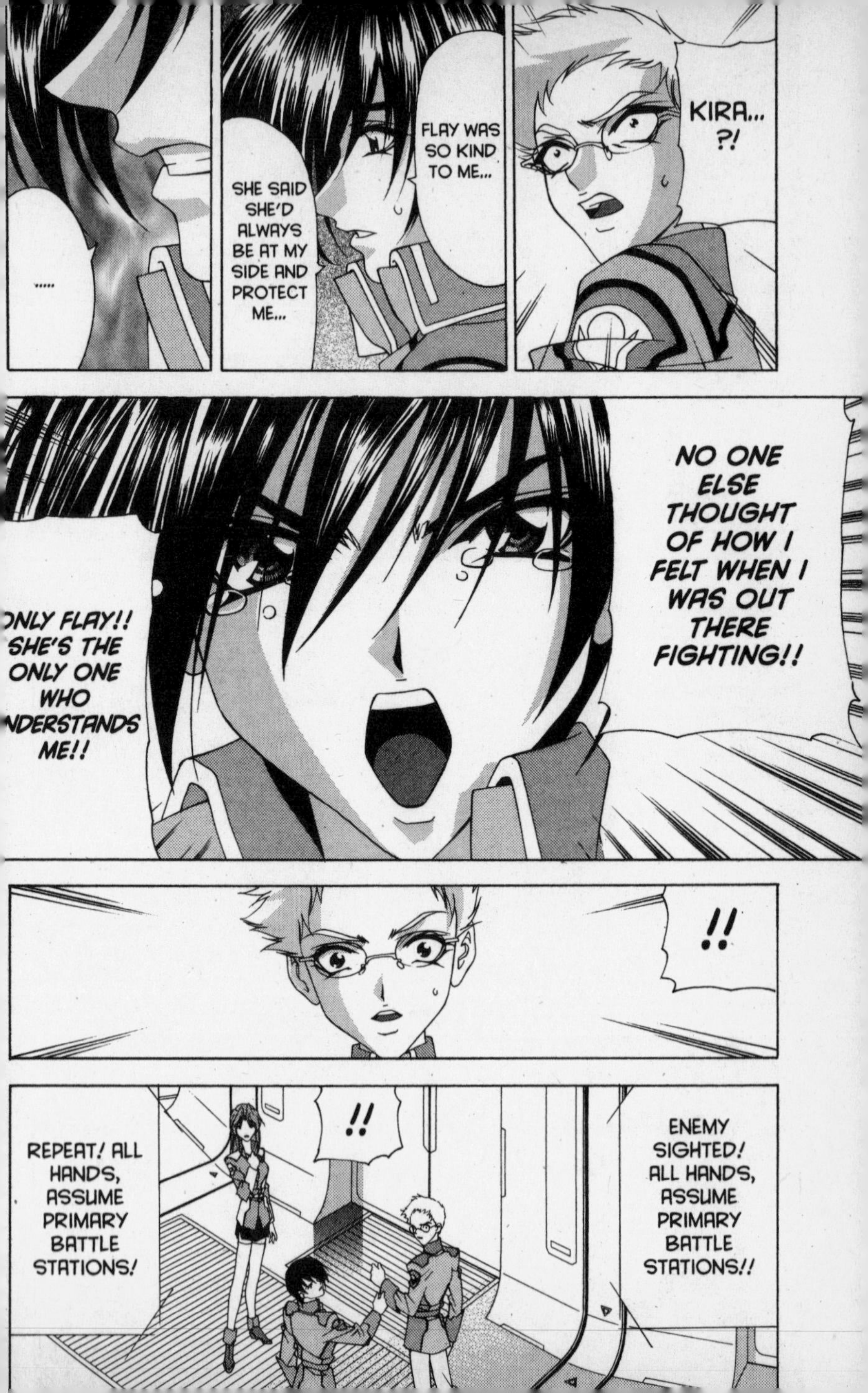
KIRA... ?!
FLAY WAS SO KIND TO ME...
SHE SAID SHE'D ALWAYS BE AT MY SIDE AND PROTECT ME...
......
NO ONE ELSE THOUGHT OF HOW I FELT WHEN I WAS OUT THERE FIGHTING!!
ONLY FLAY!! SHE'S THE ONLY ONE WHO NDERSTANDS ME!!
!!
ENEMY SIGHTED! ALL HANDS, ASSUME PRIMARY BATTLE STATIONS!!
!!
REPEAT! ALL HANDS, ASSUME PRIMARY BATTLE STATIONS!

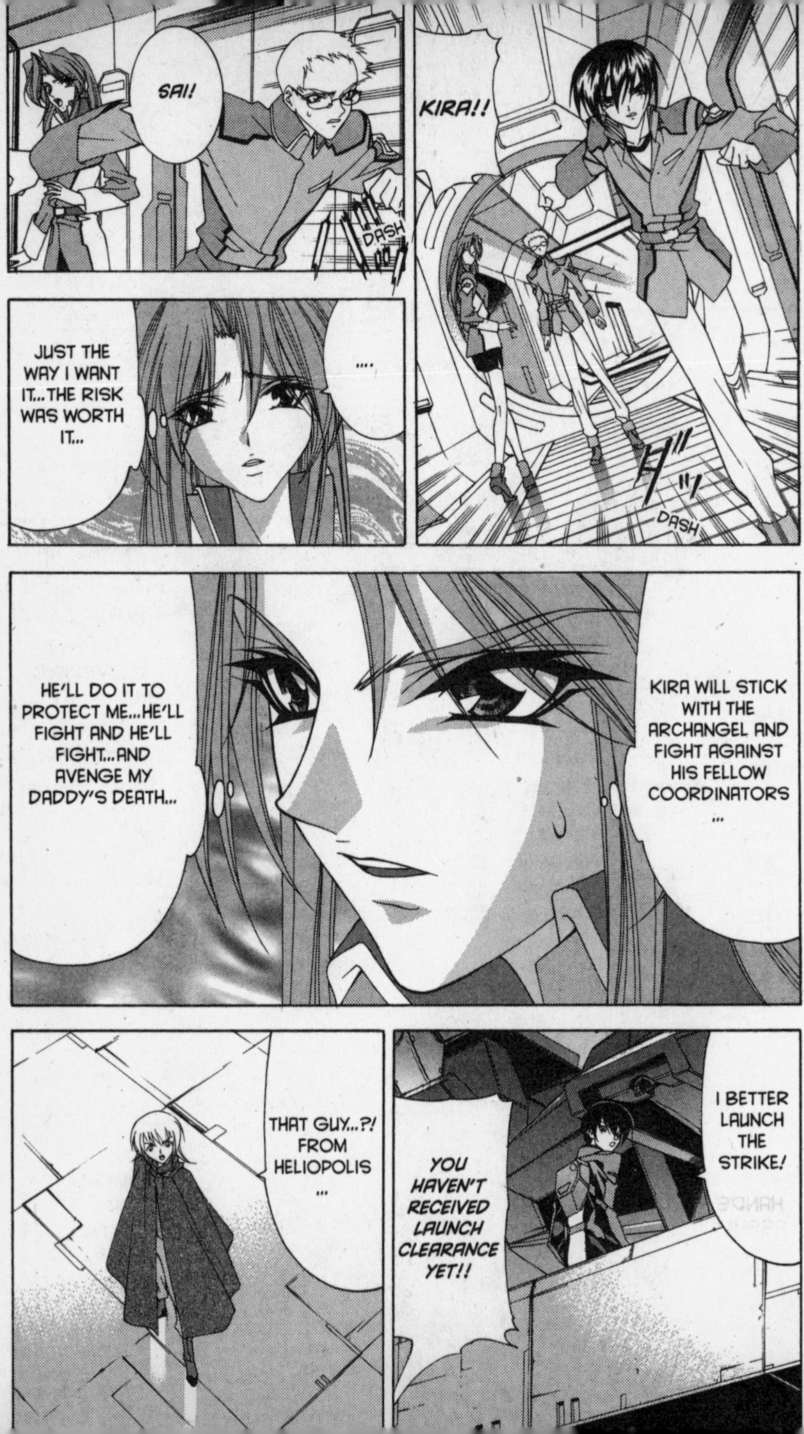
KIRA!!
DASH
SAI!
DASH
....
JUST THE WAY I WANT IT...THE RISK WAS WORTH IT...
KIRA WILL STICK WITH THE ARCHANGEL AND FIGHT AGAINST HIS FELLOW COORDINATORS ...
HE'LL DO IT TO PROTECT ME...HE'LL FIGHT AND HE'LL FIGHT...AND AVENGE MY DADDY'S DEATH...
I BETTER LAUNCH THE STRIKE!
YOU HAVEN'T RECEIVED LAUNCH CLEARANCE YET!!
THAT GUY...?! FROM HELIOPOLIS ...

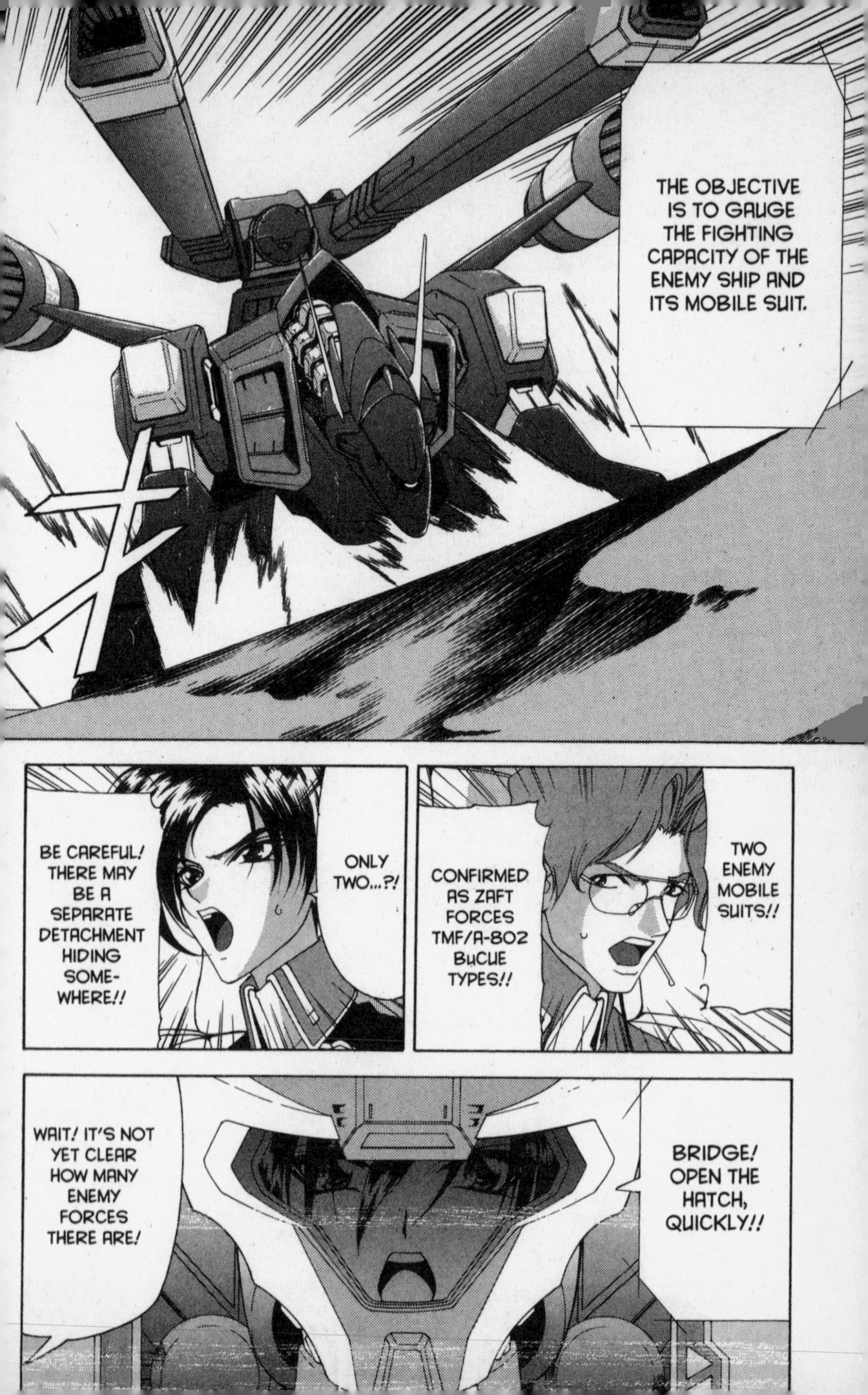
THE OBJECTIVE IS TO GAUGE THE FIGHTING CAPACITY OF THE ENEMY SHIP AND ITS MOBILE SUIT.
TWO ENEMY MOBILE SUITS!!
CONFIRMED AS ZAFT FORCES TMF/A-802 BuCUE TYPES!!
ONLY TWO...?!
BE CAREFUL! THERE MAY BE A SEPARATE DETACHMENT HIDING SOME-WHERE!!
BRIDGE! OPEN THE HATCH, QUICKLY!!
WAIT! IT'S NOT YET CLEAR HOW MANY ENEMY FORCES THERE ARE!

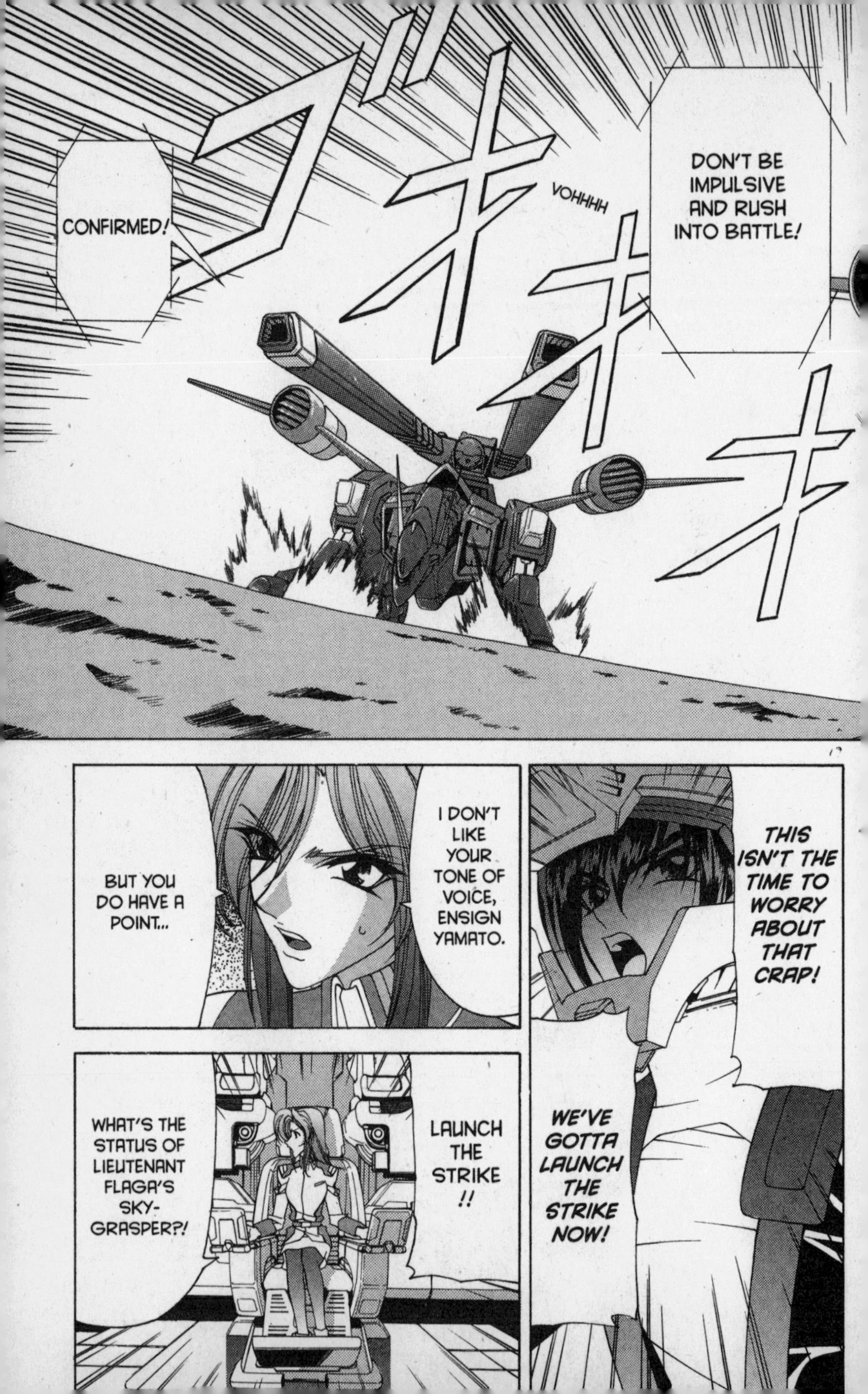
DON'T BE IMPULSIVE AND RUSH INTO BATTLE!
VOHHHH
CONFIRMED!
THIS ISN'T THE TIME TO WORRY ABOUT THAT CRAP!
WE'VE GOTTA LAUNCH THE STRIKE NOW!
I DON'T LIKE YOUR TONE OF VOICE, ENSIGN YAMATO.
BUT YOU DO HAVE A POINT...
LAUNCH THE STRIKE!!
WHAT'S THE STATUS OF LIEUTENANT FLAGA'S SKY-GRASPER?!

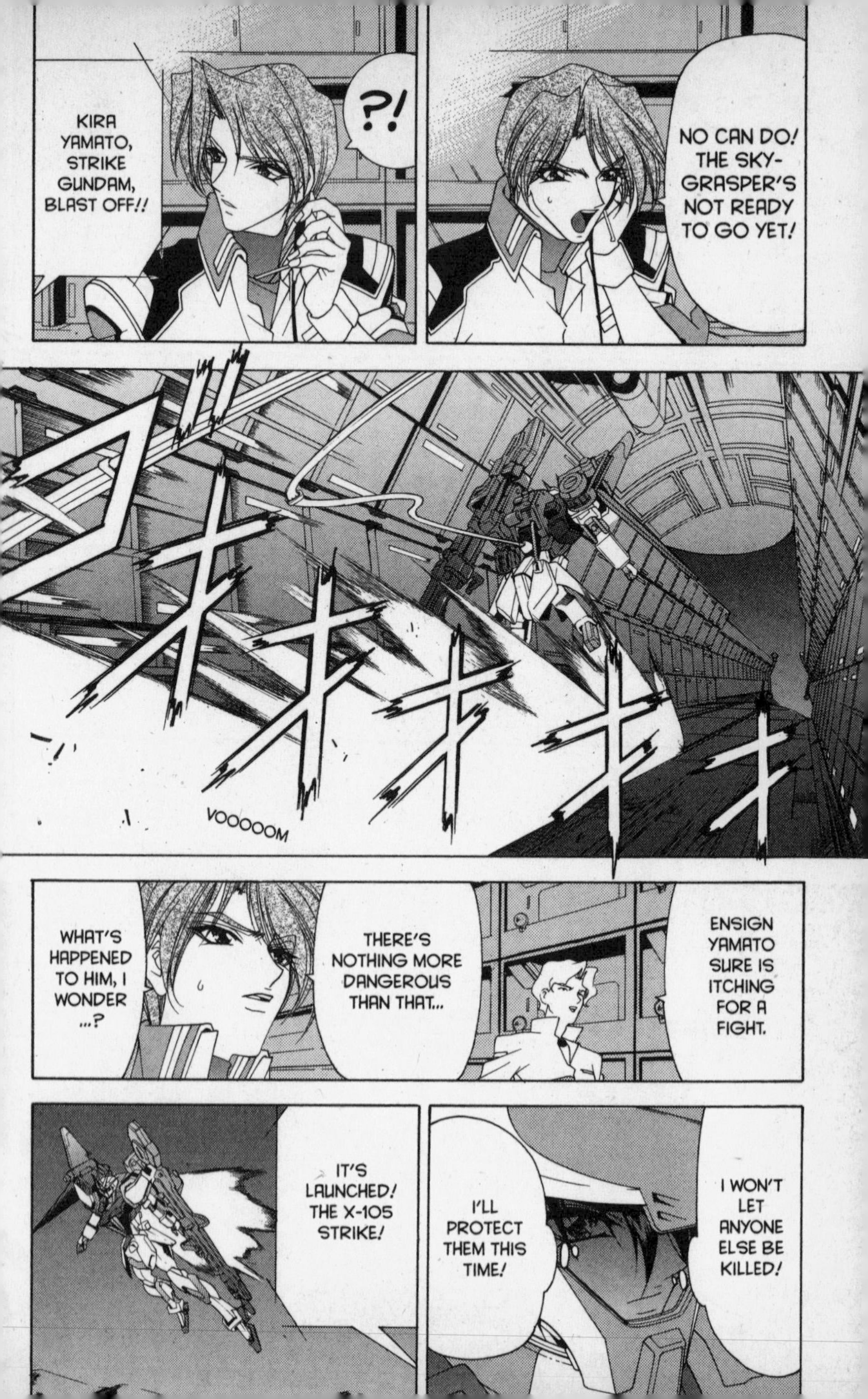
NO CAN DO! THE SKY-GRASPER'S NOT READY TO GO YET!
?!
KIRA YAMATO, STRIKE GUNDAM, BLAST OFF!!
VOOOOOM
ENSIGN YAMATO SURE IS ITCHING FOR A FIGHT.
THERE'S NOTHING MORE DANGEROUS THAN THAT...
WHAT'S HAPPENED TO HIM, I WONDER ...?
I WON'T LET ANYONE ELSE BE KILLED!
I'LL PROTECT THEM THIS TIME!
IT'S LAUNCHED! THE X-105 STRIKE!

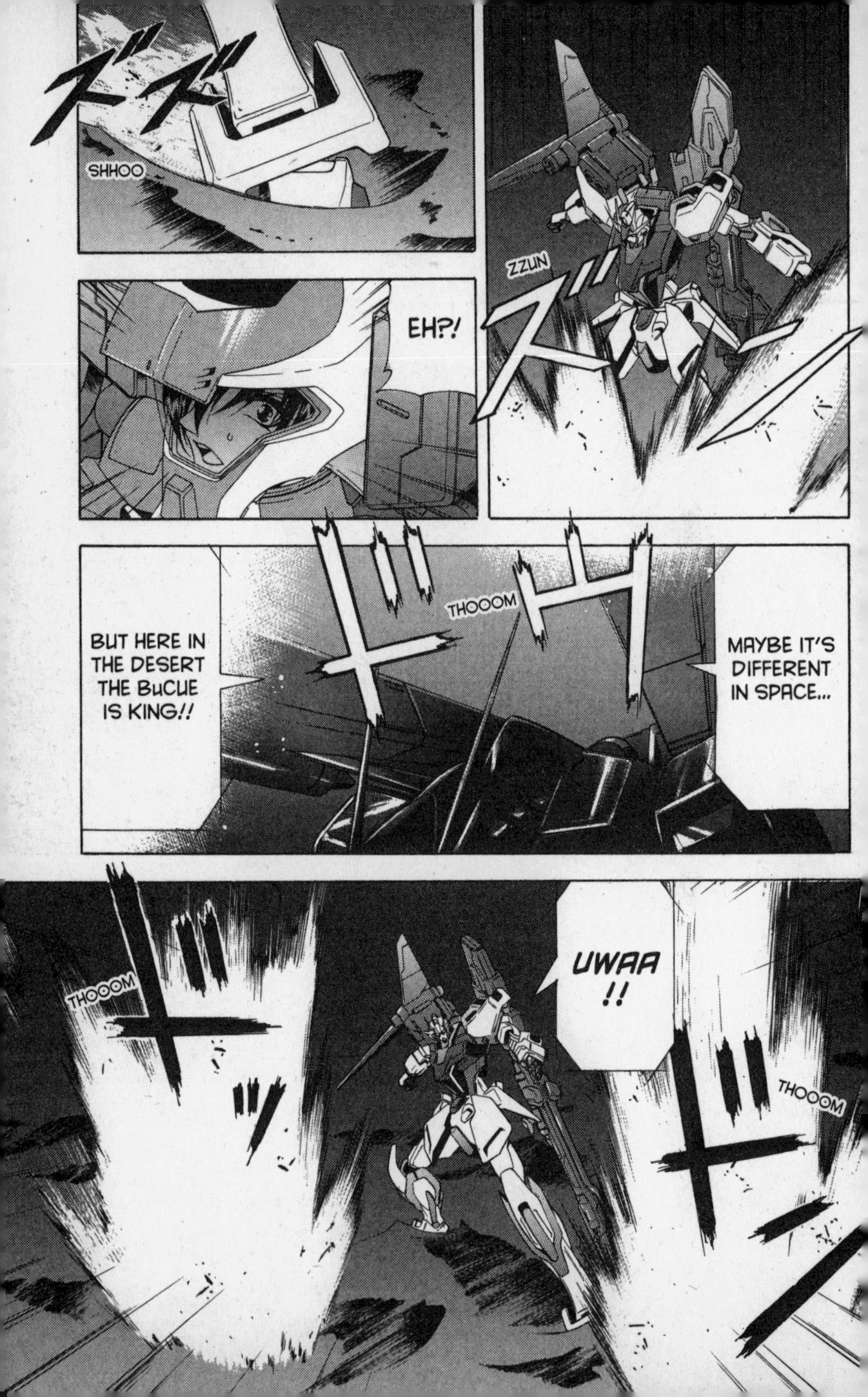
ZZUN
SHHOO
EH?!
MAYBE IT'S DIFFERENT IN SPACE...
THOOOM
BUT HERE IN THE DESERT THE BuCUE IS KING!!
UWAA!!
THOOOM
THOOOM

OH NO! I'M SINKING...

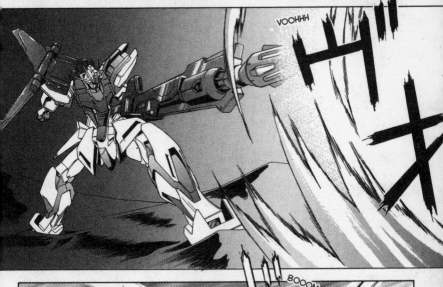

VOOHHH

BOOOM

ZZOOM

WHERE'S HE AIMING?!

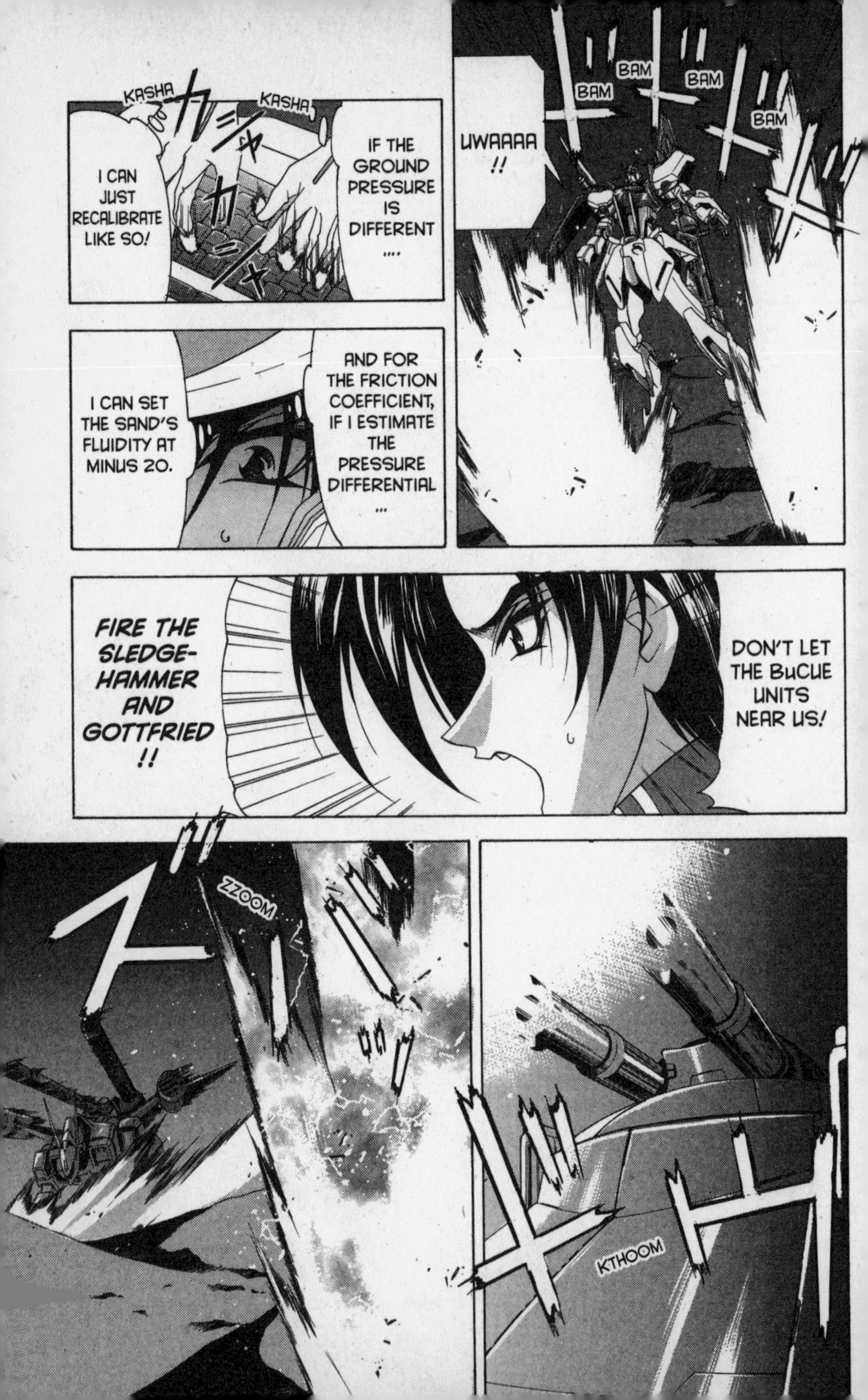
BAM
BAM
BAM
BAM
UWAAAA!!
KASHA
IF THE GROUND PRESSURE IS DIFFERENT....
KASHA
I CAN JUST RECALIBRATE LIKE SO!
AND FOR THE FRICTION COEFFICIENT, IF I ESTIMATE THE PRESSURE DIFFERENTIAL...
I CAN SET THE SAND'S FLUIDITY AT MINUS 20.
DON'T LET THE BuCUE UNITS NEAR US!
FIRE THE SLEDGE-HAMMER AND GOTTFRIED!!
KTHOOM
ZZOOM

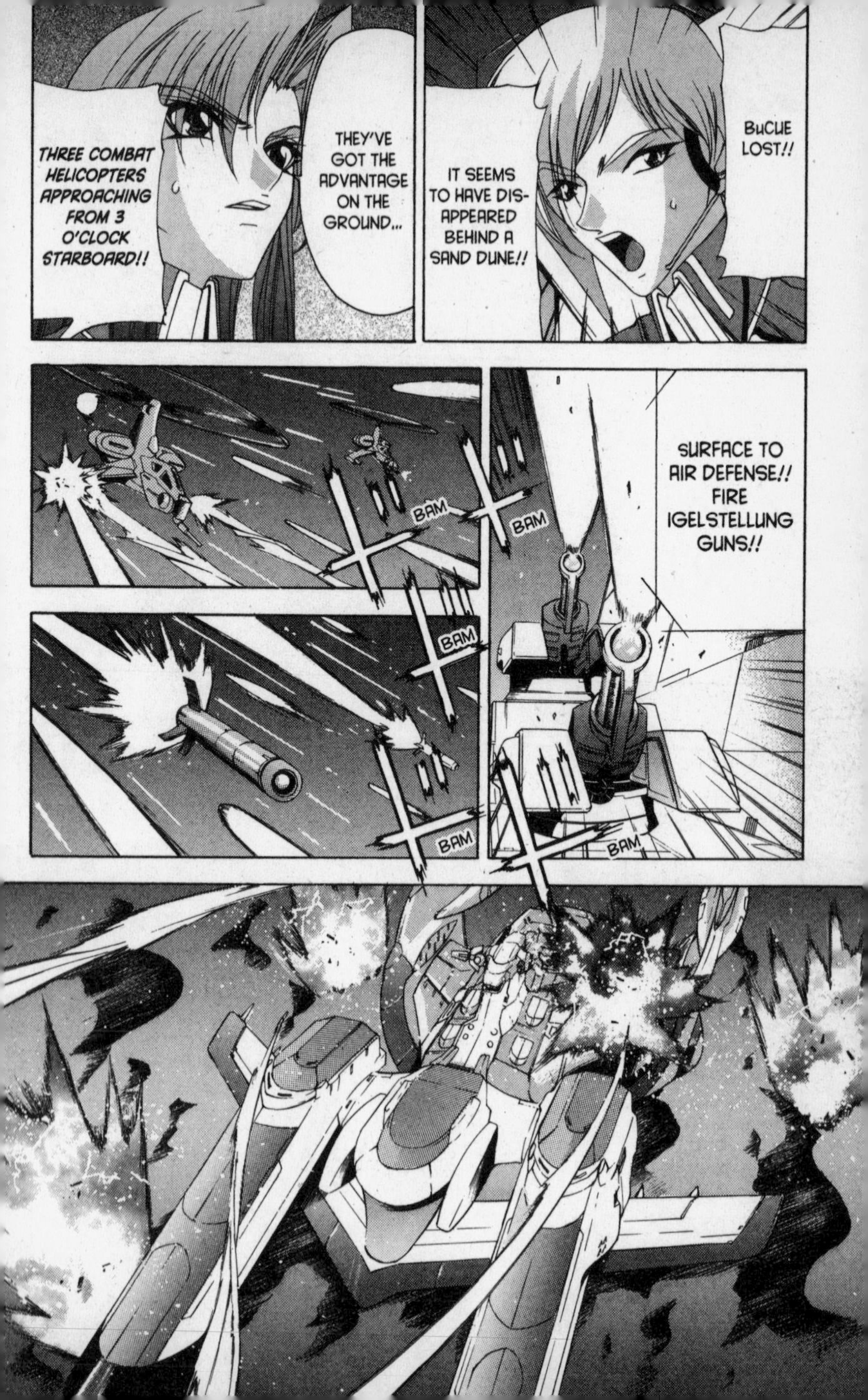
BuCUE LOST!!
IT SEEMS TO HAVE DIS-APPEARED BEHIND A SAND DUNE!!
THEY'VE GOT THE ADVANTAGE ON THE GROUND...
THREE COMBAT HELICOPTERS APPROACHING FROM 3 O'CLOCK STARBOARD!!
SURFACE TO AIR DEFENSE!! FIRE IGELSTELLUNG GUNS!!
BAM
BAM
BAM
BAM
BAM
BAM

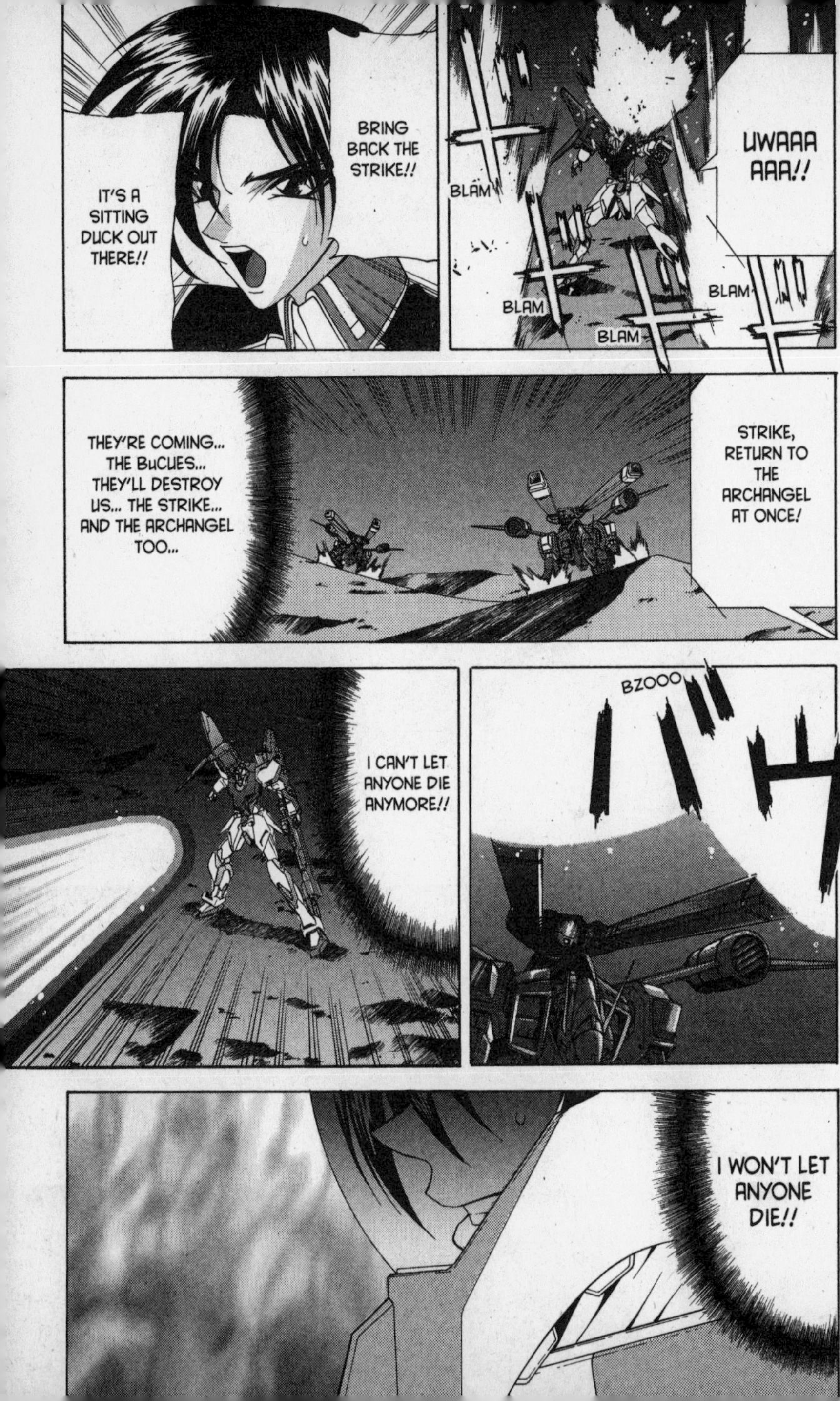
UWAAA AAA!!
BLAM
BLAM
BLAM
BLAM
BRING BACK THE STRIKE!!
IT'S A SITTING DUCK OUT THERE!!
STRIKE, RETURN TO THE ARCHANGEL AT ONCE!
THEY'RE COMING... THE BuCUES... THEY'LL DESTROY US... THE STRIKE... AND THE ARCHANGEL TOO...
BZOOO
I CAN'T LET ANYONE DIE ANYMORE!!
I WON'T LET ANYONE DIE!!

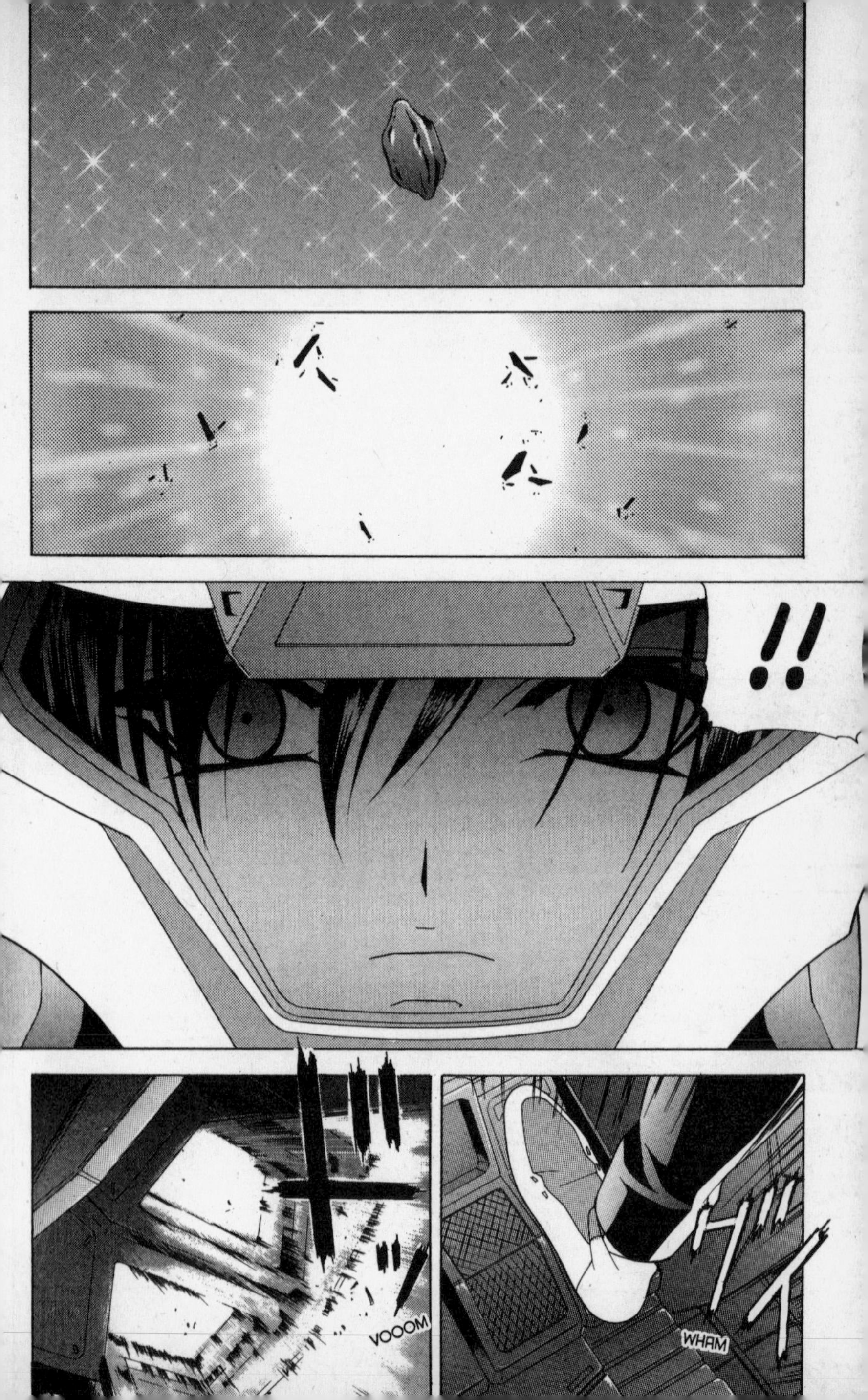
!!
WHAM
VOOOM

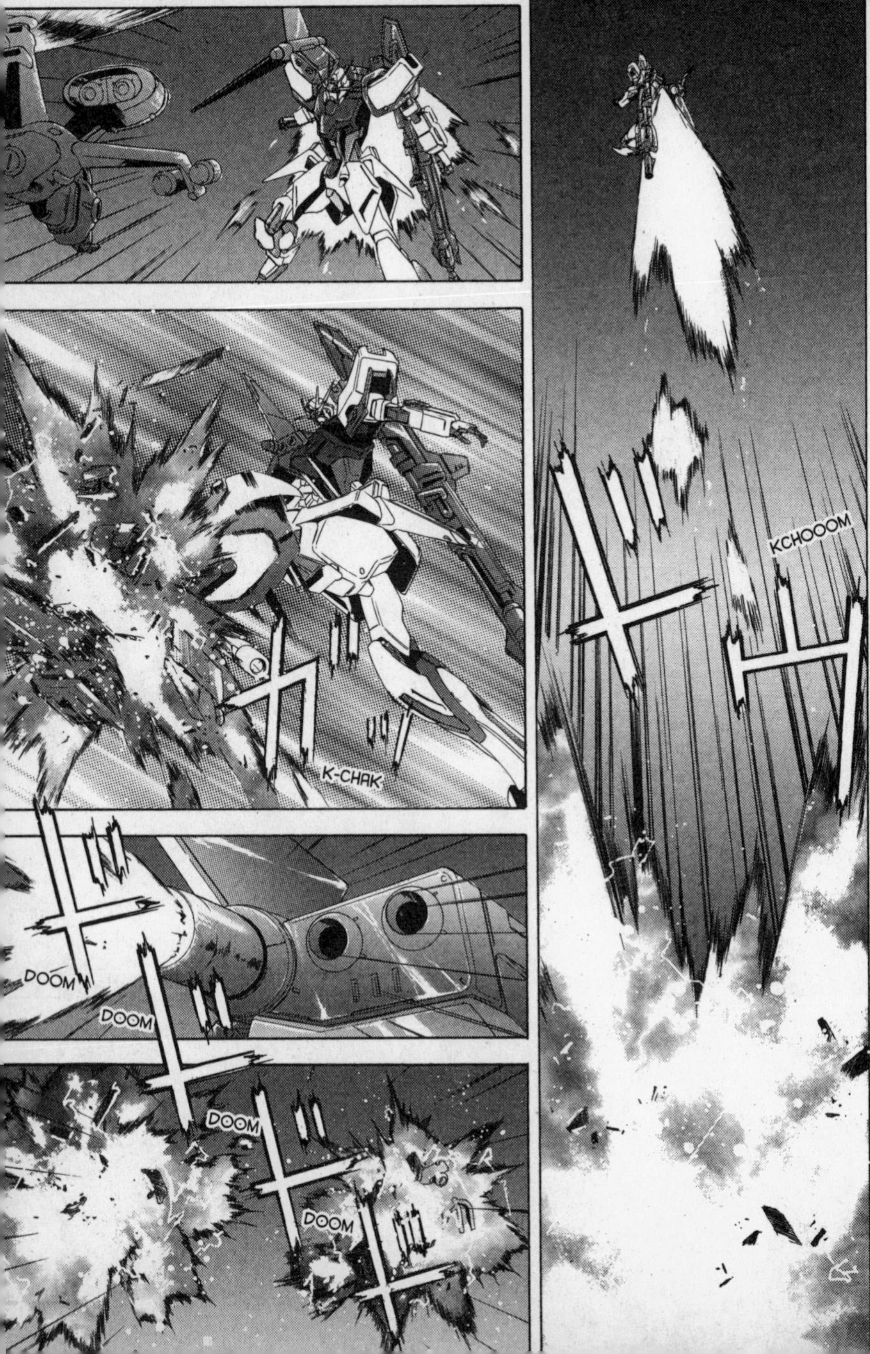
KCHOOOM
K-CHAK
DOOM
DOOM
DOOM
DOOM

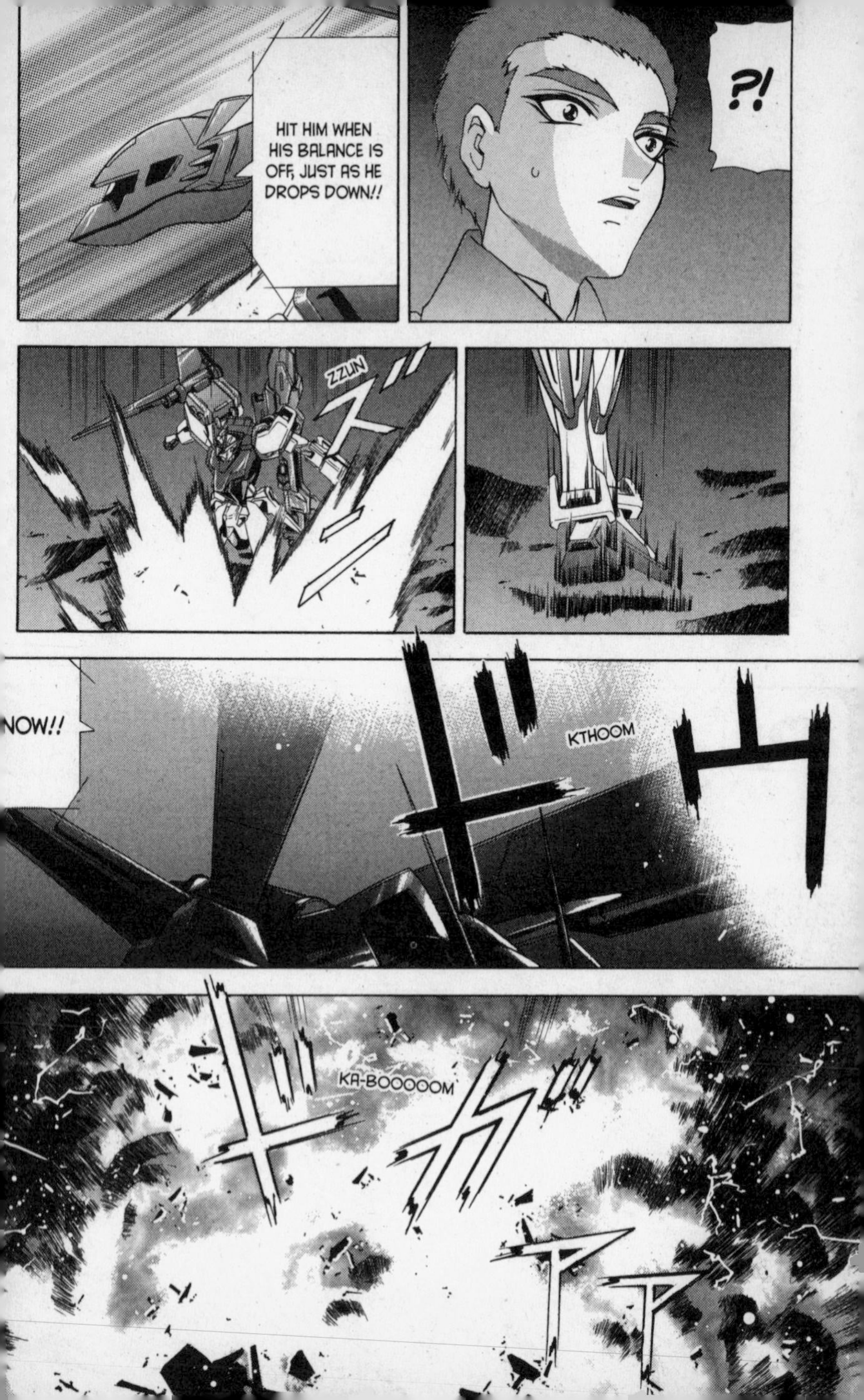
?!
HIT HIM WHEN HIS BALANCE IS OFF, JUST AS HE DROPS DOWN!!
ZZUN
NOW!!
KTHOOM
KA-BOOOOOM

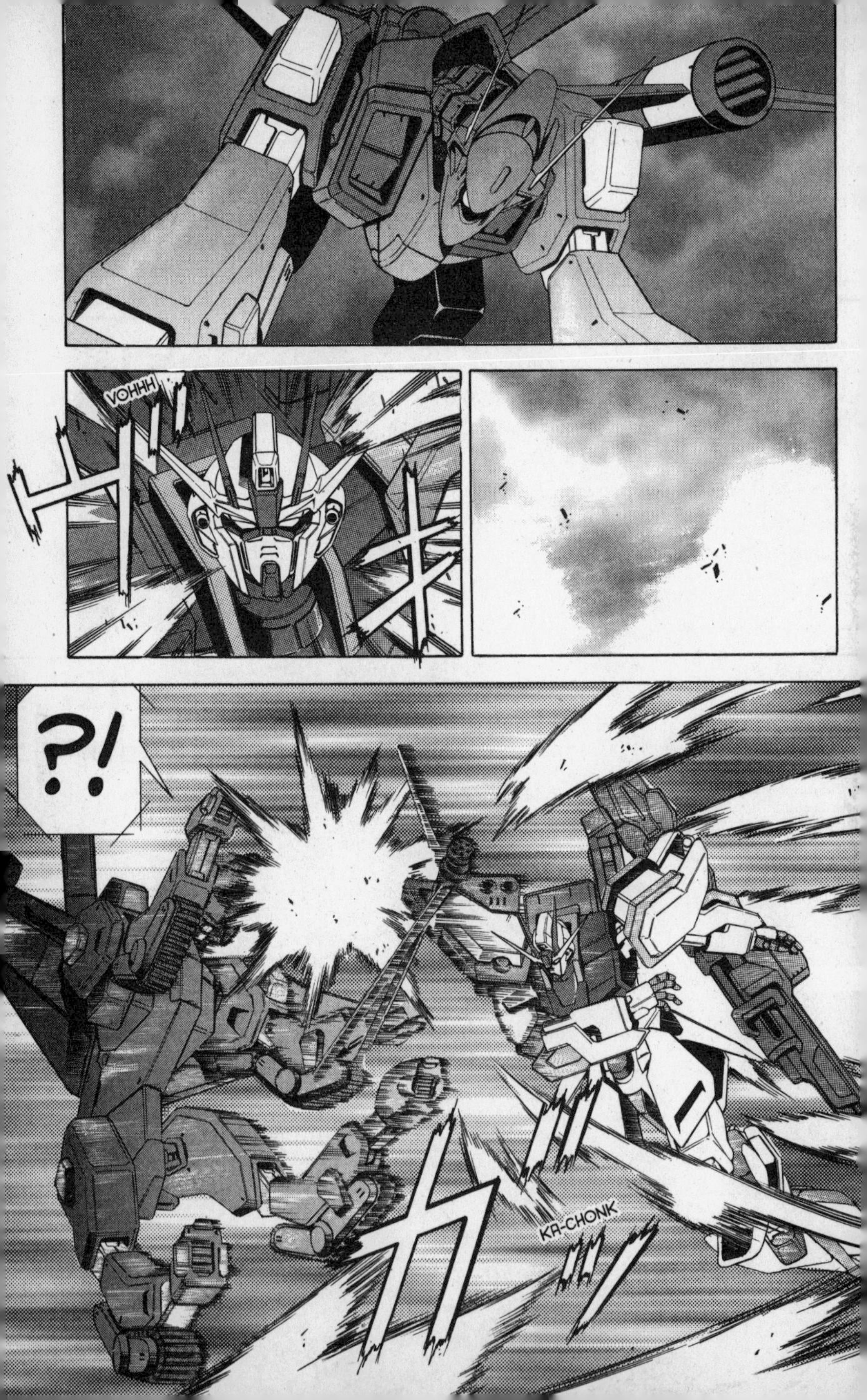
VOHHH
?!
KA-CHONK

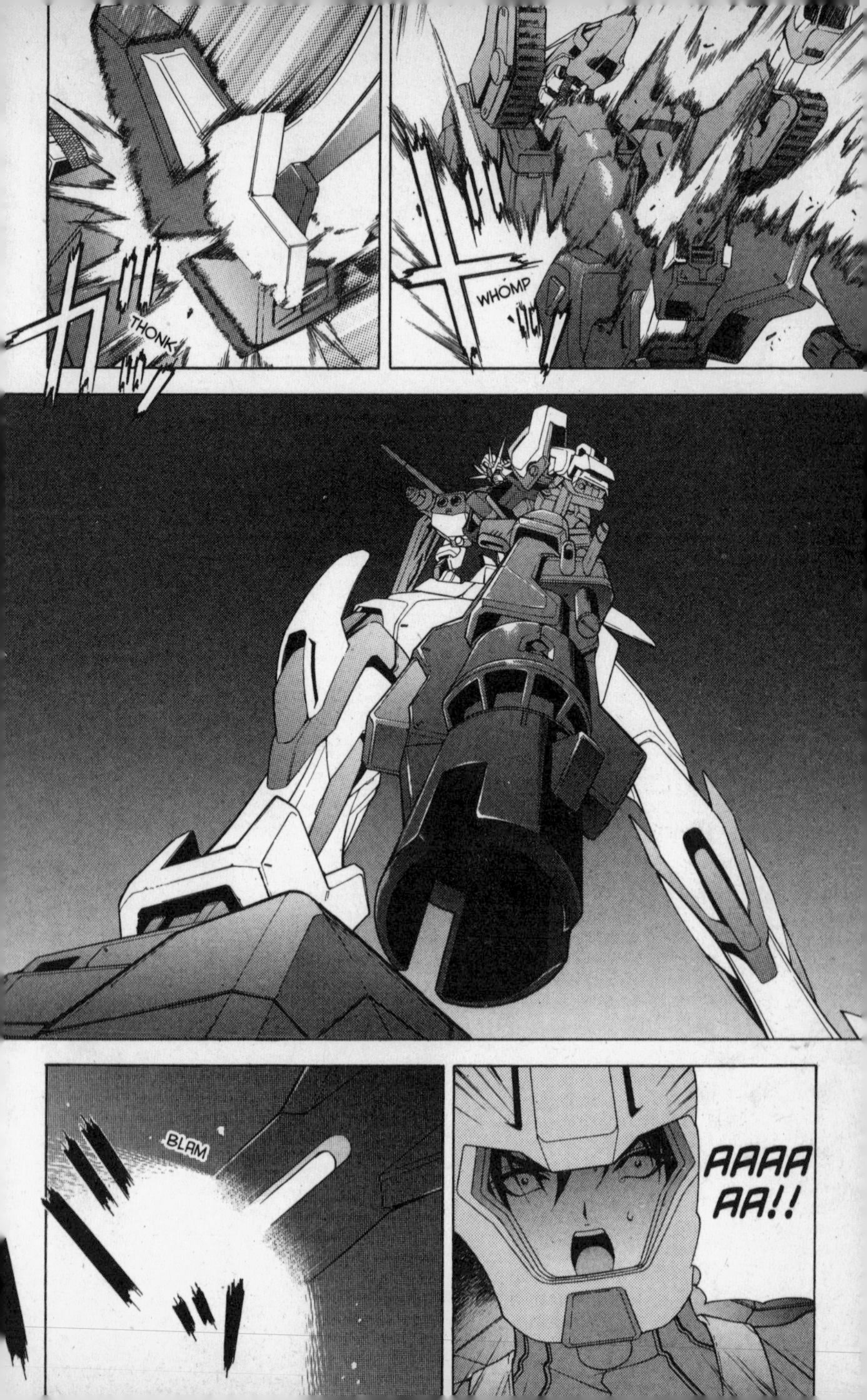
WHOMP
THONK
AAAA
AA!!
BLAM

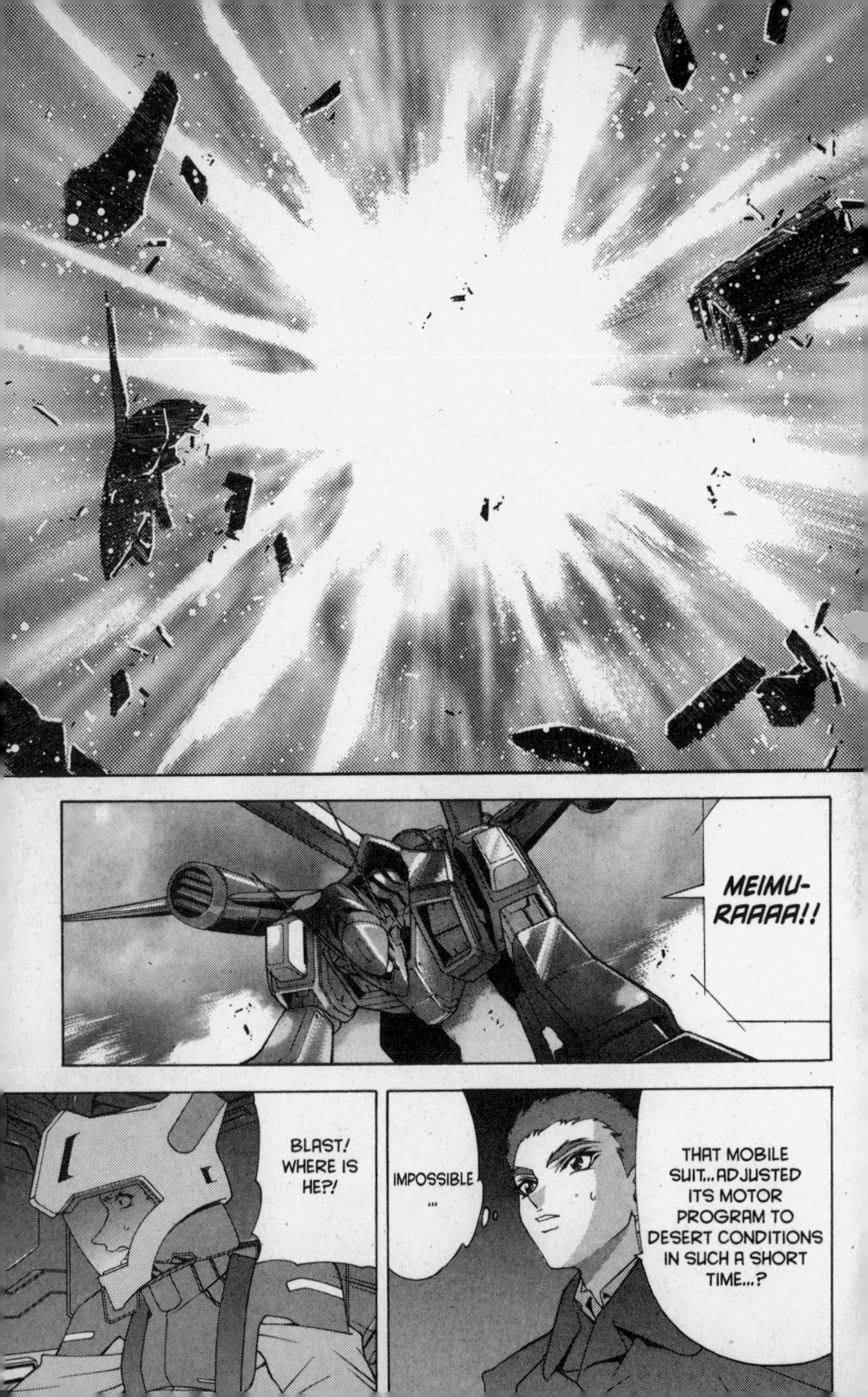
MEIMU-RAAAAA!!
THAT MOBILE SUIT...ADJUSTED ITS MOTOR PROGRAM TO DESERT CONDITIONS IN SUCH A SHORT TIME...?
IMPOSSIBLE ...
BLAST! WHERE IS HE?!

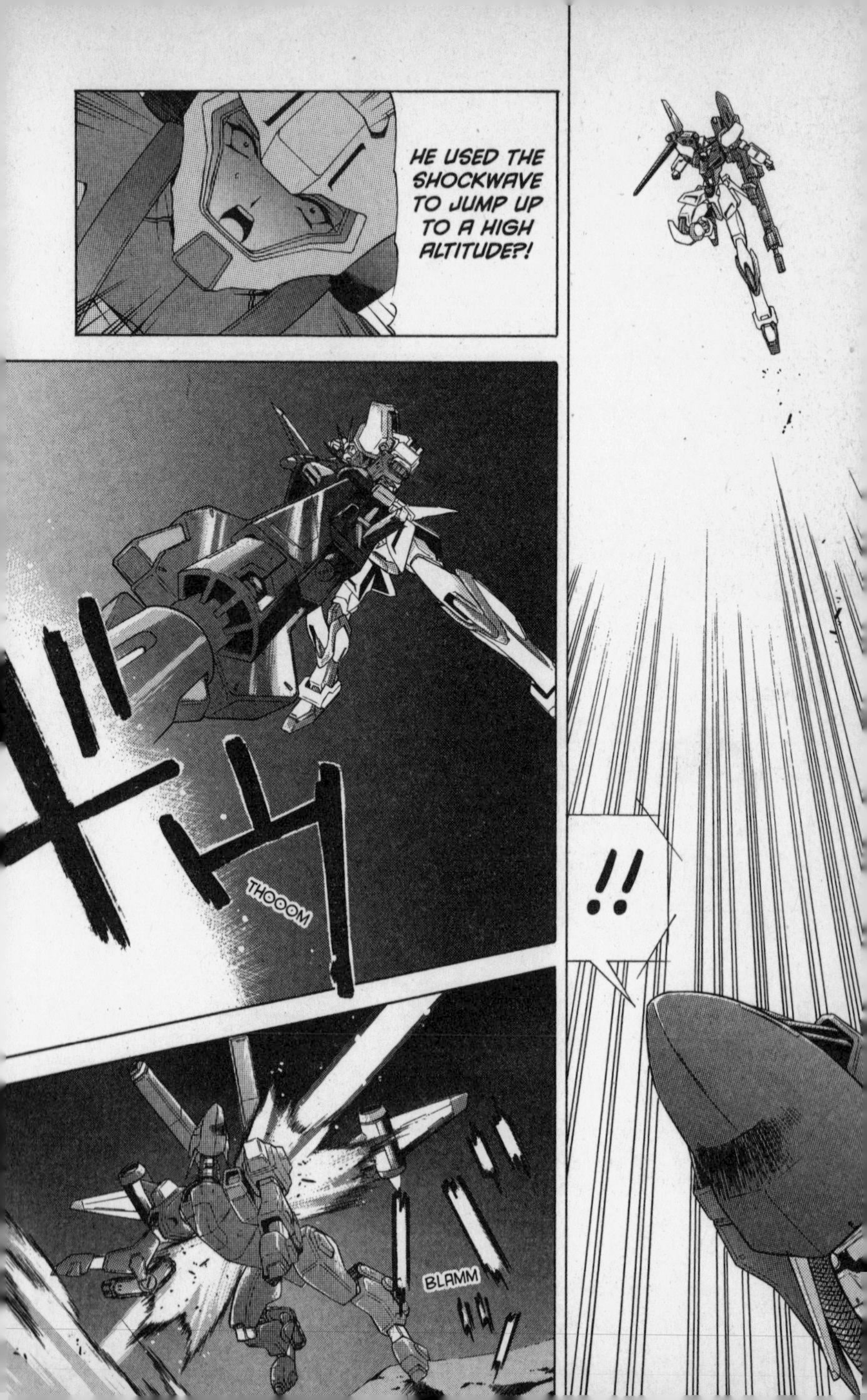
!!
HE USED THE SHOCKWAVE TO JUMP UP TO A HIGH ALTITUDE?!
THOOOM
BLAMM

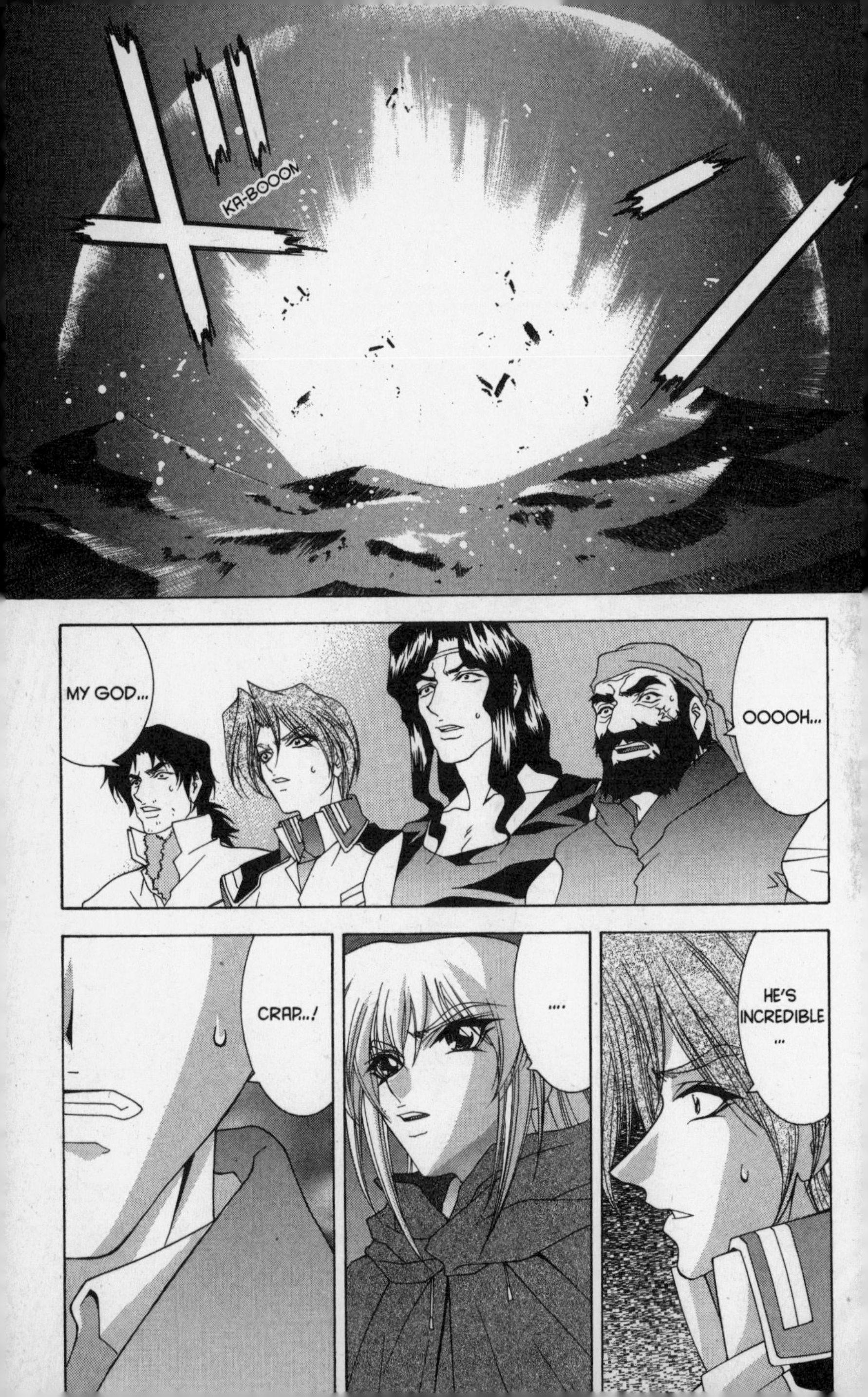
KA-BOOOM
OOOOH...
MY GOD...
HE'S INCREDIBLE ...
....
CRAP...!

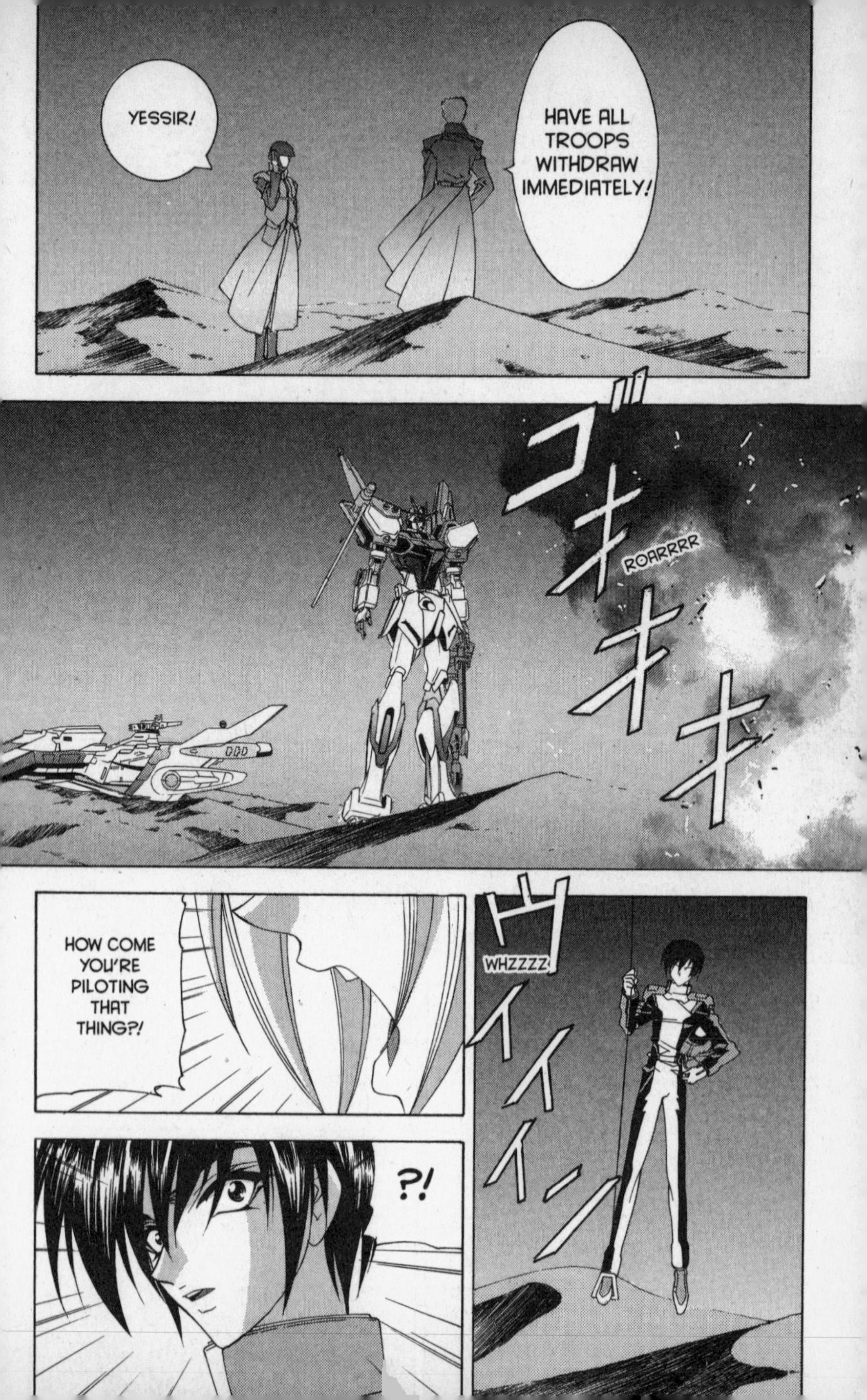
HAVE ALL TROOPS WITHDRAW IMMEDIATELY!
YESSIR!
ゴオオオ
ROARRRR
ヴィイイーン
WHZZZZ
HOW COME YOU'RE PILOTING THAT THING?!
?!

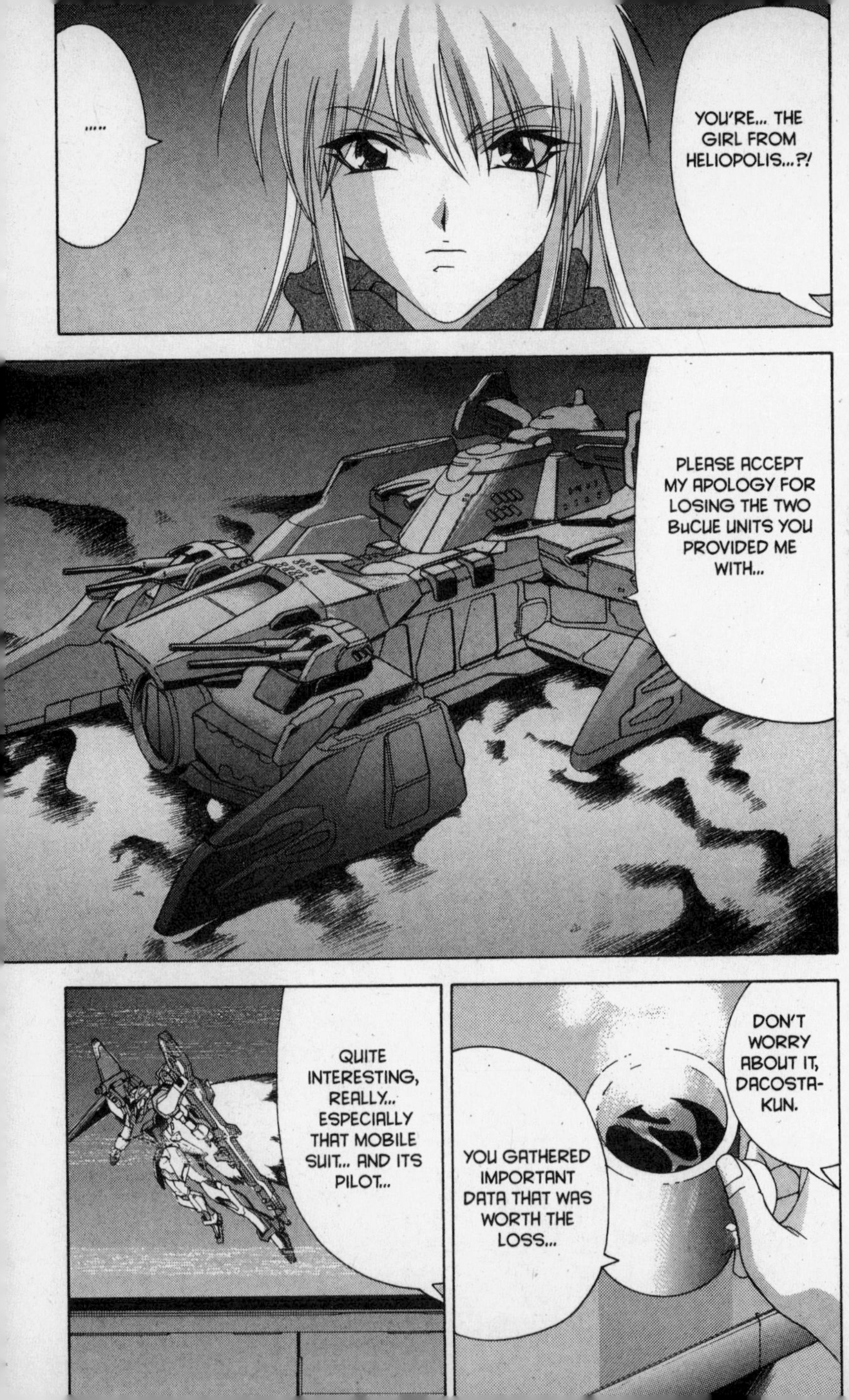
YOU'RE... THE GIRL FROM HELIOPOLIS...?!
.....
PLEASE ACCEPT MY APOLOGY FOR LOSING THE TWO BuCUE UNITS YOU PROVIDED ME WITH...
DON'T WORRY ABOUT IT, DACOSTA-KUN.
YOU GATHERED IMPORTANT DATA THAT WAS WORTH THE LOSS...
QUITE INTERESTING, REALLY... ESPECIALLY THAT MOBILE SUIT... AND ITS PILOT...

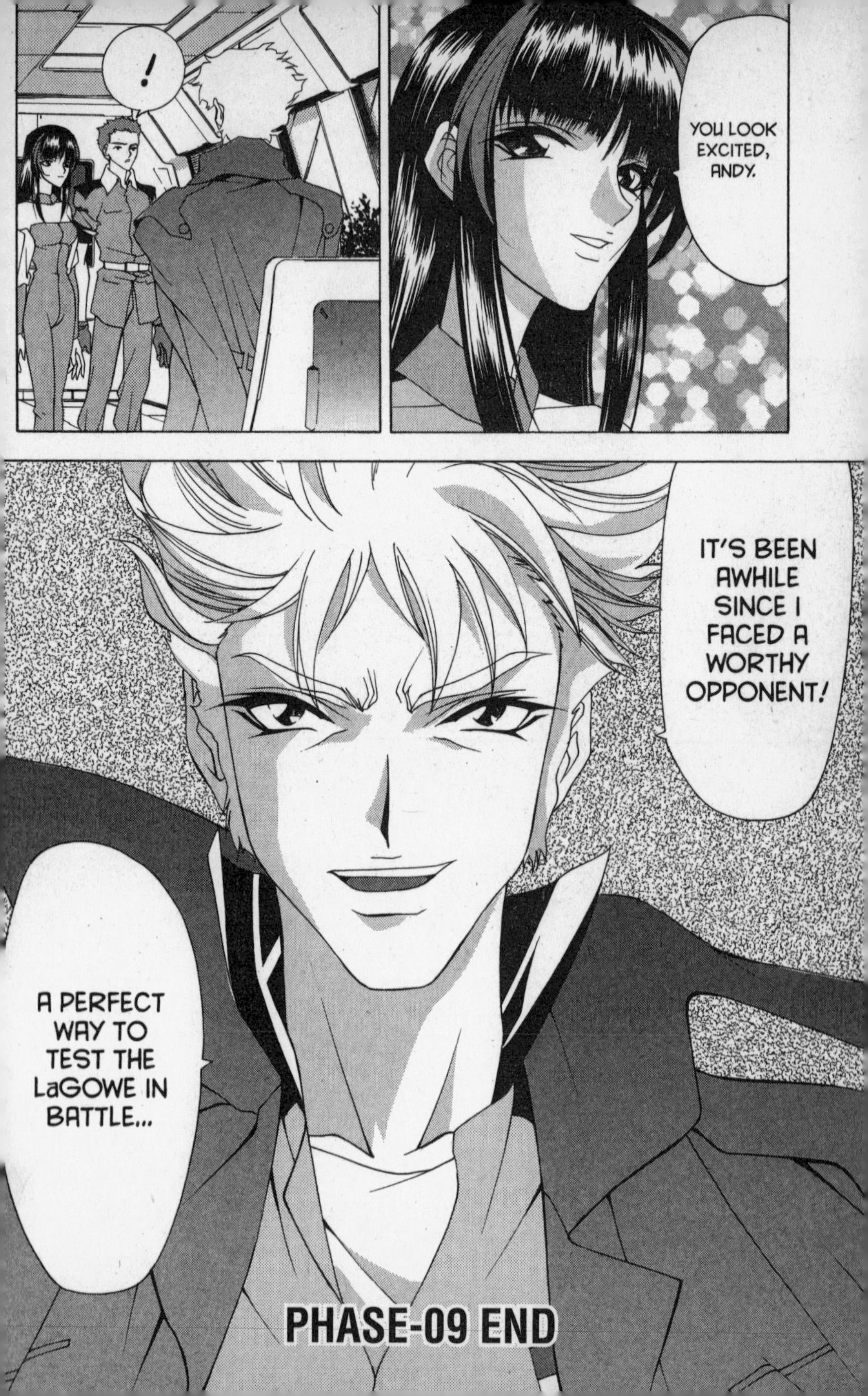
YOU LOOK EXCITED, ANDY.
!
IT'S BEEN AWHILE SINCE I FACED A WORTHY OPPONENT!
A PERFECT WAY TO TEST THE LaGOWE IN BATTLE...
PHASE-09 END

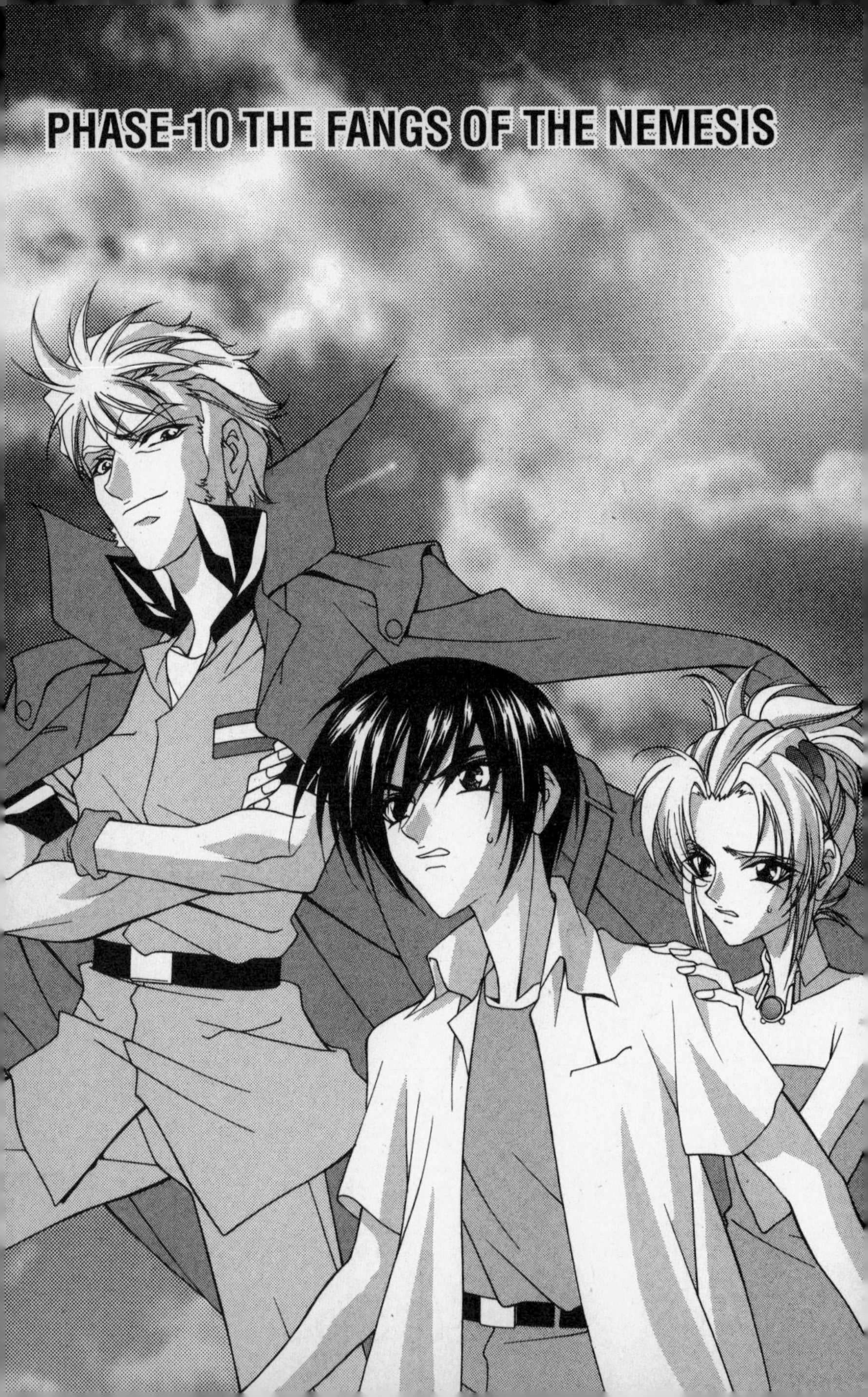
PHASE-10 THE FANGS OF THE NEMESIS

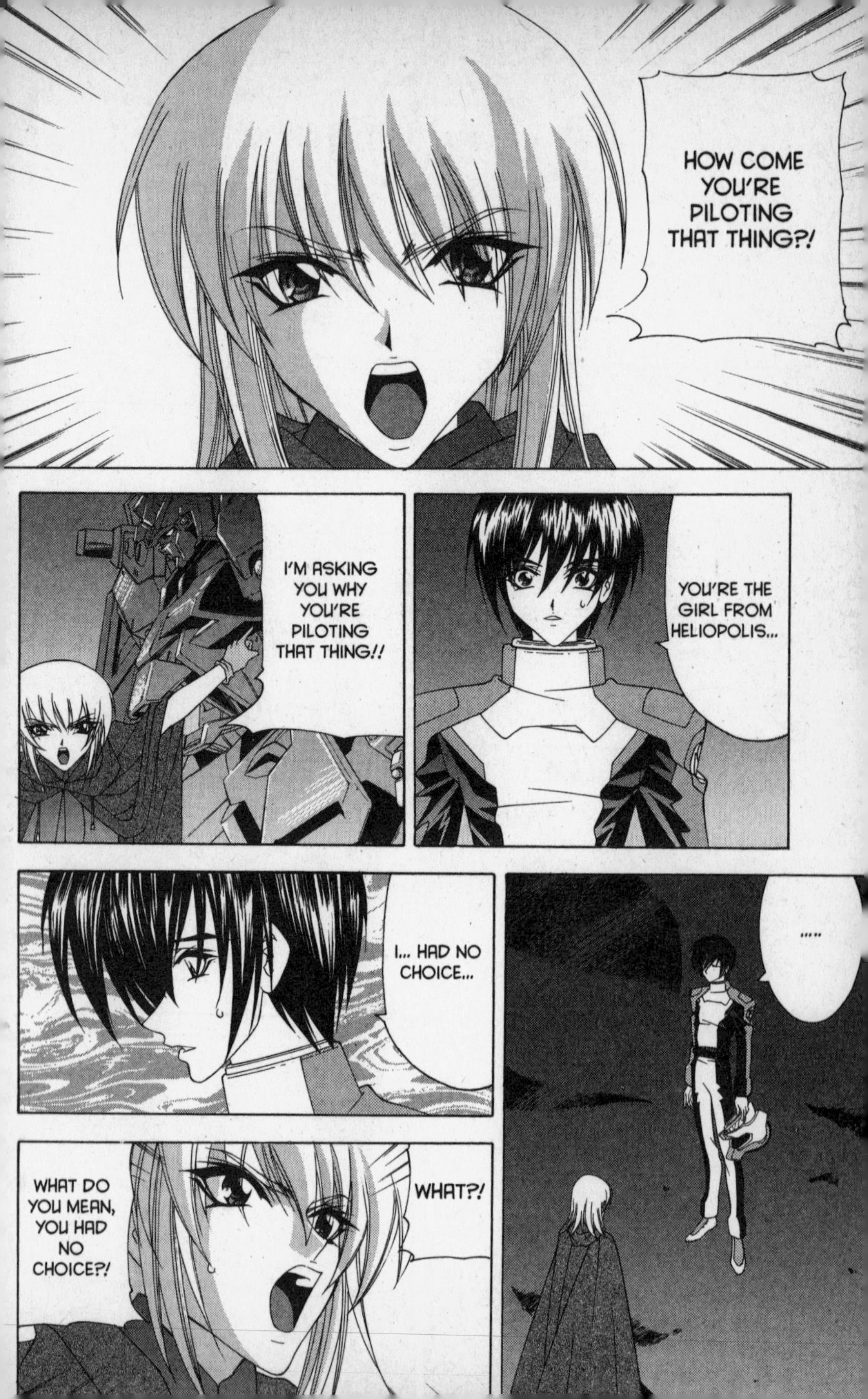
HOW COME YOU'RE PILOTING THAT THING?!
YOU'RE THE GIRL FROM HELIOPOLIS...
I'M ASKING YOU WHY YOU'RE PILOTING THAT THING!!
.....
I... HAD NO CHOICE...
WHAT?!
WHAT DO YOU MEAN, YOU HAD NO CHOICE?!

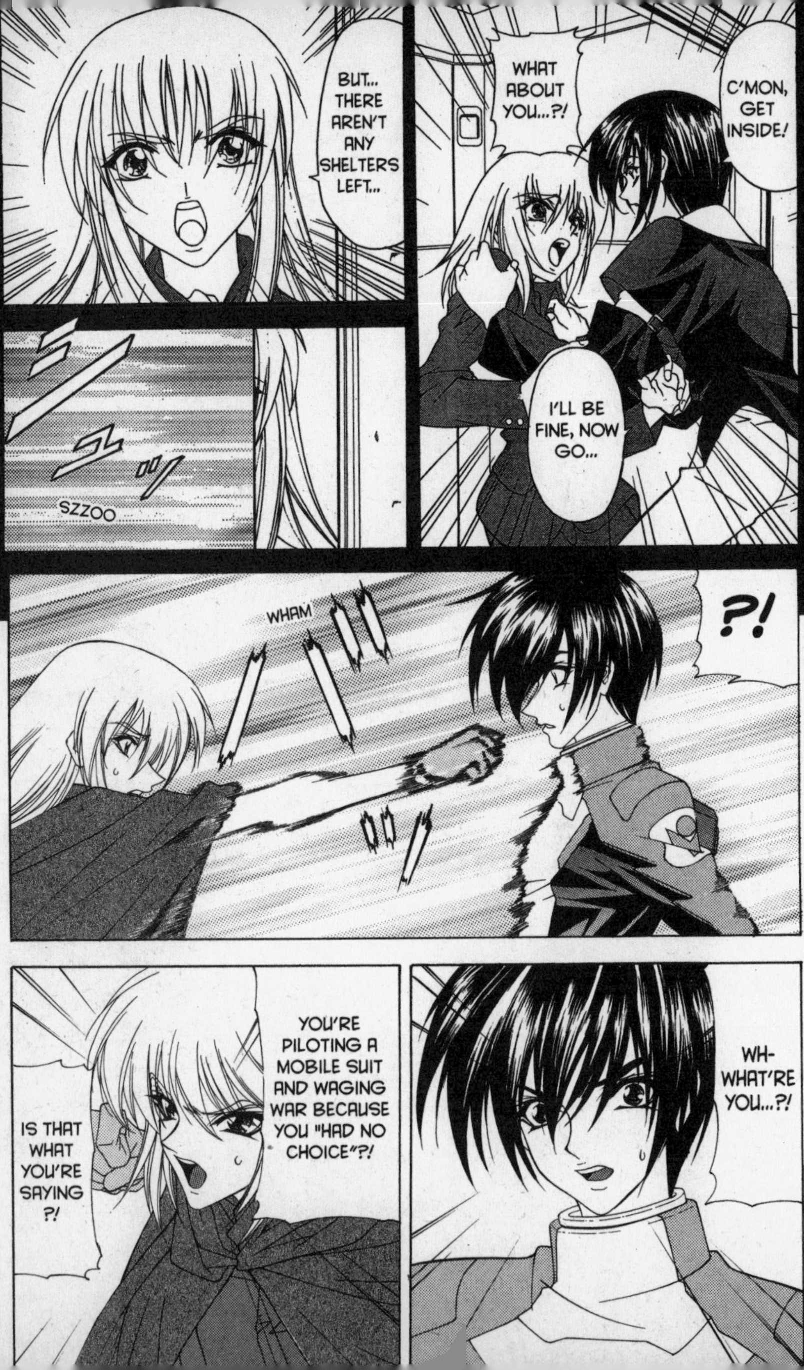
C'MON, GET INSIDE!
WHAT ABOUT YOU...?!
I'LL BE FINE, NOW GO...
BUT... THERE AREN'T ANY SHELTERS LEFT...
SZZOO
?!
WHAM
WH- WHAT'RE YOU...?!
YOU'RE PILOTING A MOBILE SUIT AND WAGING WAR BECAUSE YOU "HAD NO CHOICE"?!
IS THAT WHAT YOU'RE SAYING ?!

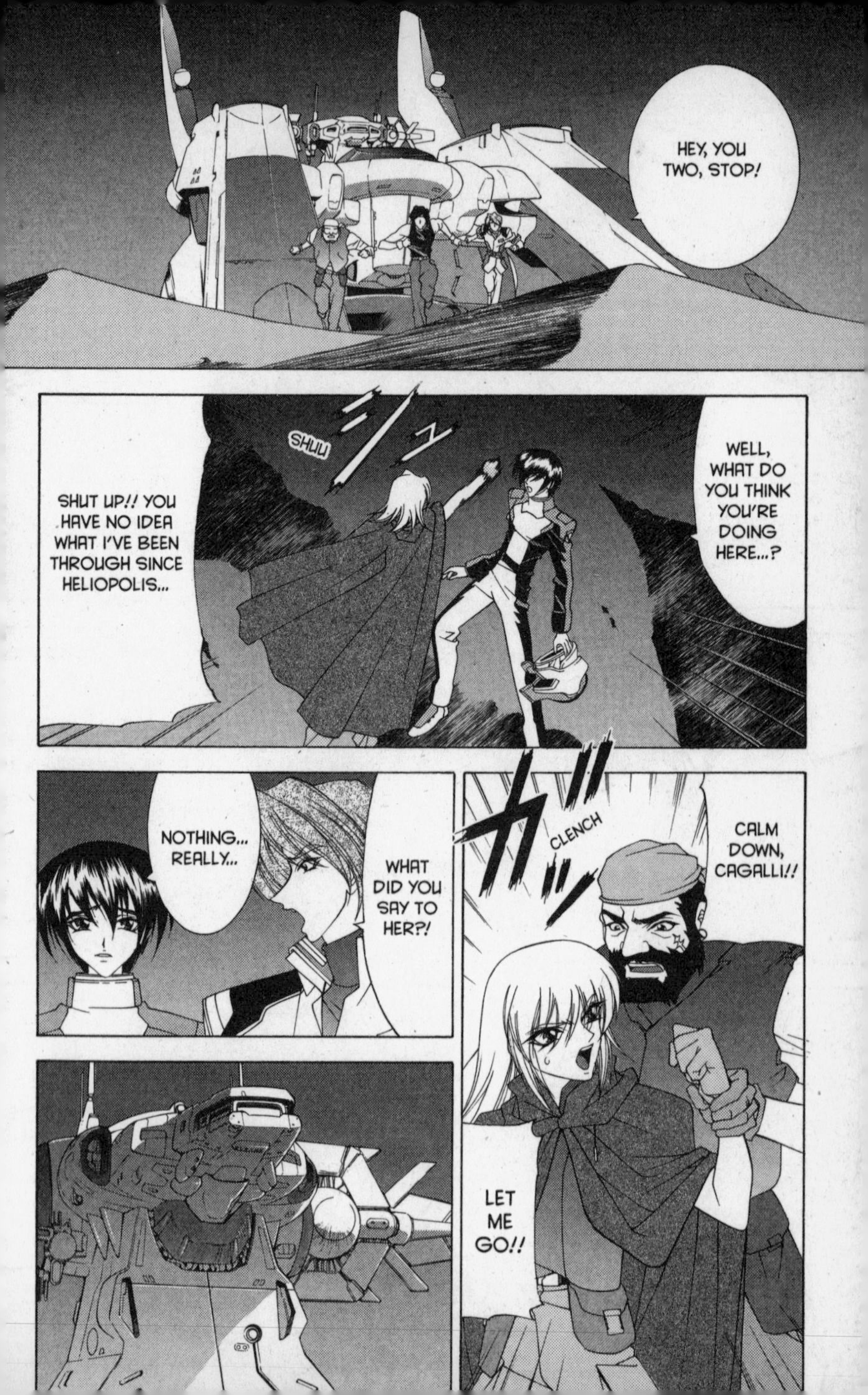
HEY, YOU TWO, STOP!
WELL, WHAT DO YOU THINK YOU'RE DOING HERE...?
SHUU
SHUT UP!! YOU HAVE NO IDEA WHAT I'VE BEEN THROUGH SINCE HELIOPOLIS...
CALM DOWN, CAGALLI!!
CLENCH
LET ME GO!!
WHAT DID YOU SAY TO HER?!
NOTHING... REALLY...

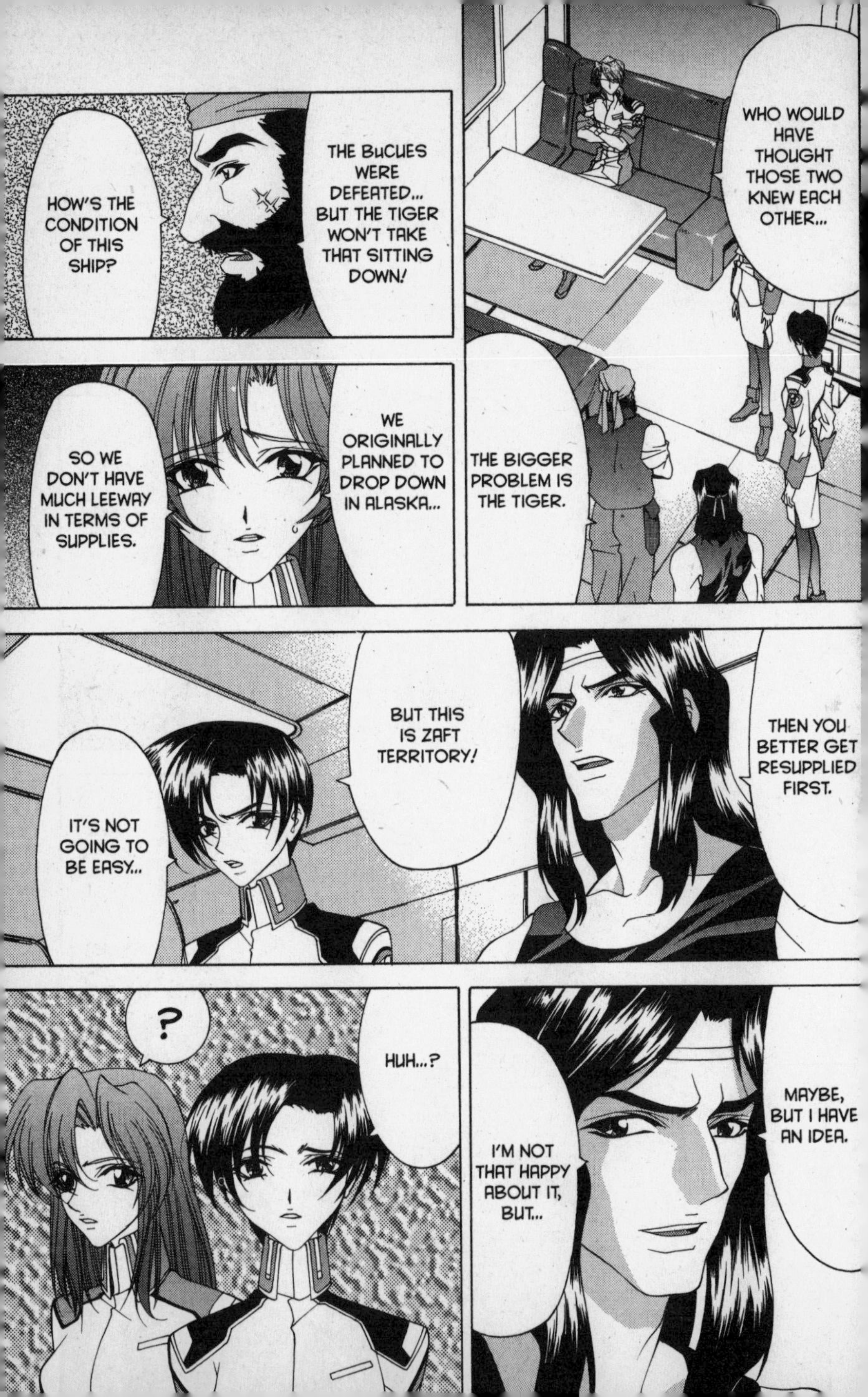
WHO WOULD HAVE THOUGHT THOSE TWO KNEW EACH OTHER...
THE BIGGER PROBLEM IS THE TIGER.
THE BUCUES WERE DEFEATED... BUT THE TIGER WON'T TAKE THAT SITTING DOWN!
HOW'S THE CONDITION OF THIS SHIP?
WE ORIGINALLY PLANNED TO DROP DOWN IN ALASKA...
SO WE DON'T HAVE MUCH LEEWAY IN TERMS OF SUPPLIES.
THEN YOU BETTER GET RESUPPLIED FIRST.
BUT THIS IS ZAFT TERRITORY!
IT'S NOT GOING TO BE EASY...
MAYBE, BUT I HAVE AN IDEA.
I'M NOT THAT HAPPY ABOUT IT, BUT...
HUH...?
?

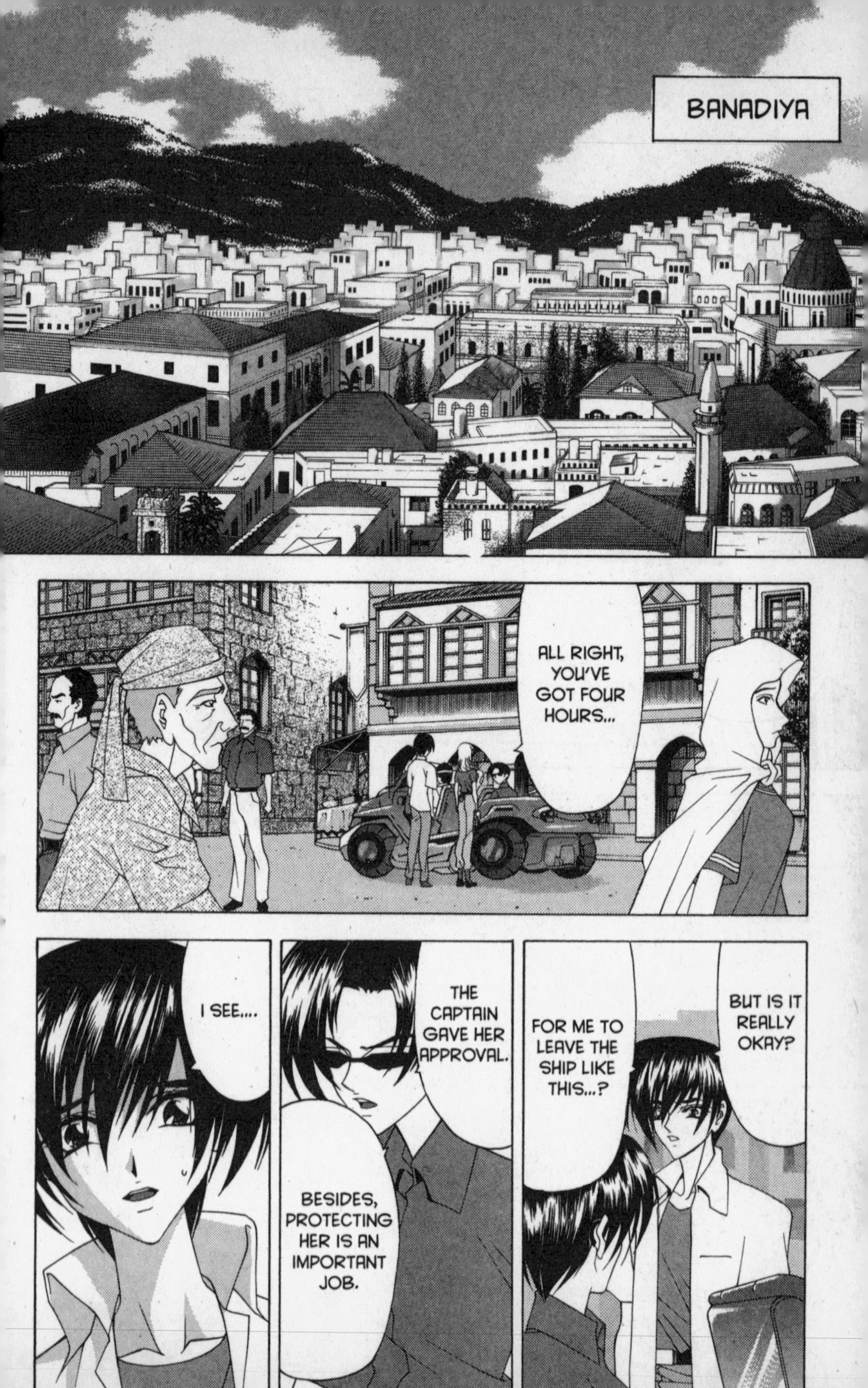
BANADIYA
ALL RIGHT, YOU'VE GOT FOUR HOURS...
BUT IS IT REALLY OKAY?
FOR ME TO LEAVE THE SHIP LIKE THIS...?
THE CAPTAIN GAVE HER APPROVAL.
BESIDES, PROTECTING HER IS AN IMPORTANT JOB.
I SEE....

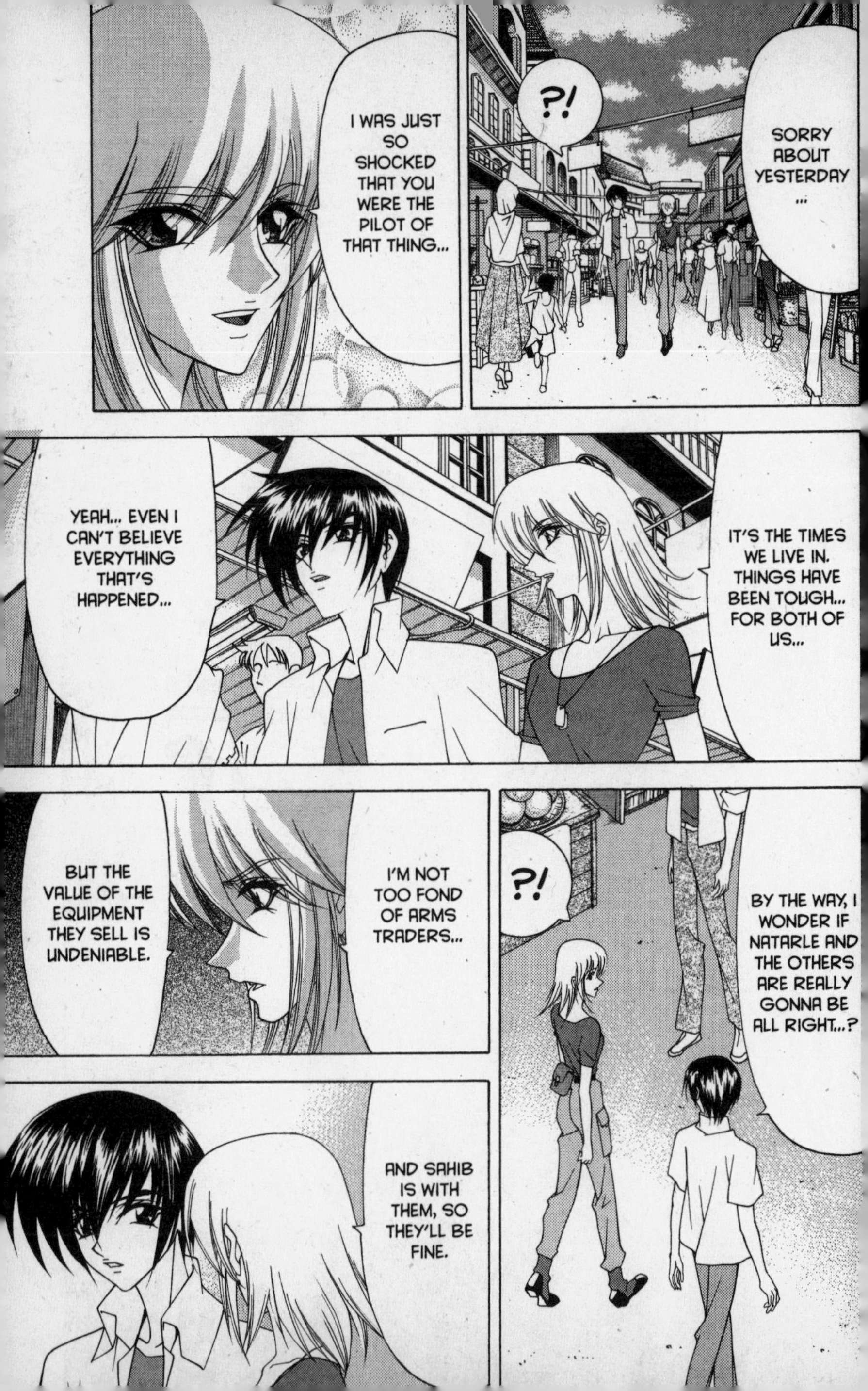
SORRY ABOUT YESTERDAY ...
?!
I WAS JUST SO SHOCKED THAT YOU WERE THE PILOT OF THAT THING...
IT'S THE TIMES WE LIVE IN. THINGS HAVE BEEN TOUGH... FOR BOTH OF US...
YEAH... EVEN I CAN'T BELIEVE EVERYTHING THAT'S HAPPENED...
BY THE WAY, I WONDER IF NATARLE AND THE OTHERS ARE REALLY GONNA BE ALL RIGHT...?
?!
I'M NOT TOO FOND OF ARMS TRADERS...
BUT THE VALUE OF THE EQUIPMENT THEY SELL IS UNDENIABLE.
AND SAHIB IS WITH THEM, SO THEY'LL BE FINE.

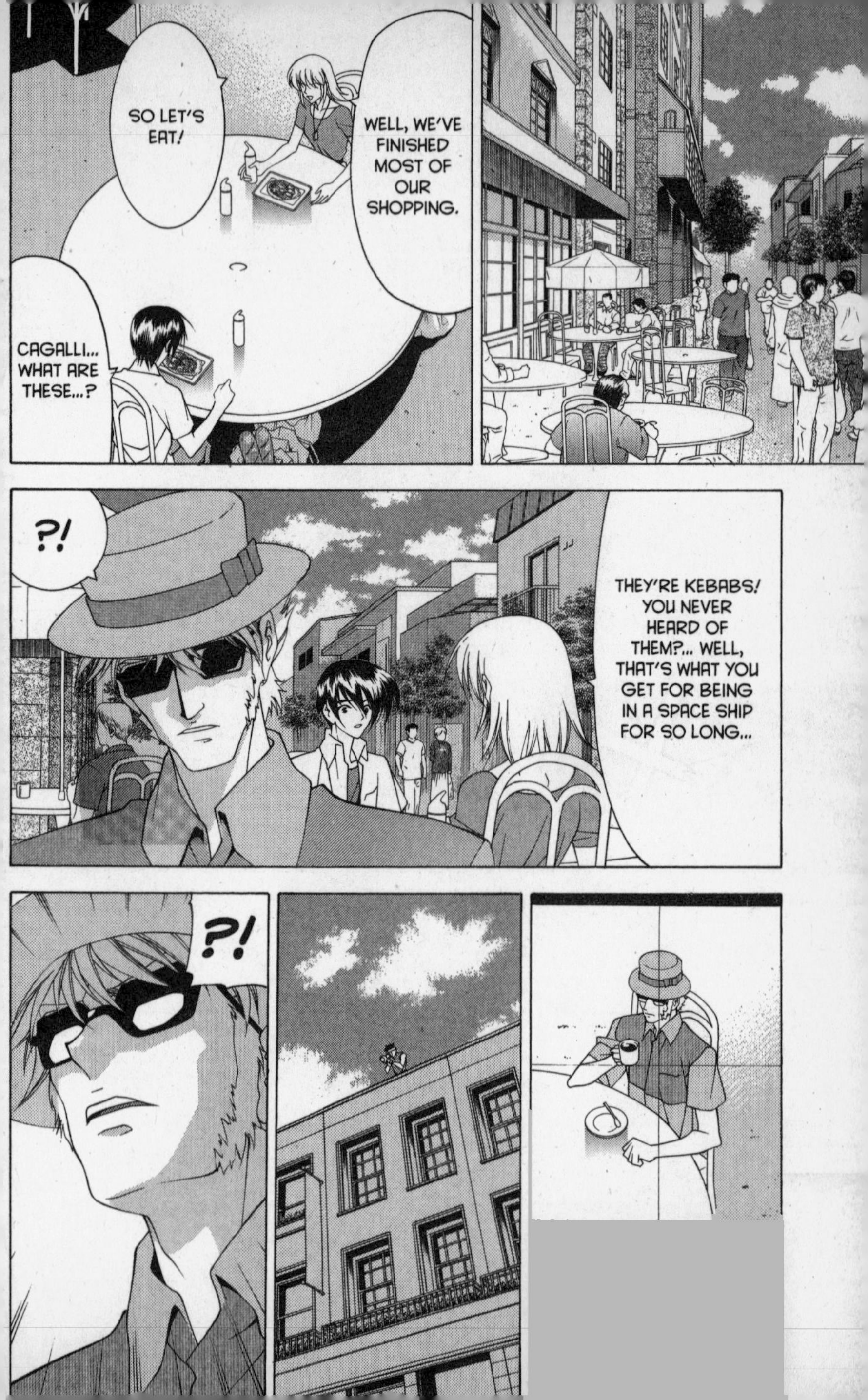
WELL, WE'VE FINISHED MOST OF OUR SHOPPING.
SO LET'S EAT!
CAGALLI... WHAT ARE THESE...?
THEY'RE KEBABS! YOU NEVER HEARD OF THEM?... WELL, THAT'S WHAT YOU GET FOR BEING IN A SPACE SHIP FOR SO LONG...
?!
?!

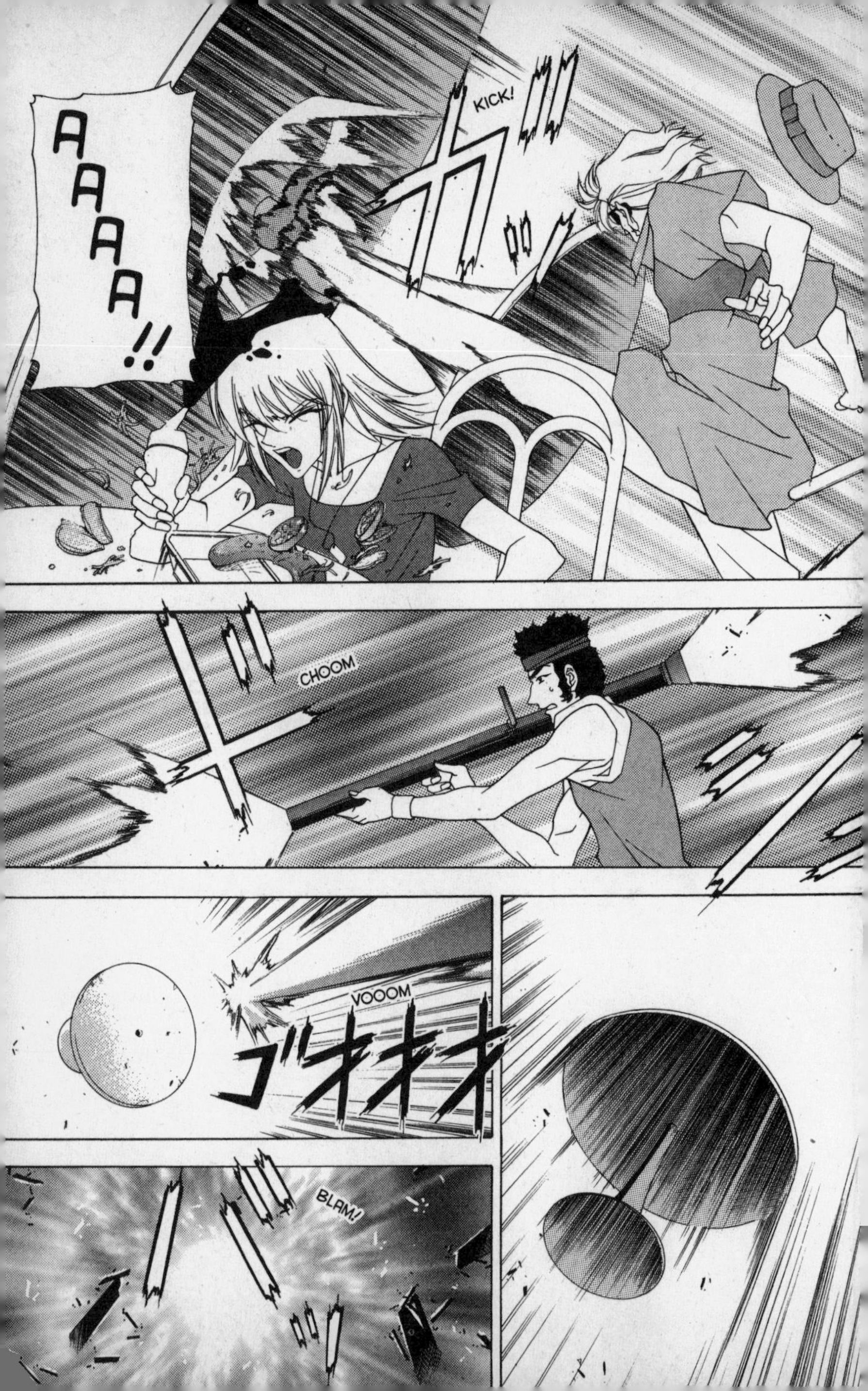
KICK!
AAAAA!!
CHOOM
VOOOM
ゴオオオ
BLAM!

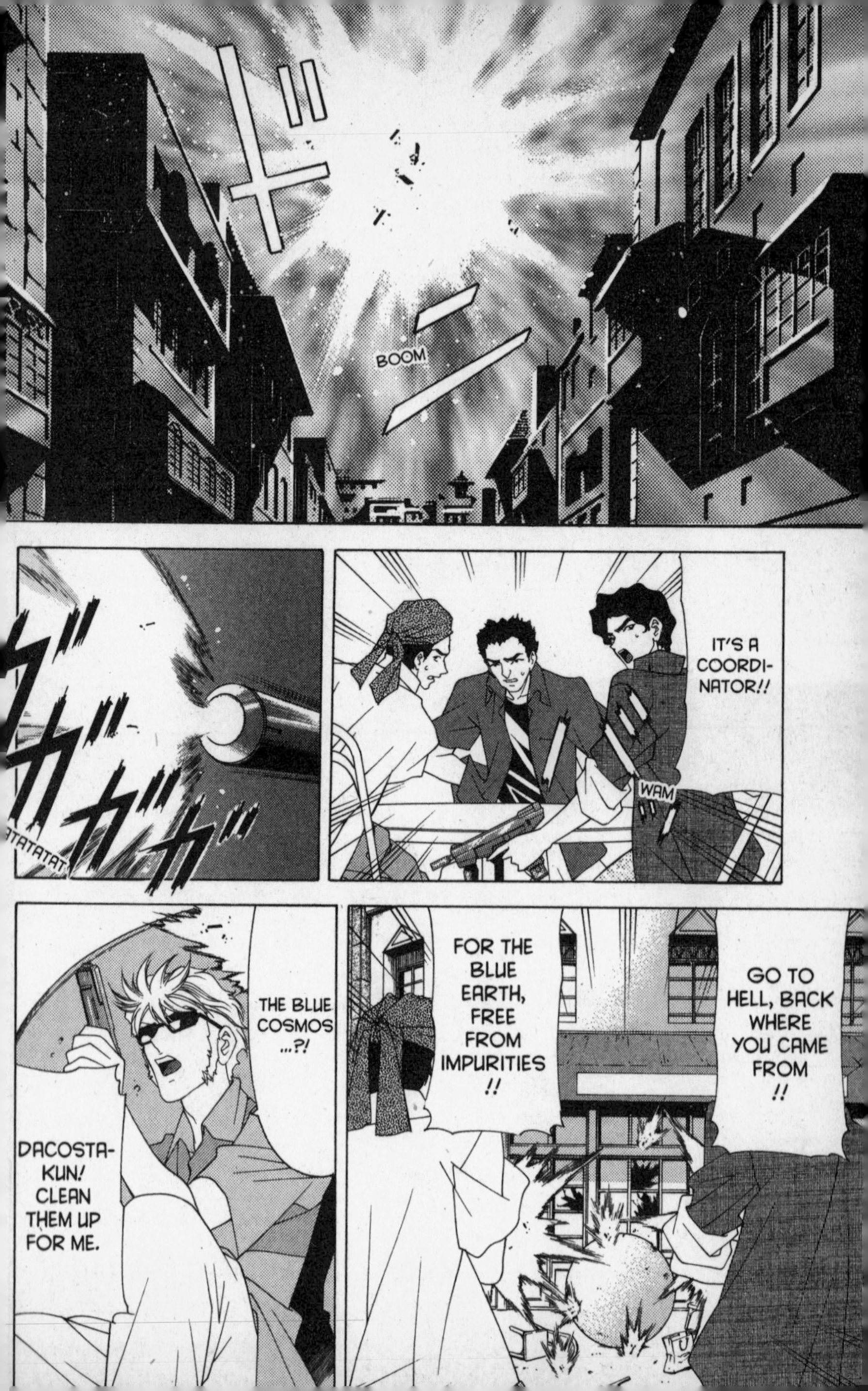
BOOM
IT'S A COORDI-NATOR!!
WAM
TATATATAT
GO TO HELL, BACK WHERE YOU CAME FROM !!
FOR THE BLUE EARTH, FREE FROM IMPURITIES !!
THE BLUE COSMOS ...?!
DACOSTA-KUN! CLEAN THEM UP FOR ME.

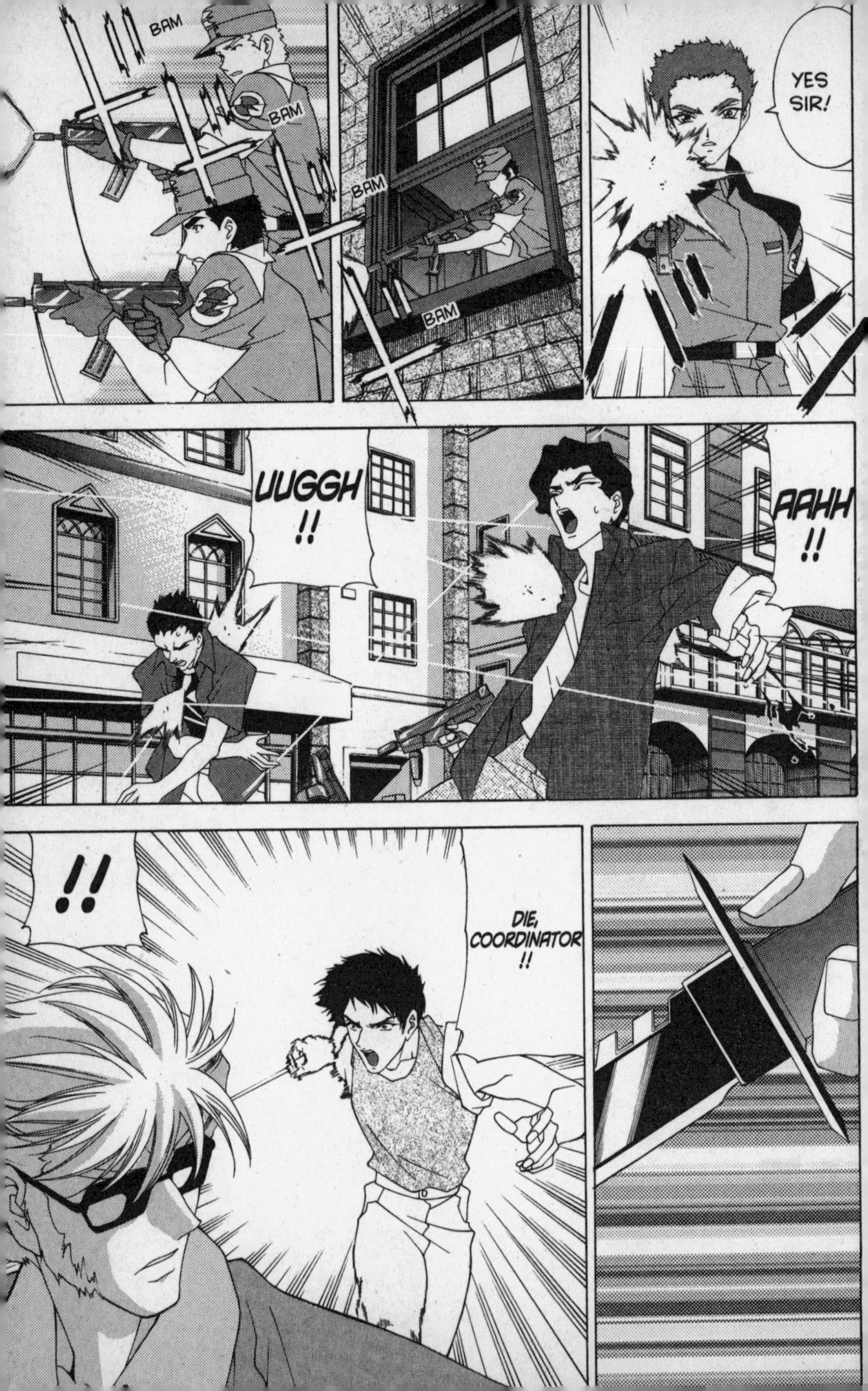
YES SIR!
BAM
BAM
BAM
BAM
AAHH !!
UUGGH !!
DIE, COORDINATOR !!
!!

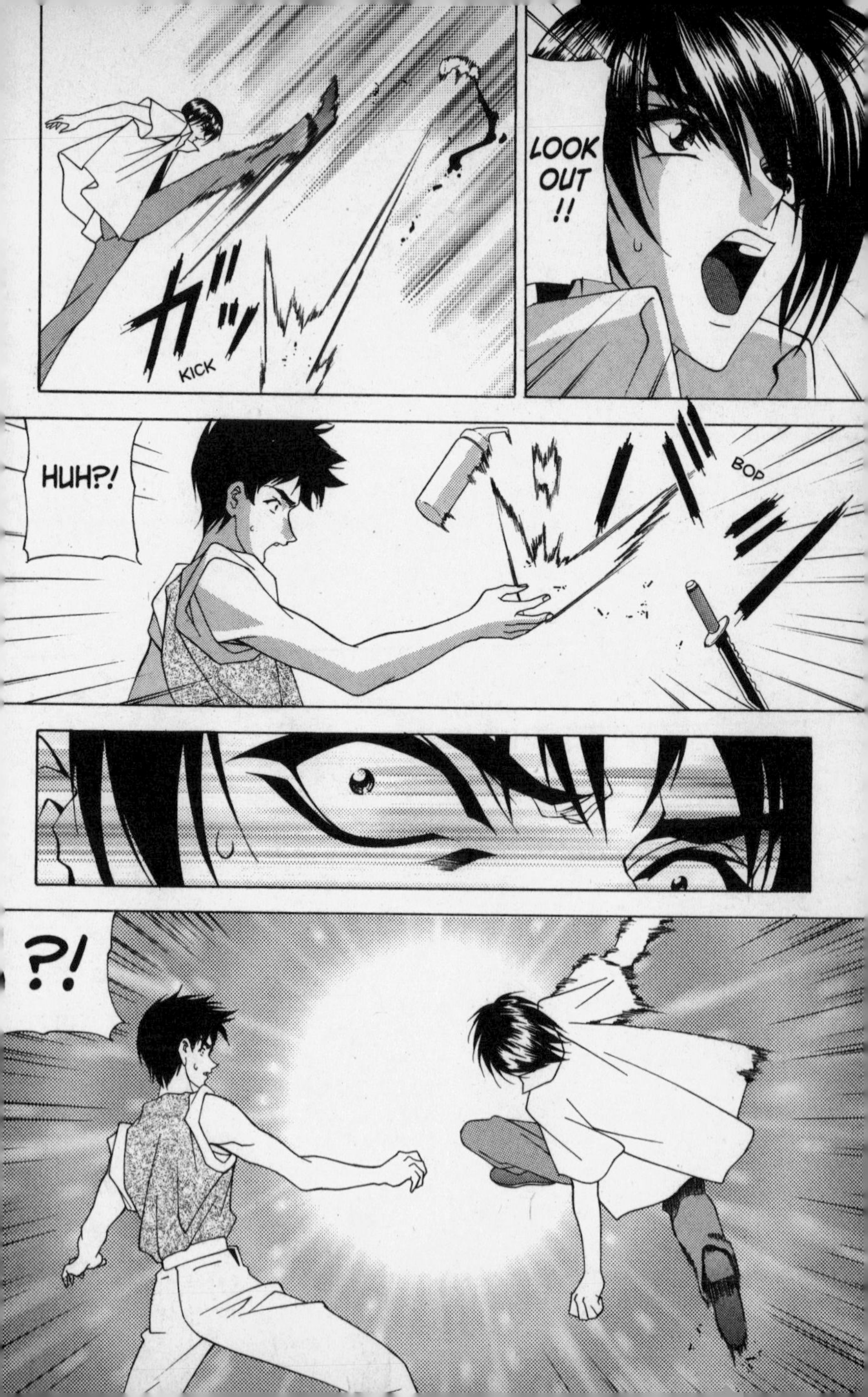
LOOK OUT !!
ガッ
KICK
BOP
HUH?!
?!

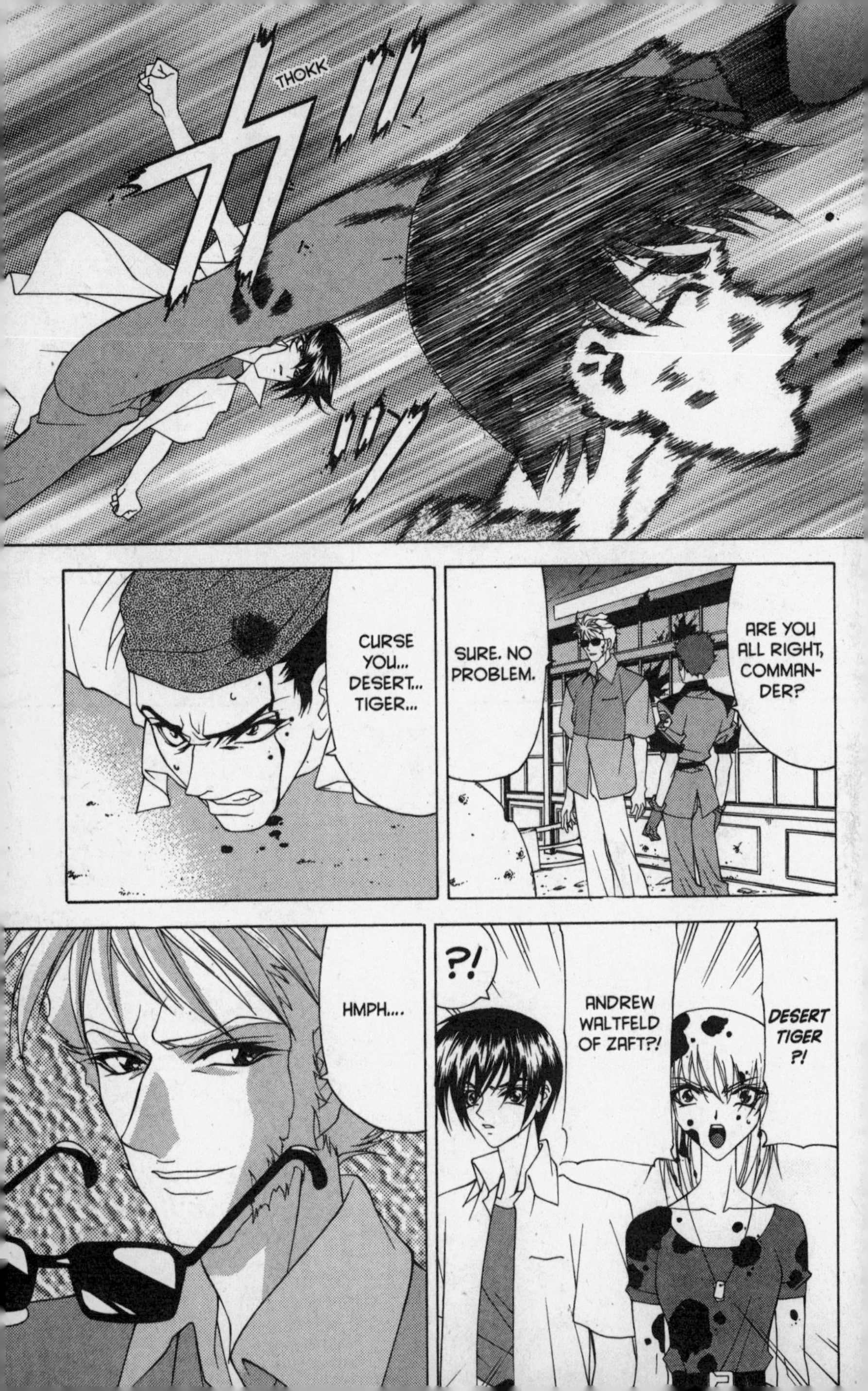
THOKK
ARE YOU ALL RIGHT, COMMANDER?
SURE. NO PROBLEM.
CURSE YOU... DESERT... TIGER...
DESERT TIGER ?!
ANDREW WALTFELD OF ZAFT?!
?!
HMPH....

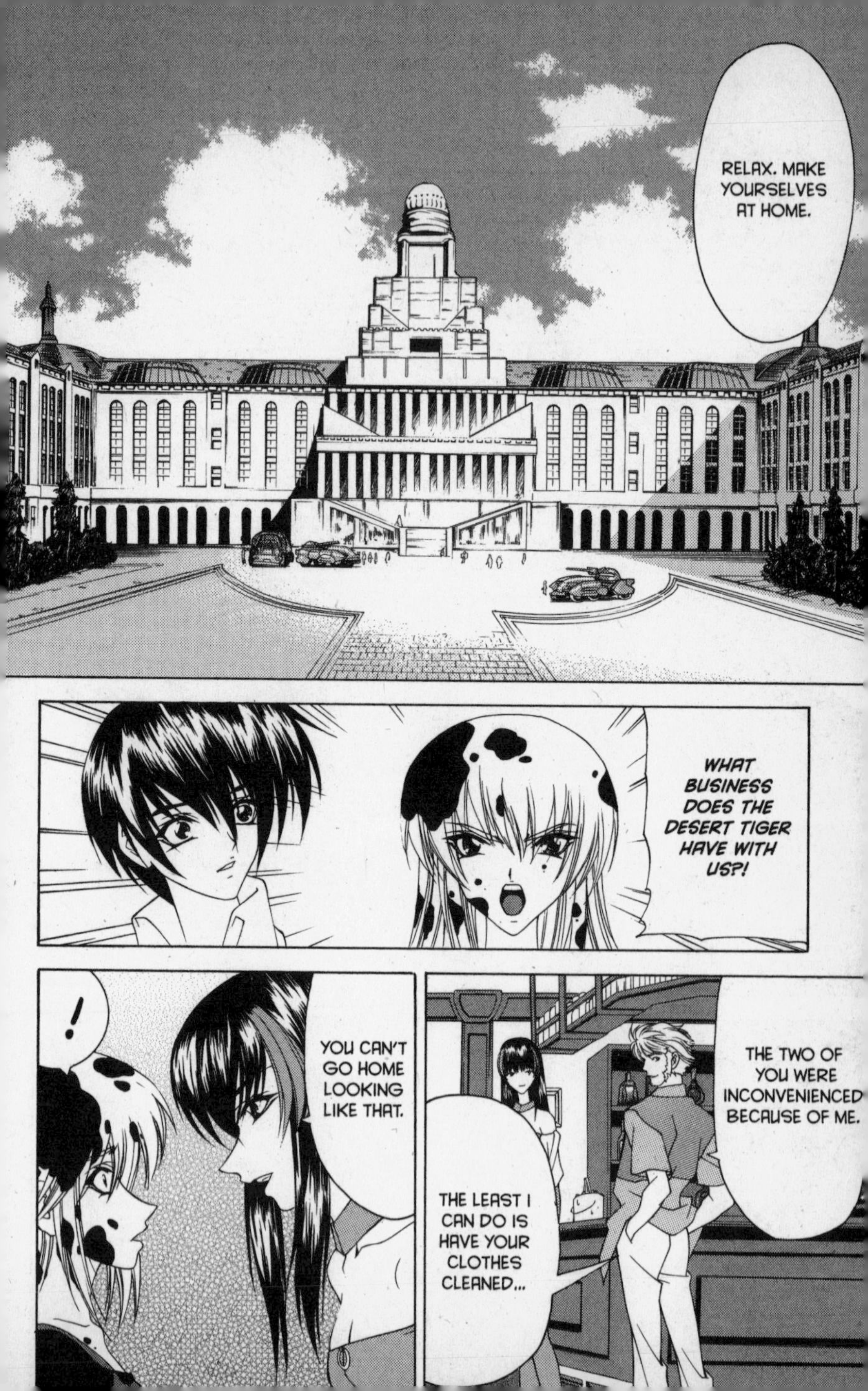
RELAX. MAKE YOURSELVES AT HOME.
WHAT BUSINESS DOES THE DESERT TIGER HAVE WITH US?!
THE TWO OF YOU WERE INCONVENIENCED BECAUSE OF ME.
THE LEAST I CAN DO IS HAVE YOUR CLOTHES CLEANED...
YOU CAN'T GO HOME LOOKING LIKE THAT.
!

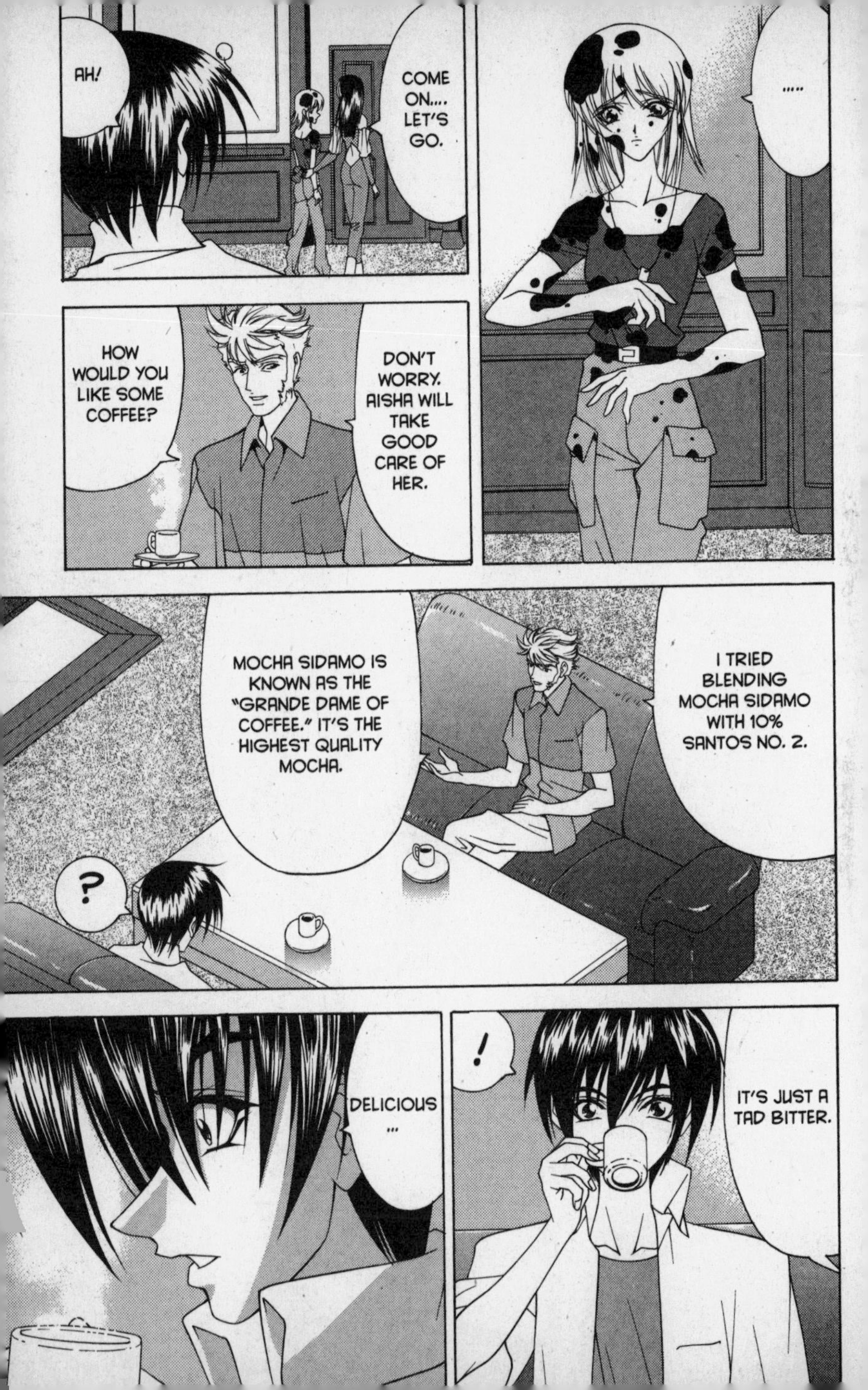
.....
COME ON.... LET'S GO.
AH!
DON'T WORRY. AISHA WILL TAKE GOOD CARE OF HER.
HOW WOULD YOU LIKE SOME COFFEE?
I TRIED BLENDING MOCHA SIDAMO WITH 10% SANTOS NO. 2.
MOCHA SIDAMO IS KNOWN AS THE "GRANDE DAME OF COFFEE." IT'S THE HIGHEST QUALITY MOCHA.
?
IT'S JUST A TAD BITTER.
!
DELICIOUS ...

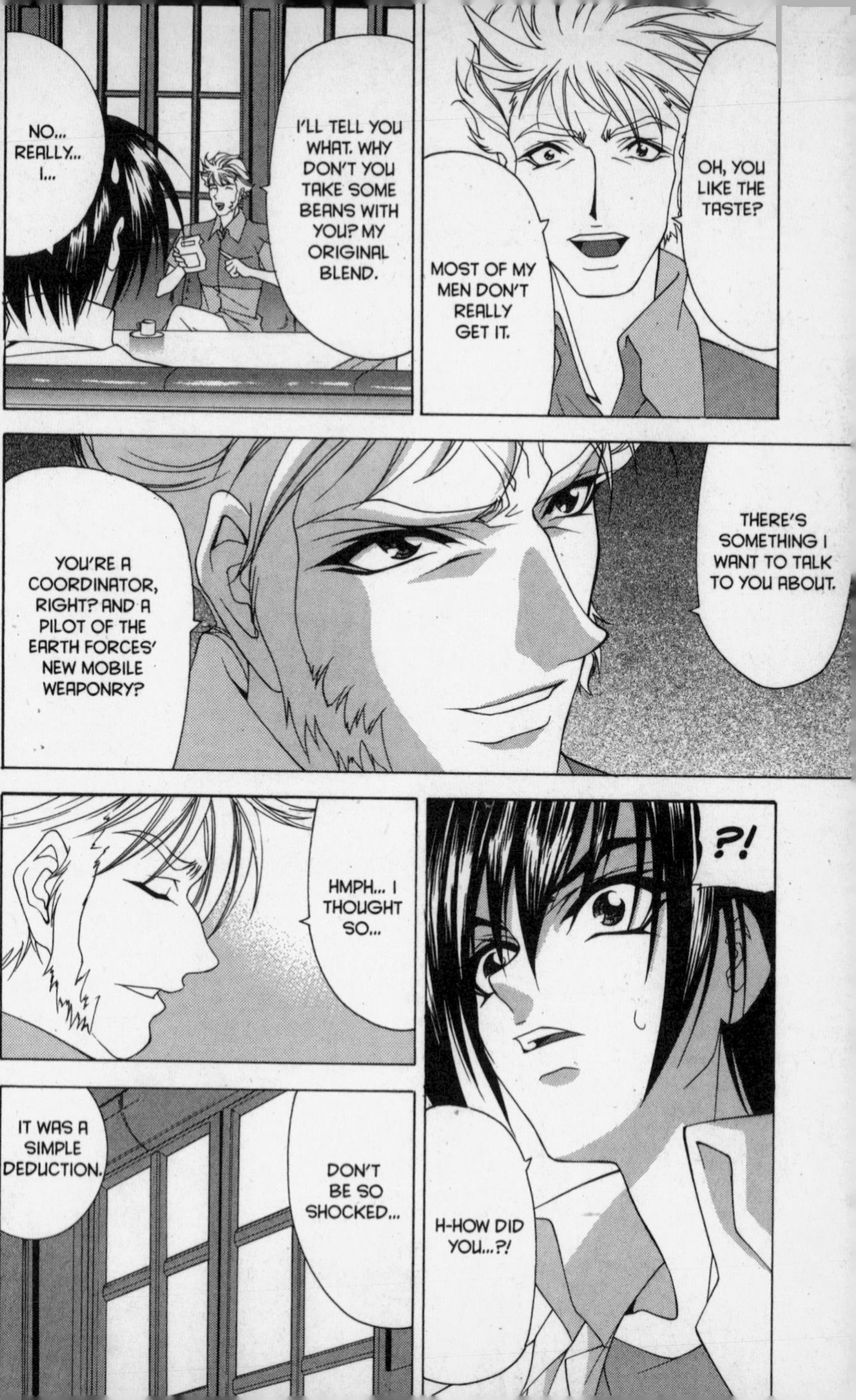
OH, YOU LIKE THE TASTE?
MOST OF MY MEN DON'T REALLY GET IT.
I'LL TELL YOU WHAT. WHY DON'T YOU TAKE SOME BEANS WITH YOU? MY ORIGINAL BLEND.
NO... REALLY... I...
THERE'S SOMETHING I WANT TO TALK TO YOU ABOUT.
YOU'RE A COORDINATOR, RIGHT? AND A PILOT OF THE EARTH FORCES' NEW MOBILE WEAPONRY?
?!
H-HOW DID YOU...?!
HMPH... I THOUGHT SO...
DON'T BE SO SHOCKED...
IT WAS A SIMPLE DEDUCTION.

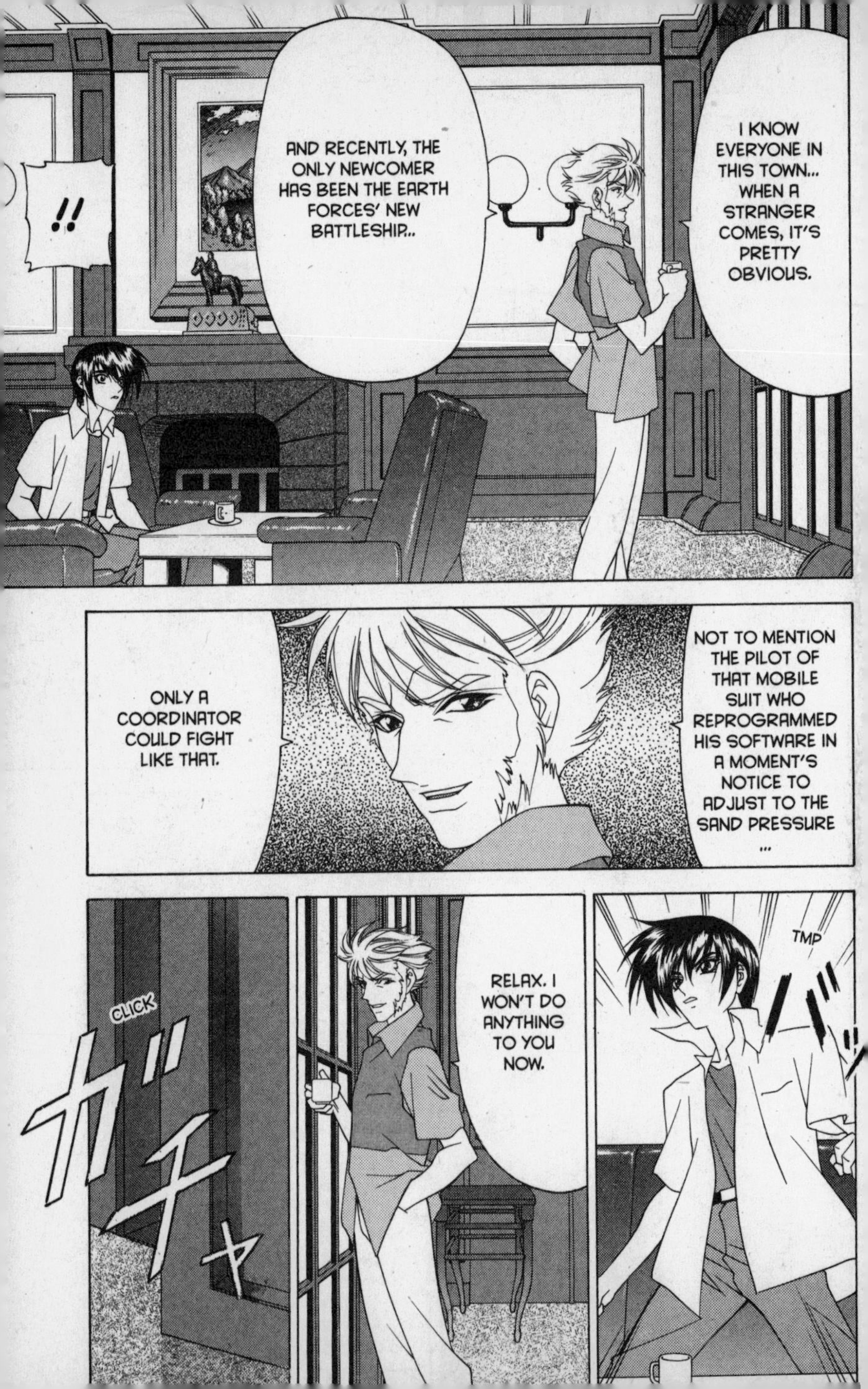
I KNOW EVERYONE IN THIS TOWN... WHEN A STRANGER COMES, IT'S PRETTY OBVIOUS.
AND RECENTLY, THE ONLY NEWCOMER HAS BEEN THE EARTH FORCES' NEW BATTLESHIP...
!!
NOT TO MENTION THE PILOT OF THAT MOBILE SUIT WHO REPROGRAMMED HIS SOFTWARE IN A MOMENT'S NOTICE TO ADJUST TO THE SAND PRESSURE ...
ONLY A COORDINATOR COULD FIGHT LIKE THAT.
TMP
RELAX. I WON'T DO ANYTHING TO YOU NOW.
CLICK
ガチャ

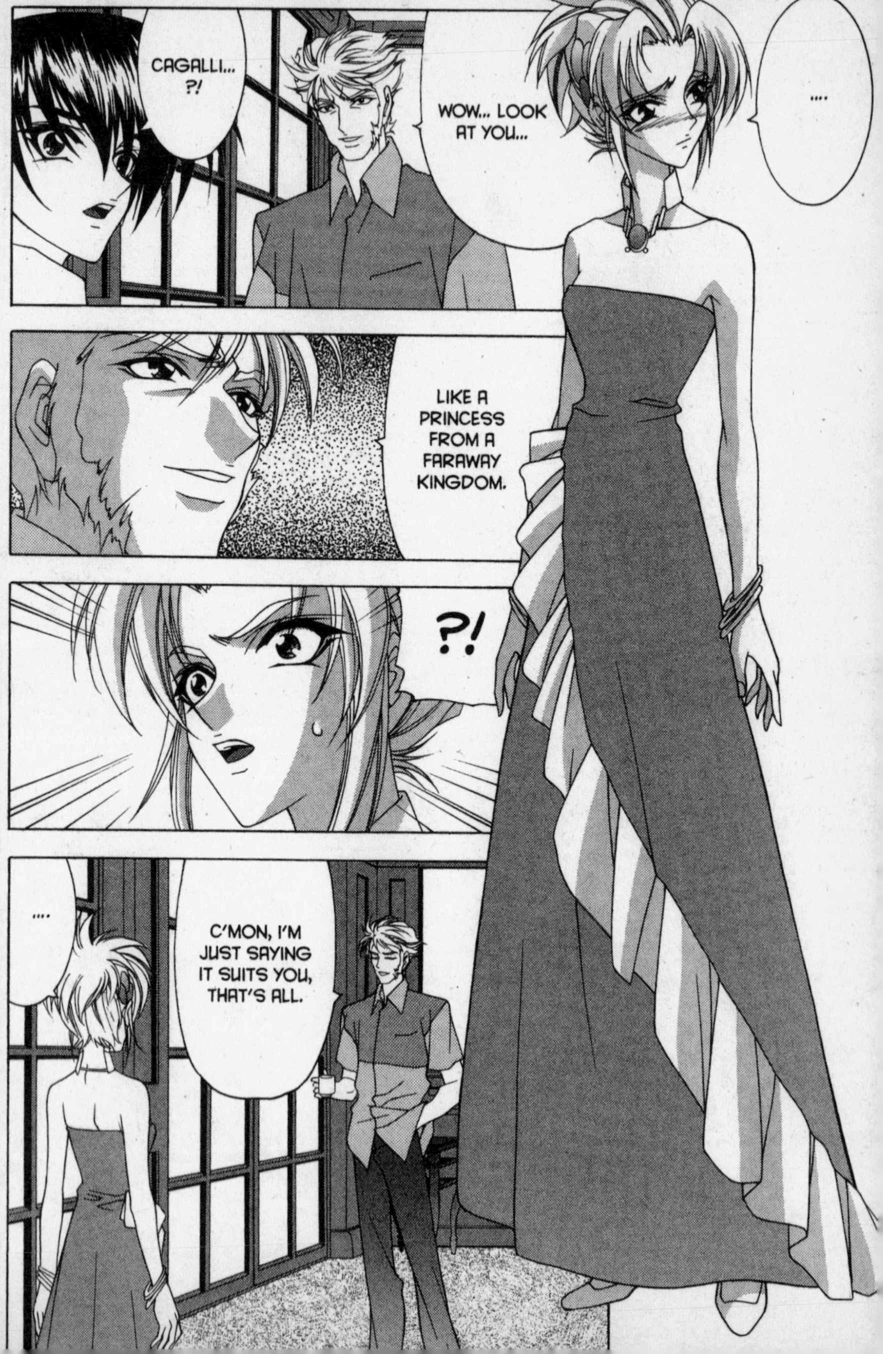
....
WOW... LOOK AT YOU...
CAGALLI... ?!
LIKE A PRINCESS FROM A FARAWAY KINGDOM.
?!
C'MON, I'M JUST SAYING IT SUITS YOU, THAT'S ALL.
....

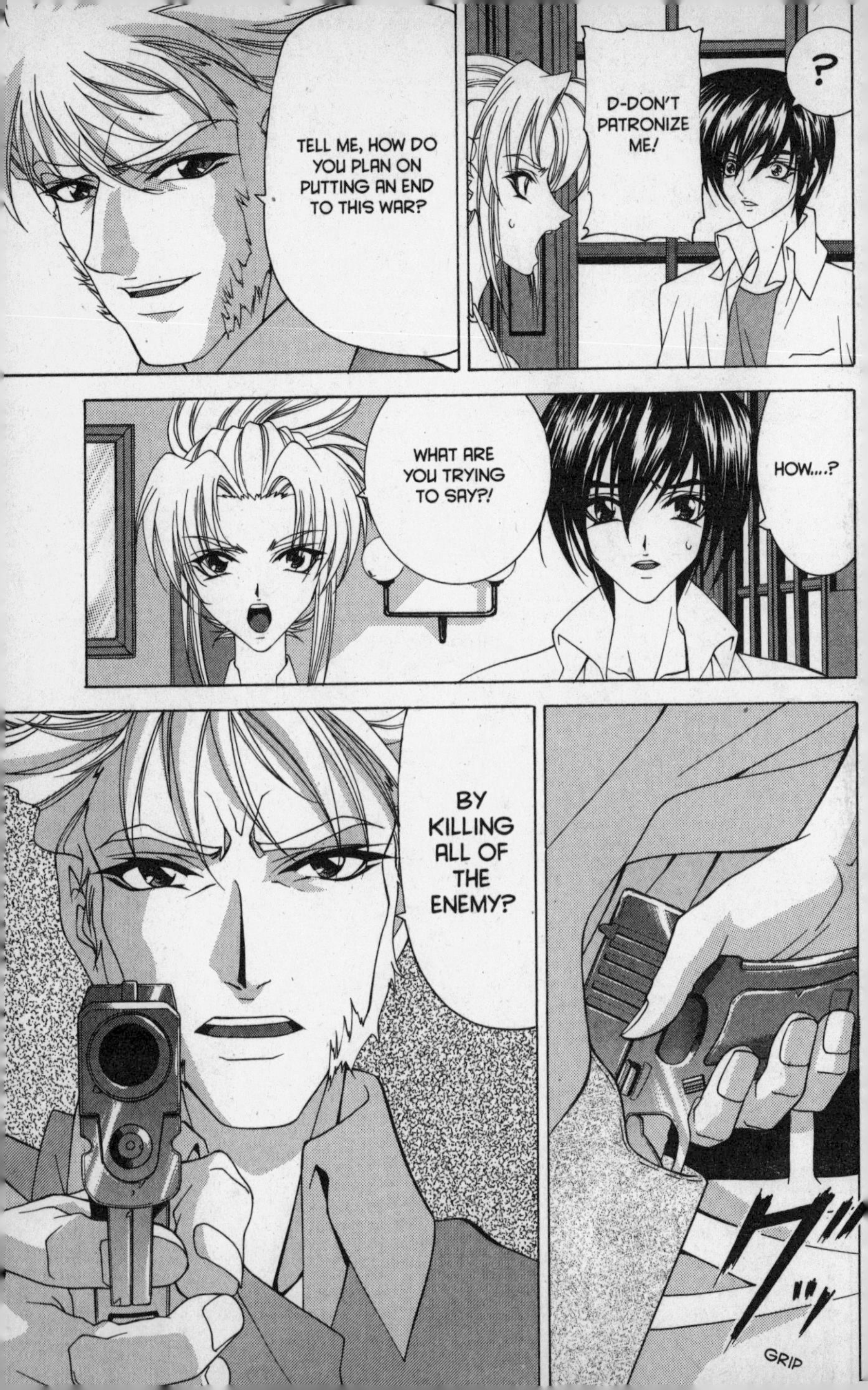
?
D-DON'T PATRONIZE ME!
TELL ME, HOW DO YOU PLAN ON PUTTING AN END TO THIS WAR?
HOW....?
WHAT ARE YOU TRYING TO SAY?!
GRIP
BY KILLING ALL OF THE ENEMY?

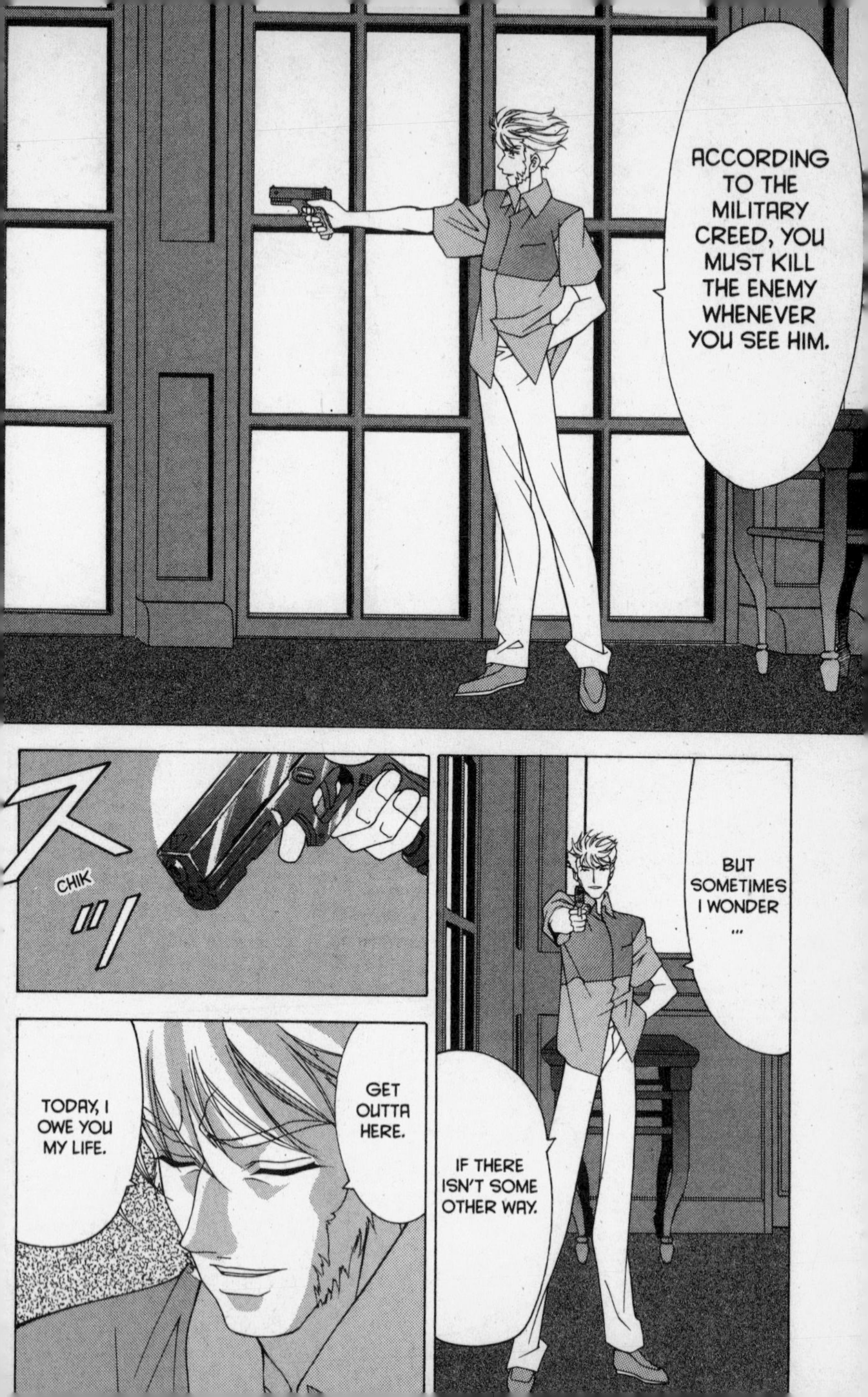
ACCORDING TO THE MILITARY CREED, YOU MUST KILL THE ENEMY WHENEVER YOU SEE HIM.
BUT SOMETIMES I WONDER ...
IF THERE ISN'T SOME OTHER WAY.
CHIK
GET OUTTA HERE.
TODAY, I OWE YOU MY LIFE.

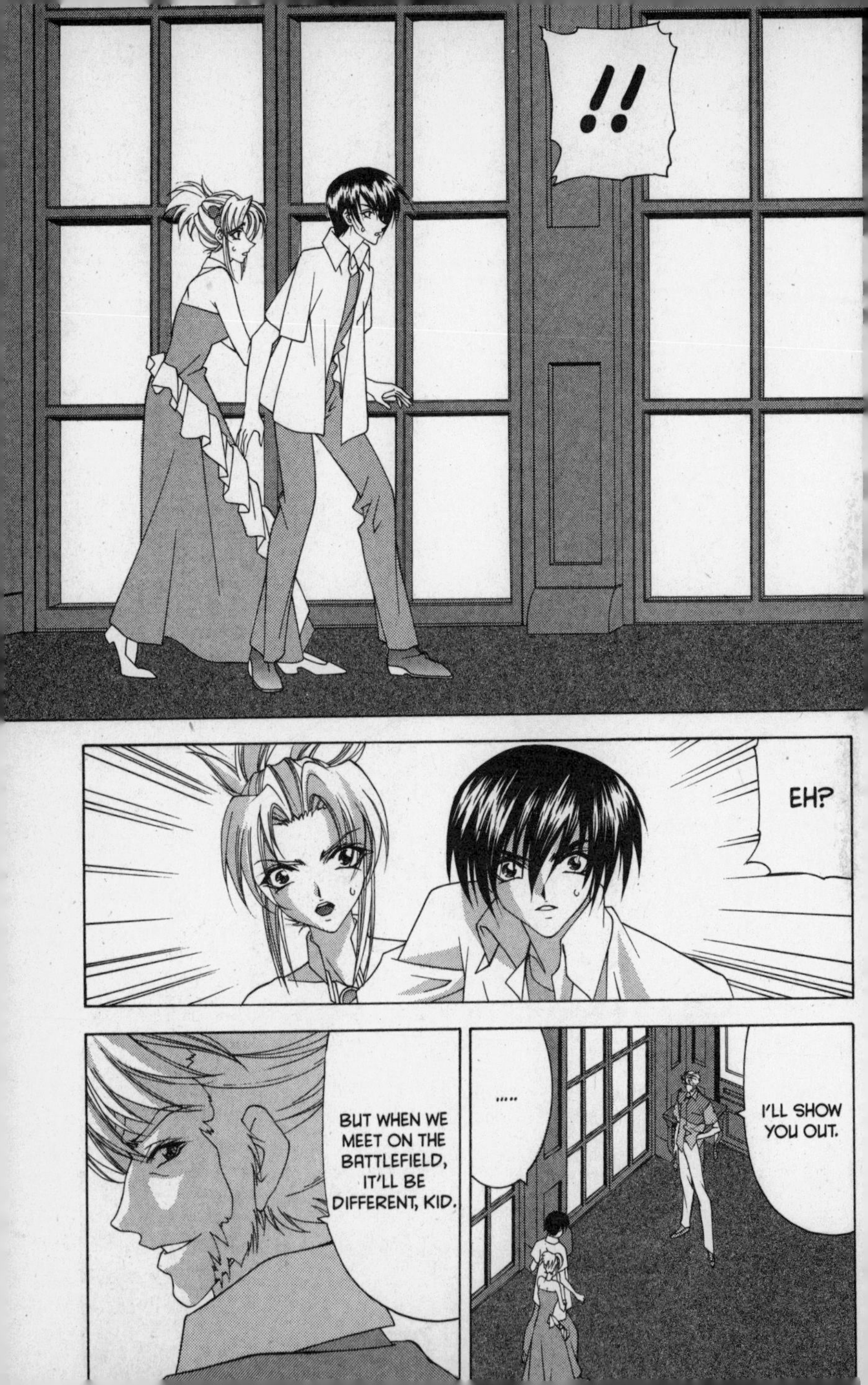
!!
EH?
I'LL SHOW YOU OUT.
......
BUT WHEN WE MEET ON THE BATTLEFIELD, IT'LL BE DIFFERENT, KID.

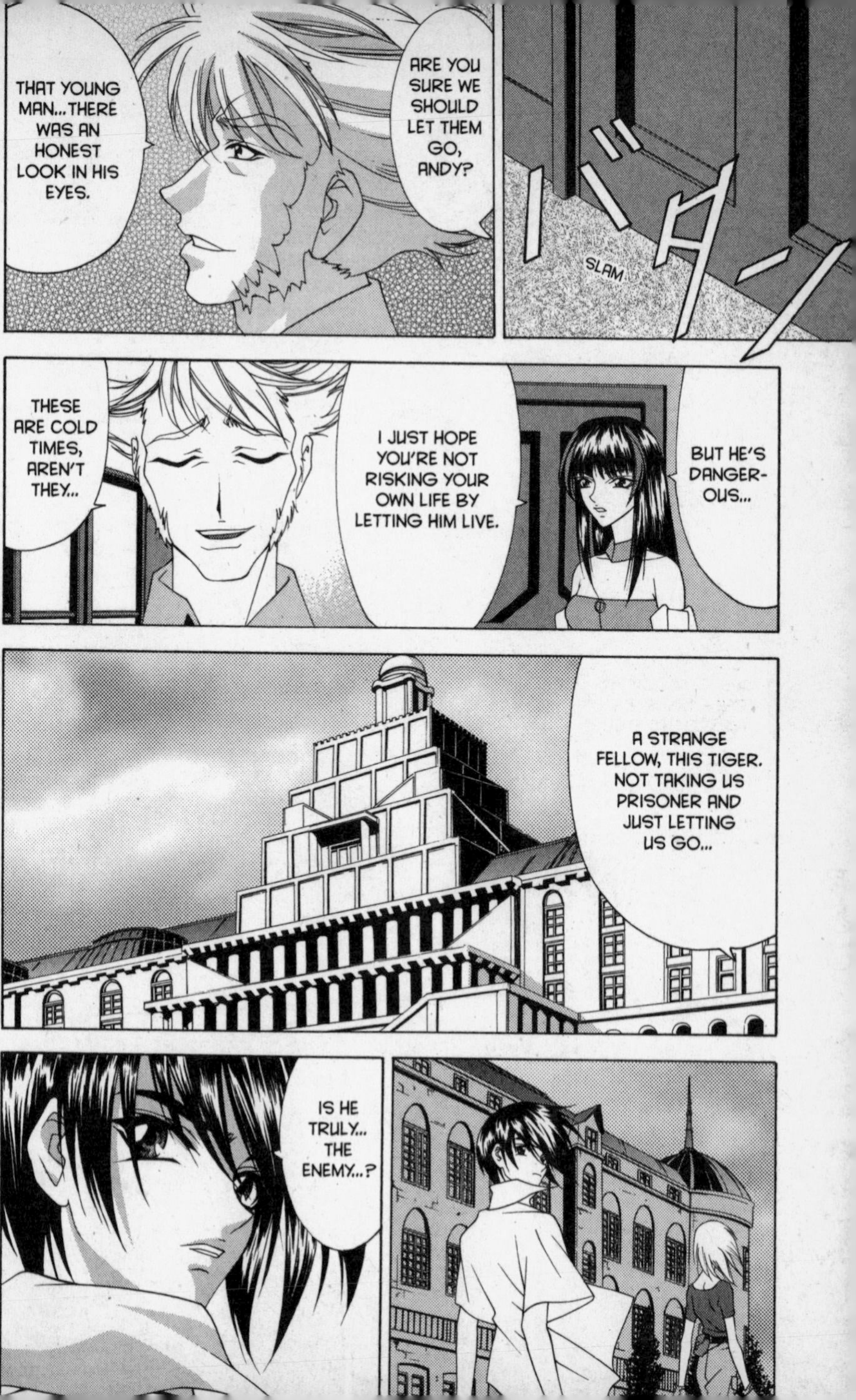
SLAM
ARE YOU SURE WE SHOULD LET THEM GO, ANDY?
THAT YOUNG MAN...THERE WAS AN HONEST LOOK IN HIS EYES.
BUT HE'S DANGER-OUS...
I JUST HOPE YOU'RE NOT RISKING YOUR OWN LIFE BY LETTING HIM LIVE.
THESE ARE COLD TIMES, AREN'T THEY...
A STRANGE FELLOW, THIS TIGER. NOT TAKING US PRISONER AND JUST LETTING US GO...
IS HE TRULY... THE ENEMY...?

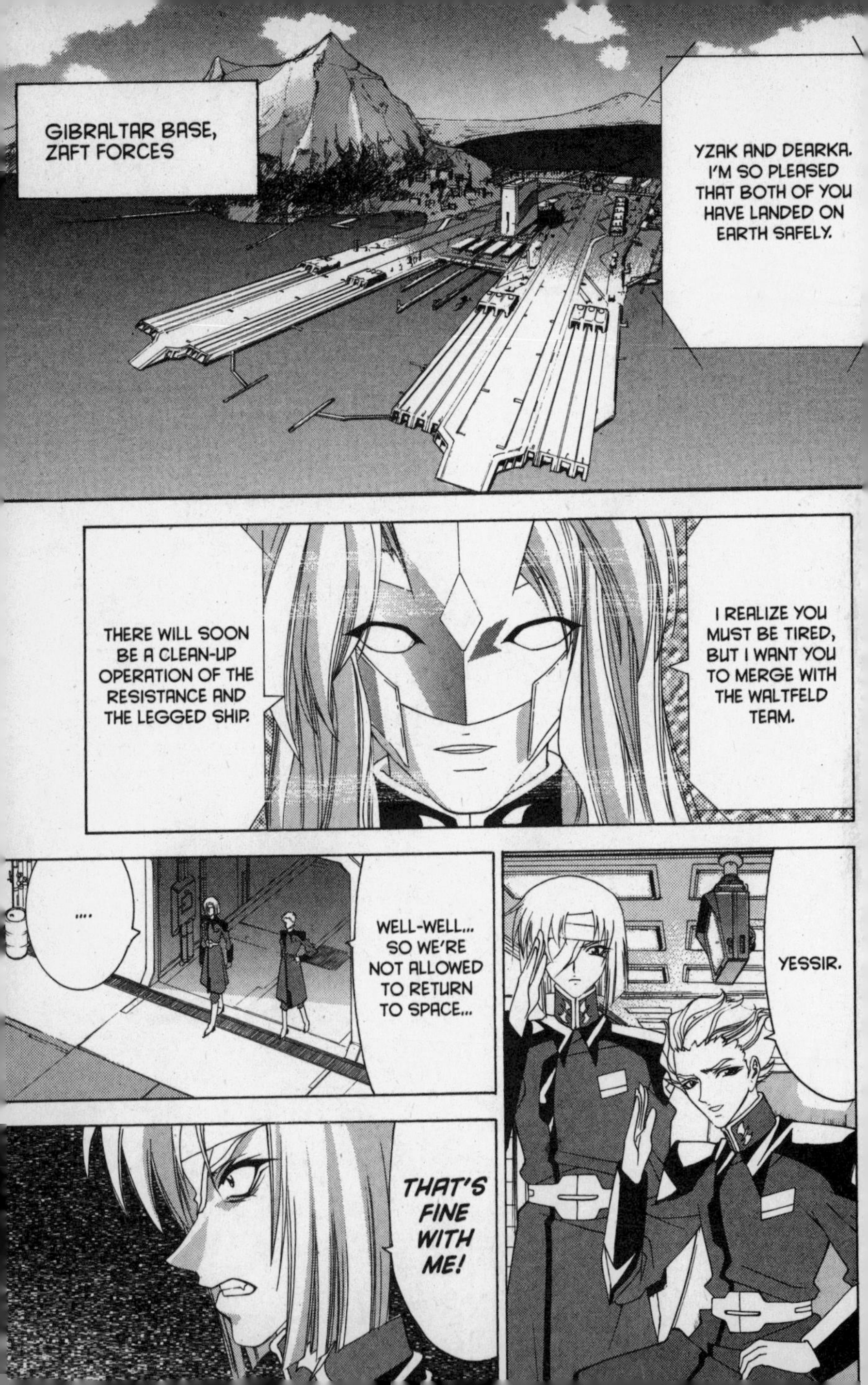
GIBRALTAR BASE, ZAFT FORCES
YZAK AND DEARKA. I'M SO PLEASED THAT BOTH OF YOU HAVE LANDED ON EARTH SAFELY.
I REALIZE YOU MUST BE TIRED, BUT I WANT YOU TO MERGE WITH THE WALTFELD TEAM.
THERE WILL SOON BE A CLEAN-UP OPERATION OF THE RESISTANCE AND THE LEGGED SHIP.
YESSIR.
WELL-WELL... SO WE'RE NOT ALLOWED TO RETURN TO SPACE...
....
THAT'S FINE WITH ME!

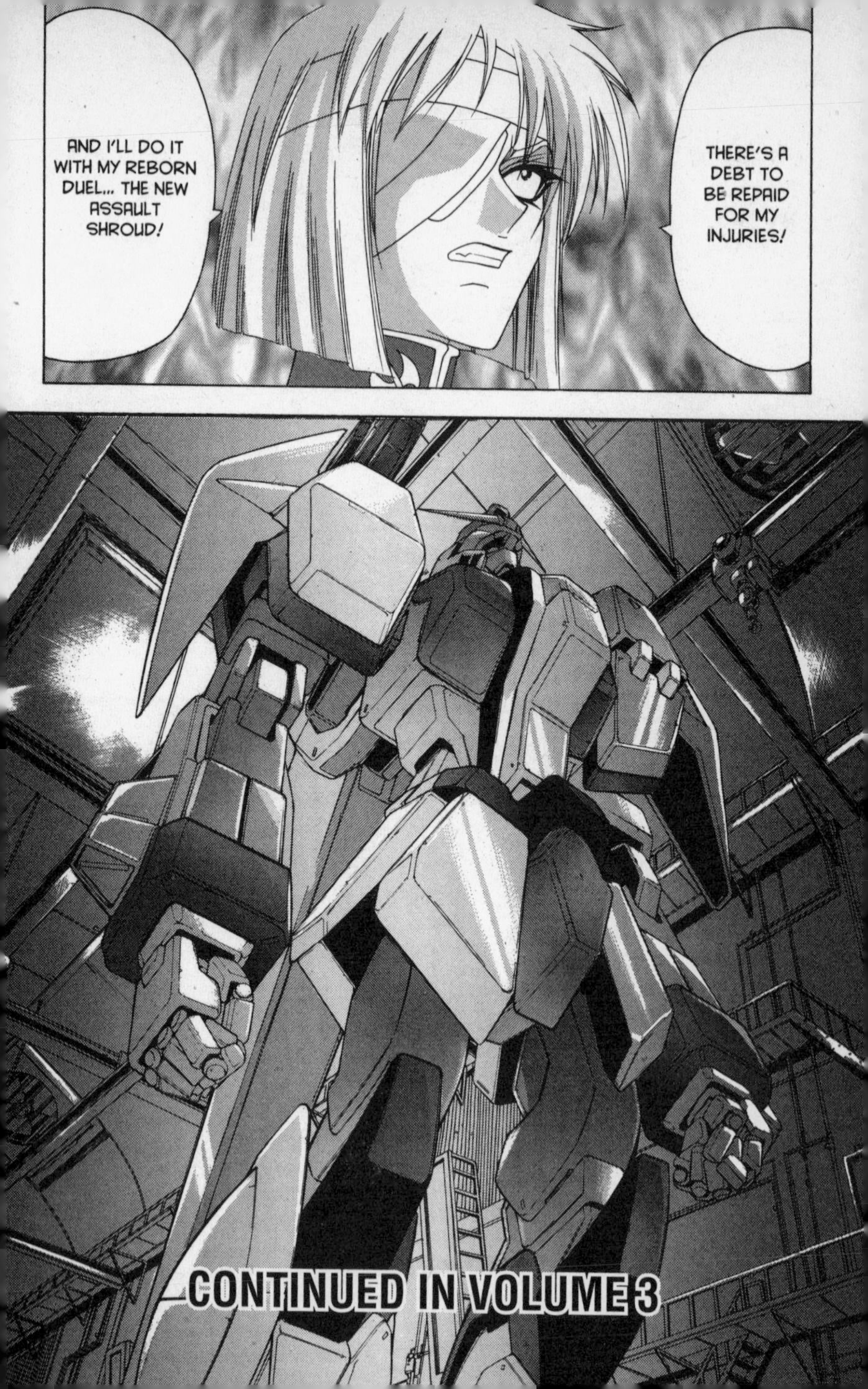
THERE'S A DEBT TO BE REPAID FOR MY INJURIES!
AND I'LL DO IT WITH MY REBORN DUEL... THE NEW ASSAULT SHROUD!
CONTINUED IN VOLUME 3

A Brief History of Gundam
Part 2: The Themes of *Gundam SEED*
By Mark Simmons

In the *Gundam SEED* television series, director Mitsuo Fukuda set out to reinvent the original Mobile Suit Gundam for the twenty-first century. The visual differences are immediately apparent, as *Gundam SEED* is packed with complex, detailed machinery, and the characters—designed for the animated series by Hisashi Hirai, and reinterpreted here by artist Masatsugu Iwase—have the sleek, stylized look of modern anime. The dialogue, with its abundance of military and technological jargon, also contributes to the atmosphere of realism. In addition to these stylistic elements, the creators also made some topical changes to the story's underlying themes to update the classic *Gundam* premise for a new era...

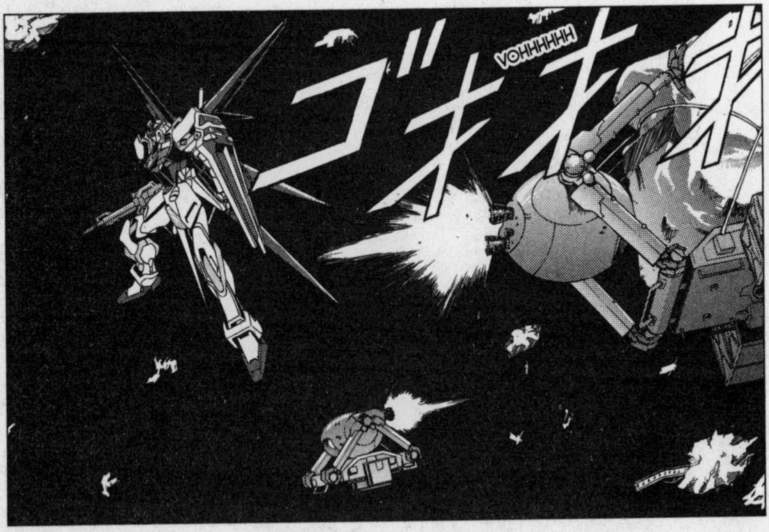
VOHHHHHH

A New Breed

For twenty-five years, the Gundam saga has returned again and again to the premise of a conflict between Earth and its rebel space colonies. Usually, these struggles are purely political in nature, with a population of space colonists growing tired of living under the control of distant rulers and launching a war of independence, not unlike the American Revolution.

In *Gundam SEED*, however, the war is also an ethnic conflict of sorts, fought between genetically engineered Coordinators and unmodified Naturals. The Coordinators made a new home in the space colonies to escape the jealousy and persecution of the Naturals, only to find themselves in economic bondage to the Earth nations which funded the construction of the colonies. This war of independence is thus the end result of genetic discrimination, and the differences between the two sides are a matter not just of where they live, but of who they are. As the fighting escalates, radicals on both sides hope to bring about a clash of civilizations that will leave only one human species.

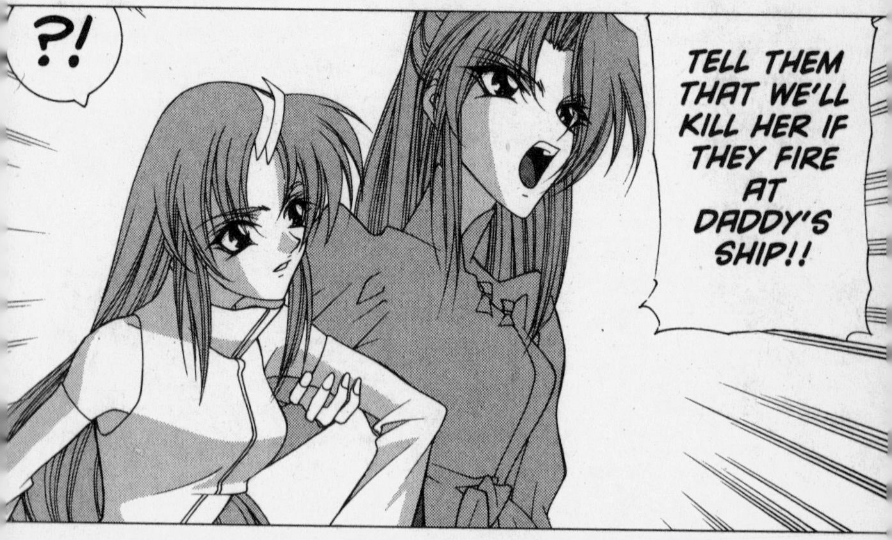
TELL THEM THAT WE'LL KILL HER IF THEY FIRE AT DADDY'S SHIP!!
?!

The concept of the Coordinators, a new breed of humanity with amazing mental and physical abilities, also echoes previous Gundam series. According to Gundam lore, the new environment of outer space may bring about a new stage in human evolution, represented by so-called Newtypes with vastly expanded powers of awareness and intuition. But *Gundam SEED's* Coordinators have no such spiritual gifts, and since their superhuman abilities are the product of artificial genetic modification, they are children of science rather than of natural evolution.

Uneasy Alliances

Gundam SEED also reflects the modern era in its complex political setup. While previous series assumed that the Earth of the future would inevitably be ruled by a single world government along the lines of the United Nations, in *Gundam SEED* the Earth Alliance which represents the Naturals is actually a joint enterprise of several different terrestrial superpowers, which scheme against each other even as they cooperate against the Coordinators.

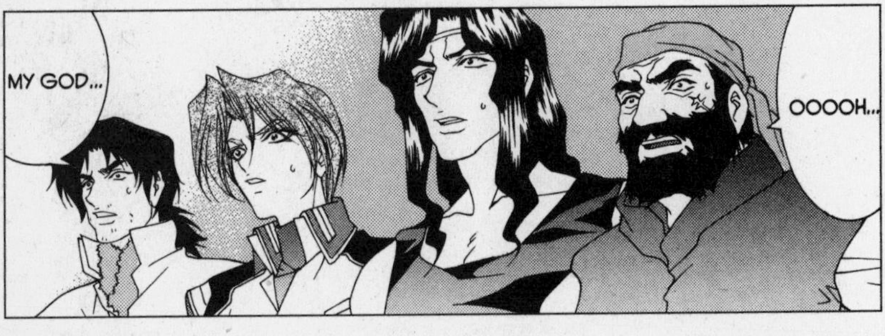
OOOOH...
MY GOD...

The Atlantic Federation, based in North America, is the leading power of the Alliance and the creator of the prototype Gundams. Among its rivals are the Eurasian Federation, which corresponds to Russia and the modern-day European Union, and the Republic of East Asia, made up of China, Japan, and Korea. Earth is also home to countless smaller nations, of which some side with the Coordinators and others remain strictly neutral.

Weapons of War

The humanoid fighting vehicles known as mobile suits are another mainstay of the Gundam saga. Although the mobile suits of *Gundam SEED* are superficially similar to those of earlier series, their technological basis is rather different. Thanks to the widespread use of devices called Neutron Jammers, which suppress all forms of nuclear fission, these mobile suits rely on batteries for their power supply. For the prototype Gundams, with their energy-guzzling beam weapons and bulletproof Phase Shift Armor, this power limitation proves to be a recurring Achilles heel.

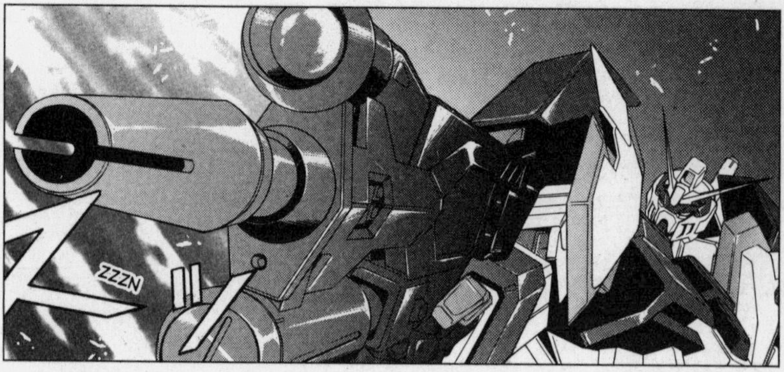
ZZZN

Continued in Volume 3!

Coming from Del Rey Manga December 2004.

About the Creators

Yoshiyuki Tomino

Gundam was created by Yoshiyuki Tomino. Prior to Gundam, Tomino had worked on the original *Astro Boy* anime, as well as *Princess Knight* and *Brave Raideen*, among others. In 1979, he created and directed *Mobile Suit Gundam*, the very first in a long line of Gundam series. The show was not immediately popular and was forced to cut its number of episodes before going off the air, but as with the American show *Star Trek*, the fans still had something to say on the matter. By 1981, the demand for Gundam was so high that Tomino oversaw the re-release of the animation as three theatrical movies (a practice still common in Japan, and rarely if ever seen in the U.S.). It was now official: Gundam was a blockbuster.

Tomino would go on to direct many Gundam series, including *Gundam ZZ*, *Char's Counterattack*, *Gundam F91* and *Victory Gundam*, all of which contributed to the rich history of the vast Gundam universe. In addition to Gundam, Tomino created *Xabungle*, *L.Gaim*, *Dunbine*, and *Garzey's Wing*. His most recent anime is *Brain Powered*, which was released by Geneon in the United States.

Masatsugu Iwase

Masatsugu Iwase writes and draws the manga adaptation of *Gundam SEED*. It is his first work published in the U.S. The manga creator is better known in Japan, however, for his work on *Calm Breaker*, a hilarious parody of anime, manga, and Japanese pop culture.

Translation Notes

Japanese is a tricky language for most Westerners, and translation is often more art than science. For your edification and reading pleasure, here are notes on some of the places where we could have gone in a different direction in our translation of the work, or where a Japanese cultural reference is used.

Yo, Dirtbag!

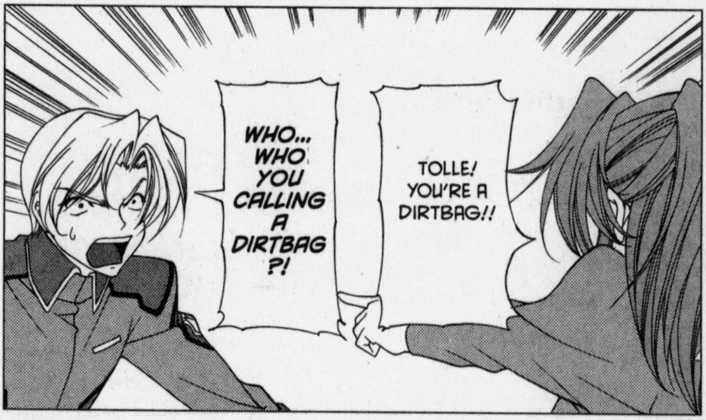
TOLLE! YOU'RE A DIRTBAG!!
WHO... WHO YOU CALLING A DIRTBAG?!

In this panel, Flay is calling Tolle a "hentai" in Japanese. A "hentai" is someone who is perverted or twisted, but the term pervert usually has different connotations in English. So instead of going with "Tolle, you're a pervert!" the translator thought "dirtbag" would be more appropriate here.

And Not a Drop to Drink

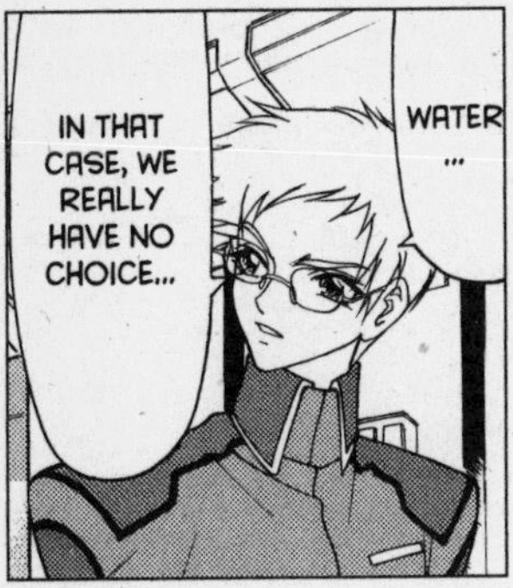
WATER
...
IN THAT CASE, WE REALLY HAVE NO CHOICE...

We have quite a few proverbs and sayings in English that would make no sense if translated literally into a foreign language. The same holds true for Japanese. Sai is quoting a Japanese proverb here. "Se ni hara wa kaerarenai" literally means "You can't change your back for your stomach." In other words: "You can't have it both ways." In the current context, the translator thought "We really have no choice" would make more sense.

I Will Bother You

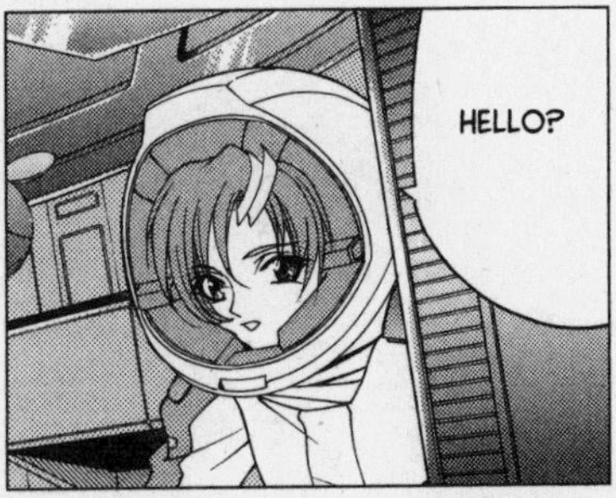
HELLO?

In English, we have greetings that aren't meant to be taken literally. For example, saying "How do you do?" when meeting someone is not a question meant to be taken literally and is usually met with the response "Fine." Here, Lacus is using the Japanese expression "Ojama shimasu," which is pretty much untranslatable. It literally means "I will bother you," or more loosely, "Sorry to disturb you." In Japan, before entering someone else's home or personal space (such as a car, a room, or an office), one frequently says "Ojama shimasu." It's used so often in Japan that it's become a greeting more than anything else, which is why the translator chose to translate it as "Hello" in this context.

The Legged Ship

HMMM.

THE LEGGED SHIP HAS MERGED WITH THE ENEMY FLEET. WE EXPECTED THEM TO HEAD FOR THE MOON BASE.

In Japanese, the Zaft frequently refer to the Archangel as the "Ashi-tsuki" which literally means "legged" or something that has legs. In the beginning, it's because they don't know its name. Later on, even after they find out it's called the Archangel, they (especially Rau) refer to it as "the legged ship" with a "you're not important enough for me to use your real name" kind of attitude. This is similar to how the Zeons kept calling the White Base "the Trojan" in the original *Mobile Suit Gundam*.

BUT WHO IS IT THAT HAS BRUTALLY SMASHED THAT HOPE?!

WAM!

Wam Bam Thank You...

Sound effects remain one of the most difficult elements of manga to translate. In English, we expect sound effects to be onomatopoeic—to resemble the sounds they're making. In Japanese, the effects are more subtle and complex. Here are two examples: First, on page 35 Zala stands up abruptly to make his point more forcefully. The effect can actually be translated as "the sense of standing suddenly."

And on page 170, as these three men stand up with guns drawn, the effect can be translated as "giving the sense of taking out their guns."

IT'S A COORDINATOR!!

WAM

Preview of Volume Three

We are pleased to present to you a preview from *Gundam SEED*,
Volume 3. This volume will be available in December 2004.

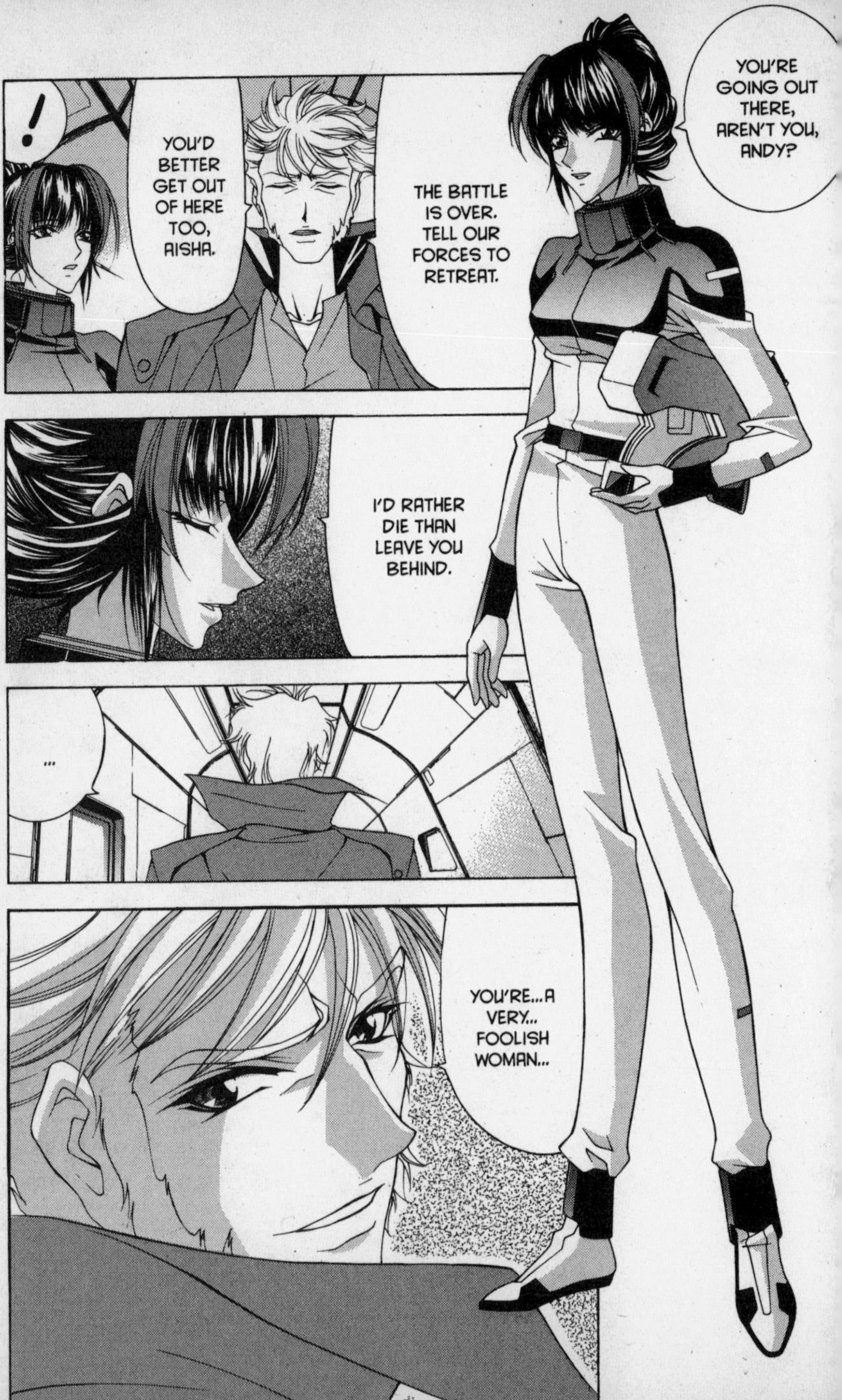
YOU'RE GOING OUT THERE, AREN'T YOU, ANDY?
THE BATTLE IS OVER. TELL OUR FORCES TO RETREAT.
YOU'D BETTER GET OUT OF HERE TOO, AISHA.
!
I'D RATHER DIE THAN LEAVE YOU BEHIND.
...
YOU'RE...A VERY... FOOLISH WOMAN...

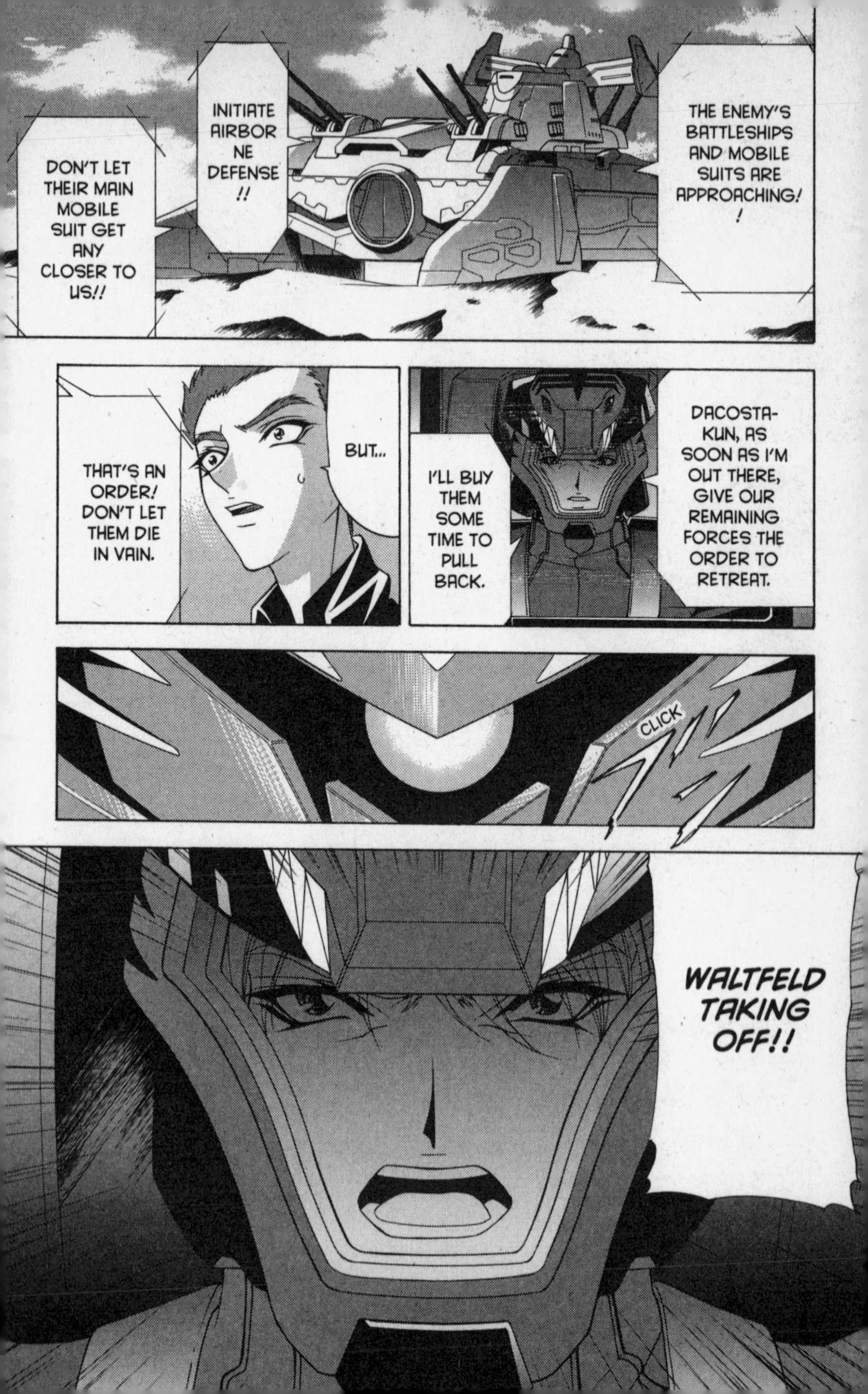
THE ENEMY'S BATTLESHIPS AND MOBILE SUITS ARE APPROACHING!!
INITIATE AIRBORNE DEFENSE!!
DON'T LET THEIR MAIN MOBILE SUIT GET ANY CLOSER TO US!!
DACOSTA-KUN, AS SOON AS I'M OUT THERE, GIVE OUR REMAINING FORCES THE ORDER TO RETREAT.
I'LL BUY THEM SOME TIME TO PULL BACK.
BUT...
THAT'S AN ORDER! DON'T LET THEM DIE IN VAIN.
CLICK
WALTFELD TAKING OFF!!

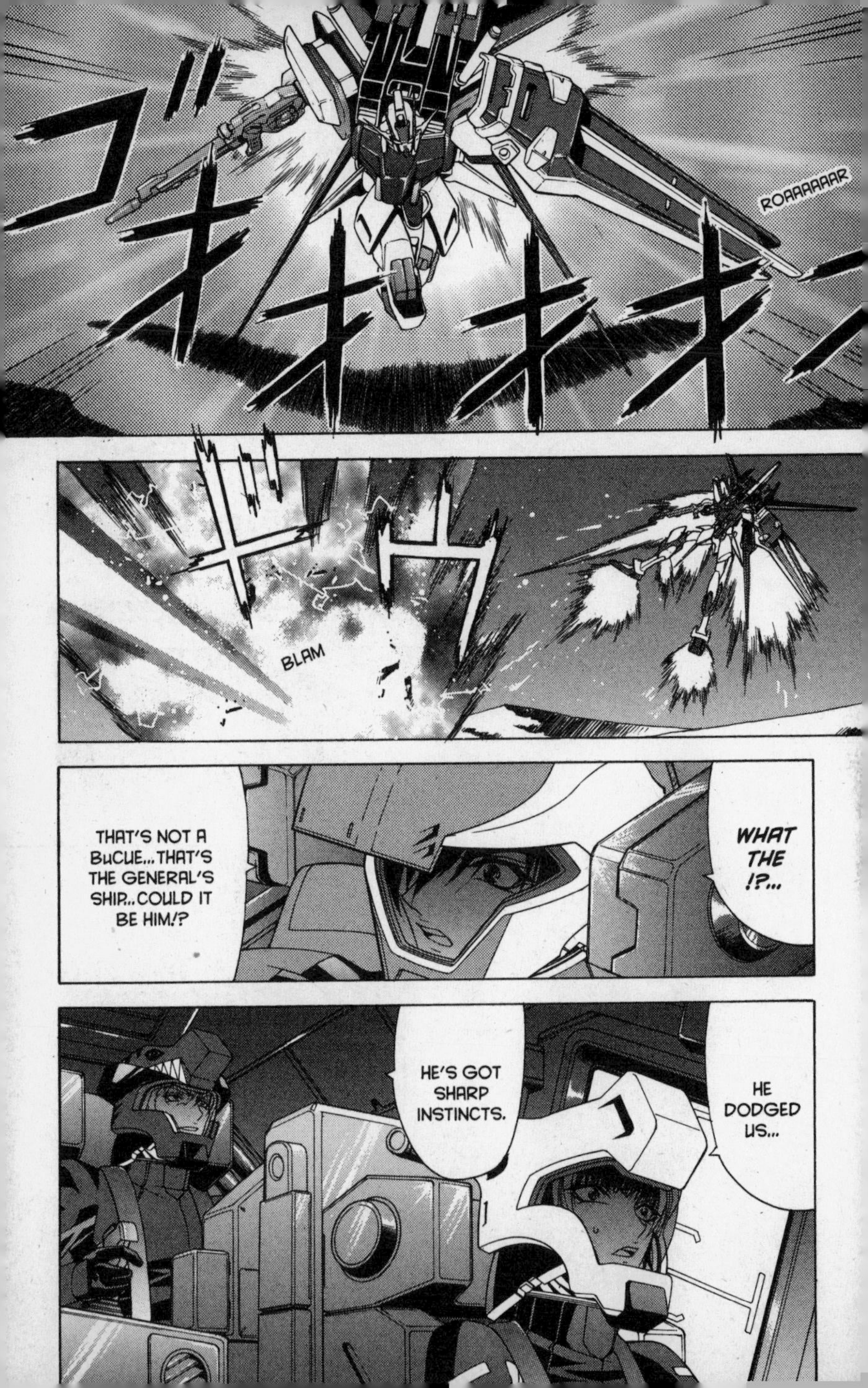
ROAAAAAAR
BLAM
WHAT THE !?...
THAT'S NOT A BuCUE... THAT'S THE GENERAL'S SHIP... COULD IT BE HIM!?
HE DODGED US...
HE'S GOT SHARP INSTINCTS.

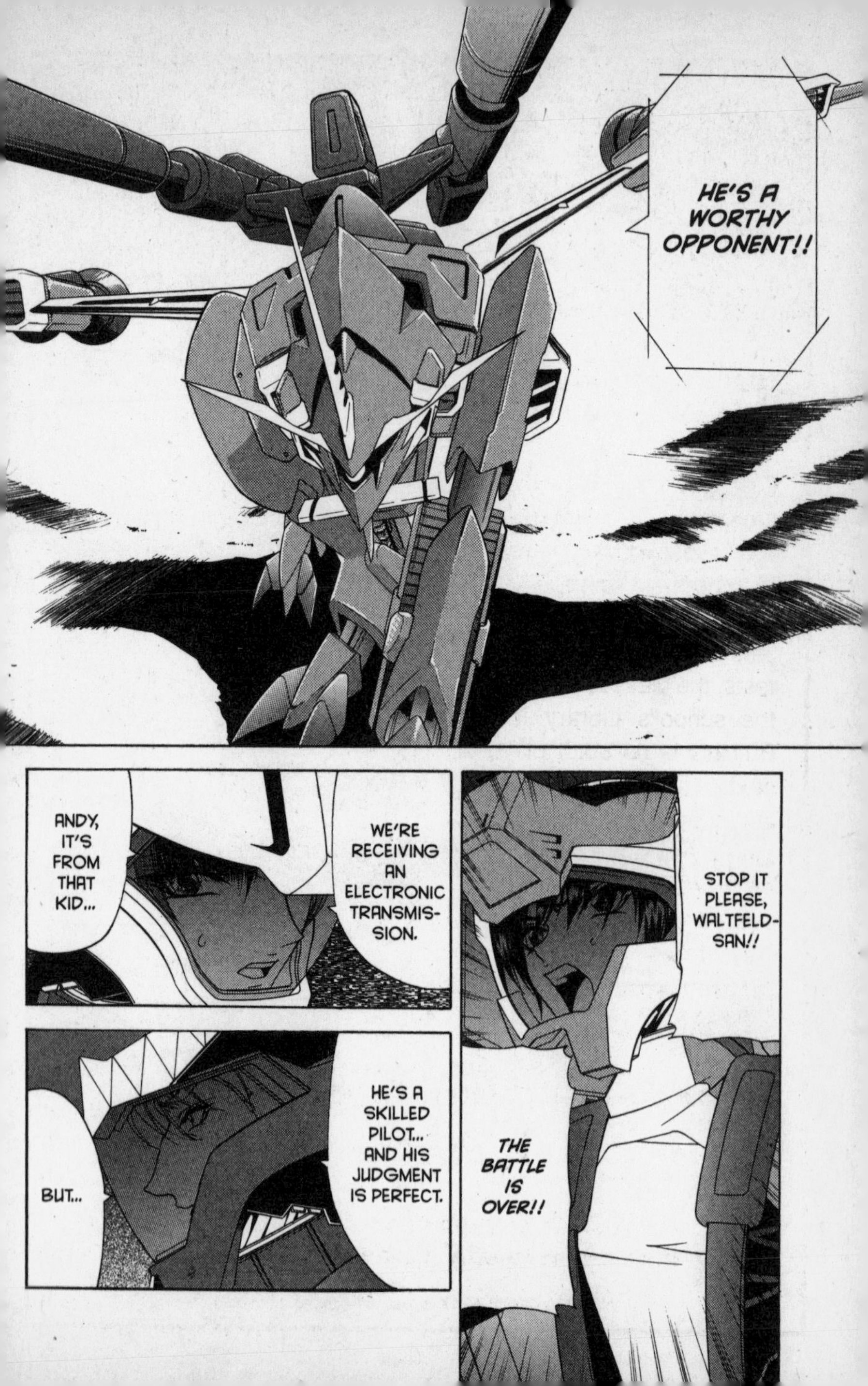
HE'S A WORTHY OPPONENT!!
STOP IT PLEASE, WALTFELD-SAN!!
THE BATTLE IS OVER!!
WE'RE RECEIVING AN ELECTRONIC TRANSMIS-SION.
ANDY, IT'S FROM THAT KID...
HE'S A SKILLED PILOT... AND HIS JUDGMENT IS PERFECT.
BUT...

NEGIMA!

VOLUME 2

BY KEN AKAMATSU

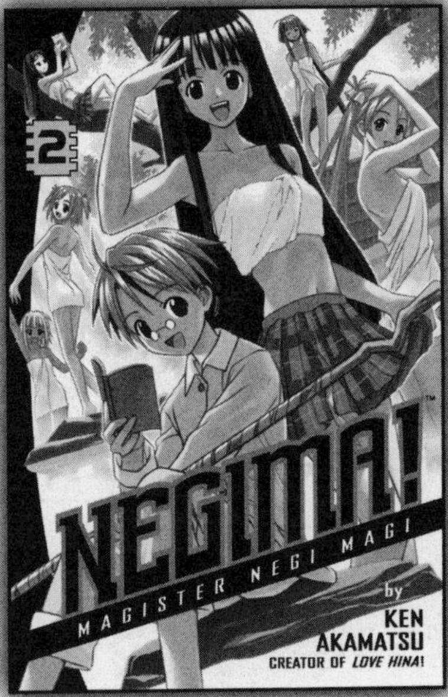
2
NEGIMA!
MAGISTER NEGI MAGI
by
KEN
AKAMATSU
CREATOR OF *LOVE HINA*!

For ten-year-old teacher Negi Springfield and his all-girl class, it's time for final exams! If his students manage not to end up with the lowest scores in school, the principal has promised to make Negi an official teacher. To prepare for the tests, the class takes a trip to the school's Library Island. But this is no quiet place of study . . . stone golems, traps, and secret passageways are the norm throughout the enormous library building. With all of these distractions, can Negi's class hope to climb out of the cellar—both academically and literally?

VOLUME 2: On sale August 2004 • VOLUME 3: On sale October 2004

DEL REY

For more information and to sign up for Del Rey's manga e-newsletter, visit www.delreymanga.com

Finished already?
Try these titles from
Del Rey!

THE SWORD OF SHANNARA
by Terry Brooks
A young boy who is the last of his bloodline is the only one who can wield the mystical Sword of Shannara!

DRAGONFLIGHT
by Anne McCaffrey
On the planet called Pern, the magnificent flying dragons and their human riders are the only protection from the deadly rain called Thread. . . .

BLACK HORSES FOR THE KING
by Anne McCaffrey
Where did King Arthur get warhorses large enough to carry his heavily armored knights? A fascinating and fast-moving historical novel.

SECRET OF THE UNICORN QUEEN
by Josepha Sherman and Gwen Hansen
Sheila McCarthy accidentally falls through a portal into another world—and finds herself part of a band of warrior-women! Two complete novels in one book!

Published by Del Rey
www.delreydigital.com
Available wherever books are sold

TOMARE!

[STOP!]

You're going the wrong way!

Manga is a completely different type of reading experience.

To start at the *beginning*, go to the *end*!

That's right! Authentic manga is read the traditional Japanese way—from right to left. Exactly the *opposite* of how American books are read. It's easy to follow: Just go to the other end of the book, and read each page—and each panel—from right side to left side, starting at the top right. Now you're experiencing manga as it was meant to be.